THE
WARLORD

GENA SHOWALTER

THE
WARLORD

ISBN-13: 978-1-335-92666-1
ISBN-13: 978-1-335-46297-8 (Walmart Exclusive Edition)

The Warlord

This edition published by arrangement with Harlequin Books S.A.

For questions and comments about the quality of this book, please contact us at
CustomerService@Harlequin.com.

HQN
22 Adelaide St. West, 40th Floor
Toronto, Ontario M5H 4E3, Canada
www.Harlequin.com

Printed in U.S.A.

To Jill Monroe and Mandy M. Roth
for the laughs, encouragement and brainstorms.
And to Naomi Lane and Marie Dowling
for every assist—you are treasures sent from above!

THE
WARLORD

"Um, guys? *Guys!* You might want to pay attention to me and gear up, because really bad stuff is about to go down. Like, the-asteroid-is-hitting bad. Oh, never mind. This will be fun...to watch."

—Neeka the Unwanted

PROLOGUE

Excerpted from The Book of Stars
Author unknown

They are ancient warriors, evil to the core and loyal only to one an-
other. Known as the Astra Planeta, Wandering Stars, the Warlords of
the Skies—the beginning of the end—they travel from world to world,
wiping out enemy armies in a single battle. Drawn to war, they finish
even the smallest skirmish with pain and bloodshed.

To see these warriors is to know you'll soon greet your death.

With no moral compass, they kill without mercy, steal without qualm
and destroy without guilt, all to receive a mystical blessing: five hundred
years of victories without ever suffering a loss.

If they fail to obtain this blessing, they automatically receive the curse:
five hundred years of utter defeat.

The time has come for the next bestowing, each Astra Planeta forced
to complete a different task. To start, their leader, Commander Alaroc

"Roc" Phaethon, Emperor of the Expanse, Rock of the Ages, Giant of the Deep, the Blazing One, must wed an immortal female of his choosing. Thirty days after the vows are spoken, he is to sacrifice this bride on an altar of his own making. If she dies a virgin, even better. He and his men receive a second blessing. If not…his greatest enemy receives it.

The Commander has never wavered in his duty. He cannot. If one Astra fails to complete his task, all fail.

Little wonder Roc will cross any line to succeed.

There has never been a woman alluring enough to tempt him from his path. No warrioress powerful enough to overcome his incredible strength. No enchantress desirable enough to make him burn beyond reason.

Until her.

1

Harpina, realm of the harpies
2248 AG (After General)

The night of her ninth birthday, Taliyah Skyhawk stalked through the royal Harpinian gardens amid a chorus of buzzing locusts and chirping birds. She approached a blazing firepit where multi-colored flames crackled. Three moons painted surrounding thickets with an eerie, cerulean glow, the scent of skullflowers and smoke hanging heavy in the air, saturating her every inhalation.

Her mother, Tabitha the Vicious, stood shoulder to shoulder with her aunt Tamera the Widow-maker and her fifteen-year-old cousin Blythe the Undoing—Taliyah's idol. The armed trio created a wall of strength.

"A death squad? Just what I wanted," she quipped, but no one smiled.

Rather, her mother readjusted her pose to better show off a sword made of fireiron. A material used to battle fae and other elemental species. "Kneel," she ordered, her small fangs bright in the firelight.

Excuse me? Taliyah's gaze darted from one family member to the other. What was going on? Earlier, when Blythe requested a midnight meeting, Taliyah had expected a surprise party. Maybe a few games. Pin the dagger inside the enemy had always been a favorite.

"Kneel," Aunt Tamera echoed. She wielded a demonglass dagger, the best tool against angels and Sent Ones. Those who came from the heavens.

Blythe gave a firm nod of encouragement. "Kneel." She clutched a stake carved from cursedwood, the best defense against demons, witches, vampires and even harpies.

Screw this. Taliyah narrowed her eyes. "I'll kneel for my General because I respect the position, but only my General."

"Good answer." Her mother smiled…and promptly swept Taliyah off her feet with a brutal kick.

She crashed into a too-cold ground that never lost its chill, no matter the season, air abandoning her lungs. Without pause, she scrambled up.

Her aunt's gut punch sent her tumbling down once again. Stars winked through her vision, but still Taliyah scrambled up. No time to gloat. Blythe darted behind her and dipped low, slicing the tendons in her ankles.

Pain flared as she hit her knees, breathing more difficult. *Still* she attempted to clamber up.

Never accept a picture of defeat.

She had to pick her poison. The pain of persevering or the agony of regretting. She chose perseverance, every time.

Striving, struggling. Her lower body refused to cooperate, keeping her in a subservient position. Taliyah remained determined. You only lost when you quit.

Panting, fighting harder, she glared up at women who should rejoice that she loved and trusted them. "Someone better tell me what's going on before I rage."

Her mother's eyes glittered in the darkness. "The time has

come, daughter. In twelve months, you will leave your family to begin your combat training, just like the harpies before you. Unlike the others, you must train as you are meant to be, not as you are."

Wait. "This is some kind of ritual for status or something? Well, why didn't you say so?" The tension drained from her. Until she replayed some of her mother's words. "How am I meant to be?" Because she liked herself just fine, thanks.

Ignoring her questions, her mother asked, "What do you want most in life, daughter?"

"You already know the answer." They'd had this conversation many times already.

"Tell me anyway," her mother commanded, her expression every bit as vicious as her moniker warned.

With black hair, amber eyes and bronzed skin, the Vicious looked as fragile as an elf and as innocent as a Sent One. Even dressed in leather and chain mail, she appeared incapable of cursing, much less killing everyone around her.

The white-haired, blue-eyed, pale Taliyah shared her mother's delicate bone structure, but nothing more. Well, and her fiery temperament. "I fight to become harpy General."

These women had drilled the words into her head. At some point, the desire had become her own. For harpies, a General was the equivalent of a queen. The ruler who led her people to greatness. Who wouldn't want to rule?

Aunt Tamera lifted her chin, just as cold, beautiful and deadly as her younger sister. "What are you willing to do to achieve this goal?"

"Anything."

"List them," she insisted.

Any harpy vying to become General must accomplish ten specific tasks. "I will serve in our army for a century and win the Harpy Games." A series of contests meant to reveal strength, speed and agility. "I will convince the reigning General to do something she doesn't want to do, and also present her with the head of her fiercest opponent. I'll oversee a victorious military campaign, negotiate a major truce, steal a royal's most prized possession, win a battle with my wits alone and sacrifice something I dearly love."

"You listed nine tasks. What of the tenth?" Her mother arched a brow. "When the time comes, you must challenge the reigning General to battle, no matter who she is or what she means to you. Do you have the courage for this?"

"I do." As mandated, Taliyah would do it all while remaining a virgin, her body given to her people. Which wasn't really a hardship, because gross. Boys were big babies. Break their faces, and they cried for days. "Nothing will stop me."

"Why will you do these things?" Tabitha asked.

"Because I'm Taliyah Skyhawk, and *nothing* will rob me of my birthright." Other words her mother had drilled into her head.

As soon as she'd learned to walk, she'd begun to prepare for the privilege of becoming General. Something many harpies attempted, but few accomplished. But, from the very beginning, Taliyah had proved more determined than most.

While others searched for ways around a problem, she grabbed the problem by the balls and squeezed. Others complained when a door of opportunity shut, then waited for another to open; she beat her way through whatever door she pleased with frightening focus.

Everything happened for a reason? Yes. That reason often involved her fists.

"You aren't just Taliyah Skyhawk." Her mother offered the barest hint of a grin, as if proud of her. "You will go by many names throughout your lifetimes, daughter. To others, you are the Cold-Hearted. To us, you are forever Taliyah the Terror of All Lands."

Terror of All Lands. Tal. A grin of her own spread. "I am the Terror of All Lands."

Her mother dipped her head in affirmation. "You are stronger, faster and far more powerful than other harpies. I made sure of that by handpicking the male I wished to father my first child."

Procreating by design was a common practice among harpies. A must when you were related to demons and vampires, and everyone referred to your species as "beautiful vultures." Many armies hunted harpies for sport. Or worse!

Nowadays, the harpies who decided to squirt out a couple of kids selected powerful males who produced more powerful children.

"You speak of the snakeshifter," Taliyah said, trying to hide her eagerness. Over the years, her mother had only ever shared the man's species. For so long, she'd wondered...

"He isn't a snakeshifter. Not entirely. He is the *creator* of snakeshifters...and he's only one of your fathers."

"What?" Um... *What?* How many fathers do I have?"

"There are two, and they are brothers, one able to possess the other, something you will never mention to others. Even your sisters cannot know."

Her gaze dropped to her mother's rounded belly, where twins named Kaia and Bianka grew. She gulped.

"Do you understand, Taliyah? We must take this secret to our graves. If ever *anyone* discovers the truth about your origins, you are to kill them without delay."

"But *I* don't even know what I am now!" *Reeling.*

"I'll explain," her aunt piped up. "Before your birth, the brothers appeared in Harpina every fifty years. One terrorized our villages, and we couldn't stop him. The other mended the survivors. Sixteen years ago, the two appeared to me in secret and offered to spare us for a time...if I spent the night with them." Her tone thinned. "Though I fought to become General, I agreed to their bargain. Nine months later, I gave birth to a healthy baby girl."

Tamera had given birth only once. Which meant... Blythe

had two fathers, too? Wait. Blythe was Taliyah's sister? *Reeling faster.*

"Five years later," her mother said, her tone just as tight, "the brothers reappeared. This time, they came to me, offering the same bargain. I agreed, despite my own bid to become General. Nine months later, I birthed you."

Taliyah licked her lips. *So much to digest. Too much at once.* She centered on the most difficult to accept, trying to make sense of it. Her fathers. In history class, she'd learned about twin brothers who'd done exactly as described. Warriors so powerful, they evinced terror in everyone they faced. *Not just warriors. The sons of a god.*

"I'm a daughter of Asclepius Serpentes and Erebus Phantom, sons of Chaos." The words tasted odd on her tongue.

Asclepius was known as the Bringer of Life, a god of medicine able to raise certain immortals from the dead. He was also the creator of snakeshifters and gorgons.

Erebus was his opposite. Known as the Bringer of Death, he destroyed whatever he touched. His contribution to immortal species? The creation of phantoms. Mindless soldiers able to take both spirit and bodily form. To survive, these phantoms consumed the souls—the very life—of the living. A grotesque act to harpies. To all immortals, really.

The two were gods in their own right, yes, but they came from a greater god known as the Abyss. That meant... *I came from the Abyss.*

Well, of course I did! Frankly, she was amazing. A defender of all harpykind.

"Where are the brothers now?" Oops. Did she sound too eager? Harpies weren't supposed to care about such matters.

Her mother hiked a shoulder, the answer clearly of no importance to her. "Rumors suggest the two picked a fight with the wrong warlords, men who once served as Chaos's personal guards. They killed the brothers, but Erebus came back...wrong."

So, one father was dead and gone. The other lived, but not well. Her stomach churned. "Does Erebus know about me? Does Chaos?" Would they visit her? A flicker of hope sparked. Maybe they'd want to get to know her or something.

"If they know of you, daughter, they care not. You are nothing to them, and they are nothing to you."

"Right." Her shoulders rolled in the slightest bit. "Good riddance, I say. Who needs them?" She did just fine on her own. Better than fine! The best! The pang in her chest bore no significance to the situation.

"You're right. You don't need them. Soon, you'll wield abilities beyond your wildest imagination."

She perked up at the thought of new power. "What abilities?" And how soon?

"You won't know until you've shed your first skin for your second," Blythe told her. The black-haired, blue-eyed beauty smiled and—Taliyah gasped. Her irises! Specks of black shimmered in their depths. "If you're like me, you'll push your spirit from your body, possess others, communicate with the dead, walk in the spirit world to spy on your enemies and recover from any death...even your first."

Her *first*? She zoomed her gaze to the weapons. Realization punched Taliyah, leaving her winded. Her family planned to kill her and raise her as a phantom.

Warring impulses surged, one after the other. Flee. Protest. Cheer. Die? In the end, she bit her tongue and remained silent. What mattered more than her dream? To walk in the spirit realm and spy on her enemies, to recover from death...

She would do *anything*. There'd be no greater General.

"I, too, fight for the right to rule," her cou—sister said. "When the time comes, the two of us will be forced to battle for the honor. But it will be a fair fight. Fair and right."

"Fair and right," Taliyah repeated with a nod. "But I'm still going to win." Facts, and all.

Blythe gifted her with another grin, there and gone. "We shall see."

"Like your half sister, you will only ever use your new powers in secret." Her mother's harsh statement cut through the night, the slightest tremor shaking her. "Erebus and Chaos have enemies who will stop at nothing to apprehend and use you, if ever your identity is discovered. Do you understand? For all we know, the gods themselves will want you dead."

Though she feared nothing, Taliyah offered a clipped assertion. When had the Vicious ever trembled? "I understand."

Satisfied, her mother lifted the fireiron sword. The dark metal glinted in the moonlight. "Are you prepared to die to become the phantom you were meant to be, my daughter?"

No! "I...am?" Though she hadn't yet lived a decade, Taliyah had already participated in two major battles. The first with Sent Ones—winged assassins of the skies—and the other with wolf-shifters. She'd watched friends enter the hereafter in the most painful ways, helpless to save them.

If dying today meant better protecting harpykind tomorrow, so be it.

Harpies today. Harpies forever.

"I am," she offered with more confidence, jutting her chin.

"So be it." Her mother repositioned into a battle stance, and Tamera and Blythe followed suit. "May your end serve as your beginning."

That said, Tabitha shoved the fireiron straight into Taliyah's heart.

Searing pain exploded through her. Blood rushed up her throat and out her mouth, choking her. All thoughts of dying for a cause vanished, survival instincts kicking in. Taliyah fit shaky hands around the hilt and pushed outward. *Can't breathe. Need to breathe.*

"May your loss serve as our gain." Without a shred of mercy, Aunt Tamera thrust the demonglass next to the fireiron.

More searing pain. More blood gurgled from the corners of her mouth. Weakness invaded her limbs, and tears welled.

"May your return serve as an eternal reminder. Death has lost its sting, the grave has lost its power." Blythe slammed the wooden stake beneath the other two weapons.

The agony! Excruciating and unending. A loud ring erupted in Taliyah's ears. *So cold. Dizzy.* What little remained of her strength abandoned her in a rush. Already hobbled, she fell.

Impact rattled her brain against her skull—a skull quickly wetted by an outpour of her blood. All she could do was peer up at a spinning night sky. Dazzling stars beckoned her closer…

She fought. She fought *hard*, because she couldn't not fight. Warped by the blades, her destroyed heart raced. Slowed. Until…

It stopped.

Taliyah wheezed a final exhalation, every muscle in her body going lax. Maybe she died, maybe she didn't. A part of her remained aware, but without time. She floated in a sea of darkness, the barest pinpricks of light blinking here and there, reminding her of the stars. All pain faded.

As the sea carried her farther and farther away, panic set in. She wished to return to her family. She *would* return. Taliyah renewed her struggles, kicking and clawing.

Blink. Blink. *Fighting harder.* Lights flared faster and faster, whizzing together. Harder still. Finally—

Taliyah gasped, her eyelids popping open.

Her mother hovered over her, a calculated smile blooming. "Congratulations, daughter. You are officially the second royal harpy-phantom in existence. You'll do great things or you'll die again trying."

2

Realm of the Forgotten, a semisecret dimension
Thousands of years later

A bare-chested Taliyah perched on her knees—willingly. A first-aid kit waited at her side. Her best friend had just pierced her nipple, claiming, "It's your lucky piercing. It's going to save your life, I swear!"

Since her best friend Neeka was a harpy-oracle who'd never given a wrong prediction, Taliyah believed her.

They occupied a spacious suite in a luxurious fortress. A master bedroom with glowing crystals that dripped from the ceiling and a beast-skin rug that stretched before a crackling hearth. Furniture made from the bones of wicked men acted as a daily reminder to enjoy the little things. Family created the artwork, an eclectic mix of so-called awards Taliyah's sisters had given her and masterpieces her only niece had painted.

"A pro hack for permanently scarring an immortal. Make sure the victim—er, recipient—isn't a screamer." Neeka the Unwanted stood near the crackling hearth, waiting for the branding iron to finish heating. Firelight cocooned her, illuminating curly black hair, gorgeous brown skin and whiskey-brown eyes.

The beauty received the less-than-stellar *Unwanted* sobriquet centuries ago from her wretch of a mother. Neeks had barely learned to walk before an enemy raided their village and stabbed her in both ears. Too young to heal from her wounds, she remained without hearing for the rest of her immortal life.

"Why do I need this scar, anyway?" Taliyah asked. "Is it going to save my life, too?"

"Something like that."

Well, it couldn't hurt any less than her stars.

After graduating from harpy training camp, Taliyah had issued a formal pledge to compete for the title of General. At that time, a mystic had imbued her left wrist with ten invisible stars. From then on, a star had darkened every time she'd successfully completed a task. The agony of a star's emergence compared to *nothing.* A way to weed out weaklings, she supposed.

"By the way, thanks for not killing me when I learned your secret heritage," Neeka said.

Yeah. Her friend uncovered the truth. But then, Neeka's father was an oracle who specialized in secrets and mysteries, so of course the girl had figured it out. Kill her for it? No. "Sometimes I want to shout the news to the world. My résumé of abilities has a wow factor, and people have a right to know."

As a snakeshifter, she mesmerized and cast illusions. A skill she used to spy on any enemy at any time; it also explained her phantom ability to dematerialize, becoming as insubstantial as mist. A few drops of her toxic blood could slay many immortal species and most humans. When she wasn't wearing an enchanted ring—which was never—she heard phantoms through a mystical connection. Or rather, she heard their screams. The ring saved her sanity.

"You know what you need?" Neeka asked, a familiar glint lighting her eyes.

"No! Do not tell me I've got to have—"

"A commemorative piece of jewelry to mark this auspicious occasion!"

She groaned. Being cooped up and bored, Neeka liked to pass time making jewelry. So many beads. The rhinestones. Oh, the rhinestones. Ten of the most gaudy necklaces dangled from her friend's neck. An array of bracelets climbed up both forearms. Rings decorated every finger.

"No more jewelry." *Please!*

"Fine. Be that way," the girl huffed. "But you're going to wish you owned a one-of-a-kind piece featuring real, genuine pearls."

"A redundant assurance doesn't make it true. Those so-called pearls are teeth you pulled out of a phoenix warrior's mouth."

"Only if you lack *imagination*." Neeka leaned over to inspect the branding iron before peering at Taliyah to watch her lips. "Almost ready. Oh, by the way, Hades is tee-icked at you. Well, not yet, but soon. *You have no right to use my name, Tal, blah, blah, blah.* He started shouting, so I started tuning out."

Use Hades's name? For what? They hadn't spoken in weeks. Months? Whatever. Earlier in the year, she'd challenged him to a test of wills. Spend two months in bed with her. If he convinced her to give up her virginity, she wouldn't kill him when he bragged about it. If she refused to surrender, he must give her...seduction lessons. Taliyah pressed her tongue to the roof of her mouth. The lessons were something else Neeka swore she needed as "a matter of life and forever death."

Remaining penis-free had been difficult. Hades had skills! Who could resist his silken voice, sinful hands and wicked mouth? Don't even get her started about his incredible body. But resist she had.

Taliyah smiled slowly, fully assured of her power. She would be General or she would die trying.

She'd fought for the title her entire life. She had *died* for the title—many times. *Born to lead.* The knowledge saturated every fiber of her being. Under her command, harpies would thrive, and enemies would fall.

Never been closer to my goal.

So why am I so dissatisfied with my life?

Her mood soured. There seemed to be holes in her heart, left by the first blades to pierce the organ. Whatever contentment Taliyah managed to garner, she lost soon after.

Everything would change when she became General, though. Surely! Long-lasting satisfaction would become hers for the taking.

"So what are we going to do after this?" Neeka asked. "Watch Henry Cavill do absolutely anything? Call Jason Momoa? His number just magically popped into my mind after only hours of searching for it. Or we could update our friends' mythology online with more *facts*? Oh! Let's retool Hades's family history, so his first wife is also his sister."

"We're definitely updating Hades's history, but first I've gotta meal-prep. I'm craving Italian."

Taliyah's diet consisted only of soul, or pure energy. Unlike Blythe, who went weeks between meals, Taliyah indulged once a day. Her current fare lived in the dungeon, her version of a refrigerator. The (former) rapists had grown too feeble to strengthen her, their souls no longer regenerating. Tonight, she'd finish them off and find their replacements.

"Steal me a marshmallow sundae while you're out," Neeka said. "Make it a double. And don't let the ice cream melt. Also, make sure they know the number of cherries added is the number of fingers they'll have when you leave." Pause. "Yes! All done." She lifted the branding iron from the flames and grinned. "Time to get aburnin'."

As her friend skipped across the room, the tool in hand, and took a position behind her, Taliyah placed a thick rope between her teeth and bit down.

Inhale. Exhale. Okay. Ready.

"You're gonna do great," Neeka assured her. "On the count of three. One—" She pressed the blazing iron into Taliyah's nape.

A bellow lived and died in her throat, murdered by determination. Heat swallowed her, every ounce of her sizzling. Sweat dotted her brow and dripped from her temples. The scent of frying meat inundated the air, and she nearly gagged.

"Mmm." The other harpy smacked her lips. "If we had marinated you in butter, I would be digesting you right now."

With a wheeze-snort, Taliyah spit out the rope. "Cannibalism... always hilarious," she managed to eke out. Harpies drank blood, but only as medicine and only when needed.

Taliyah focused on her breathing. In, out. In, out. Good, that was good.

Neeka returned the branding iron to its hook before cleaning and bandaging Taliyah's wound. "Don't take this the wrong way, but I think you need to work harder and faster to earn your final stars. I'm a queen, and I want to be friends with other queens, not *average* soldier-peasants."

Another snort. Completing eight of the ten prerequisites had required extra time—because she'd doubled or tripled each requirement, just to make a point. *I can, so I did.*

The ninth, though...the sacrifice. The task she needed to complete before she earned the right to challenge the current General. So far, the task had proved impossible. She'd given things away. Killed important people. Freely offered her time, her strength and her resources to other causes. Apparently, your motives must be *pure* for the sacrifice to count. Right now, she had no ideas for a next move.

Never accept a picture of defeat. A mantra Taliyah lived by. She'd fight until she succeeded or died for real. "I believe your husband the king divorced you when you murdered him that third time," she said as her friend tossed her a T-shirt.

A while ago, Taliyah's sister Kaia found herself betrothed to a Phoenix king. The girl had already fallen for a demon-possessed dude, though, and she'd refused to wed anyone else. To prevent an all-out war, Neeka had agreed to wed the guy instead. She'd owed Taliyah a big favor. Huge! See, a few weeks before, Taliyah had killed her favorite avatar in her favorite video game to save Neeka's favorite avatar. The loss cut deep.

The wedding should have been a typical Friday night. Murder a king before the honeymoon kicked off, loot his treasury, free the immortals he'd kept as slaves and put his palace in their rearview. And they'd done it.

They'd known the king would revive, and they'd looked forward to the ensuing war. What they hadn't expected? His ability to find Neeka anywhere. Needing a secret lair, Taliyah had bargained with friends to buy time in a place known as the Realm of Blood and Shadows. There, she'd mined rare and precious bloodgold buried in the mountains, which she'd then used to purchase time in this world. The Realm of the Forgotten.

The beauty of this place? As the name suggested, everyone everywhere forgot you the moment you entered. Unless, of course, they bore a special tattoo to remember you.

"As soon as I gain control of the harpy army," Taliyah said, "we will destroy the phoenix. You have my word."

The muscles in Neeka's shoulders suddenly bunched with tension. "The collision...it's already happened."

Collision? "What are you talking about?"

"They're here." Her friend's gaze drifted far, far away, to a land unseen by others. "The game has begun."

"What game?" Taliyah asked, only then realizing the harpy was in the midst of a vision.

"He has drawn his cards. Now he plays his hand. Prepare. The next move is yours."

The bedroom door swung open, hinges whining. Tabitha Skyhawk, mother of four, matron of dishonor, merciless killer and perpetual bachelorette, stumbled inside the chamber. She looked as if she'd just escaped a blender. Battered, bruised and bloody. She clutched an arm to her chest: her hand was missing. Fear clung to her like a second skin.

Blood freezing in her veins, Taliyah leaped to her feet. Despite waves of pain and dizziness, she remained upright. Grit and resolve served her well. "What happened?"

"Harpina," Tabitha croaked. She tripped forward, leaving a trail of blood in her wake. Crimson wetted her pale, waxen skin and splattered her torn clothing. She just kind of fell onto the foot of the bed. "A fog rolled in, and a massive wall appeared. Nine monsters stood before it. The battle bell sounded, and we rushed to engage. The monsters had no weapons, yet they severed harpy hands and feet in seconds. Bodies began to vanish. So many of us, just gone. The survivors did the unthinkable. We...surrendered. I flashed out to find help."

Taliyah's stomach turned inside out. Harpies had surrendered? A horror too abhorrent to bear. She scooped up the first-aid kit and got busy tending her mother's most concerning wounds.

"Who's dead?" she demanded. Anyone she knew? Each of her sisters lived in the mortal world. Aunt Tamera had died in battle more than a century ago, too injured to regenerate, ensuring Taliyah's heart bore a scar with her name. "What monsters?"

With her remaining hand, Tabitha shoved inky strands of hair from her face. "I don't know. I...don't know," she repeated lamely.

"Nissa is dead," Neeka intoned, going deeper into the vision. "The leader killed her." A gasp. "Blythe."

"Blythe was there?" Dread slapped Taliyah. Eight years ago, Blythe had found her consort—the male fate chose for her. She'd given up her virginity, right along with her desire to become General. Seven years ago, she'd birthed a child. A beautiful little girl named Isla. Someone Taliyah loved. "Was Isla with her?"

Eyes stark, Tabitha nodded. "Yes. And yes."

Taliyah knelt in front of the woman who'd trained her to harness the worst pain imaginable and keep fighting. To fall and stand up, even if your legs were broken. "Tell me everything I need to know."

"I wish I could," her mother rasped. "All I know is that Blythe and Isla ran. Isla fell, and Blythe backtracked. I worked my way over, but I—I couldn't find them again. I don't know whose... pieces lay on the ground."

A barbed lump grew in Taliyah's throat before falling and settling in the pit of her stomach. "Whatever their injuries, they'll recover." Her sister had experienced as many deaths as Taliyah, reviving never a problem. Why would things change now?

Isla had her own phantom abilities, despite never dying.

"The monsters... I've seen nothing like them. So cold, so cruel. They shredded anyone who approached them. There was so much blood." Tabitha the Vicious peered at Taliyah with grave eyes. "Save our people, daughter. Save them all."

Seeing her powerful mother so shaken and speaking as if the world had just come to an end shook her to the core. "I'll go to Harpina and assess the situation, yes." Forget her own injury. She strode to the closet to collect daggers, a crossbow and a pair of short swords. Strapping those swords to her back proved excruciating, but she didn't care. "Whatever these monsters are, they'll die begging for mercy."

"Use my key." Motions more awkward by the second, her mother removed a chain, where a small, dagger-shaped pendant hung.

Realm keys, no matter their incarnation, allowed a holder to flash, moving to a new location with only a thought. She could land in any location of her choosing. The key to the Realm of the Forgotten would facilitate her return. She'd had it tattooed on her lower back, an hourglass set to vanish when her purchased time ran out.

After securing the chain around her neck, she double-checked her enchanted ring. The metal screws anchoring the metal to bone held steady. Excellent. The older she'd grown, the louder the phantom screams had become, until even a few seconds had threatened to push her off the cliff of madness.

She turned to Neeka. "Any helpful hints for me?"

Her friend tilted her head, as if digging deeper into her vision. "You should say *yes*."

Say yes to what? "Anything else?" Maybe something she understood?

No answer was forthcoming, the oracle lost. Very well. Taliyah nodded goodbye to her mother, then forced her body to mist. Frigid cold washed over her, weightlessness settling into her bones.

Deep inhalation. She clasped the key to Harpina. With only a thought, she flashed to the other realm. The bedroom faded…

Heartbeat, heartbeat…

The palace formed around her, and she exhaled. Murals covered gold-trimmed walls, featuring General Nissa in the midst of battle. Multiple chandeliers dangled from the arched ceiling. Gold bricks paved the floor.

Usually chattering harpies filled this area. Today? There were no harpies and no chatter. Just dead silence.

Rage sparked in Taliyah. *Someone will pay.*

A massive set of double doors loomed before her. The throne room waited beyond them. Tall, muscular guards stood sentry, both males clutching a sword—the weapon of choice for immortals with sensitive ears. There were other men present, some marching down hallways, others guarding different doors. Vampires, wolfshifters and banshees, all natural-born enemies, worked together. What she didn't see? Monsters.

Taliyah wrapped her fingers around the hilt of a dagger, preparing to strike. In this form, no one could see, hear or even sense her. Appearing, striking and vanishing would be easy. But why solidify, leaving dead bodies sure to set off an alarm? Why not spy first?

"Who is the bloodthirstiest among you?" a rough voice called from the throne room, brutal in its intensity.

She stiffened. A monster?

Let's find out. Wasting no time, she ghosted through the closed doors…

3

Taliyah drew up short. Hundreds of soldiers surrounded her. Other vampires, wolfshifters and banshees stood alongside other natural-born enemies. Elves, warlocks, merfolk. Goblins, minotaurs, centaurs. Trolls, fae, shifters of every kind. Gorgons and even a handful of creatures she couldn't identify. Everyone focused on... She couldn't tell yet, the crowd too thick.

She ghosted forward, passing through bodies until— Taliyah gasped. Ten harpies knelt before the royal dais. With their hands chained behind their backs, the metal links connected to their ankles, they couldn't protect themselves, much less stand. Their wings fluttered like crazy as they struggled for freedom without success.

Rage growing hotter... Where were the other harpies?

Directly behind the captives—each a contender for General— were four men.

The monsters, no doubt about it.

They were enormous, both incredibly tall and stacked with muscle. A wealth of tattoos covered their torsos— Whoa. She did a double take. Did those tattoos *move*?

They did. But why? What did it mean? She needed a plan.

What would a General do? Aid the captives or hunt for the others?

At the moment, the invaders were distracted by…whatever this was. They remained unaware of the powerful phantom lurking in their midst. There was no better time for a search and rescue. Also, there was strength in numbers. The other harpies could help her save these captives.

What did these men have planned for them, though? Rape? Murder? A little of both? Hatred seethed inside her.

Better stay put.

Where did these monsters come from? What were their greatest strengths? Their weaknesses?

They reminded her of berserkers. Extra-large mutant berserkers on a steady diet of the bones of their foes. Each man wore an elaborate headdress. A mythological creature's bottom jaw rested on their shoulders, the upper part on their skulls, with saber teeth creating a cage-like effect around their faces.

Taliyah curled her hands into fists. Bloodstained claws extended from their nail beds.

"Come, ladies," a man called. The man. The one she'd heard before. "Surely someone wishes to claim the title of Blood-thirstiest Harpy?"

That deep voice with its smug undertone drew her gaze toward the throne, where a fifth male reclined.

How *dare* he claim the General's seat?

He exuded aggression and arrogance, the ferocity of him awe-inspiring. His headdress was bigger than the others. *He* was bigger than the others, with a crap ton more of those moving tattoos. Except for a fist-size patch above his heart, the images covered every inch of exposed skin.

I'm going to kill him. The decision solidified, becoming a mission. He would be the first to fall by Taliyah's hand.

He drummed black claws on the arm of the golden throne. "The bloodthirstiest will be released from her bonds. The rest will spend the next month imprisoned in the dungeon below. Any takers now?"

The girls took turns belting out replies, their tones sugary sweet.

"I'm like walking cotton candy. I practically dissolve in your mouth."

"Don't listen to her. She once drove a car into my face! *I'm* the sweetest."

"Sweetest? You just admitted to liking the taste of your own face. Bloodthirsty!"

As the women did their best to nominate each other for freedom, the leader continued to drum those claws.

Wanting a better look at him, Taliyah floated closer. Not materializing and fighting to free her people destroyed her.

As soon as she reached the edge of the dais, the leader shifted.

"Did I forget to mention," he grated, "the bloodthirstiest harpy earns the right to challenge me?"

New assurances rang out.

"Me, me, me! You heard about my face smash, right?"

"Jacoline be nimble, Jacoline be quick, Jacoline will impale you with a candlestick. Hi. I'm Jacoline."

"I will cut you open and remove your organs one by one—with my teeth." The threat came from Mara, a woman who'd earned her ninth star. Blonde like Taliyah, and equally pale.

The leader stood, silence descending upon the onlookers. "I believe I've found who I seek."

Not yet. Challenge him? *Sign me up.*

She had to be careful, though. If someone noticed Taliyah's appearance, they might suspect she'd keyed in. They might realize she'd misted, might discover her true origins. So, Taliyah returned to the double doors. A quick scan proved every eye remained on the leader. Replacing a dagger with mini-crossbows, she materialized at last. The barest tendrils of warmth unfurled through her limbs.

No time to waste. She shouldered her way to the front, commanding, "Out of my way."

All eyes zipped to her. Some men stepped out of her path, confused. Others had to be pushed. Most glowered at her, but didn't retaliate.

In this form, she smelled the blood and sweat of the men. "I hear you're holding auditions for Bloodthirstiest Harpy, and I'm here for my reading."

"You," the leader said, his tone...reverent? Thick shadows cast by the headgear kept his features in hiding, but she *could* feel the burn of his gaze upon her icy skin.

He recognized her? Had they met before? Perhaps he followed her on social media. *Can't blame him.* Her posts chronicled her steps to become General.

Guards drew their swords, suddenly intent on stopping her by any means necessary.

"Do not touch her." The leader stated the words simply, but every weapon got sheathed in a hurry. Men *leaped* out of her path.

The authority he wielded, to control so many with a lone statement... Envy swept her up.

"Allow me to introduce myself," she announced. "I'm Taliyah the Terror of All Lands, the Cold-Hearted, the Enemy of Enemies. My hobbies include listening to the screams of my foes, collecting the bones I sever and avenging the deaths of my people."

Bypassing the bound harpies a second time required great effort; for the greater good, she managed it. Only when she reached the royal dais did she halt. *Your move, monster.*

Move he did, lifting the headdress. Powerful biceps flexed, igniting flutters of anticipation in her chest. What would she find? An average Joe? A hideous beast? Maybe a handsome fairy-tale prince?

A thick tracery of veins led her gaze to the tattoo of a beautiful Amazon warrior on his—

A sudden spike of dizziness rocked Taliyah, and she swayed. Her eyesight dimmed, the throne room fading. *What's happening?*

Though she fought, a scene opened up inside her mind... A memory?

I stalk through a garden, trailing an Amazon dressed in a blood-splattered ivory gown.

The girl from the tattoo, Taliyah realized with shock.

As she stumbles and flees to the right, then the left, warriors wearing those monstrous headdresses step into her path, forcing her to continue straight ahead, where a massive structure looms. An onyx monstrosity with steps, a raised platform and an altar.

A crowd stands behind it, a thirtysomething male in the center. He exudes supremacy. Two small women in sheer gowns stand at his sides. To the right is—

Taliyah gasped. Erebus. Her father looked just like the drawings she'd seen. Fair, with curling hair and black eyes.

Stretched behind him is an army of phantoms, each soldier motionless, silent and female, draped in an ill-fitting black gown.

The Amazon throws a panicked glance over her shoulder and chokes on a sob. When she reaches the altar, I—no, the leader clasps her by the nape with a large tattooed hand, his claws at the ready. She grapples with tremendous skill, but she loses quickly.

"Stop! Do not do this!" she pleads in an ancient language.

Without hesitation or guilt, he forces her to lie flat upon the altar.

"The first is startling, I know." The now familiar voice sent ripples through the...vision?

As she struggled to escape it, her sight remained dark. Her other senses screamed to life, at least. Incredible heat engulfed her, and the most divine fragrance filled her nose. Notes of spiced rum and melted sugar—or foreplay—made her mouth water. But…

Why can't I see?

"You are reliving my memory," the male said.

Him. The leader. He was responsible for this. Air sawed in and out of her mouth as she continued to struggle, shudders working through her wings. "I'll peel you from my brain if I must. I'm getting you out, whatever it takes."

"Relax, and it will finish playing out, then dissipate."

Relax? Around foes? Not happening. She fought with more force until finally, finally light came, the memory dying prematurely. The throne room appeared first, and so did the leader. He had closed the distance and now towered over her.

Taliyah's jaw went slack. He wasn't an average Joe or a hideous beast, that was for sure. No, he was all chiseled perfection and raw sex appeal. Prince Charming with a rap sheet.

His tattoo-free face boasted flawless, bronze skin, a proud, patrician nose and sinfully plump red lips. The softest-looking mouth she'd ever seen. He cropped his hair military-short, but he also sported a beard in need of a trim. Spiky black lashes framed magnificent gold irises with striations of gray.

Realization 1: the heat and scent came from him.

Realization 2: he was studying her just as intently as she studied him.

Even as oxygen lodged in her throat, she feigned nonchalance, canting her head to the side. "I call foul. You're supposed to count down before you initiate a staring contest."

"A countdown is your responsibility, harpy. When I turn my attention someone's way, they should know they have five seconds to convince me *not* to kill them."

Good one. She'd be using it. Offering him a bright smile, she said, "How adorable are you?"

Beneath his eye, a muscle twitched. "I am Alaroc Phaethon."

Phaethon. Fey-uh-thuhn. Familiar. Where had she heard that name?

"You may call me Roc."

Oh, she may, may she? "Thanks, but no thanks, Alaroc."

He reached out and sifted a lock of her silver-white hair between two fingers. She let him, curious to know his game.

"Where are the rest of the harpies?" she demanded when the seconds ticked by and he did nothing else.

"Alive. At the moment, that's all you need to know."

"Alive? When their hands and feet litter the palace grounds?" Pairing a conversational tone with hate-filled eyes—was there a better combination?

"I killed your General. No other."

Though her mother had already warned her about Nissa, shock and sorrow inundated Taliyah. She hadn't been the General's biggest fan, but her respect for the position had never diminished. Nissa had earned her spot.

For the first time in history, harpies were without a leader.

"Those who attacked us lost their appendages before being tossed into another realm," he continued, "where they will stay and heal."

That couldn't be true. Could it? No one possessed the ability to throw others into *another freaking realm*. Right?

Uncharted territory...

A sense of purpose settled over Taliyah. The purpose for her birth was upon her. Her motivation to train without ceasing and forgo pleasures of the flesh. Her moment to shine.

My sisters need me more than ever.

"Prove my harpies are alive," she demanded. "Take me to them. Let me see them with my own eyes."

"I will. Once you earn the right." He dragged his gaze over her body, his pupils expanding over those amazing golden irises. "You are the Bloodthirstiest Harpy, are you?"

"I am." Truth was truth.

Phaethon... The name continued to poke and prod at her calm.

"And what gives you the right to bear this title, hmm?"

She leaned toward him, as if she had a secret to impart, while sneaking a dagger closer to his groin. "The fact that I'll be using your testicles as a new coin purse, perhaps?" She shoved the weapon deep into...his thigh?

He'd guessed her intent and shifted his leg, the blade embedding in muscle. He hadn't flinched or cried out.

She huffed with irritation. Centuries spent on the battlefield had honed her instincts, and right now those instincts were shouting, *To win, you must use tricks you've kept secret.*

"You were saying?" he asked, nonchalant.

"A girl's gotta swing and miss a few times, right?" Shrug. "Next time I'll hit your balls out of the park. Promise."

He examined her, betraying only the slightest hint of eagerness. "You are a virgin, Taliyah?"

Whoa! What did that have to do with anything? With a forced smile, she asked, "Does playing just the tip count?"

He stood motionless, never broadcasting his intentions. Blink. He clasped her by the shoulders and spun her around. Suddenly, she faced their audience, his muscular arm slung beneath her breasts, locking her in place.

His body heat! This close, he threw off intense waves of warmth. His skin actually burned hers...and she thought she might like it. Humiliating!

She looked over the crowd, but no one peered her way. The warlords had forced the harpies to the floor, facedown.

The powerful warrior behind her let his mouth hover just over her ear. "Let's make sure, shall we?"

That voice...the audible equivalent of a whorehouse. Capable of pleasuring every inch of your body, as long as you paid for it.

What was he planning? Rather than raging out—her usual MO—she forced herself to melt against him. What did he have planned and why? "Baby, this mouth and these hands have *done* things."

"Have they, then?"

Her breath hitched as he slid his free hand underneath her shirt, just above the waist of her pleated skirt. His heat intensified, his palm scorching her skin. She didn't move. She couldn't. Shock held her immobile. Surely he wouldn't—

He did.

He thrust his hand under her panties, through the tiny thatch of curls at the apex of her thighs, and thrust two fingers deep inside her. A moan nearly escaped. The warmth! Being filled… He needed to stop this. He needed to stop this *now*. Before she—

With a curse, he yanked his fingers out and stepped away.

Rational thought returned quickly, her cheeks burning with mortification. He'd made her forget their audience. She'd gotten wet for him.

Wet.

For him.

How dare he! She spun and threw a savage punch, her fist connecting with his rock-hard jaw.

His head didn't move an inch. Meanwhile, her knuckles cracked against his bone and pain rocketed up her arm. Not fair!

He wasn't reacting the way she'd hoped. Wait. Even through the haze, she noticed the way he fisted a hand and flared the other. The one with wet fingers.

Some part of him had enjoyed touching her. She grinned, pleased. A much better outcome—for her.

He nodded, as if he had just reached an important decision. "Yes. I do believe you're the woman I seek."

Then. That moment. Remembrance came, and her stomach bottomed out. Phaethon wasn't a name but a rank.

This man was Commander of the Astra Planeta. The most brutal army ever to live.

Reeling all over again. She'd discovered the Astra Planeta while researching her fathers. The army consisted of twenty warlords, some living, some dead. Each male bore more than a hundred different titles. They'd once served as personal guards to Chaos, her secret grandfather. Motivations and objectives unknown, they'd killed his sons.

Reports claimed Chaos supported both his returned son, Erebus, and his former guards, refusing to pick sides as the two warred millennia upon millennia.

Would Erebus return to Harpina now? Did he know about her? She'd always wondered. Would Taliyah meet him at long last?

Did she want to?

If tales were to be believed, the Astra Planeta conquered worlds in less than twenty-four hours. They sometimes entered a state known as *anhilla*, a time when they killed without thought or mercy. Similar to what the berserkers experienced, only ten million times worse. Which made sense, since the Astra created berserkers.

They lived war and embodied conquest. Their favorite prey? Phantoms.

Tremors rushed through Taliyah's limbs. Had the Astra come for her and Blythe?

No. No way they knew about the phantom daughters of their most despised enemy. If they'd had any clue, they would have struck at Taliyah already.

I might not walk away from this. I might have to crawl.

Alaroc exuded smug satisfaction, and it grated on her every nerve. "I see you've realized what I am."

"Yes." No reason to deny it. "You are Astra Planeta, primeval warlords fueled by planets. You travel from realm to realm, eradicating those who refuse to serve you. The evidence of your kills stains your skin, allowing others to observe the horrific nature of your crimes. No weaknesses, some say. Considered unbeatable, most proclaim."

Despite her concerns, she grinned slowly, coldly. He liked threats? She'd give him a vow. "I will pop each of your individual vertebrae out of your mouth. You'll be my own personal Pez dispenser. Afterward, I'll wear your skin like a prized suit. I'll call it the Husk of Defeat." Her grandfather could take his favored soldiers and shove it.

The Astra's nostrils flared with...not hostility. With a sizzling glare, he stepped into her personal space, pressing his body against hers.

Taliyah had a choice. Sever contact or let more of his heat chase away her cold, her pierced nipple aching with increased vigor every time she breathed.

Lucky piercing, Neeks? Really?

She craned up her face—and stayed put. Death before retreat.

Aggression charged the air.

Without looking away, he called to his men, "Bring the witness. The wedding happens today."

4

Do not lick your fingers.

Yes! Lick.

Fool! Don't you dare.

Commander Roc Phaethon assessed the ethereal beauty before him, desperate to forget the feminine honey that coated two of his fingers. He should wipe it away, ending temptation.

Yes, he should.

But he wouldn't.

Taliyah Skyhawk had scrambled his thoughts.

Had he ever beheld such delicate features and fathomless eyes? Eyes a stunning shade of blue, reminding him of a frozen ocean, with depths unknown. Thick slashes of kohl rimmed spiky black lashes, providing a carnal frame.

Plaited silver-white locks created a crown effect, turning the harpy into a queen. Pale, silken skin gave an illusion of fragility. And her body... *Exquisite.*

Slender and toned, she wore a leather halter, with a built-in breastplate. A short skirt revealed long, lean legs strapped with multiple weapons. Her only other adornments were a plain metal band circling her left index finger and a small dagger hanging from a chain around her neck.

Her best and worst attribute was her scent. She smelled like frostberries. Like...home. Every inhalation made his chest clench.

She must *be my bride.* He was to pick whoever attracted him most. Therefore, no other would do.

When you sought greatness, you pushed and tested yourself. You didn't choose the easy path. Rather, you endured hardness. Taliyah definitely qualified as a hardship. He'd known it the moment he'd first spied her.

Exactly twelve months ago, Roc arrived in Harpina. He'd walked the grounds undetected, taking notes, crafting the perfect battle plan, when this pale beauty had exited a shop in the market, across the street from him. The sight of her had arrested him. Then she'd turned, revealing small iridescent wings. His blood had heated, and he'd morphed into a living furnace.

She'd reminded him of home then, as well. Having spent the first part of his childhood in a frozen tundra, he'd looked at her and thought, *She's a winter wonderland.*

He'd never enjoyed the cold, but he'd always adored the fire-warmed rooms in his parents' palace. His older sisters had read him bedtime stories before a popping hearth.

Chest clenching, he shut down any thoughts outside the present. Securing Taliyah Skyhawk as his bride mattered, nothing else.

"Wedding?" she choked out.

He waved away her question. "You are part snakeshifter, yes?" Every time he'd come to Harpina, he'd looked for her. While he hadn't come across her a second time, he *had* caught a thread of gossip about her. Well respected among her peers and highly protective of her family and friends. Bloodthirsty to the extreme.

"Wedding?" she repeated.

With the exception of phantoms, snakes were his least favorite species. Born liars with a seducer's nature, all of them. Usually cowardly when pressed. Flattery spilled from their tongues without cease. They tempted and lured, happiest when they inspired misery. However, Roc was willing to tolerate this snakeshifter on a temporary basis. Hardships and all.

"Wedding," he finally affirmed. She would be his most hauntingly beautiful bride yet. A shame he must sacrifice her to his god in thirty days. "Ours, in case I wasn't clear."

"Me? Marry *you*?" The harpy bristled. "I would rather— Oh... no. No, no, no." She paled and whispered, "Say *yes*? Really, Neeks?"

Neeks? "You *will* agree, Taliyah." For multiple reasons. Mostly because he commanded it. Roc expected absolute compliance from everyone at every moment. If someone refused to obey him, he quickly taught them the error of their ways.

He never received a second refusal.

"You really don't want to marry me," Taliyah told him with gritted teeth. "I have a temper only a consort can calm." She flared her claws. "Want to guess if you're my consort?"

Calm her? Roc had never calmed anyone from anything, not even himself. "Want to guess if I dread your temper? Harpies might be stronger than giants, but only as long as their wings are free. Pin them, and you're all as weak as wee pixies."

Oh, she didn't like that bit of truth. She bared her fangs and snapped, "I will *never* marry you. Not even for the honor of making myself a widow."

Where was the cowardly side of her snakeshifter nature? "When you say yes, and you will, I'll grant you thirty days to kill me. An honor no one else receives. Succeed, and you'll become Commander of my men. When you fail, and you will, I'll sacrifice your virgin body to my god."

"Sacrifice? You're a killer by nature. How does ending your wife qualify as a sacrifice?"

She had no idea. More than anything, Roc wanted a family of his own. Wanted to protect his loved ones. To provide for them.

He proceeded as if she hadn't spoken, ready to get this done. "Don't think to seduce me or another warlord to disqualify yourself. I'll kill you anyway, and your people with you." Let there be no misunderstanding between them. He wasn't a good man.

The muscles in her shoulders knotted with aggression. Not an unusual occurrence in his presence. Despite this, she did something no other prospective bride had done. She pressed a hand against her heart and fluttered her lashes. "Murderous threats against my people? Finally! The romance my life has been missing. Should I say yes now or wait until you describe exactly how you're going to kill everyone? You know, to really flood me with desire."

Were her wings fluttering? He wondered how they'd feel against his flesh. He barely stopped himself from running a hand up the ridges of her spine. "At some point, you *will* beg me to take your virginity. It's only a matter of time."

"I'll beg you for nothing!" she spit.

That was her only point of contention? "Your attempt to seduce me will only waste your time and erase my respect." Brides would do *anything* to disqualify themselves from the sacrifice. But then, they didn't know the truth.

Roc didn't actually need a virgin. He preferred them.

Sacrifice his bride, and he and his men received a mystical blessing to win every battle they waged for the next five centuries. Sacrifice his *virgin* bride, and they received a mystical blessing plus a powerful weapon. Of course, he couldn't claim either prize until the other Astra Planeta had successfully completed their own tasks. Everything from finding lost cities to crafting powerful weapons.

Neither Roc nor his men required the blessing. If they fought, they won. Period. Unless they were cursed.

He straightened his shoulders. If a single Astra botched his task, a curse came automatically upon the entire group, ensuring they *lost* every battle they waged.

"Right," Taliyah said with a nod, exchanging fury for wry humor. "Because boning the man who injured and imprisoned my people is super high on my bucket list."

"I'll be sure to remind you of these words the first time you crawl into my bed."

"Darling, if you find me in your bed, you'll be too busy dying to remind me of anything."

Did she ever back down?

"I will resist you," he continued, "because I have a higher purpose." Long ago, the god Chaos created his own personal army. Demigods with the potential to ascend, becoming gods themselves. To do this, he'd purchased twenty children from his fellow Greeks. Young boys he'd raised with a stern hand, teaching the ways of the ancients. *Might makes right.*

Roc and his biological brother were part of the twenty, and at first, they had despised Chaos. The male had seemed to enjoy the pain he'd inflicted upon each of his charges...

To be remade, you must first be broken. To shed weakness, you must defeat the pain you fear. I'll break you in ways you can't imagine and hurt you in ways you'll never forget. For centuries to come, you'll curse my name, but when you look back, you'll thank me for it all. You'll be stronger than you ever dreamed possible.

Chaos had kept his word. Under his tutelage, Roc had strengthened in a thousand different ways. He was *still* strengthening. Now he protected the people under his charge by any means necessary.

No one took what belonged to him.

Soon, he would ascend for the second time, reaching new heights. Becoming a god far greater than the parents who'd sold him. Far greater than the enemy he loathed with every fiber of his being.

Nothing would stop him from achieving this goal. Nothing.

"Hey, Alaroc?" Taliyah batted her long lashes at him as she nibbled on her plump bottom lip. "Are you *sure* I'll be wasting my time trying to seduce you? Absolutely, positively sure your higher purpose matters more than your desires?"

He laughed and patted the top of her head. "I'm sure, harpy." He harbored zero uncertainties.

In the beginning, Celestian "Ian" Eosphorus, had been the Commander. Roc's brother. But Ian had failed to sacrifice his first bride, bringing the curse upon the Astra. They'd lost two men the first hour and had to make a retreat. A humiliation seared into his memory.

They'd spent the next five hundred years in hibernation. Upon awakening, they'd discovered Ian's demotion, another warrior given the Commander's helmet. A ruthless barbarian named Solar.

Solar, once the leader responsible for wedding a virgin bride. Time after time, he'd done it without complaint. Then he'd met the siren. He'd made the mistake of taking her to bed and everything changed.

"She is my *gravita*," he'd said. The female who spun his world out of orbit. Who both rushed and slowed time for him, her pull too strong to deny. "I produce stardust for her."

Stardust was a sparkling powder produced in an Astra's palms, toxic to all but its creator and his *gravita*.

In the end, Solar had spared his bride, exactly as Ian had.

Both males lost their females, anyway. On the very same day as the sacrifice. Solar had died minutes after his bride, leaving the remaining Astra to fight on without him.

Bitterness coated Roc's tongue, old fury flaring. What leader had the right to choose a bride over his men?

"Yes, but are you sure you're sure?" Taliyah asked. "Like, no doubts or anything?"

How much plainer could he make this? "In thirty days, you will die a virgin."

"Yes, yes. That's very believable. Except..." She motioned to his groin. "One of us has a raging hard-on, and it isn't me. I left mine at home."

He ground his molars. "Today's takeover proved unchallenging. I released no battle heat. Now my body seeks other methods for expulsion." Nothing more.

"*Suuure*. Follow-up question. When do I get to shove two fingers into *you*? You know, to check for *your* virginity."

"You're welcome to try whatever you'd like." He had to admit, he admired her spirit. But then, all brides exhibited spirit in the beginning. Once the overconfidence wore off, fury took over. Hope quickly followed. Then desperation. Finally, she would accept her doom and soothe herself with hatred. "Like the others before you, you have nothing I need."

"Oh, really?" Her eyes lit with calculation, contrasting with the innocence of her haunting beauty. Stepping closer, she pressed a cold palm over his heart. "Women are interchangeable?"

He silenced a hiss, discomforted by her chill. Her boldness. Few brides had ever dared handle him without first seeking permission. "You are."

"What if I promise to be *really* nice to you?" A rosy flush spreading up her arm. Because she absorbed his body heat, his warmth conquering new territory? "Would *that* help my cause?"

Could he melt her entire body? At the thought, his erection... throbbed.

Scowling, Roc pushed her hand away. "Enough, harpy."

She grinned at him, slowly, wickedly. "I could have you if I wanted you, warrior."

Despite his odd reaction to her, he laughed again, the very

idea of his capitulation ludicrous. "I like sex. I use it to purge excess aggression. But I've lived a long time and taken many females, one orgasm as good as the next. Whatever I might want from you, I'll accept from my concubine. Yes, she's here, and yes, she will see to my needs."

"I'll wed you, Commander," another harpy called.

Without removing his attention from Taliyah, he held up a hand, a command to his men to keep the audience silent. He would allow no distraction with his chosen female.

"Your concubine is welcome to you with my compliments." Taliyah furrowed brows surprisingly as dark as her lashes, deep in thought. "Let's pretend I'm a fool who says yes to your proposal, just because my best friend told me to. Why the thirty-day stay of execution?"

He had no reason to tell her. Still, he said, "My determination and fortitude must be tested."

"Will I be locked away those thirty days?"

"Obey my rules, and you'll have unlimited access to the palace."

"Let me guess the first rule," she replied, her tone flat. "Never leave said palace."

"Exactly right. If you attempt to leave, I'll know, and I'll come get you. Trust me when I say you don't want me to come get you, harpy."

She searched his gaze, as if trying to fit squares into circles. "You don't fear me at all, do you?"

"Your need for clarification baffles me." He feared losing the blessing for his brothers-in-arms, nothing else. If he had to commit a cold-blooded murder to save them, if he must live with the consequences of his deed for the rest of eternity, so be it.

The harpy's death would be a blow to his enemy.

Soon, Erebus Phantom would find him. The god would arrive in Harpina with a single goal: to make the Astra miserable.

Even thinking his name boiled Roc's blood. Chaos's eldest

son was the most vile, corrupt being in existence. The miscreant knew there was no better period to strike than the months before the bestowing of a new blessing, when victory and defeat were not guaranteed.

The male despised the members of his father's army and always had, his envy unchecked. The mind-boggling atrocities he'd committed against the Astra over the years...

He'd struck out once too often, and the Astra had finally retaliated. Back then, Roc had worried about losing Chaos's respect. The god loved his son dearly. But Chaos also loved the Astra. In the end, he'd opted to support both sides equally.

Roc loved Chaos, as well. He admired the male for his unwavering devotion to those under his care. A failure of his own parents.

"Uh-oh. Did someone hit a land mine in their head?" Taliyah's smooth voice mocked him, and his scowl returned.

He *had* lost track of his surroundings in the presence of a foe. "Harpy, you should know the male you taunt. I can rip you into more pieces than anyone can count."

To his consternation, she remained unflapped. "You can try." She released an airy sigh. "I must admit, I'm intrigued by the notion of ruling your men. Do you think I'll be the first dictator to slaughter her own army?"

The most beautiful of his brides, and the most stubborn, it seemed. "No matter what you throw at me, I'll overcome. I must. Your death is the first step to earning a blessing from my god."

She didn't miss a beat. "Oh, yeah? What kind of blessing?"

This time, he offered no response. With the Astra, you had to earn the right to question someone of higher authority. Roc had humored this woman enough. "I'll hear your answer now, Taliyah."

The gleam of calculation returned to her ocean-water eyes. "Slow your roll, Rocaby-baby. I'm not done getting *my* answers yet. You implied you've experienced wedded bliss before. So, how many times have you gotten hitched and ditched?"

That gleam… Why did he like it so much? "Many." Perhaps he wasn't finished humoring her after all. He beat a fist into his shoulder, saying, "I wear their deaths in my skin." The *alevala* acted as an outward sign of his inner commitment, his unwavering determination and his willingness to cross any line to achieve a goal.

He regretted nothing.

Except one.

He fisted his hand to stop himself from rubbing the patch of perfectly healed flesh above his heart, where he'd removed a fist-size circle of skin just this morning—as he did every morning. The patch was beginning to stain again. Sometime in the night, a full image would appear, revealing the worst of his crimes.

"Lucky," she muttered, shocking him.

He raised his chin. "In thirty days, I'll wear your death, too." A warning, challenge and promise. "Unless you defeat me, of course. Or shall I offer this gift to another harpy?" As soon as the bluff registered, he had to bite his tongue to stop from reversing himself.

A part of him had hoped to avoid Taliyah today, but here she was. If he must wed the woman he wanted most, he must wed her. What if she agreed to let him pick another?

"Let someone else have a crack at you?" In her irises, sunlight glinted off the ice. "Your death will be my honor, and mine alone."

He exhaled with relief and fought a smile. The desire to mete justice was the downfall of every bride. Of any species, really. Did she have a right to feel this way? Absolutely. He'd harmed and imprisoned many of her kinsfolk today, then threatened her life and touched her without permission. But right or wrong, Roc couldn't, wouldn't, change his plans.

"Do you accept me, Taliyah Skyhawk? I'll hear the words."

Still she resisted, saying, "If I do, you must free the harpies."

Bargaining wasn't uncommon among his brides, either. In the beginning, they pushed and pushed to learn his limits. It was a smart move—with anyone but an Astra.

Reach my limit and die screaming.

"You have no power and no leverage." Already he'd made a major allowance. Usually when he conquered a new world, he killed the soldiers who attacked him, only imprisoning those who stood down. Those he could later mold. For her and her loved ones, he'd merely injured and tossed. Just as he'd claimed.

He owed this woman no other favors, yet he added, "Give me no trouble today, I'll let you *see* the captives." He did this because...just because. He wanted this over and done as quickly as possible, and this presented the swiftest route.

As believable an excuse as any.

A pause. Then a grated, "What are the rules of engagement?"

His relief returned. She engaged rather than taunted. Progress. "The rules are simple. I will show you the same respect you show me. A room of my choosing remains designated as neutral territory. In it, you are to commit no acts of violence. You won't speak to my men. You'll limit your attacks to me and only me. I'll sleep with anyone I desire, anytime I wish. You'll practice the art of abstinence." Something he would be helping her with...

The corners of his mouth began to lift. A smile? But why?

She flicked her tongue over an incisor, staying silent, and smiling ceased being an issue for him. She would say yes *now*. Allowing her to drag this out smacked of weakness.

"Do you agree to wed me, Taliyah? I won't ask again."

Finally, she offered him a curt nod. "Yes. I agree to wed you."

Roc bit his cheek to silence a shout of victory. And a flash of...was it grief? No, couldn't be. All was going according to plan. For better or worse, Taliyah Skyhawk would be his bride. Guaranteed she tried to kill, seduce and guilt him, in that order.

For thirty days, Roc had only to defend, resist and ignore her. And try not to enjoy the battle between them, as he had during this first encounter.

Despite his…stronger reaction to her, he wouldn't waver in his objective.

A beautiful female with blue-green hair and brown skin etched with glowing, starlike symbols appeared beside Roc and Taliyah. The witness, his sister Aurora. As always, this rare glimpse doused his internal organs with acid.

They spoke to each other every five hundred years, when he wed, when they saw each other at the sacrifice and occasionally when he visited Chaos's realm. Something he could only do by invitation.

He missed his two sisters more than a limb, remembered playing games and huddling together for warmth…remembered his inability to save the pair from being sold by their parents.

His hands drew into tight fists. If not for Chaos… The god had saved the pair, winning them from the males who'd originally bought them, accepting them as acolytes.

Aurora wore typical acolyte garb: sheer scarves as black as a starless night, the hem dancing at her bare feet despite her stillness.

"Who are you?" Taliyah demanded, and Roc tensed. "Because I just watched you passively observe another woman's murder."

"You will watch your tongue, harpy, or you will lose it."

His soon-to-be bride didn't flinch at his harshness. No, she studied his sister with new intensity. Trying to put pieces of a puzzle together?

With a frown, Aurora removed the blade from his thigh. Oh, yes. He'd forgotten it was there.

"My thanks." *Dear one.* When he extended his palm, she offered the hilt and a quick, private smile, and his stinging chest clenched.

Voice as wispy as wind, she said, "You may begin."

"What?" the harpy shrieked. "This is happening *now*?"

"Now."

A bit hysterical, she called, "But where's my toaster? My barely remembered bachelorette party? Where are the strippers?"

She teases me? He clamped his large fingers around her small wrist, then lifted her palm to the light; she remained stationary, opting not to fight him. Not by word or deed did she react as he ran the blade from the base of her index finger to the middle of her wrist.

Blood welled and pooled. "You'll regret that," she said with a cold smile.

"Why? Because you are a venomous snake?" He sliced open his palm next, then linked their fingers, mixing their blood. "I'm immune."

She gasped as if he'd singed her. Maybe he had, the difference in their temperatures startling. She tried to wrench away, but he held on, her strength no match for his own.

Determined to finish this, he gazed into her frosty eyes. "I take you as my bride, Taliyah Skyhawk, the Terror of All Lands. You are mine." His voice had heft and carried throughout the room, lingering long after he'd spoken. As Commander of the Astra, he needed to say nothing more to cement this union. He merely required her acceptance. "Repeat the words," he instructed, tightening his grip.

She didn't repeat the words. Not right away. She glared up at him and huffed, "I'm going to enjoy killing you. So you know what? Yeah. Let's do it. Let's War-of-the-Roses this sitch. I take you as my bride, Alaroc Phaethon. You are mine...to murder."

Aurora accepted the words, calling, "The marriage is acceptable to Chaos. The clock starts." She cast Roc a final glance before vanishing.

He couldn't halt a familiar pang of loss. *Focus.*

Taliyah smiled up at him, the tone of it different from her

others, rendering him momentarily mute. If ever evil had a face… "This is the moment we kiss, right?" If ever seduction had a voice…

He dropped his gaze to her lips, the action automatic and unstoppable. *So plump and pink.* A heart-shaped masterpiece, with a center dip in the bottom one. Impossibly lovely. He cleared his throat. "There's no reason to kiss. Our word is our bond."

A gleam of calculation appeared in her eyes. "I disagree. I'm not married until I'm kissed."

True in some cultures, but not his. "My blood runs through your veins," he grated. "You are *very* married."

"No kiss, no marriage." All simmering seduction, her eyes swirling and mesmerizing, she glided her free hand up his chest. The snakeshifter had decided to work her wiles. "Stop me when it's too much for you…"

Her temperature shocked him into immobility. That must be the problem. He did nothing to dissuade her when she freed her other hand from his and twined her fingers at his nape… nothing to stop her when she hauled her body against his, jumping up and winding her legs around his waist.

No, he reached up to ghost his fingers over her wings. They fluttered swiftly, brushing his knuckles again and again. His lungs squeezed.

He would set her on her feet. He would.

"Practically begging for it," she muttered, leaning her face toward his. Slow, so slow. Giving him time to protest as her gaze challenged his.

His shaft throbbed harder. *Rebuke her. End this.*

He remained quiet. She had something to prove—but so did he. She expected him to turn away. He would not.

Would she?

Almost upon him… Contact. She pressed her lips to him, and he sucked in a breath. She jolted.

Wanting consumed him as they lunged in unison. Their

mouths crashed together, tongues thrusting. A moan left him. How sweet she tasted. How sweetly she tasted *him*.

As the seconds, minutes, hours ticked on, neither willing to stop, he thought he might be losing his mind. When the first flame of a wildfire ignited, he fisted her hair. He loved the way the soft strands felt between his fingers. Angling her head, he deepened the kiss. She let him.

Want more of her. Must touch. His control wavered.

No! Heartbeat thumping, he peeled Taliyah off his body and set her on her feet, ending contact. Her frostberry scent clung to his skin, and her sweetness lingered on his lips. He wiped his mouth with the back of his hand. He needed her sweetness gone *immediately*.

"Never do that again," he snapped. "You have thirty days left to live, Taliyah. Anger me at your peril."

5

I'm…married? It was a state Neeka had urged Taliyah to accept. A state she'd never planned to be in, outside of a joke. Maybe a dare. But she'd kinda sorta done it for real.

To be honest, she'd expected her ninth star to appear right after the vows. Getting hitched to the big bad in order to save harpykind was a huge sacrifice, right? Apparently not huge enough. The star remained invisible.

Now she had thirty days to figure out the perfect game plan and murder her husband. The game plan was optional.

I can do it. I must. She had to. The second Alaroc breathed his last, she could instruct the Astra to free the harpies. Did she believe the towers of beefcake and hostility would actually follow her orders once she proved victorious against their leader? No. But also yes. She didn't know! Some of the more ancient warriors honored their word, no matter the cost.

What she did know? The warlords could use her people

against her at any time. Therefore, she must find and free the harpies as soon as possible.

Her goals realigned. *Harpies forever.*

The fact that this guy thought to sacrifice *her*? A secret phantom? Good luck. She'd just resurrect. Maybe? Probably? What if he utilized some kind of special weapon? She remembered reading about a powerful blade the Astra employed against all phantoms. Although, Taliyah wasn't some mindless being. She was royal, practically a goddess. Maybe she'd still resurrect.

She feigned nonchalance. "Do make sure there's a vegetarian option at the reception, darling. Did you remember to order a cake?"

His pupils pulsed, and it was the oddest thing she'd ever witnessed. Perhaps one of the hottest, as well. What did it mean? Fury? Passion? Or both?

Maybe she shouldn't have kissed him. But oh, he'd been so smug. She'd *needed* to oversee his defeat. Any kind of defeat. And yes, she was the kind of person willing to impale herself on a pole, as long as she impaled her foe, too. Alaroc hadn't wanted the kiss, so he'd gotten it. But this… She hadn't expected to like it. Her lips tingled from the softness of his. His taste proved as amazing as his scent, all spiced rum and melted sugar. Like the piña colada she'd once sampled. Something she thought she might…crave.

"There will be no reception." Alaroc maintained a blank expression. No big deal. He'd never be able to erase the memory. Whether he admitted it or not, a part of him had liked the kiss, too. "You'll wish to settle in and plan your first attack, I'm sure. Allow me to escort you upstairs, so that you may begin." A polite request that wasn't really a request.

No time to respond. He grabbed her healed hand and marched her across the throne room. The executioner and his prize. His men dived out of the way. The harpies watched her with envy.

To her bafflement, the warlord's grip remained firm, never

bruising. They entered the hallway, the guards she'd spotted before standing in place. *Should have killed them while I had the chance.*

Alaroc led her around a corner, and she noted the blood-splattered walls. The blood of her kind. Furnishings were overturned, priceless vases broken and scattered over a cracked marble floor.

Fury reignited. Harpies might be a bloodthirsty lot, but they valued their treasures. "How did Harpina draw the short stick? What made you decide to wed a harpy?"

"I'm always mystically drawn to the world I must conquer."

Mystically drawn? "By whom? Your god?"

"Perhaps him. Mayhap fate."

He has drawn his cards...

"Well, fate dealt you a bad hand this go-round." Taliyah wanted so badly to study Alaroc's tattoos and learn from the mistakes of past victims. But she resisted the urge, knowing the distraction would cost her. "Hey! How do you know your way around the palace?" Men like him were never allowed inside. Plus, he'd arrived today.

"I arrived a year ago, unbeknownst to the citizens."

"Excuse me?" An entire year?

"I trekked every inch of the realm, collecting data. My knowledge allowed me to create a duplicate realm. That's where your people currently reside. Today is merely the day I revealed myself."

Taliyah listened, agog. A duplicate realm? As storage?

Um, how was she supposed to defeat a *creator of worlds*? And what was that strange sensation working through her? That couldn't be dread, could it? Nope. Impossible!

"Why not pick a timid mouse and guarantee a victory?" she asked.

"Neither mouse nor lion has the power to defeat me." A pause. At a lower volume, he admitted, "I've never desired a timid woman."

And he must desire his wife?

As they ascended a staircase, she realized they were headed for the General's suite. A big nope from Taliyah. She dug her heels into the marble, barely slowing his progress. "I'm not staying in Nissa's room."

"Correct. I am." He didn't bother glancing at her, just kept dragging her along. "You'll stay next door."

Teeth grinding, she asked, "You don't feel guilty about claiming the bedroom of the woman you just murdered?"

"Hardly. She chose to die. I honored her decision."

"Hold up. You didn't just say she *chose to die*."

"She attacked me. She chose to die," he verified, his tone flat.

"And you *honored* her decision," she repeated, *her* tone dry.

"Is there any greater honor than dying for your cause?"

"Yes. Living for it."

He frowned over his shoulder, and she schooled her expression to say, *Go ahead, deny it.*

"Perhaps you're right," he said with a shrug. "I gave her the second-best honor."

Such a paragon of virtue. "If honor really matters to you, you won't cheat on your brand-new wife." Since sex purged him of aggression, she considered herself the royal wet blanket. The more on edge she kept him, the more mistakes he'd make. "If you truly respect a person's position, as I do, you'll respect mine and abstain from sex for the next thirty days."

The muscles in his shoulder bunched as he said, "You manipulate me. At the moment, I'm willing to play along. So yes. I will remain celibate on your behalf. If you think you've won a battle, however, you are mistaken. You alone will suffer my wrath."

"For your information, I've won two battles. This pledge and the kiss. Admit it, you're hungry for more of me. Starved!"

The slightest noise left him. A growl? A grin spread. Oh, yeah. He wanted more.

Now she would needle him about it for the rest of his very short life.

They reached the master suite, where two guards stood sentry. Without a word exchanged, the pair opened up, allowing Alaroc and Taliyah to stride inside without pause.

"You may go," he said, giving Taliyah a nudge as disciplined as his handhold.

With a quick scan, she memorized the layout of the room and noted every object she could use to her advantage. Basically: everything. The teapot in the sitting area before the hearth. The vase of flowers on the dresser. The massive chandelier hanging over the bed.

When she pivoted to face him, he kicked the door shut, sealing the two of them inside.

"Okay, Mr. Drama Queen." Was she supposed to cower now that they were alone? Why not test his reflexes? After all, he hadn't even bothered to discard her weapons.

She strolled closer, grateful she'd taken Neeka's advice and trained at the hands of a sensual master. Voice throaty, she asked, "Whatever do you plan to do with me?"

"Whatever I want." He stalked closer, as well…only to bypass her without ever making contact.

Jerk! "I'm assuming the *whatever I want* goes both ways?"

He snorted. A starting bell. Taliyah didn't bother pondering the best attack. She simply grabbed a dagger and slammed the blade into his brain stem. Except, he twisted and latched on to her wrist, stopping her before she made contact.

Their gazes connected, her breath hitching.

"There's something you should know," he told her, utterly calm and casual. "I sense the slightest thrum of aggression."

"Are you saying I inadvertently broadcast my intentions?"

Nod.

"Something to work on, then."

He narrowed his eyes. "Drop the dagger."

"No, thanks." She gripped the hilt tighter.

"Drop it."

"No. Obviously, I have a point to prove." Nothing would stop her. Not now, not ever.

He squeezed her wrist, and it hurt. Tomorrow she'd wear his bruises. Still she held on with all her might.

"This bedroom is our neutral zone. Attacks aren't allowed in here." He punctuated every word. "I'm not angered by your actions—yet. You didn't know. Now you do. Next time… Do not let there be a next time." His tone sharpened into an audible blade. "Drop the dagger, Taliyah. Now."

Not angered by her actions yet? Liar, liar. The man *seethed*. "Sorry," she quipped, "but this is a therapy dagger. The law says I get to take it everywhere, no questions asked."

He stepped closer, entering her personal space until the blade rested against his collarbone. Teeth clenched, he told her, "Listen well, harpy. From this moment on, *my* law is your law. If I must remove your hand to oversee your cooperation, I will."

The most delicious warmth radiated from him, threatening to weaken her resolve. As a phantom and snake, she existed in a state of total cold, regardless of the situation. She didn't like it, but what could she do? How did this man continue to heat her up, something Hades, a king of Hell, had never managed?

"Does anyone ever disobey you?" she asked conversationally.

"Never more than once."

Arrogant male. Sexy. Too bad, so sad. *I will* make *him concede*.

Her sexuality worked before. Why mess with perfection? "Are you saying…" She flattened her other palm on his pectoral. "…that you don't want me to touch you?"

The muscle jerked, drawing her gaze. Down she looked. Along the way, a moving tattoo snagged her attention.

Dizziness invaded, and she groaned. Not this again.

She tried to tear her gaze away. Too late. A new memory claimed center stage…

A trembling banshee stands before a massive black altar. A savage wind gusts, dancing locks of red hair before her face as the hem of her ivory gown billows. Tears well in her beautiful eyes. She bows her head, defeated, and climbs atop the altar, where she stretches out. A sob leaves her.

Behind the altar is a silent crowd. The black-robed man occupies the center, set apart from the others. The same two females stand at his sides. Erebus is feet away, seething with fury, an army of phantoms fanned out behind him. Each embodied female wears a somber black gown.

Alaroc approaches the banshee and places a hand just over her heart. "You have served me well, female. Worry not. Your death will be painless." Apologetic words, monotone voice.

The banshee sniffles and croaks, "Please, don't do this."

"You were dead the moment you wed me. You knew this. I made no secret of it."

In the distance, a bell tolls the midnight hour. Ding.

He maintains his stance, his hand pressed against her, and the banshee whimpers. Then… Black lines spread through her pale skin. Ding.

She goes quiet. Her eyes close, and her head lolls to the side. Ding.

A strange blue glow shoots from Alaroc. A near-blinding pulse that blasts from his being. Ding.

The light fades, revealing—

Taliyah gasped. The banshee had turned to stone. That stone crumbled into ash. Handfuls of it floated up and twirled away.

As the memory dulled, a final ding sounding, she tightened her grip on the dagger. Did Alaroc plan to ash Taliyah at month's end? She knew she'd recover from the loss of any limb or internal organ; she'd survived a myriad of poisons, starvation and any number of other horrors. But stoning and ashing? Could she recover from something like that?

Yes, yes. Of course. She'd even survived a beheading!

Reveal nothing. Batting her lashes, she asked, "Do the Astra Planeta ash all their wives, or did I luck out and marry the best one?"

"Release. The. Blade."

"Why do you stone and ash your wives?" she asked, resting her free hand over the other. A double hold. Take that!

He scowled. "Stone and ash prevent anyone from coming along and reviving the body or spirit, undoing the sacrifice."

She gulped. "How do you kill non-wives?"

"With a three-blade. A weapon made of trinite. Most of my enemies are phantoms."

Trinite? The special weapon, most likely. She could guess the trio involved. Fireiron, demonglass and cursedwood. "And what does trinite do to phantoms? Because I've never heard of it, and I'm something of a weapon aficionado."

"Trinite bestows the final death to phantoms, causing their bodies to evaporate into nothing." Without a pause, he added, "Release the blade."

The fingers curled in, a defensive action to guard her enchanted ring. Alaroc could never learn she was a phantom.

Had she come back from the dead after tangling with the toxic trio? Yes. The first time. Would she revive a second time? Her mother didn't think so.

Dude. "So how long have you been getting your little Rocs off by murdering brides?"

A flicker in his irises. "My brides died for a purpose, with honor."

Had she struck a nerve? "Dying with honor cannot trump living with it. Soon, I'll prove it to you."

Another flicker in those golden eyes. "Each death saved countless lives. Without the Astra, phantoms would roam the worlds unchecked, feasting on everyone they encounter."

"So the sacrifice to your god and your survival are connected. Good to know."

Oh, he didn't like that he'd revealed more than he'd intended, she could tell. Once again, he tightened his grip. "My patience wears thin, harpy."

Ripples of pain shot up her arm, each stronger than the last. Inhale. Exhale. "Why do you hate phantoms so much? Word is, they're just mindless spooks controlled by a master."

Malice contorted his features. "Phantoms are parasites. Being fed on…" His lips curled in disgust. "Pray you never experience such a horror. There's no worse sensation." He squeezed with more force. "Although, losing a hand might come close."

Ouch—in more ways than one. He hated phantoms beyond reason. So much he might kill a phantom bride before her time was up…

She had to go at him with her biggest guns, then. Her own phantom abilities.

Astra hunting season kicked off today. Duration: thirty days. Method: any available weaponry. No daily bag limit.

A game plan formed. Tonight, she would feed on Alaroc. Mindless phantoms couldn't hide their feeding. Taliyah could. She could drain him to death while he slept, unaware of his impending doom. Or try to drain him to death. He was a big guy with a lot of power, and her body had a threshold. She could only contain what she had room to contain. If she failed to drain him to death, she'd have to settle for weakening him. Let him fade slowly without ever understanding why.

"That's it?" *Ignore the pain.* By strength of will alone, she maintained an uncaring expression. "That's your big beef with phantoms? They sucked your soul a little too hard? Wow. Sensitive much?"

He ran his tongue over straight pearly whites. "Phantoms are an extension of their master, a god who has overseen the Astra's suffering for more than twenty thousand years. We've endured ambushes, losses, abuses and untold agonies." He bent down, putting the tip of his nose against hers. "I'm done answering your questions. I'll tell you about myself instead, for you should know the beast you provoke. I'll put myself and my men first in all ways, at all times. If that means burning a world and everyone in it to the ground, so be it. I've never been a hero. I've never wanted to be. I make a better villain. To me, women are receptacles, one the same as another. Sometimes a female isn't even as good as my hand."

Unfazed, she told him, "I'm certain bad lovers everywhere agree with you. No wonder you have to pay for it."

He huffed a breath. "You'll find it difficult to push me to my limit, but woe to you if ever you near it. I can cause you pain in any way imaginable. I won't constrain myself to your punishment, either. I'll visit your crimes upon your loved ones. So, now that you know me better, do explain why you continue to hold a dagger on neutral ground."

"Because I can." If he wanted the dagger out of her hand, he'd have to break her wrist and pry it out. And even then he'd have a fight.

"Taliyah—"

"I'd rather die," she snapped.

With an animalistic snarl, he released her.

Pressure on her bones released all at once, sharper pains rushing up her arm, but Taliyah practically floated on clouds. She'd won a third round with the Commander.

I've got this. I'm unstoppable!

He stalked into the closet. In no way, shape or form did he look remotely civilized. No, he looked… Oh, man. She hated to say it, but he looked good. Very, very good. She'd never had a thing for beards but…

I might have a new fetish.

Okay, so maybe Taliyah was high from victory. Which was strange. Usually, her dissatisfaction returned in seconds.

He emerged from the closet with a small crystal in hand. "Anytime you wish to see the harpies in the duplicate realm, hold this." In the center of the spacious bedroom, he stopped and extended his arm, offering the crystal.

She glanced from the crystal to the calculated smile-not-smile playing at the corners of his lips. His entire being screamed, *Come and get it.*

Oh, that burned. He knew he held something she wanted, and he was forcing her to close the distance in a willing act of submission. The warlord had her, and they both knew it.

Left with no other choice, she sheathed her dagger and marched across the distance. No use putting off the inevitable. He smirked when she snatched the crystal.

Heavier than she'd expected. She shook it, frowned and shook it again. Uh... "What do I do with it?"

"You must only peer into it."

Really? Suspicious, she held the crystal to her eye and— Oh, wow! Okay. Taliyah gazed into a whole new world. Forty harpies in different stages of healing slept on cots in a large room. Wait. This room? She seemed to be standing in the middle of a body.

With a yelp, she hopped to the side. Her movement changed the crystal's angle, blurring the other world and real life together. They were so different, yet exactly the same.

Were they the same? Was she *seeing* into the duplicate realm from where she stood? Did it matter? A duplicate realm was still just a realm. Anyone with a key possessed the means to enter.

Taliyah tweaked her mission objective. *Find a key to save harpykind, kill Alaroc.*

Through the crystal, she watched as an Astra strode through her new husband's body. A warlord she hadn't seen before. So far, she'd clocked six of the nine her mother had mentioned.

The new guy gently lifted a sleeper and carried her out of the bedroom.

"Hey!" Taliyah shouted, ready to give chase. "What are you doing with her? Put her down!"

"He can't hear you. I'm sure he's merely taking her to a healer to speed up her recovery. My men are under strict orders. None will disobey."

That she kind of believed. Taliyah searched the faces of the remaining harpies, on the hunt for Blythe or Isla. No luck. "Everyone is resting so soundly, despite their injuries."

"They're in hibernation."

"Hibernation?" She seriously needed a better understanding of the man she'd just agreed to battle to the death. "Explain."

Alaroc turned, silent, presenting her with his back, making it clear he'd meant what he'd said; the guy didn't fear her in the slightest. Worse, he all but dared her to attack him in the no-go zone.

Was this a test?

He unsheathed and tossed several daggers upon the bed. Oh, yeah. Definitely a test.

"If you're planning to put *me* into hibernation for the month—"

"I'll take your life, harpy, but I won't take your right to choose your end. Surrender or fight me. You decide."

Never in a million years would she admit this aloud, but he'd just made her heart leap. His ferocity convinced her he'd meant what he'd said. He was offering her a fair fight.

The best warrior would win.

Okay, so, that was kind of burn-the-house-down sexy. Peering at him, considering the challenge and the victory, she felt every pulse in her body, blood rushing through her veins as if a dam had burst wide open. Not a hint of dissatisfaction.

Leaving his weapons on the bed, he headed for the door, grating, "I'll be eating in the dining room in an hour. If you'd like to join me, you may. If you'd prefer to avoid me, you may. As with everything, the choice is yours. What you won't do is surprise me. I'm prepared, whatever you decide." He exited, shutting the door behind him.

Where was he going and why? She would find out.

While she yearned to scour the palace for Blythe and Isla, she had to seize any opportunity to learn more about her opponent.

A pre-General had to make tough calls, putting the good of

the people above everything, even family. Besides, if Alaroc had told the truth, Nissa was the sole casualty. Which meant Blythe and Isla were resting. Healing, even.

Maybe she'd luck out and Alaroc would reveal a key to the duplicate realm. What if he revealed a weakness or vice? Or lied? He might be on his way to his concubine even now.

I must know.

This phantom was going to risk big and spy in a palace filled with phantom assassins…

6

Roc could've flashed to the throne room, appearing in an instant, but he opted to walk and ponder the mystery of Taliyah Skyhawk. The harpy might prove a tad more tempting than his other brides. The languid way she moved. The inherent rasp in her voice. The permanent glint of wickedness in those ocean-water eyes. She possessed a core of iron, and he found himself more intrigued than before. A strange state he didn't like... because he liked it.

He was a male who had reduced war to a series of chores and checklists, winning hundreds of worlds without a problem or hardship. Yet a harpy dared to hold on to a dagger, forcing him to break her wrist or retreat, and he developed a permanent hard-on?

The look she'd given him as he'd squeezed her wrist had shocked him. Taliyah the Terror of All Lands had very clearly preferred to lose a hand than a battle.

He should have followed through. He'd warned her; empty threats would only make things worse for him. But... What right did he have to punish such bravery?

Now, however, she'd earned gloating rights. She'd forced an Astra to retreat. The Commander, no less. On day one. During hour one. Twice! As her frostberry scent had invaded his nose, she'd left him trembling like a lad. He'd reveled as a flush spread over her skin, his heat chasing away her cold.

Where was his titanium core?

From now on, he needed to be stern with Taliyah. No more touching her. No more kissing, no matter how badly he craved her sweetness. The woman schemed to oversee his murder, nothing more. Who *wouldn't* want to save their people and lead the Astra? He fully expected an ambush before the end of the day. Perhaps even an *impressive* ambush.

What would she do?

Steps suddenly lighter, Roc entered the throne room. The place was empty, as expected. Ian had the unique ability to flash entire armies at once. An ability he used each time Roc shepherded a new bride away. The soldiers were transported beyond the trinite wall, allowing the rest of his men to deposit the rejected harpies into a cell in the dungeon.

The wall acted as a first line of defense against Erebus and his phantoms. When combined in such large quantities, fireiron, demonglass and cursedwood emitted waves of energy, creating a dome-like sphere of protection impossible for the living dead to bypass.

—*Ian.*— Roc projected. Astra often spoke into each other's minds, either collectively or individually. Sender's choice.

—*Yes, Commander. You desire your report, I'm sure.*— His brother's tone carried bite today.

Understandable. Once the first Commander, now the least ranked. Though eons had passed, he'd never forgotten the taste of power. Who could? The weddings served as a reminder of what Ian had lost.

His brother told him, —*Halo now patrols the wall. No sign of soulsuckers yet. Silver is working on your personal project, and Roux guards the harpies in the dungeon. I'm working on palace fortifications.*—

Halo Phaninon, the Ringed One, was a disciplined warrior and master strategist. With an array of mystical objects, he kept watch over the entire realm, both inside and outside the palace.

Silver Stilbon, the Fiery One, was a merciless metalworker, with an ability to read hundreds of minds at the same time. Though it cost him dearly.

Roux Pyroesis, the Crazed One, was their torture master. The horrors his broken mind cooked up for their foes... Roc shuddered.

Some men had a moral compass. The Astra Planeta lost theirs long ago.

—*How much did the prisoners protest their new accommodations?*— Roc asked.

—*They screamed insults, vowed to wipe out our entire familial line and clawed Roux's face when he stepped too close to the bars, so nothing out of the ordinary.*—

He sighed as he eased onto his newest throne. The women would act as an insurance policy, keeping Taliyah tied to the palace.

—*I have a job for you, brother. I told my bride that we'll be eating dinner in an hour. Therefore, you must plan and prepare a dinner. In less than an hour, in case that part wasn't clear.*—

Ian sputtered for a moment. —*Your black heart is showing. You know that, right?*—

—*Make it a feast. I wouldn't host anything less.*—

Grumbling filled his head before the connection dropped.

Roc loved his men, but he *loved* his brother. Teasing him provided endless entertainment.

He and Ian were sons of Dawn and Dusk, both born at the

moment night crashed into day. Mostly ignored by their parents, they'd spent their days with Aurora and Twila.

Raised by unconcerned, often cruel nannies, the siblings learned to rely only on each other.

After Dawn and Dusk had sold the girls, Roc had been racked with more guilt and rage than any man could bear, much less a little boy. He'd frothed at the injustice, the helplessness, desperate for change. The moment Chaos entered the picture, he'd gotten his wish.

At first, Roc hadn't just despised the god. He'd despised the god as much as Dawn and Dusk. The male had touted daily beatings, endless trials and constant battles as *training*. The moment Roc defeated his first opponent, however, he'd understood the god's methods. Hardness bred strength. The stronger you were, the less you lost.

Never, for the rest of eternity, would Roc be weak, unable to protect and defend what belonged to him.

Ian's voice cut into his musings.

—*I have an army of chefs installed in the kitchen. Your bride will have her feast.*— He paused before asking, —*You reacted to the harpy a bit strongly, eh?*—

His mouth turned down at the corners. —*What do you mean?*—

—*You're going to make me say it? Very well. Your hard-on nearly busted your leathers open.*—

—*It did, didn't it?*— Wasn't like he could deny it. —*That kiss… won't happen again.*— Taliyah's virginity didn't just purchase Roc a weapon. Her untouched state prevented *Erebus* from receiving it.

Any and every loss came with consequences of the worst kind.

In all his years as leader, Roc had only parted with a lone weapon. The Blade of Destiny. A dagger able to cut into the threads of fate, helping the wielder advance his agenda. The forfeit rankled even now.

Roc wasn't sure how Erebus had used the blade against him throughout the centuries; he only knew the god had used it.

He drummed his claws into the arms of the throne, a habit he'd developed since coming to Harpina, and cast his voice into Silver's head. —*How is the chastity belt coming?*—

Oh, yes. He planned to lock Taliyah in a belt by morning.

He'd lost the Blade of Destiny when Erebus sneaked in and secretly slept with his bride. The male could've killed her instead, as he'd attempted to do to so many others, but he hadn't. He'd allowed Roc to complete his task, discover the truth after her death.

At the time, Roc hadn't understood the man's motivation for such an act. Why settle for half when you had the means to enjoy the whole? Only later had the answer become crystal clear. Erebus wanted Roc defeated—but only after he'd ensured his misery.

Now Roc kept his brides in belts. As soon as Silver finished fitting the device to her species-specific strengths, she would sport one.

How would Taliyah react when Roc sealed her up?

And once again, he shot harder than steel. His blood heated, his every nerve pulsing with arousal.

—*How do you feel about lemon tartlets?*—

Roc focused on his brother's ridiculous question and inhaled. Exhaled. Some of his tension ebbed, but not all. Not even close.

—*Do you want to lose your tongue, brother?*—

Ian laughed, a nice sound to hear today of all days. —*You seem on edge. Shall I flash your concubine directly onto your lap?*—

He pinched the bridge of his nose before grudgingly admitting, —*I'll be…seeing to myself this month. I gave my word.*—

His brother laughed harder. —*You'll want to tell the concubines you have no need of their services, of course.*—

Not particularly. Why bother? Concubines signed on for two hundred and fifty years of service, traveling the realms with the warlords. They were free to bed whomever they desired. Partners changed often.

A grinning Ian appeared mere feet away. Like Roc, he'd removed his helmet, revealing long black hair, light brown skin covered in *alevala*, and black eyes that looked like stars anchored in an abyss. He stepped to the side and swept out his arm. The concubines appeared in unison.

Roc glared at the scourge before focusing on the women. They were an array of sizes, colors and species, dressed in everything from tank tops and panties to formal gowns. Some of the concubines were in the midst of a conversation, others in the middle of some kind of action. As soon as they realized they'd been flashed—a common occurrence among the Astra—they quieted.

Spotting him, they curtsied and awaited his command.

In a mimic of him, Ian arched a brow. —*Do you think your concubine looks like someone we know? A certain bride, perhaps?*—

He looked to the elf he'd chosen last year, mere weeks after visiting Harpina for the first time. Tall and slender, with long blond hair, blue eyes and pale skin. Frowning, he said, —*I don't see it.*— Taliyah commanded attention. She…was here? He sniffed. Did he smell frostberries?

Was she able to flash?

He leaped to his feet, his hands fisted. Ian caught his aggression and palmed a three-blade. A minute passed in silence. Two. Taliyah never materialized, and his frown deepened.

Roc shifted to the right. Had the fragrance of frostberries grown stronger in this area? It must have; he heated, his body suddenly determined to warm her. But again, the female never appeared.

Had his shirt picked up her scent when she'd rubbed against him?

He scowled and faced his elf…whatever her name was. "For

the next thirty days, you aren't to enter my room. Or approach me. Just stay away entirely."

Not the least bit bothered, she curtsied, saying, "Yes, Commander. Your every whim is my greatest desire."

He nodded with irritation. Which irritated him further. All of their so-called conversations flowed in this direction: he spoke, she agreed, and that was that, just the way he liked it. No part of him wished she would call his bluff.

"Just...return them to their quarters," he instructed Ian.

Ian huffed before sending the females away. "How are you able to ruin my fun so quickly?" he asked before vanishing.

Roc walked to a tall, arching windowpane bordered by stained glass and surveyed Harpina. The palace overlooked a garden maze filled with bushes and statues of past Generals. A meteorite graced the center. With it, he would construct Taliyah's altar.

Beyond the garden, in the center of the market courtyard, a massive tree bloomed with red flowers, shading every shop.

When he'd first arrived, the streets had brimmed with chatty females going about their day. Now those streets were empty, his men stationed behind the wall. By sunset, patrols would march about town.

The scent of frostberries had faded, he realized with a jolt. Meaning, he didn't carry the perfume on his clothing. Meaning... what? Taliyah was nearby, watching and listening?

What ability did she wield? Was Taliyah here, casting an illusion of invisibility, as only the strongest of snakeshifters could do? If he could catch her...

Excitement—

—*Commander?*—

—crashed. Roc sighed. He knew Roux requested an audience. The hunt for Taliyah must wait.

—*You may enter.*— He glanced over his shoulder, nodding at Roux in greeting when the warlord appeared. A beast with pale hair, golden skin, and yellow eyes with striations of pink, gray and brown—until his temper sparked and red took over. He gripped a kneeling wolfshifter by the hair. The beast held on to Roux's wrists with razor-sharp claws, but he didn't fight.

Well. The wolf had figured out the strategy to possibly surviving an encounter with the Astra: remain calm.

Roux muttered something about seeing and not seeing a woman, his gaze darting for a moment. Though he appeared somewhat crazed, he was the most intelligent Astra. Too intelligent. The way his brilliant mind worked often staggered everyone else.

Once he'd figured out whatever mystery currently plagued him, the muttering would cease.

Unlike other Astra, Roux didn't possess moving *alevala* outside of battle. In fact, his *alevala* did the opposite. For some reason, the images moved *only* during battle.

Face-to-face, Roc preferred speech to thought. "You've brought me a present?"

"Yes."

Roux must have caught the shifter attempting to free the harpies from their cell.

Wolves were a dangerous species. The essence of their beasts rose from their bodies, like a demon exiting a host, the thick shadow transposing itself over their features.

"He's a consort, I'm sure." Roc faced the window again, peering out. Perhaps he'd keep this world after Taliyah's death. "Put him with—"

"What do you plan to do with the harpies?" the shifter demanded, cutting Roc off. "Tell me! They are—"

Without turning his head a second time, Roc palmed the small crossbow sheathed at his side, extended his arm and nailed the male in the center of his throat, severing his vocal cords. Then he turned his head, his body following the new direction at a slower pace.

As the shifter gasped for air he could no longer catch, his face darkened to a deep purple. Blood leaked from his mouth.

"Had you let me finish speaking," Roc calmly explained, "you would have heard me instruct my warlord to put you in the cell next to the harpies."

He watched, uncaring, as the wolf fell over, twitched, then sagged onto the floor.

To protect your people, you maintained order. To maintain order, you took decisive action. *Exactly as he'd done since dispensing with his first bride. Precisely what he'd do in thirty days.*

He met Roux's gaze. "Before you return to the prisons, display his head on the front lawn."

Roc ain't here to mess around. He's here to murder brides and slay wolves. And he's all out of wolves.

Taliyah gaped at the male she'd married. She'd entered the throne room with just enough time to scope out a couple of the concubines. Then he'd murdered someone's consort without a shred of remorse—without even looking at the guy—because of an interruption. No, he'd struck because the shifter had disrespected him.

Honor and respect mattered to Alaroc to an insane degree. And his power...

Am I turned on by the thought of besting him...or by the man himself? Because hello, exhilaration. Her veins fizzed like never before.

She had no business desiring the dude who planned to kill her. The "monster" who'd already conquered her world and imprisoned her people.

Floating closer, she studied him more intently. He remained alert, his eyes brightening. Something had excited him, too. The kill? Or something else?

What would the brutal male do next?

What would *she* do?

Alaroc wandered about the throne room, silent. Ugh. Did he have to move so seductively? Muscles flexed. Despite his incredible size, his motions remained as fluid as water.

Again and again, he switched directions, closing in on her, as if he sensed her. *Wait. What if he sensed her?*

To gauge his reaction, she gathered her resolve and walked *through* the warlord. Upon contact, he grunted and planted his feet.

Oh, yes. He sensed her. Did he suspect the truth of her origins?

A minute passed. Two. He scanned the room, looking past her. His excitement remained. Well. That answered that. If he suspected the truth, he would project hatred.

Finally, he gave his beard a couple of strokes and flashed.

Where had he gone now? Did it really matter? In thirty minutes, he'd be in the dining hall. Why not join him? The man clearly enjoyed a type, his concubine basically Taliyah's doppelganger. She could resume her inquisition. He was too smug to guard his words. If she asked nicely enough, he might even *tell* her where he kept a key to the duplicate realm.

Another win for the bride.

Her exhilaration redoubled, keeping her usual dissatisfaction at bay as she raced to the bedroom reserved for special guests. There, a closet overflowed with garments of every size and type.

My honey had a hard day at work, overtaking a realm. He deserves a delicious meal and a gorgeous companion at his side.

"You can't surprise me, Taliyah," she mocked, brushing her fingertips over sheer silk. *Watch me, warlord.*

7

Roc sat at the harpy General's table, in the harpy General's hand-carved chair, his plate piled high with the harpy General's food. The scent of roasted meat, butter-drenched vegetables and freshly squeezed lemons saturated the air.

Colorful tapestries decorated the walls, depicting General Nissa's victories, of which there'd been many. Those tapestries hung alongside cases displaying the skulls of her enemies. Vases and other ornaments sparkled in the light, each piece adorned with precious gems. The table itself was molded from solid gold. The floor possessed a pearlescent sheen. A room fit for the most beloved of queens.

Would Taliyah show up?

Anticipation shaped his every breath, honing molecules of air into razors, slicing at his calm. Because he had questions for his lovely bride, and the strength to insist on answers, not for any other reason.

Three Astra occupied seats at the other end of the table. Halo, Silver and Ian. Roux had chosen to remain with the prisoners, social occasions often too difficult for him to navigate.

"Is this supposed to be a celebration? Very well. To Roc and his new bride." Halo lifted a goblet of mead, his eyes aglow as yellow, green and brown striations revolved around his irises. Over the years, the stubborn male with unflappable calm had proved to be an excellent second. There was no task he couldn't complete in record time, no man he couldn't break when the occasion arose. "May her death bring us new life."

Silver lifted a goblet, as well. "May she accept what she cannot change and never change what she cannot accept." Roughly the same height as Roc, he possessed long black hair, bronze skin and eyes like mirrors. A scar bisected his left brow.

The last one raised his goblet in solidarity. Roc merely bobbed his head once. As much as he loved these men, he rarely joined in their fun. At any time, any Astra had the right to challenge his rule. A battle would then take place. Whoever won earned the Commander's helmet. If the loser survived, he received the bottom rank. A position none wanted.

Ian, who sat at the foot of the table, proclaimed, "Five minutes past the hour." He tsk-tsked. "The way the harpy challenged our fearless leader made me believe she would join us."

Same. Roc shot his gaze to the double doors. Hopefully they would open any moment...

He gnashed his molars.

Earlier, as he'd stalked his prey through the throne room, he'd confirmed his suspicion. Taliyah cast an illusion of invisibility. Twice he'd brushed against her cold skin. Thrice he'd felt the graze of her hand on his body.

What other illusions could she cast? What other abilities did she wield? Could she mesmerize with a glance, as so many snakes attempted? Could she tempt a man beyond reason? She must. Despite their separation, his veins burned hotter.

Tone curious, Halo asked, "What do you think harpy history books will say about us in a hundred years?"

Silver, the most cynical of the bunch, hiked his shoulders. "That we kill for entertainment, care about little and disregard the suffering of others."

"So the truth for once?" Ian deadpanned.

Throughout the ages, many stories had been written about the Astra Planeta. Most were told by embittered descendants of those they'd conquered, the tales twisted. Many immortals believed the Astra to be extinct, bested by lesser beings like Cronus, Zeus and Ares. Please. Those so-called gods never ascended to a higher level, far too busy playing with mortals to care about power.

His lip curled with disdain. *Nothing matters more than ascension.*

With his next ascension, he would graduate from the blessing and curse. For his first deed, he would kill Erebus once and for all. Afterward, Roc would wed for real and experience peace for the first time in his existence.

Until then, the cycle churned on. The Astra created realms at will and destroyed worlds as warranted, their conquests legion. And if Taliyah didn't join them for dinner, she wouldn't eat! Roc wouldn't pander to her, just because he intended to kill her. He'd never done so with his other brides, and he wouldn't start now.

He glanced at the double doors before lifting his fork to his mouth with an angry swipe. The dish, whatever it was, had a decent flavor but— His ears twitched. He straightened with a snap. Did he hear the click-clack of a woman's footfalls?

He waited at the edge of his seat, his heartbeat quickening.

The doors parted at last, the harpy-snake strolling into the dining room, her head high, her shoulders squared. The moment her gaze found his, she paused. He drank her in—in gulps. Gone was the traditional war garb. Two pieces of ice-blue material clung to her curves, leaving her midriff bare. The top offered a deep V between her breasts, while the bottom cinched her waist and free-flowed to her ankles in varying lengths.

She had bathed, her white hair unbraided, the glossy waves like a waterfall, framing her exquisite face. The viper had added thicker slashes of kohl around her eyes, making them appear sleepy, as if she'd just roused from bed and desired a lover *immediately.*

He didn't shoot hard as steel this time. He shot harder. All that pale skin…

Hot before? No. Sweltering, Roc pressed his tongue to the roof of his mouth.

A deep shade of red stained her lips. Lips she'd slanted over his only an hour ago. Soft lips. Luscious. The kind a man craved wrapped around his—

Enough!

As she glided forward, locks of hair swished over her breasts, playing hide-and-seek with her nipples. Nipples puckering beneath the fabric of her top. Did he detect the ridge of a piercing?

He swiped his hand over his mouth and willed her dress to burn away. *Must see.*

Must? The word echoed in his mind, the fork in his hand bending. Nipples were nipples, pierced or not.

A few feet away, she paused once more to look him over, her cool expression giving nothing away. "Have I earned your respect yet?" Running a fingertip between the valley of those magnificent breasts, she made a little noise of dismay. Definitely pierced. "Or should I strip?"

She'd asked a question, and Roc had an answer. *Yes!* She should strip. *No!* She should change into a gown with chin-to-toe coverage. Which, which? He couldn't think. He scented her now, the frostberries like a potent wine. Lust hijacked his good sense.

"Join us as you are," he said with more force than intended.

Seduction so soon? Not likely. What was her purpose? What did she hope to gain with this? Was she wearing panties?

"By the way," she purred, a rosy flush burgeoning in her cheeks, "if anyone sees me naked later, mind your business. I'm just wearing my wifely uniform."

His men displayed different degrees of amusement.

Did she feel Roc's heat despite the distance between them? "Sit," he said, waving to the chair at his right.

She didn't sit. "I should probably apologize for my tardiness, and I will, just as soon as I'm sorry. As your men are proving with their nine-inch salutes, I'm totally worth the wait. Well, he's giving me ten." She winked at Silver. "Bravo, sir."

Irritation spiked. "You know you aren't to speak with my men. You know because I told you. Consider this your first and only warning." Because of her position as his bride, their sense of honor demanded they obey.

Far from cowed, she resumed her pout. "Is my new hubby the jealous type?"

Never. "Do you seek to arouse us so we'll fight over you? Is that what this is about?"

"Of course not." She blew him a kiss with a hint of fang. "That's just a bonus."

"Sit," he demanded.

Of course, she resisted. "I think I'd rather fill a plate and go. With everyone congregating at the other end of the table, I've got to assume you're terrible company."

"When you resist, I will assist. Then I'll force." He stemmed a stronger tide of irritation, stood and held out her chair. *I won't reach for her. Won't shake her…or haul her into my lap.* "Don't pretend to misunderstand the ways of warriors. You fight to become General. A title that will set you apart from those you lead."

"Apart, yes. Not above."

"Questioning my leadership?" Others had died for less.

"Wow. I didn't realize you were so sensitive. But just to be clear, yes, I'm questioning your leadership. I'll definitely do things differently when I'm in charge." Movements as fluid as water, she eased into the offered chair at last. "Be honest. You beat off to thoughts of me as soon as you left the throne room, didn't you?"

Sensitive? "You admit you used an illusion of invisibility to follow me?" Why part with a rare advantage?

She grinned, smug assurance pulsing from her. "Well, I *am* part snakeshifter. What did you expect?"

The woman's confidence remained unsullied. She truly believed she could best him. Perhaps he should show her the error of her ways.

She shouldn't play with a man who is stronger, faster and far more determined.

Fueled by the irritation—only the irritation—Roc half rose, leaning over the table to grip her by the waist. As he sat back down, he pulled her onto his lap, using his knees to force her legs apart. He shackled her arms behind her back as her wings fluttered against his chest.

Slits in her dress caused the material to gap, revealing silken skin and a dagger inside its sheath.

To his consternation—yes, only consternation—she relaxed against him, smashing her wings, as if he'd put her exactly where she'd wanted to be.

Her game rolled on, whatever it was. Perhaps she merely hoped to drive him mad?

"Please feel free to correct me if I'm wrong," she said, "but I do believe I feel my leverage growing."

Well, he had his answer. She did indeed hope to drive him mad.

Roc bit his tongue, tasting blood. As every astonished gaze watched their byplay unabashed, he rumbled straight into her ear, "I told you what happens when you provoke an Astra. Now I'll show you. Tit for tat. Challenge me in front of my men, and I'll do the same to you."

★ ★ ★

Taliyah cut off a groan as the Astra reached under her skirt and thrust two fingers deep into her core. Alaroc's incredible scent surrounded her. His heat engulfed her, and the incomparable strength of his body thrilled her.

You started this. See it through. "This is your idea of punishment, warlord? Or did you decide to seize the first excuse to finger me?" She'd come here planning to act nice and ask questions while he leered at her. The moment she'd spotted his erection, she'd switched gears. Why not poke at his pride until he bragged about his strengths, the realm key and anything else she wished to know?

He didn't stand a chance.

As he slowly plunged those fingers in and out, he nearly wrenched another groan out of her. "What do you think you're doing, flirting with me, harpy? I want to hear you admit it."

"I'm tricking you into a public fondling. Obviously." Oh, how she hated her breathlessness. "By the way, it took me thirty seconds. Are you embarrassed?"

He growled and nipped her earlobe. "What are you doing?" he insisted.

"I'm proving you not so secretly desire me and showcasing my ability to make you do my bidding. What else?"

Low and gruff, he asked, "Do you truly believe *anyone* can force me to do something I don't want to do?"

"I do. Very easily." Arching her back, she gifted him with a better look down the deep V of her dress. "I just have to make you want to say yes more than you want to say no."

Leaning into her, letting his thick beard stubble abrade her cheek, he stroked her clitoris. "Why don't I prove how much you not so secretly desire *me*?"

A gasp left her, her pleasure undeniable. *Control!*

When rational thought resumed, she gave a husky laugh. "If no one can force you, you *want* to finger me."

"Would you complain if I stopped?" His next exhalation

tickled her skin, rousing goose bumps. "Why don't I make you *scream* your surrender?"

"Please do," she rasped. "I'm not shy, coy or modest. Maybe I'll *like* getting off in front of our audience."

"I think you'll like getting off, period." Again, he ran her earlobe through his teeth. "Feel how wet you are for me."

Smug warlord. She should respond. She shouldn't continue staring at the arm pressed against her belly, marveling as soft, golden light illuminated his tattoos. He was so much darker than her, so much bigger, and the contrasts proved hypnotic.

Whoa! Hypnotic? Had she lost her freaking mind? She must have. Like a fool, she rolled her hips, greeting his next inward plunge. *Convince him to stop that. Never stop that. Argh!* The ache!

"If you're giving free orgasms, I'm placing an order for two. Make me come right now. Prove you can." He would fail, and she would gloat. He should know by now—Taliyah refused to break. "I'm sure your men will enjoy the show. Maybe they'll do me a solid and record it. I think I'll enjoy watching it later."

One warlord pulled at his collar and another shifted in his seat, as if uncomfortable. The third grinned and glared. But none looked away.

Alaroc's inhalations grew more labored. But so did hers. Soon, they were panting. Did he halt those wicked strokes between her legs? No. Her aches intensified.

Finally, he demanded, "Have you no shame?"

"Why? Are you hoping to give me some of yours?" She wouldn't moan. She wouldn't! *I. Will. Not. Break.* Upping the stakes, she reached up to cup her breasts. "I noticed you looking at these. Do you want to see them? Or do you prefer sensation to sight? Go ahead. Cup and knead them. I want you to…"

Would he do it? *Come on, Astra. Cave.*

He gave her clit a firm press, and unrivaled pleasure shot through her. Hot shivers cascaded down her spine, her hips arching of their own accord, seeking more of him without permission from her mind.

Growing desperate, she asked, "Do you think your men are lusting after the Commander's wife?"

He must have made a face at the others, because they looked away from her in unison.

Another chuckle left her, huskier than before. "Jealous Astra."

"Tell me why you're pushing for this," Alaroc demanded. Did he project more strain? "What do you hope to accomplish, exactly?"

"Besides a happy ending, you mean?" Taliyah lifted just enough to flutter her wings. A boost of strength allowed her to maneuver his hand out from under her skirt and spin.

Time to take this up a notch.

She straddled him, grinding her sex against his. The sudden pressure shocked a groan from both of them.

Had she just made a huge mistake? She wanted to rub against him. She *needed* to rub against him. Remaining immobile required every ounce of her willpower.

"There. Isn't that better?" Excellent. She'd sounded teasing rather than needy. She gifted him with another wicked smile. "Now we can come *together*."

He knew what she knew. Either he did as he'd threatened, suffering the consequences right along with her, or he retreated yet again.

"Feels so good," she breathed, rocking against him.

He stared at her with those blazing irises, as intense and motionless as a predator about to strike. What would he do next?

What did she *want* him to do?

His heat tempted and lured. His intensity delighted. Finally, he moved again. Gaze steady, he gripped her hips and urged her into a steady grind. She gasped, struggling to remember why she must resist him.

"You are—" He shifted, grinding on her right back. "You…"

Just as she softened, he gave another growl, lifted her and put her back in her chair.

Disappointment blended with satisfaction, the combination sparking anger. She'd won another round. She should celebrate. And she would, as soon as she stopped aching.

He slammed his palm on the table, rattling the dishes. Dark red liquid splashed from the rim of his cup, but he didn't seem to notice as his gaze revisited her.

"*Such* a drama queen." Taliyah tsked, feigning irritation.

He pursed his lips. "I'm not—"

"You are." She donned a disapproving expression. "You're a tease, too. Sorry to tell you this, but no one likes a tease."

"Are you sure?" He lifted his hand to his mouth and licked his fingers. The two wet with her essence. "I think you liked it very much."

Sexy, sexy Astra. Did he like the taste of her?

His eyes hooded. Oh, yes. He liked.

Taliyah squirmed in her seat, the urge to return to his lap a shocker. In a moment of self-preservation, she concentrated on the food, doing what she'd sworn she wouldn't: withdrawing from battle. Maybe he wouldn't notice.

"Now that we've established my leverage," she said, "I want my people released. Today."

"You won't win the war against me, harpy." His smugness returned, making a mockery of hers. Meaning, he'd noticed. "Your leverage is already disappearing. As I told you, I'll release the harpies on the thirtieth day, when my enemy can no longer use them against me."

Her leverage disappearing? She ground her teeth. "Maybe you're right about the harpies." Erebus, warring with the sisterhood again… Yeah, maybe they *were* better off sleeping. "But you're wrong about me. I promise you, I'll find a way to win. I'm already ahead. Your tally is one. Mine is currently five."

Leery, he asked, "Five what?"

"Boner pops."

★ ★ ★

The things this woman said! The things she did. Roc had no idea how to proceed with her. Laugh? Curse? Simply enjoy the ride?

He couldn't erase the feel of her from his mind, either. And the taste of her...

Sweeter than honey.

He bore an attraction to her, and she knew it. She'd decided to simulate a seduction, using his own body against him. Just to force him to surrender to her will.

Never again.

Ian, the traitor, failed to contain his laughter. The others sneaked glances at the harpy as if she were some kind of strange creature who'd emerged from a far-off galaxy. Even the cynical Silver.

Needing a distraction, Roc heaped different kinds of food onto Taliyah's plate. "Eat, never mention boner pops again, and I'll answer your questions. I'm sure you have many more." Maybe, if he kept her eating and relaxed, she would cease smoldering, daring him to grab her again.

She examined the selection of food and grimaced, but dutifully forked a bite of rice. Which she pretended to eat while dumping the contents in a waiting napkin. Did she think he dosed her food with a sedative, to make her more pliable?

Roc rolled his eyes, reached out and stabbed something from her plate to prove she could eat without worry. "I will never poison you."

"Yes," she responded, her tone dry, "you prefer to tear your victims to pieces, don't you?"

"When necessary." Where had she stood during this morning's battle? He'd looked for her.

"Ugh. Lame response." She shook her free hand up and down, making a crude motion with her fist before pretending to take another bite of food. "How are you planning to spend the next thirty days while I'm busy killing you? Help me understand what's on tap."

The ability to predict her reactions and responses exceeded his skill set. "I'll kill phantoms and build an altar."

Roc's chest clenched, and he rubbed the *alevala*-free spot above his heart. Almost *alevala*-free. More of the image now stained his skin. Not that Taliyah could see it beneath his shirt. A garment an Astra wore only in the presence of nonthreats. The warlords *wanted* their enemies to witness what they'd done. To know the being they fought.

"I've heard of phantoms, like I said, but I've never combat any," she admitted with an odd inflection. "You mentioned the leader of them. Rumors claim Erebus Phantom is dead."

Did she fear the only living son of Chaos? Roc...didn't like that. His own bride shouldn't fear Erebus and eschew Roc himself.

This was what he got—what he deserved—for refusing to make Taliyah come in front of everyone. Follow-through mattered.

"Erebus is their leader, yes. We did kill him, but he revived." Next time, Roc intended to stone and ash him for good. The only way to truly end a god with his abilities and powers.

"You guys killed him?" She couldn't hide a thrum of... What was that? "How?"

"Tell you so that you may use the information against me? No."

She smiled so sweetly, a fox in the guise of a lamb. "So the information *can* be used against you. Good to know."

He *pfted* a breath.

"Did you know Erebus terrorized Harpina before I was born?" she asked, shuffling her food around her plate. "His brother Asclepius helped doctor the survivors."

"I doubt Asclepius helped your kind. In his quest to create new armies and ascend, he and Erebus worked together to terrorize many femalecentric species." The brothers liked to dress those females in widow's weeds to remind the Astra of the bride ceremony. Even after Asclepius's death, Erebus continued the tradition.

Taliyah's gaze flipped up, meeting his. "Did you ever slaughter an army of phantom-harpies?"

He didn't hesitate to offer the truth. "My guess is yes, most likely, but I honestly don't know. I fight, and I kill. With phantoms, you don't consider any other origin, their old life dead and gone."

She thought for a moment. "What do you mean by *ascend*? You can go higher?"

"Always. Among the gods, there are myriad ranks and levels of power. To reach a new height, we must toil and fight until it occurs."

"Ah. Like the fight for harpy General. As we do all that toiling and fighting, our power grows. We prepare for leadership."

"Exactly."

She returned her attention to her food, mixing, mixing. Why didn't she eat? "Will Erebus come to Harpina? Will Chaos?"

"Chaos will attend the final ceremony." He made no effort to hide his affection for the male. "Erebus and his phantoms, too." Or his hatred. "But you have nothing to fear from either. I will protect you."

"Fear?" She lifted her gaze, and her head followed, only at a much slower pace. "You take that back right this instant. I fear nothing."

"You *should* fear Erebus and his phantoms," he told her, and yes, he contradicted his earlier assurance of protection. He was aware. "They want you dead before the day of sacrifice."

Her icy irises glittered with malice, the waters beneath that frozen surface clearly churning. "Since you killed our current General, I'm merely a single star away from being the next harpy General. I can handle a god and his puppies. Now. Do. You. Understand?"

Magnificent female. She embodied rage.

He suspected he'd learn nothing else until he responded to her query. "Let this stand as an official proclamation by the Astra Commander. Taliyah Skyhawk fears nothing."

Pride assuaged, she relaxed into her seat.

"I haven't forgotten what you said in the throne room." Words spilled from him, a question suddenly troubling him. "With whom have your hands and mouth...done things?"

She didn't miss a beat. "I used a temporary boy toy whenever the occasion suited me. His name is Hades. Why?"

"Hades, a king of the underworld?" A master seducer, according to reports.

"You've heard of him?"

"The male has won major wars and slain countless enemies. Yes, I've heard of him." Roc settled his fingers over and around the arms of his chair, slowly gripping the wood.

Taliyah and Hades.

Hades and Taliyah.

Hmm. "Do you miss him?" How could *any* male leave her a virgin, when the fate of his loved ones didn't hang in the balance?

Her lips formed a wide O, and she sputtered again. He hated that he'd stooped low enough to ask. The answer mattered not at all. In no way would her emotional state affect Roc's plans. But he didn't like the thought of *his* bride pining for another male in *his* palace. The disrespect of it... Yes, the disrespect. The *only* reason this bothered him.

He would hear her response, and he would hear it *now*. "Answer me, harpy."

"You really are jealous," she gasped out. "You are! We've been married a hot minute, and you're already foaming at the mouth with jealousy." Mirth softened her features, highlighting her delicacy. "Astra are possessive, then? No, don't try to deny it. Envy is practically seeping from your pores, darling."

In that moment, Roc kind of hated her. "I'm merely curious

as to why you risked your chance to become General to get off with a man like Hades."

"Here's the thing," she said, and judging by the calculated gleam in her eyes, she planned to eviscerate Roc. "I didn't just get off with him. I had my world blown. Repeatedly. No other has ever come so close to winning my V-card."

A god of the underworld had nearly taken what belonged to Roc. Little red dots sparked throughout his line of sight, every inhalation like a stream of fire in his nostrils.

The first signs of *anhilla*, a time when nothing could stop him. Anyone who got between him and his enemy died screaming.

—*Dismiss me, and I'll finish constructing the chastity belt before dinner ends. I've only a handful of adjustments to make.*— Silver's voice broke through the haze, alerting Roc to how quickly he was burning through his control.

He gripped the arms of his chair tighter, swung his gaze to his warrior and offered a clipped nod.

—*Do it.*— The sooner Roc put Taliyah in her belt, the better. Not because he feared he would lose his mind and bed her. Please. No matter how badly he wanted her, he wouldn't take her. But, if he had to suffer without a concubine tonight, she would suffer without relief of any kind.

Silver stood and marched out of the room.

"What was that?" A frowning Taliyah skidded her gaze over the warlords. "Do you guys communicate telepathically like Sent Ones or something?"

"Eat," Roc snapped.

"I've nearly cleaned my plate!"

"Yet you haven't consumed more than a bite." He needed time to calm. She needed sustenance. They might as well stay here while he awaited the belt. "We aren't leaving this room until you've dined, Taliyah. If I must feed you by hand, I will. That, I swear to you."

8

Taliyah recognized a challenge when she heard one. Alaroc *wanted* her to refuse to eat dinner. Any excuse to punish the woman who'd unearthed a weakness: his primitive sense of possession. Oh, he wasn't a raving envymaniac because he'd fallen for her or anything like that. She carried his name now. He considered her a piece of property. In his mind, he had an exclusive right to her body.

At the moment, he spoiled for a fight. How he must lament his inability to summon his concubine. For the next thirty days, Taliyah was his only outlet. Therefore, she shouldn't fight him on this. What the Commander wanted from her, he would not get.

Smirking at him, she spooned a bite of something creamy. Oh, ew. Had masticating always been this revolting? She much preferred her diet of souls. They went down nice and smooth. At least she didn't have to steal or earn food in order to enjoy it, like other harpies. Her phantom half overrode the necessity.

Roc glowered at her. Because her drama queen couldn't help himself. "If you dislike a dish, pick another."

"Why so huffy, husband? Bad day at the office?"

He said nothing, just studied her as if he were taking notes for their coming battles, planning where he'd put his hands.

With her next bite, she got the hang of things, adapting to the sensations and flavors. She absolutely, positively didn't squirm as she watched him watch her. The guy confused her, that was all. He was brusque and high-tempered, expecting obedience in all ways, at all times, but he was also...normal.

He'd softened when he'd spoken of Chaos and bristled at the mere mention of Erebus. How would he react to her familial relationship to the males? She supposed it depended on what was stronger, his love or his hate.

With Erebus scheduled to revisit Harpina, she decided to keep the information in her pocket.

A bomb could only be detonated once.

Today, she had to settle for screwing with Alaroc. Shocking him from his stoic demeanor was amusing, at least.

"Just curious," she said after she swallowed. "Are we spending our honeymoon in my bed or yours?"

Reclining in his seat, he adopted a casual pose. Nice try. Aggression like his couldn't be masked. The black shirt hugged massive biceps flexed and ready. Beneath the sleeve, a tattoo frothed and writhed with greater speed.

Avoid the trap! She redirected her attention to his too-rough, too-beautiful face. Now wasn't the time for another trip down Murder Lane. "Well?" she prompted.

"I'll sleep in the General's suite. Alone."

So. He required sleep, like everyone else. He wasn't all-powerful.

Operation Night Gorge is a go.

"Since harpies only use beds for sex and laundry storage," he said, "I'm sure you'll spend each night plotting my downfall."

"You aren't wrong." Until a consort was found, a harpy refused to rest in expected places or near an enemy. "You're not afraid I'll ditch you?"

"I'm able to destroy the duplicate realm with the harpies inside it. No, I'm not afraid you'll ditch." He delivered the threat as calmly as he'd delivered everything else, a warlord confident of his strategy. As he should be.

The strategy was sound. She couldn't delude herself into thinking he merely called her bluff. If she left and he caught her, he would absolutely destroy the other realm. But he was wrong about something. The knowledge wouldn't stop her.

First rule of war: never let trepidation about what could be stop you from doing the right thing.

If Taliyah wished to confer with Neeks, she'd freaking confer with Neeks. If she did her realm-hopping after she'd fed, the sleeping Alaroc would never know she'd jumped ship for a bit. If he even survived the feeding, of course.

His soul was going to taste so good, she just knew it.

"What motivation do I have to leave you, hubby dearest?" She batted her lashes at him. "A pre-General deserves to savor every second of her starter marriage."

His gaze dropped to her wrist. "What makes you think you'll become General before the other harpy? The one I first selected. She has more stars."

Annoyance prodded her. "That might be the dumbest question you've ever said. Mara fought General Nissa and lost. She's out of the running until the new General is crowned."

Taliyah figured those with nine stars would battle it out. Once she herself completed her sacrifice, she'd challenge the winner. Not to brag, but she could beat Mara while blindfolded, with both hands and feet bound.

"Why do you wish to become General?"

"I'm the best woman for the job." Truth was truth.

"And what makes you think you're the best?"

Curiosity layered his tone, nothing else, but for some reason she reacted as if he'd thrown a gauntlet, sputtering and shifting. No one had ever asked her a follow-up question about this. "For starters, I'm strong."

"So are the others."

"I'm—" Argh! "I was born to be General, so I'll be General." *And your constant dissatisfaction? What of that?*

Alaroc's head tilted to the side, his gaze moving past her. She glanced over her shoulder, following his line of sight. Nothing jumped out at her. No changes. Oh, wait. He must be communicating with his men.

He jumped to his feet as if he'd been ejected and held out his hand. "Come." A shocking mix of anger, arousal and excitement emanated from him, electrifying the air. "I have a special gift you *will* accept."

Beyond curious, she almost accepted his help to stand. "No, thanks. I'm ready for dessert." He would get nothing he wanted today.

With a grunt, he hefted her to her feet and restrained her against his chest.

Her heart drummed as they peered at each other, silent. Rebellion blunted, desires switched and honed. "Are *you* my dessert, Astra?"

He cursed and flashed her from the dining hall, an unfamiliar bedroom forming around her. Less space than the master suite, with fewer valuables. The canopied bed, claw-foot tub before the hearth and desk with golden turtles anchored beneath the legs suited her tastes.

Alaroc released her, separating from her so abruptly she stumbled.

Okay, so she could add flashing other people to his résumé of skills. She glared up at him, only to lose her train of thought. The silver striations in his molten-gold irises were spinning.

"Now," he said, unveiling a sardonic smile. "We do this my way, nice and easy, or we do this your way. *Not* nice and easy."

Different parts of her quivered as she scanned the bedroom, on the hunt for what could possibly cause this kind of reaction in— *Oh, screw that!* A beautiful but treacherous chastity belt waited on the mattress. She recognized the design.

A thin metal band decorated with swirling symbols fit around her hips. Two flat links of chain hung from the band's center, one in front and one behind, both delicate in appearance. They held a small, curved metal sheet in place.

No wonder Alaroc exuded sizzling excitement. With this "gift," he better secured his investment, ensured his bride remained untouched and punished Taliyah for taunting him at dinner.

Anger glimmered within her. Definitely anger. Not an excitement comparable to his. "You need help to resist me? How sad for you."

He paid no attention to her words. "For once, harpy, I'm hoping to do this your way."

Hot shivers trekked her spine, pings of exhilaration—er, hotter *anger* singeing every nerve ending. "How do you feel about regifting? I think the belt will really make your erection pop."

"Either I put it on you with your cooperation, or I just put it on you." Guttural tone, unwavering resolve. "Decide."

Her mind raced. Man, she'd really poked the bear with her jealousy comment, huh? He'd been itching for this fight ever since. Accepting the belt would discombobulate him, but giving up a personal freedom without a battle wasn't her style.

Why waste an opportunity to witness his combat skill?

She toed up to him. "Looks like you're getting your wish, Astra." His delectable scent muddled her thoughts, but she forged ahead. "Let's see what you've got."

A slow grin bloomed. "With pleasure, bride." In a motion too swift for her to perceive, he swept her into his arms and threw her atop the bed, right next to the chastity belt. Before she even stopped bouncing, he lifted her skirt and ripped off her minuscule panties.

She gasped as cool air kissed her heated core. "Well, well, well. You have moves. Not bad."

"There's more to come."

"I'm sure there is."

To her consternation, he didn't pounce. He moved to the side of the bed. Gaze locked on her, he rolled his head left and right, popping bones in his neck. Preparing. Muscle and tendon flexed, and she gulped. All that carefully banked power was doing strange things to her concentration.

Inner shake. Taliyah propped her weight on her elbows, smiled with invitation as he leaned toward her—and kicked his face with her six-inch stilettos.

He caught her ankle, but only after she'd cut his cheek. Blood trickled from the wound already healing.

"I have moves, too," she said.

"I'm sure you do." He grazed his thumb over her heel, tickling, popping the shoe off. "Have you ever worn a chastity belt?"

Do not moan. "Only in nightmares."

A husky, sardonic chuckle met her answer. "You'll wear mine."

How could a voice remind her of sandpaper and silk at the same time? "You'll have to subdue me first. Can you?"

His gaze dropped to the apex of her thighs as a bead of sweat trickled from his temple. "I think you like the idea."

She didn't. She couldn't. The madness! "I like the possibility of your defeat," she said, her voice hoarser than usual. How humiliating.

No more conversation. Erupting, Taliyah kicked him with her other foot. Harpy speed allowed her to nail him once, twice, thrice. Could he have stopped her? Probably. But he didn't even try. He held her stare, the stiletto's heel sinking into his shoulder with each strike.

"The way your breasts jostle..." Pulling himself from his stupor, he plucked the shoe from her and pitched it behind him.

When he reached for her, she punted him in the throat. He stumbled a single step, and she jolted upright, punching him in the same spot she'd last kicked him. Her knuckles cracked with the first blow and shattered with the second, his trachea like steel. She didn't care; she swung again.

He flashed before the next blow landed, disappearing. Heat behind her! Taliyah rolled back and punted her legs. Contact! He grunted, blood seeping from the corner of his mouth.

"You've had your fun. Now I'll have mine." He dived for her.

Just before he landed, she rotated. He crashed on the mattress, but launched up with purpose.

She rolled and kicked. He latched on to her ankle and tugged. They grappled on the bed, the floor, knocking into furniture and shattering knickknacks. She fought dirty, her entire body engaged in the battle. Wings fluttering, fists like hammers. If an opportunity presented itself, she took it, poking at his eyes, crushing his throat and bruising his balls.

The only skill she didn't utilize: misting. Maybe he'd consider it an illusion, maybe he wouldn't. The reward didn't outweigh the risks. Misting required energy, and Taliyah had yet to feed. She was already tiring, weakness invading her limbs.

Gah! How much more could she dish?

To her astonishment, he didn't throw a single punch. He merely defended himself.

She panted and wheezed as she shouted the many ways she hoped to kill him. All the while, he used his superior strength to herd her back to the bed. The beginning of the end for her, and they both knew it.

In minutes, he managed to pin her to the mattress. With her wings smashed, her strength dwindled faster.

"Concede, harpy. I've won." He hovered over her, damp with sweat. A vein bulged in the center of his forehead.

Some of her animosity drained. His tension… She might have lost this battle, but she'd won something else. "Why don't you look victorious, warlord? Because you want me more than ever?" A massive erection had popped the button of his leathers, rising from the waistband, the head slick with arousal.

Silent, he held her down and slid the belt up her legs nice and slow. He couldn't mask his tremors as he anchored the belt in place, his fingers lingering on her skin.

The big, bad Astra trembles for me?

Ignore your wonder. "You like tit for tat, yes? Guess I'll have to make you insane with unrequited desire before I kill you."

He didn't back down. A single twist of his wrist bolted the belt in place.

The ominous *click* and the cold bite of metal should have infuriated her. Lying there with a two-hundred-plus-pound enforcer between her legs, she felt…vulnerable. And she liked it.

Something was seriously wrong with her. A General should *never* enjoy a foe's victory.

"Do you see now, harpy?" Satisfaction oozed from him. "You can't beat me."

Determined to lord *something* over him, Taliyah snapped, "All I see is a man without a concubine who just lost fingering privileges with his wife."

9

A mess of conflicting emotions, Roc flashed to the master suite next door. He *needed* to escape Taliyah's addictive chill...titillating scent...defiant gaze...wanton mouth...the excitement and thrill she roused with her very presence.

As he'd peered down at her in the belt, he'd felt invincible. A heady sensation. He'd only craved more.

Fighting with her was exhilarating. She possessed incredible skill, speed and a cruel streak. His balls ached from repeated contact with her knee. Yet undeniable pleasure had consumed him every time he'd touched her. Her lush femininity had beguiled him.

When he'd pinned her, ribbons of silver-white hair had spilled over the pillows. Beneath the dress, her nipples had puckered, the ridge of the piercing daring him to pinch and suck hard. As his body had burned a flush into her skin, his resistance had crumbled.

The temptress made him crave more, more, more.

He'd yearned to kiss her a second time. Had longed to thrust his fingers deep and bring her to a swift climax. Just one. Her last. As her husband, he *owned* that climax.

Possessive again? He cursed. Already she worked her wiles on him. The true danger of a snakeshifter. They schemed and maneuvered and lured. You never realized you'd crossed your own boundaries until it was too late.

Had Solar felt torn apart like this?

Roc stomped to the closet—non-dramatically—to armor up. No more thoughts of Taliyah. Tonight, he guarded the wall. Phantoms usually showed up the day after his wedding.

As he selected the night's arsenal, he blasted a command to all of his men.

—Report.—

Halo spoke first, his right as second-in-command. —*I have returned to the wall. No sign of phantoms.*— He paused. —*This bride is…feisty. Is that the word for lightning in a body?*—

Roux's rumbly voice filled his head next. —*The harpies revolted when they heard your battle with your bride. I reminded them you won't be murdering her for thirty days, but my reassurances failed to calm them. I'm assuming mass execution remains off the table?*—

Silver told him, —*I have the armies split into groups, dispersed throughout the realm and in formation, ready for anything.*—

Excellent.

—*I've resumed palace fortifications,*— Ian said. —*Oh, and I should probably inform you the soldiers are gossiping like old ladies. Word about your humiliating interaction with the harpy has spread. Thanks to me. Jokes are being crafted. You're going to love to hate them.*—

Roc flicked his tongue over an incisor as he reached for a three-blade. —*Laugh it up. I look forward to the day I return the favor.*—

As he exited the closet, he glanced at the door dividing his and Taliyah's bedrooms. Was she inside, attempting to remove the belt?

Still hard, he cursed. He cursed again as he marched to the exit. Before he clasped the knob, searing heat blistered his nape. The exact spot Chaos had branded a symbol into his flesh.

An official summons.

Roc didn't resist as an unseen hand reached out to yank him through different realms. He might be a Commander used to complete control, but he served Chaos by choice.

Around him, scenery blurred, walls replaced by trees…water… buildings. Faster and faster, the objects blurred together. The deeper he traveled, the more his brand cooled.

When he stopped, he hovered in the midst of an endless night sky—a private room within the god's home. No sign of his sisters.

He stemmed his disappointment. Suspended nearby was the enigmatic god known to many as Ocean of the Dark.

"Roc."

"My lord," he said, bowing his head in a show of respect.

Chaos possessed rich black skin, his eyes a perfect match. When the sun rose, those eyes lightened, tinted with hues of pink, yellow and blue. By midday, his irises turned a blue so pure they rivaled the purest body of water. Then the process began all over again. A cloud of white smoke encompassed his hair. He wore a black robe, the ends covered in frost.

Roc's curiosity magnified, but he said nothing more. The highest-ranked warrior should start a conversation. Something Taliyah had yet to learn.

He stabbed his hands through his hair, as if he could scrub her from his mind. *No thoughts of the harpy.*

Finally, the god began. "You are wed again." Chaos's voice boomed, a lightning storm contained in every word.

"I am, yes." He offered no more. With Chaos, silence proved

wiser than chatter. The god often used your own declarations to teach you a painful lesson.

"My son remains determined to break you."

"I'm sure." Roc didn't understand why Chaos loved the male, after everything Erebus had done to the Astra, to others. On the other hand, Roc admired his mentor for loving his son the way Roc's own parents should have loved him and his siblings.

"You chose Taliyah the Terror of All Lands. The Cold-Hearted." The god never asked questions, even when he asked questions. He stated, his unwavering gaze boring into Roc's soul, sifting through his innermost thoughts. "She draws you as no other ever has, yet you will slay her. Other warlords might have wed another and kept the Terror for themselves."

Seemed he'd be thinking about the harpy after all. *Careful. Admit as little as possible.* "The harpy-snake makes the better sacrifice."

"I'm told the preferred term for a harpy-snake is snarpy."

Taliyah...a snarpy. Yes, he liked the label very much.

"If given a chance to start over, to choose another female, my Roc of the Ages will change nothing."

Another question without being a question. "You are correct." Anything less than the best was an insult to the male who'd saved his sisters and spent centuries overseeing Roc's advancement. Repay greatness with garbage? Never.

Roc desired Taliyah, yes. In a few short hours, she'd excited him in ways no other female ever had. A part of him eagerly anticipated their next sparring match. But that anticipation wouldn't save her. Nothing could.

"You will waver in your duty." The statement chilled him. "The only facet of this I don't know is whether you'll refuse to kill her."

Waver? No. "I'll do my duty without delay or excuse. I *will* kill her." He must.

The god floated closer, gliding around him. A trail of frost glittered in his wake, the frigid temperature sizzling over Roc's skin. "You will kill her...even if Taliyah the Terror of All Lands is your *gravita*."

Horror stirred within him, quickly conquered by disbelief. His *gravita*? The bride he could never replace. No, absolutely not. "An Astra produces stardust for his *gravita*. I've produced none."

"No, you haven't. Yet."

The final word hovered between them, a black hole of destruction.

Heat and aggression filled Roc, his muscles expanding. Taliyah...his gravita... *Was* it possible? It explained the intensity of his attraction to her. Not to mention his unwillingness to harm her as they'd sparred. The way he hungered for her, even now. "I... No. She isn't, and she won't be."

"Or she is, and she will always be."

No. He would prove it. "I won't change my mind about her or my duty." He wasn't like Solar. He wouldn't put a bride's life before his men, heaping a curse upon their heads.

"I suspect you lie to us both." In front of Roc once again, Chaos smiled, revealing razor-sharp teeth. "Perhaps, with her death, you'll finally ascend."

His greatest desire. Will do anything.

"We shall learn the truth together." A wave of Chaos's hand, nothing more, yet Roc tumbled into the next realm and the next, hurling to Harpina before he fully processed the god's words.

His momentum barely tapered by the time he accessed his bedroom. He stumbled about, slamming into a wall and cracking the stone. His brain rattled against his skull. Dust plumed the air and tickled his throat.

When he stilled, he cast his gaze to the door that separated his bedroom from Taliyah's.

The urge to close the distance nearly overpowered him, but he resisted. Taliyah *wasn't* his *gravita*. No need to contemplate or debate the notion. He hadn't lied to his god. Duty came first, no matter the consequences. For his men, for the blessing—for the downfall of Erebus—Roc performed his duty *always*.

Would he ascend, as Chaos predicted?

The possibility of achieving his goal at long last…didn't thrill him as it should have. He scowled, his default expression since meeting the snarpy. Why couldn't he rejoice at the thought of surpassing Erebus's level of power? Of annihilating every phantom in existence? Of making his parents regret their actions toward him and his siblings? Of escaping the endless cycle of wedding and killing?

Although, if he murdered his *gravita*, he might find himself embroiled in a far worse curse.

10

Stupid chastity belt! Taliyah stomped through the palace, crystal in hand, on the hunt for Blythe, Isla or a key. With every step, the metal plate rubbed a very sensitive spot, keeping her on edge. No doubt the designer hoped to torment as much as guard her precious virginity.

She'd tried to remove the belt with a blade, but she'd only sliced herself. Didn't help that the weakness she'd experienced during the battle with Roc lingered, gaining new ground. And yes, she called him Roc now. No need to make a big deal out of it. The shorter pronunciation saved time, that was all.

Anyway. As soon as Roc fell asleep, she'd rid herself of the weakness. Feeding and feeding and feeding. All would be well.

Her wings rippled with anticipation. If everything went according to plan, her widowhood kicked off before sunrise. If she merely managed to fatigue him, so be it. She had plenty of time to ensure her win.

Snaking around a corner, she entered a hallway with six doors. Three on the left, three on the right. No sign of her sister or niece among the sleepers but... *Hmm, that's new.*

At the other end of the hall, someone had framed the windows with... What was that? Some kind of stone? She glided closer to the arching pane of stained glass.

She reached out, the hairs on her nape standing at attention. The substance, whatever it was, was gunmetal gray and jagged, pulsing with energy. Upon contact, a thousand invisible bugs crawled over her skin, biting and stinging. A sensation she recognized.

Taliyah faltered, her stomach roiling. The Astra had bordered the window with a combination of fireiron, demonglass and cursedwood. Trinite, Roc had called it. *My kryptonite.*

Well, after she finished her search, she'd just have to even the playing field.

Determined, Taliyah headed for the last room on tonight's list. The library, an enormous, three-tiered room filled with countless books about harpies and the many different species they warred with. Among other things. The first floor gleamed like a lake of fire, the second like a layer of ice, the third a combination of the two. Flanking the heart were statues of past Generals.

With the crystal in hand, she discovered row after row of cots lined the library in the duplicate realm. Harpies slept here, there, everywhere. Still no sign of Blythe, Isla or a key.

Disappointed but more determined, she switched her efforts to Roc's destruction. Taliyah rigged a chandelier to fall within the next twenty-four hours, messed with electrical wires to fry whoever flipped the switches and loosened select balcony rails.

As she finished up, a short, dark-skinned brunette and a tall, fair-skinned blonde with curlers in her hair rounded a bookshelf. Concubines.

Taliyah paused. Dressed in bathrobes, the pair perused the

vast array of tomes while drinking canned soda from a straw and whispering between themselves.

Could they be used for intel?

Approaching, she tried for a friendly greeting. "Hey, guys. It's me, your Commander's new bride or whatever. How about a chat?"

In unison, they drew up short. Neither projected fear. Fools. She'd changed out of her dress and into battle regalia. Roc's discarded weapons were strapped all over her body.

Yeah, she'd sneaked into the neutral zone before beginning her hunt. He'd been long gone.

"You are Taliyah, yes?" the brunette asked.

"Yep. The one and only." How loyal were they to the Astra? Could they be bought? "What're your names?"

The brunette introduced herself first. "I'm Teriella. Teri."

The blonde—the one who resembled Taliyah—took a sip of soda and belched into her hand. "I'm Kindred."

Up close, Taliyah clocked their differences. Kindred was a couple of inches shorter, with pointy ears. Her rosy skin resembled polished pearls. An elf, then. She smelled like a lilac garden.

"We thought we'd grab some books," Kindred said, "but we'll leave you to your…whatever you're planning."

"Stay. I can help you find the best books. Is there a particular subject you're interested in? We have a couple shelves devoted to romance novels, if that's your thing."

"Lookit, I don't want to be rude or anything, but you aren't winning us over to your side." Teri edged away. "We won't help you escape, and we won't harm our men on your behalf."

"As if I need help." She kept her focus on Kindred. "You are in love with Roc?"

The elf laughed. "Lady, you've got it all wrong. I'm living my dream life. Fierce protectors, good sex and great friends. I'm not giving it up for a dead harpy walking."

Taliyah shrugged. "Go ahead, bet on the wrong horse. This year's participation trophy is the Astra's head."

Teri tugged on the other girl's arm. "Let's go. We shouldn't be talking to her."

Well, good riddance. She had better things to do.

As Taliyah set traps for the Astra in other rooms, her empty stomach folded into itself. More strength drained. Soon, the sun would rise. Surely Roc had returned. Surely he slept.

Her mouth watered. *So hungry.* Before she got busy with the Astra, she might as well collect the gun every General stashed in the library. Everyone needed a plan B.

She rushed back and scanned the area. Alone. Excellent. Taliyah approached a life-size portrait of Nissa that hung at eye level. In it, the former General crossed her arms over her chest, a semiautomatic resting against a shoulder.

Can already smell the gunpowder. Another scan of the area. She reached out, her hand ghosting through the image. Not because she had misted; she hadn't. Harpies often traded mercenary work for magic. Any harpy could do this. When her fingers curled around cold, hard steel, she grinned.

Bullets might not kill Roc, but they'd definitely slow him down. Pair the gun with the crossbow and daggers he'd left on his bed and she could do major damage.

Once she'd sheathed the gun, she sneaked into the proper hallway as quietly as possible. The guards posted at the master's door earlier were long gone.

Because her room offered a private entrance, she didn't have to pass through Roc's. Taliyah set the gun on the nightstand, alongside the other weapons she'd pilfered from him. Had he even noticed their loss? In the small time she'd known him, he'd treated his arsenal as disposable. The exact wrong thing to do, according to Tabitha Skyhawk's school of successful warring.

Her mother used to tell her, "When your strength fails, your weapons excel."

Roc's strength was about to fail him.

He's gonna taste so good. Trembling with a mix of hunger and excitement, she settled on the bed, boots and all, preparing to do a little *soulsucking.*

Soulsucking, a term often used with great derision, interchangeable with *feeding.* It occurred physically or mystically, diner's choice. Most days, Taliyah preferred live and in person, body to body. When dealing with an Astra, exceptions had to be made.

Let's do this. Inhale. She pushed her spirit from her body, bit by bit. A painful process, every time. Like amputating a limb. Deeper cold washed over her as bone, muscle and flesh separated from spirit. Almost there...

Every immortal possessed a spirit, soul and body. The body acted as the house. The soul contained the mind, will and emotions—the power—while the spirit acted as a vessel for the soul, linking it to the body. A spirit could function outside the body, but a body couldn't function without the spirit.

She hated leaving any part of her behind and vulnerable and wished she could mist to feed. Alas. She must ensure a part of her spirit connected with Roc's, no barriers between them.

As soon as the creepy process completed, she glided across the room and slipped through the wall. And there he lay, the Commander of the Astra. He *was* asleep, tossing and turning.

Almost giddy, Taliyah glided closer to the bed. *Bon appétit.*

When he shifted in her direction, a beam of cerulean moonlight bathed him and she froze. Had he sensed her?

His eyes remained closed, his long lashes casting spiky shadows over his cheeks. If not for the lines of strain around his mouth, he would have looked boyish.

"No," he barked. He kicked at the covers and whipped his head.

Bad dreams? How very...normal. And kind of cute. It humanized him a bit.

She licked her lips as she completed her approach and eased upon the side of the bed.

He thrashed his head again, and an urge to comfort him caught her unaware. What troubled a warlord as fierce as this one? What bothered a killer who proudly wore his worst crimes on his skin?

Are you…softening? Recalling his purpose for her, she had no trouble hardening her heart. Comfort the man planning to kill her? No. Right now, she lived for his torment.

Taliyah leaned into him, letting her mouth hover over his. Her eyelids sank low. Mmm. She already scented his soul, all that spiced rum and melted sugar. Was she drooling? She might be drooling.

Had she brought a cell phone, she might have snapped a picture of her meal and posted it on her social-media platforms.

The caption would read *About to dive into an all-you-can-eat buffet of 100% Grade-A Astra beef.*

For a moment, Taliyah merely savored him. When hunger eclipsed everything else, she cupped his jaw, shocked by the fervency of her tremors. Tremors that worsened as she pressed her lips against his and extracted…nothing.

She frowned. Had she done something wrong? Tightening her grip, making sure her spirit brushed against his, she refit her mouth over his, extracting…nothing. She sucked with more force. Nothing. She sucked with so much force her cheeks hollowed, then sucked even harder. The only thing she received? A dance with dizziness.

Flabbergasted, she dissolved contact by small degrees. Somehow, this big, beautiful slab of power had blocked her. While sleeping!

He deserved… She was going to… Argh!

Fuming, she returned to her bedroom and reentered her body. As the different parts of her reconnected, limbs tingled and chilled. Mind racing, she eased into an upright position.

Okay. All right. Forget feeding. With so little time before sunrise, she couldn't hunt his army to consume a soldier. She'd have to go another day without a meal. Perfectly doable. Tomorrow night, she'd visit the army first thing.

Today, she'd settle for striking at Roc in other ways. She had the gun and crossbow. Why not set a trap? At the very least, she'd learn how he reacted to bullets and arrows and how quickly he healed.

Decision made, an idea already taking shape. Taliyah got busy arranging a very bad morning for her husband.

Once she'd figured out all the kinks, she grinned. He wasn't going to like this at all...

11

As soon as sunlight streamed through the bedroom windows, Roc rose from bed. He'd gotten no sleep. First, he'd stalked the streets of Harpina, on the hunt for phantoms. From there, he'd tossed and turned, plagued by dreams of his sisters, reliving the day his parents sold the girls to the highest bidder. The helplessness of fighting and failing to save them...the sheer terror etched into their little faces... Ian's tears as the two were carried away...

At some point, Roc had lost himself in a vision of Taliyah. A memory of her flawless body splayed across a bed, flushed and panting, daring him to do whatever he desired as he slid the chastity belt up her legs.

From *there*, he'd battled a raging hard-on.

Roc glared down at his hands. As expected, no evidence of stardust glittered there. "She isn't my *gravita*."

Chaos sought to teach him a lesson, that was all.

And what would that lesson be, eh? How to obsess over a woman?

Sullen, he grabbed a dagger and stomped into the bathroom. Needful of a distraction, he sent a command to Ian, rather than the other warlords.

—*Report.*—

Only seconds passed before his brother obliged. —*The bride used the crystal for most of the night. I lost track of her multiple times as I framed windows, but I know she had a run-in with the concubines. I don't know what was said.*—

No telling what the unpredictable Taliyah would do to the women in an attempt to hurt him. —*Move the concubines to Halo's quarters near the wall.*— A pause. —*Anything else?*—

—*Why? Do you want there to be something else, brother?*—

—*Never mind. Forget it.*— Conversation was a bad idea.

Roc stripped out of his underwear and entered the shower stall with the dagger clutched tight. Cold water sprayed from the overhead spout, quickly warming. Steam filled the enclosure and coated the glass.

As warmth rained over him, he glared at the spot just over his heart. The *alevala* had regrown, his most hated memory on display. How he wished he could remove the mark permanently. The best he could do was forget for a little while.

Eager, Roc pushed the dagger into the image, into muscle, and slowly rotated the blade in a wide circle. His lips pulled tight over his teeth. Rivers of crimson trickled down, down, joining the stream of water and whirling into the drain. Inhale. Exhale. Good. Some of his tension drained. He'd done this every day for centuries, the pain now a welcome part of his day.

What would Taliyah think, if ever she spotted—

He shut down the thought before it fully formed, the answer moot. She'd never view this particular memory, and that was that.

When a bloody, fist-size flap of flesh plopped to the floor, Roc sighed with relief. Better. Within minutes, he grew new skin unstained by *alevala*.

He tossed the dagger to the side, the metal clinking against another dagger. With quick efficiency, he washed up and exited.

His gaze strayed to the door to Taliyah's room. What was she doing in there?

He scowled. He had a thousand things to do today, and none of them involved seeing the snarpy.

"*Not* my *gravita*," he snarled. After dressing in a plain black T-shirt, leather pants and spiked combat boots, he collected his favorite set of chisels. Perfectly constructed altars didn't grow on trees. He had twenty-nine days to create a masterpiece worthy of his god—and the sacrifice herself.

What *was* she doing? Didn't he have a right to know? He was her husband. Her master. Depriving himself of the information only helped *her* cause. Since she hadn't ambushed him yesterday, he assumed she'd do so today.

Why not get their next clash over with?

Roc flashed into her bedroom, not bothering to knock and announce his intentions.

The bed was made, nothing out of place.

His hands balled into fists. "Tali—"

A tendril of aggression brushed his skin, his body burning in seconds. He braced for a strike. A split second lasted an eternity as he noticed his crossbow anchored to the wall, a cord wrapped around its trigger. Taliyah braced herself in a corner of the opposite wall, a set of claws embedded in plaster, an arm extended. She'd tied the opposite end of the cord to the trigger of a semiautomatic, the barrel aimed at him.

She grinned, a temptress without equal, transfixing his gaze.

He held himself motionless—barely. "Impressive."

"I know." *Boom!*

Whoosh. A bullet ripped through his heart at the same instant an arrow cut through his shoulder. He had no time to process what she'd done before she launched her next strike.

Boom, boom, boom! Whoosh, whoosh. Three new bullets and

two new arrows battered him. He stumbled forward, then back, toppling over something he hadn't noticed before. Trip wire? He crashed into the floor, falling like a cannonball.

He thought he might admire her the *tiniest* bit.

"My motto?" She dropped from the corner, landing with spectacular grace. Walking toward him, she swayed her hips, lifted the gun and fired off another round. "Why wait to kill your enemy tomorrow when you can kill him today?"

Only admire her the tiniest *bit, Roc?*

He remained on the floor, ignoring the pain. "There are few ways to kill an Astra, wife, and this isn't on the list."

"I figured. So I brought a sword." The gun thudded to the floor. A whistle of metal sounded. She reached his strike zone and swung.

He didn't attempt to dodge. He caught the sword in his hands. The blade sliced skin and muscle, hitting bone with a clink.

Her lips parted, and her breaths quickened. "I'm fighting a *robot*? Dude. You have no idea how much sense this makes."

He frowned. She considered him emotionless? "I promise you, I'm all man. My threshold for pain is unsurpassed, my ability to heal unmatched." Blood poured from the wound, but the newest flare of pain barely registered. "Are you done with this ambush, or do you have more planned? I have duties."

His feigned boredom provoked the desired response. Fury exploded inside those ocean-water eyes, some of the ice melting. The loveliest color bloomed in her cheeks.

"You're going to pay for that," she grated.

She. Was. Magnificent. He hardened. He throbbed.

Intense waves of heat emanated from him, the urge to yank her closer nearly irresistible. To hold her, if only for a moment. To kiss her again. The last time. To touch. To...protect?

He rejected the notion without taking time to analyze it.

Her gaze slid over his body, a virtual caress, and she licked her lips.

His shaft throbbed harder.

"Do you know what I'm going to do to you, Roc?" She met his gaze.

He couldn't stop his next words. "Tell me."

"Absolutely nothing." Hips swishing gracefully, she stepped out of range. The sultry way she moved… "My work here is done."

She must have rendered him stupid, because he struggled to understand. "What do you mean?" What work?

A grin of delight bloomed. "You crave me. Even now, you ache for me. Do you know how much *I* crave *you*? Zero point zero."

A lie. "I make you wet, and we both know it."

She tsked. "Are you sure it was you? Or my thoughts of Hades?"

Jealousy shattered what little remained of his calm. Disgusted with her, with himself, Roc snapped, "You are not my *gravita*," and flashed away.

12

Gravita? What did that even mean?

Taliyah made her way to the dungeon, tumbling the question through her mind. *You are not my...downfall? You are not my... friend? You are not my...good girl?*

The answer remained at bay.

When Roc first appeared in her bedroom, she'd sensed his irritation and assumed he'd stumbled upon some of her traps. But as they'd peered at each other across the sword's blade, something had changed. For a moment, he'd observed her as if she were the answer to his prayers. Then, of course, he'd turned into a snarling beast.

Whatever. His opinion hardly mattered. Like him, she had duties. Namely, coming up with a new game plan. It was nonoptional now.

Plan A, feeding, had failed. Plan B, shooting and beheading Roc, had also failed. So far, plan C eluded her. That was why she wanted to talk with the harpies below. She'd scope out the other prisoners, too. Maybe she'd come upon the perfect snack. Hunger gnawed at her more forcefully than she'd expected.

Taliyah descended dark, dank steps and entered a wide corridor with crumbling stone walls and flickering torches. Water dripped in several places. A horrid odor of mold and death coated the air, creating a fetid perfume. In the dungeon, the ground remained cold all year around, just like in the garden, freezing her feet inside her boots.

Navigating the corridors, she eyed every cell. Most contained a prisoner who'd committed a terrible act against harpykind.

Hmm. Not a great selection, to be honest. Despite their varying species, no prisoner displayed hints of strength. Even if she tapped out the entire lot, she doubted she'd fill her tank halfway.

The General contenders occupied the cell at the end of the farthest corridor. The only way in or out of it was flashing, a skill these harpies did not possess. They had no strength, either. Metal bands pinned their wings, crisscrossing above and below their breasts outside their shirts.

The sight gutted Taliyah, and she curled her hands into fists. Along with everything else, Roc would pay for this.

The women huddled together, whispering. An Astra stood sentry nearby. The guy with long white hair. Striations of pink, gray and brown ringed his yellow irises. He wore a T-shirt and leather pants, like Roc, and he didn't move in the slightest bit. But his gaze darted constantly, as if he saw things that weren't there. He mumbled his words. "There and not there. When? When did they vanish?"

She tuned out the warrior and focused on the harpies. Hey! They were talking about her.

"Is Tal already dead, do you think?" someone asked.

"You heard yesterday's fight, right? Girl struck and missed, and boy retaliated. We're on our own now. As the warrior with the most stars, I'm in charge."

That voice Taliyah recognized. Mara had best watch herself, or she'd get hers, too.

The Astra didn't rebuke Taliyah as she closed the distance, but he did shut up and stare when she stopped in front of him. Embers of red flared and died in those amazing irises.

"I'm here to check out the one-room abode with natural flooring and guaranteed security. Gotta say, the curb appeal isn't what I was hoping."

"Why am I happy to see you?" he demanded.

"Because I'm awesome?"

"Why, why, why?" His gaze slid away from her. "Why don't I remember? She was there. *They* were there, then nothing. What don't I remember?" He resumed his mumbling, then his pacing, seeming to forget her presence altogether.

A possible weak link in the Astra chain? Could he be used against Roc?

Gasps sounded from the harpies. "Taliyah!"

"Our MVP! Never doubted you'd survive."

She darted past the jailer, hurrying to the bars to greet the girls. Grins and cheers abounded. No one bore any wounds or bruises to signal physical abuse. They wore plenty of dirt, though.

"Is their leader dead yet?" Mara asked, her superior tone suggesting she'd have this thing won and celebrated by now.

Of course she went there. "Trust me, I'm working on it. I plugged the Commander full of bullets and arrows, and he barely felt it. He caught my sword blade and all but yawned."

"Bed him, his men, or a vibrator for all we care," Mara belted out. "We all heard him. He needs a virgin. No hymen, no sacrifice."

The exact plan Roc claimed every bride had endeavored to enact at some point. "Aw. Is Mara afraid of a wittle competition?"

"Aw. Is Taliyah afraid she'll fail to get it and quit it? The Commander didn't seem impressed with your goods and services."

"Only because you weren't looking low enough," she snapped. The woman had landed a direct hit. What if she...couldn't?

If these girls ever found out about the chastity belt, they'd tease her for life.

"Wait. Are you blushing?" Mara gasped.

"Guys! T-bone is blushing!"

Speculations about the reason ebbed and flowed, blending together.

"I'll kill him, okay?" How? *How?* "Don't worry. I just came to tell you guys the rest of our people are being kept in a duplicate realm. Some or all of the Astra have a key. We need one."

"On it!"

"We've got this!"

"I'll nab Officer Mumbles's key, guaranteed. I think I'll take his heart while I'm at it. Everyone needs a keepsake."

Harpies were the best. "I'll send food you can steal from Mumbles," she said, then pivoted on her heel and stalked past the Astra. He made no comment.

Where was her dear, darling husband right this second? What was he doing? Should she track him down to make another play for his head or wait?

Wait and stick with her original plan, she decided. Return to the Realm of the Forgotten while he slept, feed, strengthen and clear her head. Tomorrow, she'd launch her next attack.

For the rest of the day, she'd...what? Try to learn more about him, to unearth another weakness? Challenge him in a sexual way to keep him off-kilter?

You are not my gravita.

Gah! What did that even mean?

When Taliyah entered the master suite, she noticed a constant, rhythmic clink. The noise came through the private balcony, so she padded over. Open doors allowed a soft, rose-scented breeze to waft past the dancing curtains. At the railing, she scanned the royal gardens.

Oh, wow. Okay. A shirtless Roc sat before a massive chunk of black rock, his big, tattooed body bathed in sunlight. Pieces of the rock fell as he chiseled. Sweat trickled down ridge after glorious ridge of flexing muscles. Fury and determination tinged his expression.

Beautiful monster. Powerful beyond imagining. Dangerous in ways she'd never thought possible. In a single day, he'd trained her body to react to his, the mere sight of him enough to fill her with heat.

For some reason, her mind replayed the way he'd tossed and turned and shouted as he'd slept. A fearless warrior, plagued by bad dreams.

Ugh. Was sexy, stoic and secretly tormented her new type?

She couldn't count the number of times Roc had inspired arousal in her...or the times he'd made her forget her dissatisfaction. That one rankled. She might kill him for it alone.

She *was* going to kill him. That was mission objective number one. He believed failure waited in her future. He also believed that she, like the rest of his brides, would try to seduce him at some point—and bomb. Even Mara had lost faith.

Would Taliyah bomb if she gave seduction her best? Roc had hardened for her this morning, yes, but the look on his face after she'd baited him about Hades... The Astra might keep his distance from her for the remaining twenty-nine days. She had enraged him, the urge to throttle her pulsing from him.

Her confidence dwindled. Suddenly, she had...doubts. Not just about the seduction but the war. His special skills were stacking up. The ashing. Her inability to feed from him. His resistance to pain and lightning-fast ability to heal.

Doubt? Me?

Never accept a picture of defeat. Especially in the middle of a war.

What had her mother used to tell her as a child? *Doubt is fear in disguise. All fear must be rooted out and destroyed or it will only grow again.*

Taliyah refused to fear anyone, even a white-hot monster with sex appeal seeping out of his pores. But…what if she did fail to kill him and this marriage came down to the wire? What if she had no other option *but* seduction? Shouldn't she lay the groundwork for success, just in case? Shouldn't she shake *his* confidence?

Roc was more of a threat than she'd expected. Orchestrating his death would be difficult, so allowances must be made. He wasn't like other men. He was a thousand times more stubborn, with a literal god complex. Unlike most guys, he wasn't out for a quick nut: he had his own mission objective, with a guaranteed prize waiting at the end of his rainbow. But…

Stupid *but*! How she hated the word. But. Wasn't it her duty as his wife to show him how wrong he was about everything always? Shouldn't she prove her ability to take him by the balls and lead him anywhere she wished?

Hades had trained her for this. Her eyes widened. *That's right.*

One day, you're going to require the skills of a seduction master, Neeka had told her.

Hello, one day. And really, it wasn't like Taliyah had to go all the way with Roc. She just had to make him admit how much *he* wanted *her.* In the process, she might discover other weaknesses or gain an opportunity to strike.

She returned her gaze to his muscular, tattooed build, a shiver racing over her. At the very least, pitting her ability to seduce against his ability to resist might rid her of the chastity belt.

Justifying your actions, girl?

Maybe. But until she fed, she wouldn't win a physical altercation with him. A vengeful seduction without benefits was currently the strongest arrow in her quiver. So…

Yes. She would do it. The decision solidified, and she crafted a quick plan. First, she'd log in more time with the crystal, searching for Blythe and Isla, as well as mentally charting names and identities of other harpies she recognized. Then preparation for hubby dearest could begin…

Roc would learn. War with a harpy and suffer.

13

Roc perched on a stool, working in the hot Harpina sun, surprised and disappointed as the hours passed and neither Taliyah nor phantoms interrupted him. A battle might do him some good. Release a little tension. *Any* tension. Inside him, pressure continued to build. At this rate, an explosion seemed imminent.

Usually, he summoned his concubine before he reached this level of aggression. But even if an interlude were an option, he didn't want his concubine.

Though Taliyah wasn't his *gravita*, his treacherous body craved her alone. Because his *mind* craved her alone.

Women are a receptacle, Roc? One as good as any other? If ever words returned to bite him...

Fierce Taliyah was unlike any other. More stubborn, defiant and rigid...until aroused. Then she melted for him. Or pretended to. He cursed.

Roc yearned for her, while she yearned for another.

"Zero point zero," he spit.

With a huff, he adjusted the erection that refused to deflate. *No more thoughts of the snarpy.*

He dipped his head and hiked his shoulder, wiping sweat from his brow before he resumed chiseling his chosen meteorite. A six-ton beast shaped like a half-moon. Big enough to fill his new bedroom. The best of the best, without crack or blemish. The better the meteorite, the more honor he bestowed upon Chaos. More than a sign of his great respect for the male who'd helped shape him, the meteorite served as a sign of his commitment. Something Roc took seriously. How else did you thank the god you served?

Usually he worked as if he handled handblown glass. Today, he put too much force behind his blows, his temper boosting every strike. Large hunks of debris rained to a ground covered in frost. A Harpinian anomaly he despised, for it reminded him of Taliyah and—

No thoughts of her!

Thunk, thunk. Thunk, thunk. A larger section of rock fell, a crack forming in the piece left behind. He ground his teeth and switched his efforts to erasing the damage. Perhaps he *should* think of the snarpy. List the many ways he despised her.

Yes, he liked this plan. For starters, Taliyah Skyhawk, Terror of All Lands, refused to follow orders even to save her life. She turned everything into a contest of wills, forcing him to do the same. The excitement of those contests didn't matter. The woman refused to bend, a trait *only* estimable in an Astra. With her presence, her scent, her everything, she made him burn. He loved—*hated* to burn. He valued control in every area of his life.

Control equated to power. Life without power equated to misery without equal.

Cursing, Roc dropped the chisel and resettled on the stool, his elbows on his knees, his head in his upraised hands. A petite temptress was walking all over the Commander of the Astra

Planeta, and he was letting her do it. He *invited* her rebellions, because he liked the end result. His hands roaming over her body. His fingers inside her.

Even now, he panted for more.

Could he make her moan? Would she beg for his kiss, his touch—or Hades's?

Roc's claws shaded from gray to black, the tips becoming razors. For pride's sake, he should *make* Taliyah crave him. He had something to prove.

Taking her to bed was practically a duty. He didn't require her virginity, only her pleasure.

Yes! He jumped to his feet, certain of his brilliance. He'd make her come all night long.

Deny my effect on you then, harpy.

Before he'd taken a step, he recalled the day Solar used a similar excuse to be with *his* bride. He eased into his seat.

Back then, Roc had believed the idea smacked of "pure foolishness." Did it?

Or did he know better now?

Better. Definitely. With Taliyah, the scales were unbalanced. In her favor! He desired her, but she didn't desire him in return. She had power over him. An unacceptable situation. No one should have power over him, especially a bride.

Might equaled right.

Roc wasn't some inexperienced youth who lost his mind in the midst of passion, forgetting his purpose. He had the skill to pleasure Taliyah as much as he pleased, without crossing that final line. As he released the worst of his tension, she would learn to never again taunt him.

The perfect plan. Flawless.

With measured strokes, he petted the key he'd hung around his neck before coming to the gardens. The only way to open the enchanted chastity belt. Taliyah didn't know the skills he possessed in the bedroom. But she would learn. Laugh at him? No, oh no. She'd be too busy screaming.

Arousal singed muscle and bone. He wanted Taliyah screaming.

He would have the harpy in his bed *tonight*. By morning, the scale would tip in *his* favor.

—*May I approach, Commander?*—

Roc wasn't in the mood for company, but his station came before his mood. Had phantoms been found? —*You may.*—

His brother appeared and leaned a broad shoulder against the meteorite. Rather than offer a report about phantoms, as expected, he said, "You look more tormented than usual."

"That means I look better than I feel," Roc grumbled. He picked up his chisel to eliminate what remained of the crack. "What do you need?"

"Lack of sex isn't getting to you *at all*."

He opened his mouth to lament the trials of being wed to the world's most sensual bride, only to snap his teeth together. Soon, Ian would begin his assigned task. As the least ranked, he was forced to do something so horrific Roc shuddered at the thought. *Let him have his fun while he can.*

"I'll be better tomorrow, you'll see." Sizzling desire raged as he imagined Taliyah naked in his bed. "Much better."

No reason to inform his brother of his plans. A worried soldier led to a worried army. A worried army was a defeated army. What's more, their concern had no bearing on the situation. No matter how many times the snarpy begged and pleaded for Roc's possession, he would refuse, his resolve steadfast.

Ian whistled. "You realize you're stroking the key like a lover, yes?"

Again? He returned to his task.

"Perhaps I should retain possession of—"

"Mine!" The word burst from him, a command, warning and

claim all at once. Realizing how crazed he sounded, he scoured a hand over his face. "My apologies."

Ian blinked at him. "You're...sorry? You?"

What if she is your gravita?

No! Roc had endured thousands of years without a fated mate. The odds of finding his *gravita* were low. Lower than low. And if not, well, Taliyah's station still didn't matter. He couldn't divorce her and sacrifice another; the ritual prevented it. When the time came, Taliyah would die. Perhaps he would ascend immediately afterward. His dream of slaying his enemy and enjoying a happy, peaceful life realized at last.

For the first time, the thought brought no triumph.

Tone flat, he told his brother, "I'll keep the key."

Ian held up his hands in a gesture of surrender. "I thought you should know the harpy rigged traps throughout the palace." He reached over his shoulder to pluck a large, bloody shard of glass from his flesh. "I met with each of the men this morning. Silver was shocked every time he flipped a light switch. A floorboard caved in and sliced Roux's tendon. Knobs fell off doors every time Halo touched one. A chandelier came down on my head. Twice."

An inventive and interesting strategy. None of his other brides had sought to annoy everyone to death. Roc ignored the sliver of pride working through him.

"The harpy doesn't play nice," his brother said, amused rather than angry.

"I'll deal with her after I've completed this section of the altar." He knew just what to do...

"Also," his brother said, "I should probably mention she visited the prisoners earlier today. The whole group plans to swipe a realm key from Roux, and they aren't being secretive about it."

His lips twitched. He had to admire Taliyah's initiative. He'd threatened to destroy the duplicate realm, and she'd launched a search and recover mission as soon as possible.

Only another Astra brandished the strength and talent to steal from Roux. Especially when he didn't carry the item in question. Astra *were* the keys.

"What is she doing now?" he asked, doing his best to hide the intensity of his curiosity.

"After spending hours searching the palace with the crystal, she set up camp in the kitchen. I asked her what she was cooking, and she told me she couldn't speak to me without angering her snookiems, but if she *were* able to speak with me, she'd tell me she's making an elaborate meal for her pookie bear. Obviously, she's poisoning your food."

Snookiems? Pookie bear? Ian was right. She was absolutely poisoning Roc's food. A disappointing and familiar play. Many brides had gotten their hands on toxins and venoms. Not that they'd had any luck. No matter the toxin or venom, the Astra were immune. They created worlds. They were poison, and they were remedy.

He'd expected Taliyah to physically assault him. He'd... hoped.

"Did she search for someone specific?" Her mother, sisters and cousins lived in another realm. People who would mourn her death. A thought he'd never allowed himself to entertain during his other marriages. A thought he dismissed. *Doesn't matter. Can't matter.*

"I'd guess yes. The more rooms she searched, the more frustrated she appeared."

Perhaps he'd do a hunt of his own. If any of her relatives visited Harpina the day of the invasion, he'd peg them by sight alone. The mother and cousins had accompanied her that day in the market. The sisters he'd spotted only once, later that day. He could use the females as leverage. Or a gift?

A gift, Commander? Who are you?

As he stood, aggression prickled his nape. Ian felt it, too, and they tensed in unison. Someone prepared to launch an attack. Taliyah?

Just as his blood heated with excitement, a whoosh and a whistle sounded. He reached up, catching the shaft of an arrow, then cast his gaze over the garden. There. His excitement fizzled. Not Taliyah but a vampire hiding in the shade. Another harpy consort?

The bloodfiend launched a second arrow, but Roc caught it, too. With a toss and a sigh of disappointment, he returned both missiles to the vampire. Another whoosh and whistle, only faster and deadlier. The first arrow sank into the vampire's left eye. The second embedded in the right.

As the screaming man toppled, Ian flashed to his side. With a single swipe of his claws, the vampire forfeited his head.

Ever since Ian lost the Commander's helmet, he'd meted swift deaths to any who challenged him. He never hesitated to make a kill.

He returned to Roc, the severed head in hand. "Shall I display this on the front lawn with the others?"

He gave a clipped nod, but Ian didn't flash. He lingered, uneasy, as if something of grave importance plagued him.

"What?" Roc asked and heaved a sigh.

"Do you...maybe, perhaps, I don't know—" Ian massaged the back of his neck "—want a chastity belt of your own?"

Are you kidding me? Roc dropped his chin, a bull ready to charge. "Do you angle to lose your tongue? If I can't resist the urge to penetrate one little snarpy, I don't deserve to lead the most powerful army in existence."

"Are you sure?" his brother asked, mimicking Taliyah. "Allow me to demonstrate a scene from yesterday's dinner theater. In the role of Roc..." Ian banged his chest and growled, *"I told you what happens when you provoke an Astra. Now I'll show you. Me Commander."* He snickered. "Oh, and there's been no sign of phantoms. Not that you asked about our safety or anything."

One step. Roc took one step before his laughing brother vanished, taking the head with him.

Roc grabbed an icy water bottle, chugged half the contents and poured the rest over his sweaty face. A cool tide rushed over him, doing little to douse his desire for the snarpy.

Maybe he *did* require a chastity belt of his own.

No, he just needed to deal with the harpy. Ian's parting shot had set off an alarm. Not loud but noticeable. Erebus never wasted a moment to war. Why hadn't he sent a phantom to attack yet? New strategy?

Bring it. Roc had planned for every eventuality.

Except Taliyah.

He swiped a hand over his face, freeing his lashes of water droplets. Tonight he would eat the meal she prepared, whatever it was. Goading her temper while they dined was sure to lighten his mood. If she attacked him, she'd give him the perfect excuse to put his hands on her. He could *make* her want him.

He would.

14

Taliyah surveyed her handiwork. Nice. Expert-level romance. In front of a well-stoked hearth, she'd arranged a picnic-style dinner on a coffee table.

The stage for Roc's test-seduction was set.

A General should be versed in all forms of attack. Even this. Once she convinced him to remove the belt, she'd know she possessed the ability to seduce him. So would he.

Her confidence would be restored, and she'd have no trouble resuming the orchestration of his murder. All would be well.

She smoothed her hands over tonight's dress of choice: a stunner of Grecian design, sophisticated yet Gothic. The choker collar provided open shoulders and a deep V that ended just below her navel. The cinched waist led to a flowing hem with multiple slits, her sexy heels on display. Between her breasts dangled the key to Harpina.

Maybe Roc knew what it was; maybe he didn't. He probably

didn't care either way. In his mind, his threat to destroy the duplicate realm bound her here. He— Argh!

Every time she moved, the chastity belt grazed the heart of her need. Taliyah thought she'd go mad. The stupid contraption was coming off tonight. If desire got the better of him—*it must*—he would remove the belt.

Could she get him there? The challenge of it all was kind of...sexy.

Incredibly sexy.

Make him want you, future General, not the other way around.

Wait! The constant scrape of a chisel ceased. Had Roc finished his work for the day? Heart kicking into a wild beat, she hurried to the balcony and searched the gardens. The colossal hunk of rock remained, but she saw no sign of the Astra.

She averted her gaze, shifting her attention to the horizon, where his wall circled the city, a majestic but horrifying monstrosity. Did he walk the parapet? How long did she have before he hunted her?

What if he didn't hunt her?

The door opened. As if her thoughts had conjured him, Roc stalked into the bedroom, master of the manor.

She whirled, facing him fully. He'd showered somewhere other than his bathroom. Interesting. He'd donned a shirt, covering the bulk of his *alevala*. That shirt did great things for him, stretching over broad shoulders and bulging muscles. Water droplets dampened his hair, a few beads clinging to long black lashes. Harsh features appeared more pronounced than usual, strain pulling his bronze skin taut.

He strained up good. Real good.

He stopped abruptly and perused her slowly. Tremors beset her limbs. Performance jitters, nothing more.

His expression remained neutral, but his hands fisted. "I'm told you prepared my dinner."

My cue. Strolling closer, Taliyah motioned to the picnic. "My hubby had a tough day, and he deserved a little pampering."

"Yes, I can see you slaved over this delicious meal of—" he glanced at the different platters of food "—pineapple."

So cooking wasn't her strong suit. She'd gathered every pineapple in the kitchen. "I wasn't sure how you preferred it, so I spent extra time preparing it multiple ways. Sliced, smashed, crushed, kicked, choked or smothered. Husband's choice. And yes, I'm such a good wife. I know." When she reached him, she realized she had a choice. Link her arm through his and escort him to the table, or walk past him, letting him watch.

When his pupils pulsed, she opted for the latter. She paused only long enough to drag a fingertip over his chest. "Come. Eat. You must be ravenous." Strolling off...

A sudden vise grip on her arm spun her into him, smashing her breasts into his chest. An involuntary shiver coursed through her. Heat followed.

She swallowed, her bones threatening to melt. "Perhaps you have another meal in mind?"

Roc dipped his head and dragged his nose up her throat, sniffing her. As he straightened, his pupils pulsed again. A heartbeat in his eyes. "I accept your invitation to *come and eat.*" He sounded...lusty.

Uh, where was the rampaging beast she'd dealt with this morning? "You aren't afraid I'll poison you?"

"I'm sure you did, but it doesn't matter. I'm immune to poison."

"Yes, but which poison?"

"Every."

How was that possible?

Gaze steady, he glided his hands up her arms. As she struggled to catch her breath, he settled palms against her nape and toyed with locks of her hair. "We can use the time to get to know each other."

Seriously, what had brought about his attitude adjustment?

"You want to know more about the pre-General you plan to kill?"

"Why wouldn't I?" His voice dipped, his lusty smolder intensifying. "I'm fascinated by everything else I've learned about her."

"You are?" No, she did *not* just ask that. And so needy, too! What was even happening right now? He was messing with her head, screwing with her plan, and she wanted it to stop. To get them both on the right track—*her* track—she asked, "What's a *gravita?*"

He jerked and released her, looking to the table. "Let's talk of more important things while we eat." With three long strides, he reached the pillows and eased down.

Subject closed.

"May I prepare your meal?" he asked, already spooning multiple pineapple rounds onto her plate.

Now the Commander served her? "You may tell me what's going on, that's what you may do." Taliyah marched over with a huff. "You are Roc-blocking yourself, and you don't even know it."

He blinked and said, "I'd rather you tell me more about your life. I'm willing to exchange information, however."

"The big, bad Roc bargains with a lowly bride? I thought I had no leverage," she quipped.

He hiked his shoulders, adorably sheepish and utterly unrepentant. "I distinctly remember you finding leverage in my pants."

He did not just say that. "Okay, I'll take the bait. We'll exchange info." She kinda sorta wanted to know more about him, too. For the cause…mostly. "Drama queen's first. What do you want to know about my life?"

He flicked her a narrowed glance. "Tell me about your hobbies."

Easy enough. "I don't really have hobbies, because I don't really have downtime. I used to spend my few days off bailing

my sisters out of jail, but that's a chore for their consorts now."
And she wasn't jealous that the girls had found their other halves.
She'd never let herself entertain the idea of a permaguy. Why
waste time longing for what you couldn't have?

Kaia, who'd grown up to be the cruelest, sweetest sister, paired
up with a warrior possessed by the demon of Defeat. Strider
couldn't lose a single battle without suffering for days. Bianka,
the wild one, shocked everyone by falling for a by-the-book Sent
One of immeasurable power named Lysander. Her youngest sister, the indomitable Gwen, went for warmonger Sabin, keeper
of the demon of Doubt. Odd pairings, certainly, but her sisters
made it work. They'd never been more satisfied.

Since meeting Roc, Taliyah had sampled her own satisfaction.
There was no denying it. But it was a temporary thing, and it
meant nothing. Roc wasn't her consort. A harpy had to trust
her partner enough to sleep in his presence. The day Taliyah
slept near Roc was the day she signed up for another beheading. *But.* Man, she *really* hated that word. For the first time, she
almost saw the…appeal of a consort.

"Nowadays," she said, picking up where she'd left off, "I stay
busy running interference for my friend Neeka. She's evading a
phoenix king out to gank her."

Roc handed her the plate he'd prepared, and she noted he'd
chosen the best, most unmutilated slices for her. A surprisingly
solicitous and respectful gesture.

"Shall I kill the phoenix for you?" he asked.

"What? No! Are you kidding? If I can't take him out, I don't
deserve to be General. I protect what I love."

He tilted his head. "Family and friends are important to you?"

Hold up. "If you're about to threaten my family—"

"You'll hear no threats from me tonight," he interjected, all
innocence.

Why no threats *tonight*? "Is family important to *you*?" Wait.
"Do you even have a family? Besides twenty ex-wives, I mean."

Did he flinch at that? "I have two sisters and a brother," he said, his expression softening. The boyishness from before came into clearer focus. "You've crossed paths with my brother, a fellow Astra, as well as a sister."

Who... "The witness." Ahhh. His rebuke during the marriage ceremony suddenly made more sense.

"I miss her and the other," he admitted.

Ugh, what was going on inside Taliyah's chest all of a sudden, causing some kind of terrible, amazing tightening sensation? Realizing this larger-than-life enforcer might have a gooey candy center inside his hard outer shell? But, but...that was ridiculous! "You don't get to see them often?"

"Not nearly as much as I'd like. I see them no more than a handful of times every five hundred years." He popped a piece of pineapple into his mouth with sensual grace. As he chewed and swallowed, his brow furrowed. "I detect no poison."

"So?"

"So." He skidded his gaze down her dress, different emotions warring for rights to his face. Incredulity won the battle. "You didn't poison me, but you did dress up." A roguish smile grew, making her heart skip. "You're seducing me."

Her cheeks burned. "You believe I've thrown in the towel and shifted my objective? No more fighting, only banging to get rid of my virginity? Well, go on. Keep believing it." He would discover the truth soon enough. "You won't see my next trick coming."

"You don't want sex. You want an orgasm."

Ignore your stinging pride. Don't mention Hades. Teeth clenched, she asked, "What's the problem with your family? Are you too busy conquering worlds to visit your sisters?"

His smile vanished so quickly, she almost felt guilty. "There are few times I'm allowed to see them. The day of my wedding and the day of the sacrifice are guarantees. Any other sightings happen at random." A hint of sadness crept into his irises, making her chest do that weird tightening thing again.

"Allowed? You don't strike me as the type to follow someone else's orders."

"Do you think I'm the first Astra Commander? I once served others. I serve Chaos always."

That kind of loyalty was so rare. So precious. How would it feel to be the recipient of Roc's? "What do you do between weddings?"

"Hunt Erebus and his phantoms."

Reveal nothing. "Your war with Erebus has stretched across the eons. Why haven't you killed him a second time, if you're so tough?"

"I *have* killed him a second time. And a third. A fourth. He *always* revives." Roc arched a brow. "How would *you* slay him, o great and marvelous pre-General?"

Good question. How might she murder her own father? "I'd probably start by inviting him to a delicious dinner," she said, motioning to the pineapple dishes.

Roc made a *pft* sound before taking another bite.

They lapsed into silence for a bit. Not awkward, but not comfortable, either. She watched him, captivated by his movements. Every action served a distinct purpose, his control unwavering.

As she stared, he blasted intense amounts of heat. The warmer she grew, the more she...tingled. If she could just put a little more pressure on the metal plate...

The corners of his lips twitched. "Problem, snarpy?"

He knew his power over her. So irritating! But snarpy? Dude. Neeka had tried to warn her the stupid name would catch on. A crude hand gesture served as her only response, and Roc chuckled outright. Then he shocked her.

"Ask me nicely, and I'll remove the belt for a night." His voice dipped once more, and her pulse spiked.

Ask an enemy for a boon, even if it was the boon she'd sought?

Not just no, but never. He just— Whoa. Hold up. A startling comprehension dawned. Did he *want* her to ask him to remove the belt? As sweet as he'd been since entering the bedroom, he clearly wanted *something* from her.

Well, then… "What if I want to keep the belt?" she asked. "Maybe I've grown to love it."

Determination flowed over him, tightening his expression, his chest, fisting his hands yet again. If he'd come here with a game plan, he'd just tweaked it.

She was in trouble.

"Well, then," he rasped, "I suppose I'll have to do my best to make you hate it."

Blink. He was on his feet. Blink. He yanked her body to his. Blink. He eased onto his pillow, pulling her onto his lap.

She could have resisted. Instead, Taliyah straddled him. If he wanted to help with his own surrender, why complain? "So far, I'm not even feeling mild dislike." For balance, she rested her hands on his shoulders.

With a hooded gaze and wicked intent, he readjusted her to press her metal plate against his erection. A puff of air parted her lips, every ache intensifying.

Maybe if she adjusted just a little…to…the… Stupid chastity belt! The ache worsened more than expected.

"There. That's better," he said with lazy indulgence.

Get your mind in the game, girl. "Tell me, Roc." Taliyah leaned closer, letting her lips hover over his. "Do you hope I'll ask you to remove the belt so you can gloat…or because you're desperate to finger me?"

"A man can't have two reasons?" he asked in a mimic of her. Cupping her backside, he rocked her against him. "I'll make you come so hard my army will hear your screams. All you have to do is ask me to remove the belt."

Do not moan. This was a contest of wills. She'd set out to prove she had the skills to seduce him, and he'd oh, so clearly set out to prove he had the skills to seduce her. Tricky, tricky Astra. Did his poor little Commander pride need assuaging?

The game played on!

She brushed the tip of her nose against his. "Roc?"

His fingers flexed on her. "Yes, Taliyah?"

"Will you, pretty please, with cherries on top of me…leave the belt on me forever?"

His pupils did that cool pulsing thing, a galaxy of stars seeming to swim inside their depths. The first time she'd seen it, she'd wondered if it happened due to fury or passion. Now she knew. Passion. Her Astra was intensely aroused…

He rocked his straining erection against her with more force. "You want me to remove the metal. Admit it."

A shot of pleasure momentarily robbed her of sound. Drawing on iron control she'd honed on the battlefield, Taliyah ultimately countered, "You want to remove it. Admit it."

"Just for that," he said, his face almost brutal in the candlelight, "I'll make you beg for me."

Do not squirm. "You'll try. Others have. All have failed."

"I don't lose battles." As his gaze held hers, aggression charged the air between them.

With the gentlest, most shocking of touches, he grazed his hands up her sides and stopped beside her breasts. With his thumbs, he drew lazy circles around her nipples. Both drew tight; the lucky piercing made her ache. "I'll make you scream *my name.*"

Taliyah fought another moan.

Circle…circle… In the firelight, he was a painting come to life. A fabled king who ruled with an iron fist. And his scent… his scent deepened, becoming richer. He smelled like her most fevered dream. He was temptation made flesh, and she was panting. She must be soaked right now.

Circle, circle… He picked up speed.

Goose bumps spread, and she rocked herself against him. "Keep trying. I'm sure I'll scream sooner or later."

He nipped her bottom lip. "You want me to see your breasts. Show them to me."

Yes... "I'll do it because you believe you'll die if I don't." Hands shaking, she unhooked the gown's collar. The top fell, baring her breasts to his blistering gaze.

Air hissed between his teeth. "Exquisite."

Had any man ever looked at her this way, as if he'd never beheld such beauty? "You want your mouth on me," she rasped. "Do it."

"Yes...because you need me to." Appearing dazed, he lifted her, placing her piercing at the same level as his mouth. But he didn't lick. He stared, hard, his entire being promising wild, wicked things.

Taliyah hovered at the razor's edge of *suspense*? Would he? Wouldn't he?

Would she stoop to asking?

"Roc," she said, as much a command as a complaint.

"Yes." At last, he stroked his tongue over the piercing.

She gasped, inundated by an avalanche of sensation. All the heat, all the wet, all the pleasure.

When he sucked the distended crest into his mouth, he wrenched a hoarse groan from her. Taliyah was too far gone to care. "Harder." No mistaking the command this time.

Releasing a deliciously rumbly sound, he flipped her to her back, splaying her across the pillows, trapping her wings against the mattress. He pinned her arms overhead with a single hand, positioning himself above her. A warrior without equal. So big he eclipsed the rest of the world, keeping her attention centered on him.

His breaths turned choppy, his gaze fierce. With lips wet and puffy from suction, he looked wonderfully lewd. He was...

what…that scent. What *was* that? She whimpered. Had *anything* ever smelled so scrumptious?

If he smells this good, how good must he taste? Mmm. *A sip. Just the tiniest sip…* A soul-light glowed from his pores, growing brighter, leaving her dizzy.

"You snarl and you shout, harpy," he said with a husky chuckle, "but the right touch makes you mewl like a little kitten."

Both the statement and the chuckle dripped with wonder. Slowly she opened her legs to cradle his lower body against hers.

Upon contact, they both moaned. He was a furnace, his warmth a sublime drug.

She wanted to kiss him… She needed to feed… Desires warred. "Touch me, Roc."

"Yes." With his free hand, he traced the column of her neck, then her collarbone, leaving a trail of tingling heat.

"More." She tilted her head, granting him better access.

"The things I plan to do to you…" He stroked between her breasts, so tender. Was this how he treated all his lovers? So… irresistibly?

A flare of jealousy surprised her.

He kneaded her bare breast, his skin like fire, branding her as surely as the iron. Taliyah reveled, the jealousy torched.

Rubbing her knees up his legs, she croaked, "Tell me everything you want to do to me…and maybe I'll let you."

"I'll start with—" He frowned, his gaze glued to the area he'd just touched. His head tilted. His eyes widened. Rearing onto his haunches, he lifted his hand into the light, then did the same to the other. His gaze returned to her, sweeping over every spot he'd caressed.

Her pulse leaped with confusion. And maybe, just maybe, a pinch of vulnerability. "Roc?"

Almost crazed, he jumped to his feet. "You… I… Do not

leave this room, Taliyah. Do you understand? You will remain in here or you will regret it."

"What happened?" Colder by the second—*angrier* by the second—she eased upright. Fix her gown? Hardly. Let him look at what he wouldn't be seeing again. Had this been his plan all along? To get her worked up and leave her to suffer?

He shifted his gaze. "I'll return in an hour. Two hours. Possibly tomorrow. You'd better be here." With a final glance at his hands, he stomped from the bedroom, slamming the door behind him.

Stay here? Screw that! Taliyah jumped to her feet and stormed into the bedroom she'd claimed as her own, where she donned a tank top and shorts. Forget waiting until he fell asleep to visit the Realm of the Forgotten. Something had happened to him, between them, and she needed to know what. Then she would feed.

Nothing—not even a shockingly sensual Astra—would stop her.

15

A jumble of emotions, Roc headed for...somewhere at a clipped pace, his stomping steps seeming to shake the entire palace. He needed to burn off excess energy and fast.

Taliyah was... She... He hadn't wanted to believe it when he'd been in the room with her, and he hated to believe it now. But he could not deny the evidence staining his hands.

He flinched as he brought his palms into the light. A glittery powder coated his skin. Stardust.

Chaos hadn't sought to teach him a lesson: the god tried to warn him. Taliyah *was* his *gravita*. The woman who challenged him at every turn belonged to him, body and soul. No wonder she'd drawn him so strongly, so quickly.

Where was he supposed to go from here? How was he supposed to treat her? Ignore her? Enjoy her while he could? Attempt to build an immunity to her charms? Was resisting her appeal an impossibility now that he'd tongued those pretty pink nipples, sucked that piercing and heard her soft cries of pleasure?

He remembered the advice he'd once offered Solar, when his Commander had faced this very situation. *Starve your body, feed your duty. The desire will go away.*

A snarling laugh left Roc. He doubted lust this all-consuming *ever* faded.

As he stormed down a winding staircase, he rubbed the spot above his heart. The awful, horrific things he'd done to acquire the missing *alevala* teased the edge of his mind. Actions he'd taken against Solar and his siren *gravita*.

Taliyah must be payback.

Roc didn't understand how he'd found her. Why now? Why her? What had broken past his defenses and summoned the stardust to his palms? The sight of her in that slinky black dress? Finally getting his hands on her curves? Conversing with her as equals, enjoying her wit and flavor? The nipple ring? Those wings? Was it the way she melted for him while challenging him?

Whatever the reason, something *had* changed for him. The second he'd flipped her onto those pillows and run his hands over silken skin fevered by his touch, he'd simmered with heat like never before. To cool down, he'd *needed* to overcome more of her chill. To touch more—all—of her. But everywhere his fingers had traveled, a sheen of something glittery remained behind.

He'd marked her, staking an undeniable claim. Yet he must kill her. Were he to save Taliyah, the way Solar had saved his siren, he'd only delay the inevitable. The second he received the curse, he lost the ability to protect her from phantoms. Ascending ceased being an option. For five hundred years, they required hibernation to survive. And when they awoke? What then? The wedding and killing of another woman? What about the wife who lived?

No couple was more doomed.

To confess to his men or not? There might be no need. Stardust faded with time. The scent dulled. Roc had only to keep his distance from the temptress to make it go away. But the thought...didn't settle well.

He stalked around a corner and punched a wall. On impact, his knuckles split. Blood trickled over the stardust, hiding it.

He'd never acted so volatile before. Usually, he remained calm, regardless of the situation. But then, his carefully crafted world had never teetered on the brink of total collapse before.

Though his excess energy remained unchanged with his second punch, a flicker of common sense prevailed. Why worry about this? He was a warlord first and foremost, a *gravita* bride still just a bride. A sacrifice. A *gravita* bride was the greatest sacrifice of all, perhaps even the tipping point necessary for his ascension.

For the first time, he must part with something...precious. Future happiness with the woman destined to rule at his side. The family he'd so badly craved.

Punch, punch, punch. Upon his next turn, he spotted Ian. His brother toiled over a section of wires protruding from the wall. Undoing one of Taliyah's traps?

He wouldn't tell his men about the stardust, he decided. Not until he'd worked up a plan. They had enough to deal with at the moment.

So altruistic, Commander.

His brother noticed him and leaped to attention. "Phantoms have arrived?"

Roc looked ready for battle? "Not yet. I'd...like to speak with the prisoners." Yes. That. He had questions about Taliyah, and they had answers. "Continue with your duties," he said, then flashed to the dungeon.

In an instant, cold replaced warmth. A scattering of torches lined the wall, providing the only source of light. Like any well-used dungeon, centuries of torture and abuse stained every visible surface.

He stalked down a darkened corridor, cells on either side of him. Other hallways branched off here and there, offering more cells, but he remained on his current path. At last, the lockup at the end of the corridor came into view. The harpies roamed about in varying stages of undress. As some washed their clothes in a tub of water and snacked on fruits, breads and cheeses, they debated whether Mara qualified as a General. Taliyah's doing?

Roux paced in front of the cell, mumbling again. What puzzle plagued him? He usually figured things out by now. "Why don't I remember? What don't I remember?"

"Be at ease, warrior," Roc told him, using his gentlest voice.

The male jerked and stopped, then slowly turned, facing him. Their gazes met, those red irises haunted. "Some of the invasion is wiped from my memory. What did I do? Why did I do it?"

"You fought at my side." At first. Minutes before the harpies issued their surrender, Roux had frozen, doing nothing, saying nothing.

"What are these thoughts?" Roux pulled at his hair. "They aren't mine."

Were he anyone else, Roc might suggest he showed signs of a phantom possession. But no phantoms had been present during the battle. Nor did a phantom possess the power to penetrate an Astra's shields, not without time and never without the warlord's awareness.

The harpies stopped what they were doing and approached the bars. Voices rang out.

"Are you our new warden? Bummer. I liked the last one. He struggled to form a complete sentence. The best quality in a man, I always say."

"Let's see. We've gotten to interact with the brainless Scarecrow and the heartless Tin Man. Does that make you the Cowardly Lion?"

"Have you ever wondered what it's like to have your skin ripped off your body in one piece, turned inside out, then shoved on?"

He crossed his arms over his chest. "I'm here to learn more about Taliyah Skyhawk." Why not bargain with these prisoners? Surely they desired other amenities.

"Oh, what perfect timing!" a female called. "I was *just* telling the girls how much I'd love to help you get to know our T-bomb better."

"Having trouble intimidating your new bride?" another cackled. "I hope she gags you with your own testicles."

They snickered at each other, as if he were a fool for coming here. He absolutely was.

"Do I have nothing you want?" he asked.

"I'll give you a Taliyah fact free of charge." The only redhead smiled slyly at him. "She's the one who stopped the great zombie apocalypse in our nineteenth century."

He'd caught up on the world's history before invading Harpina. "There was no zombie apocalypse."

"Exactly."

"Did you know Taliyah—"

Roc lost track of her words as Silver's voice boomed through his mind.

—*We have the first phantom trapped.*—

"Stay here," he commanded Roux, wiping all thoughts of his *gravita* from his head. Using the mental link between them, he unearthed Silver's location and flashed.

Halo stood at the warlord's side. Ian appeared next to Roc. They occupied a midsize building. A bar he'd visited before, during one of his preliminary visits. The place once brimmed with harpies. Now, no bodies. Tables and chairs were pushed aside. At the edge of the dance floor, an embodied phantom trudged a continuous circle inside a prison of trinite.

Swaying from side to side, she droned, "Get inside, embody,

walk around, tell Roc. Get inside, embody, walk around, tell Roc."

Orders from her master. Whatever Erebus commanded of his creations, they repeated over and over as they obeyed. A checklist.

The phantom had pallid and waxen skin with no distinguishing marks and eyes of milky white that stared at nothing. She wore an ill-fitting gown. Widow's weeds, of course.

Erebus *always* sent his phantoms in widow's weeds. A reminder of the worst day of Roc's life.

Black lines branched from her eye sockets, a sure sign of hunger. How long since she'd fed? Years, he would guess. Until she completed her master's mission, she *couldn't* eat.

A single meal powered most phantoms for months. Erebus preferred to keep his puppets starved for decades, however. When they finally had a chance to eat, they gorged.

"She never approached the wall," Halo said, stroking his strong jaw. "Erebus must have flashed her in."

Roc gripped the hilt of his three-blade. Like the Astra, Erebus didn't need a key to enter a realm: he was a key. But he left telltale signs of his presence. A glaze of frost everywhere he stepped. Ice crystals in the air. The stench of death.

"He can't enter the realm without alerting us." A possibility: Erebus flashed the phantom without needing to touch her. A skill Roc had once believed only Ian possessed.

She hadn't dwelled here before the wall. He'd found no trace of phantoms, embodied or otherwise, during his many trips.

"Get inside, embody, walk around, tell Roc."

Seemed Erebus wished to pass along a message.

He looked to Silver. "I'll deal with the phantom. I'd like you to—" *Don't say it.* "—make and deliver a set of lightweight chains to my room. Within the hour. For the bed." *Well, you said it.*

The warrior blinked with surprise. "I see."

"The cuffs aren't meant to cause pain." He said no more. With Taliyah, Roc must be prepared for anything. The thrill meant nothing.

Silver nodded, a stiff incline of his head. He flashed from the bar.

Let's get this over with. Roc strode to the cage, appearing before the phantom.

She whizzed up to the bars, her foggy gaze locked on him. An arctic chill seeped from her, frost spreading over his *alevala*. A phenomenon caused by all phantoms.

"Tell me your message," he ordered.

Words spilled out. "You know what she is to you, but you don't know who or why she is. You don't know what." No longer did she mumble. Her monotone voice proved as chilling as her temperature. "Allow me to tell you. She is a Skyhawk, a harpy, a snake…and a phantom. You wed one of mine, Commander, but you can't kill her until the required time. Do you know what she'll do before then, Roc? Whatever I tell her. Ha ha ha. Ha ha ha ha ha."

That fake, mocking laugh… Roc struck, shoving the three-blade deep into her chest. Black blood poured from the wound as she collapsed. As seconds ticked by, she evaporated into nothing. His disgust for her remained.

Rooted in place, he snapped, "She lied." No way Taliyah was a phantom.

"As if we didn't already know that," Ian replied. "We've never iced over in her presence."

"More than that, Erebus always lies," Halo assured him.

"He sows doubt, nothing more," Ian added.

"Yes." Absolutely. Which meant the god had known Taliyah was Roc's *gravita before* Roc.

You know what she is to you…

Erebus mixed truth with lie to incite panic, nothing more. Taliyah wasn't a phantom. She was cold-blooded, yes, but he warmed her. An impossibility with phantoms. Her irises were clear. No black lines smudged the skin around her eyes, indicating hunger. She was smart. No phantom possessed the skill to fake such intelligence.

Unless Erebus had figured out how to make others like himself.

16

"Mother," Taliyah called, hurrying through the fortress. Nothing had changed in the Realm of the Forgotten. Lavish, unsullied by dirt, debris or time, and vacant. Where were her loved ones? She planned to check on Tabitha and talk to Neeka, then finish off the immortals stored in the dungeon. They'd still had a little life in them, last time she'd been here. The perfect appetizer. Soon, Roc's army would become her all-you-can-eat buffet.

Maybe Neeka knew what Roc did to her skin? In select places, she glittered. Where she glittered, she burned. Where she burned, she ached. Where she ached, she wanted.

Taliyah wanted *so bad*.

For Neeka, she flipped every switch, flickering the lights. "Mom. Momma. Mooom. Mother!"

Taliyah quickened her step, entering the library— Whoa! She ground to a halt. Her nape grew real cold, real fast.

Confused, she reached behind to pat the area. Frost? On the brand Neeka had given her two thousand years ago? Or yesterday or whatever.

"Hello, daughter."

The craggy voice came from behind the desk, where a huge leather chair swirled around, revealing a man with pale skin, black eyes and a hooked nose. Curly blond hair hung over a prominent brow. A thick beard with a wealth of braids covered an equally prominent jawline. Across his lap rested a blade with jagged edges. The extraordinary hilt seemed to swirl, as if he held a small piece of a universe.

Erebus. Here. Heart thumping, Taliyah palmed two daggers. A thousand thoughts, questions and emotions bubbled up at once. At the forefront: anger.

"You know I exist," she said, doing her best to remain conversational. For centuries, she'd wondered about the man despised by everyone who'd ever met him. A villain willing to murder his own daughter to ruin Roc. Hadn't her hubby warned her of this? "Where are my mother and my friend?"

"I did nothing to them, I assure you. They were gone when I arrived. I've no plans to harm you, either."

Truth or lie? For Neeka, she suspected he spoke true. Not because he hid an honest side. Did he? The powerful oracle saw him coming, no doubt about it. Bet she even left her best friend a message. Where... There! The mirror hanging behind the desk. In the reflection, Taliyah spotted a note on the wall, the letters painted in blood. *We're fine!*

Okay, then. She could proceed without removing her father's head.

He wrinkled his nose at her. "You reek of Astra Planeta."

That *is his first comment to me, post greeting?* "Save the commentary," she snapped. "What do you want from me? Why are you here?"

One corner of his mouth quirked up. "I bet you're maddening to the Commander. The sanctimonious Roc is so rarely challenged. I must say, I'm glad fate chose you as his *gravita*."

Her ears twitched. *Don't ask. Don't do it.* "What's a *gravita*?" Well, she'd asked.

"A mate."

She gulped. "*Mate*, as in another name for bride? Or *mate*, a term meaning…consort?"

With all kinds of relish, he told her, "Consort."

No. Nope. He lied. He must. She knew she wasn't Roc's mate. Not because he'd shouted his thoughts on the matter before stomping off and avoiding the topic altogether. But because of…reasons. He *couldn't* consider Taliyah his mate.

"You are skeptical," Erebus said. "Daughter, I knew you belonged with him before your birth. Why do you think I put you in his path?"

"Wrong. I put *myself* in his path."

He shrugged, unperturbed by her denial. "You wear his stardust. A substance the Astra produce only for their *gravitas*. It acts as a warning to others."

Stardust… Like the white-hot glitter on her skin? She *did* remember reading something about it during her studies. But she couldn't…she wouldn't… Argh! What if she *was* Roc's *gravita*? He'd marked her *without permission*.

The possibility infuriated her…mostly. Had he deduced what she was to him from the first moment? Was that why he'd blurted out *you* the first time he'd seen her? But why marry her just to kill her? Why— Wait.

"What do you mean I belonged to Roc *before I was born*?"

Her father stroked the handle of his weapon. "I…see."

He was an oracle?

Relish in full force, he asked, "Do you think Roc will die in your stead?"

Okay, enough of this. "I do think he'll die in my stead, yes, because I won't give him a choice. I won't back down, I won't give up, I won't surrender." Taliyah Skyhawk fought until the very end.

Blink. Suddenly, Erebus towered in front of her, and the brand on her nape blistered her with cold. *Calm. Steady.* She remained in place, standing her ground.

"You don't know how glad I am to hear this." A creepy smile contorted his face. "You will destroy Roc for me."

Possessive instincts swamped her. "No, I'll destroy Roc for *me*. His death is mine to mete out."

"Oh, I don't want him dead, daughter. I want him miserable, and you are my chosen tool. Why do you think I bedded your mother?"

"I'm no one's tool. And go ahead and mention my mother and threaten Roc again. See what happens." Like Roc, Erebus was a god with incredible power. But so what? She might not be a General—yet. She might be hungry and a little weak, but she had combat skills and a petty streak *no one* could guard against.

Erebus canted his head, his gaze twitching. He grinned. "The true fun is starting. Roc knows you're gone, and he's far from pleased. Enjoy your evening, daughter. I know I will."

As she lunged to strike, he dematerialized. She spun, panting, the brand cooling.

Minutes ticked by without incident. Finally, she released the pressure on her limbs and straightened, her mind reeling. What just happened?

Roc *couldn't* know she was gone. She currently resided in the Realm of the Forgotten. He didn't even remember her name. But what if he *did* know she was gone? What would he do upon her return?

A beat of apprehension left her floundering. The sooner she returned to Harpina to scope out the situation, the better.

She rushed to the dungeon to feed and— "No!" The men were gone, a note from Neeka taped to the cell door.

Cruel to be kind. Sorry not sorry!

"Why, that little…" Though Taliyah's trust in her friend remained unbroken, she struggled to find a higher purpose in this. Why leave her in a weakened state around the Astra? Especially now?

Mood souring, Taliyah clasped the key to Harpina. *Here goes nothing.* The fortress vanished, her bedroom appearing.

A battle plan formed. Find Roc. He might be sleeping, allowing her to continue on with her night of hunting and feeding. If he remained awake and impossibly aware, she needed to know it now, now, now.

Wait. Darkness encompassed the room. When she'd left, lights from the chandelier had shone brightly.

Roc's scent filled her nose. Intense heat caressed her skin from behind, and she froze. He was nearby. And he'd just caught her reappearance. He might not have known she'd left before, but he knew it now.

Heart thudding, she slowly turned…and there he was. Reclining in a chair near the hearth, enveloped by thick, black shadows.

"Would you like to explain yourself, wife?" He switched on a lamp, light chasing the shadows away, revealing harsh and quiet rage.

Going on the defensive, she snapped, "Do I *need* to explain? We're at war, and I'm using every weapon at my disposal."

Her honesty threw him.

When he opened his mouth to respond, she added, "If you complain about this, you're only admitting you're afraid I'll win."

He regarded her coldly, intently.

"Did you know I'd left the fortress before I appeared or after?" she asked. For that matter, "How did you remember me?" The Realm of the Forgotten should have wiped her from his mind the moment she'd arrived there.

"How could I forget the bane of my existence?" He straightened gradually. A long-sleeved shirt covered his arms and chest, hiding prime real estate. Leather pants hugged his thighs, and metal-tipped boots protected his feet.

"By bane of existence, do you mean fated mate?" He had his complaints, she had hers. "Or does the Black Widower refuse to acknowledge the woman he can't live without?" Lifting her top, revealing an extra glittery patch of skin, she said, "Of course, I might deny it, too, if the situation were reversed. I'm yours... but you aren't mine."

Literal sparks flared in his irises, blazing bright, extinguished only seconds later. "I can live without you," he told her, his fury barely banked. "I can also guess how you left the palace. The key dangling from your neck. Which I will be taking from you, one way or another."

Roc peered at the most defiant, exciting, challenging female to ever walk any planet and wanted only to get inside her. Once again, she made him throb. Even as she taunted him for being a black widower. Even as she eviscerated him with truth.

I'm yours, but you aren't mine.

"Take the key," she said with an airy tone. "I don't care."

He studied her. When she'd first arrived, she'd been paler than usual, her eye sockets darker than expected. Roc admitted it: he'd feared. Then his heat raised a rosy flush on her skin, and she appeared normal. Which meant she wasn't a phantom. She couldn't be. He'd never harden for a phantom.

"I'll take more than the key. You'll give me answers." He flashed to her, latched on to her arms, then flashed again, ending his journey with his bride pressed against the wall. He inserted a knee between her legs, ensuring she straddled him, the metal plate resting upon his thigh. He covered her vulnerable throat with his fingers. With his other hand, he clasped her hip bone, his grip almost...tender. "Where did you go? Tell me!" Who did she meet?

When she said nothing, his control took a substantial hit. He raised his knee, lifting her feet off the floor, forcing her weight to balance on the needy space between her thighs, relying on his body for an anchor.

She dug her claws into the wall and grinned up at him, far from cowed. "Going to try to pleasure the information out of me? Well, go ahead. I'll enjoy every second, and you'll end up frustrated, learning only what I want you to know."

Fury...passion, *something* summoned the stardust. Intense heat flared in his palms. Taliyah sucked in a breath. More proof she wasn't a phantom. The fiends had no need to breathe. But Erebus did. If the god had indeed made more like himself.

"No regard for your friends in the duplicate realm?" he asked.

She bit out, "Are you going to destroy it?"

He'd boasted he would do so, and he never reversed a decision. But as he pictured her lovely, defiant features contorted with grief and... He couldn't do it.

"The harpies are safe," he grated. "For now."

The response clearly surprised her. She frowned as she plucked her nails free and settled her hands on his shoulders, melting against him. "Truly? Why? I didn't peg you as the three strikes type."

The way her body fit his...did things to him. "With the right incentive, I can be merciful. Tell me where you went, Taliyah."

"I... No." She shook her head, stubborn to her very core.

His heart shuddered in his chest. Had black lines sped through her eye sockets as she'd moved?

Erebus toys with your thoughts, and you're letting him.

Roc tightened his grip, just a little, just long enough to feel her pulse leap. "Where did you go, harpy?"

"Mmm." A temptress to the end, she lifted her arms above her head and thrust up her breasts. "Haven't we played this game before? Remind me, darling. Didn't I win?"

This. This was what happened when you showed mercy to a foe even once. But no matter. He could make up for his previous mistake. Though he'd bent once, refusing to break her wrist when she'd disobeyed his command to drop the dagger, he would see this challenge through to the bitter end.

He would have her answer. And her thanks.

The decision solidified. He'd wondered what to do about his *gravita*. Now, with her luscious body pressed against his, he had no problem discerning the proper path. Whether he liked it or not, Taliyah *was* special to him. His body reacted to hers. Why not enjoy her while he could?

The callous thought jarred him. Enjoy the woman fate selected for him, receiving pleasure from her, before he struck her dead? *You are a prize among prizes, Roc.*

He hated himself...but he wouldn't change his path.

"Uh-oh," she purred. "Someone looks like he's just made a very important decision."

An observant woman. Smug. Challenging.

Exhilarating.

"You will talk, harpy," he told her with a voice like silk on barbed wire. "That I swear to you."

One second Taliyah straddled Roc's thigh, her weight braced against a wall; the next he flashed her to the bed. He knew he seemed to flicker above her as he moved between this realm and the duplicate of the duplicate, where he'd stored her new chains. As he collected what he needed, he moved at a speed no one but another Astra could track. By the time he finished, he had her locked tight, her wrists shackled above her head and her ankles secured miles apart.

A potent mix of fury and lust kept him on edge. "Anything to say *now*, harpy?"

Taliyah shocked him. She got comfortable, all smug assurance and wicked fantasy. "You had these chains crafted for me, the bride you can't resist, because you *wanted* to end up this way. Did you seize the first excuse to use them? Am I getting to you, Astra?"

Yes!

"If this is your version of torture," she said, feminine power impelling her to a new level of boldness, "sign me up for a morning, afternoon and evening session every day for the rest of the month. I'm sure I'll tell you *something* by then."

Want her. "I'm going to touch you, harpy. I'm going to touch you *everywhere*."

Her eyelids sank low, as if too heavy to hold up. "Is that a warning or a promise?"

Seeing her like this, a sultry seductress in chains, his stardust glittering on her pale skin, provoked a war in Roc. Continue, or stop before he fell down an endless abyss from which he might not recover?

How could he stop?

"The battle ends when you tell me what I want to know." Petting her inner thighs, his fingers inching closer and closer to the belt. Tormenting her. "You're going to enjoy this…at first."

Roc grazed his knuckles against the center of Taliyah's plate.

Bull's-eye. Taliyah barely halted a cry of pleasure. "Do that again," she rasped. "I almost told you all my secrets, honest."

He slitted his eyes, and oh, he looked magnificent. Primal. Fierce. *Fevered.* A warlord without equal, ready to die for his victory. The special scent wafted from him. The one from before. As she breathed it in, heat escalated. Perspiration dotted her skin.

When he grazed the metal plate a second time, she rolled her hips without thought, seeking more, her sex aching.

The intensity of those aches caught her off guard. She forced herself to still.

"Not so smug now, hmm?" He dragged a claw down her clothes, never scratching her flesh. Leather separated, sides popping free. "The mind shuts down and the body…needs."

"Nothing I can't handle." Did she sound drugged? So quickly?

He circled a finger around her pierced nipple. "Are you sure?"

The heat! "Very," she breathed. "No doubts." Other than a few hundred.

A predatory smile gave him a sinister air. "I must admit, I like the sight of you, naked and bound." He tugged the uniform out from under her quickly, but examined her leisurely. The more he looked, the more his pulsating pupils overtook his irises. A midnight sky lit by stars and charged by storms.

"I like the sight of you liking me naked and bound." A jest too huskily stated, too genuine. His admiration was doing terrible and wonderful things to her resolve.

A chuckle rose from him. "Your pleas for mercy will be the sweetest music." He dipped his head and flicked his tongue over her piercing.

A hard suckle left her gasping. New heat flooded her. Taliyah reached for him, wanting her fingers in his hair and her claws in his scalp. The chains caught, holding her in place, and she groaned.

"Do you *want* me to keep my secrets, warlord? If you crave answers, you'll have to try harder."

He growled against her piercing, the most delicious vibrations driving her mad. Lucky, lucky piercing indeed.

When he turned his attention to her other nipple, she knew she was in trouble. He didn't lick or suck it. No, he let his lips linger above it. Seconds stretched into an eternity, leaving her writhing with need.

She panted. Bit her tongue. Shifted and squirmed. *Do it, Roc! Just do it!*

"Do you see, harpy?" His warm breath caressed her sensitive skin, igniting wild tingles. "Deny me what I want, and one part of you will always ache."

Sensual beast. "Maybe I ache, but you do, too. Your measuring stick is about to burst."

"You mean my measuring *log*."

Oh, no he didn't. Roc didn't just tease her with a bigger euphemism, adding fuel to the flames of her desire. Humor was sexy.

He lifted to his knees and carefully drew his shirt over his head, muscled *alevala* on sudden display. With the same languorous patience, he unfastened and opened his leathers, his erection bobbing free. A bead of moisture already wetted the tip.

The moment she spied it, she gave another spontaneous roll of her hips. *Mine.*

"This is what's going to happen," he told her as calmly as if they were having tea. He drew the small silver key from his neck, all that controlled grace staggering to her. "I will do whatever I want to you, without taking your virginity. I'll come as many times as I wish, and you won't stop coming until you tell me where you traveled."

"Promise?" She knew he thought the key around *her* neck led to the other realm. In his mind, he had only to take the key and use it to get his answer. But he didn't. He *wanted* to do this.

What would he do when he discovered the second key? The hourglass tattoo.

"Tsk, tsk. You're only making this worse for yourself, harpy." With a deft flick of his wrist, he separated metal from metal. Another flick, and the belt hit the floor.

"Are you sure?" Their favorite question to each other. Cool air kissed her core. "So far you've been all talk."

"Apparently you've liked what I've had to say." His tone thickened. He never took his greedy gaze from her as he wiped his mouth with a trembling hand. "You're already soaked."

Leaning forward, he fixed that hand near her temple and wrapped an arm under her knee, forcing her legs to part further. He seemed to simmer with purpose and anticipation. Then he rotated his hips, rubbing his erection against her core, and thought fled. They were male to female, nothing between them.

A choking sound lodged in her throat. Pressure felt incredible. *He* felt incredible. His rigid length seared her and she gasped.

"Try to last, harpy. I plan to drench myself in your honey before I accept your surrender."

His unfounded confidence deserved a stinging retort. Yes, yes. Definitely unfounded. Except, he stirred his hips in a clockwise motion that very nearly disseminated her control.

Doubts surfaced, one after the other. Emerging the winner of this round might be a scooch more difficult than she'd assumed, but win she would. Whatever proved necessary.

17

Roc drank in the winter queen beneath him. A pale incarnation of every dream he'd never known he had, naked but for her jewelry, bathed in firelight and scented with frostberries and stardust. A female with a bounty of curves, his for the taking. A seductress who wielded more power over him than any other bride ever had. An assassin who refused to bend because she didn't yet understand the depths of his determination.

Before the night ended, she would.

He'd left a new print of stardust on her vulnerable throat, the sight more satisfying than the hardest-won victory. For the next twenty-nine days, Taliyah belonged to him.

He returned to his knees, contact with her minimal. A mewl of protest split the soft, red lips he intended to conquer, the sound like kerosene to his internal flame. He burned for this woman. Even now, a yearning to make her bow to his will warred with a need to give her whatever she desired. But he hadn't lied. Stopping would occur only after she'd given him what he wanted. Answers...her pleas...

That icy gaze tracked his every move as he fisted his shaft and stroked up, down. Up, down. "Do you see something you like, harpy?" Would she admit it?

Her inhalations shallowed. "I'd tell you if I did or didn't, but so far I'm not feeling real chatty." Brave talk delivered with a trembling voice.

Confidence in his success soared. She was flesh and blood and desire. A woman with desires could be... How had she phrased it? *Handled.*

"That's all right," he said. "I've thought of a better use for your mouth." He slanted his mouth over hers and dipped his tongue, seeking.

She welcomed him inside, their tongues thrusting together. Two matches, one strike. Unstoppable wildfire spread.

He kissed and kissed and kissed her, withholding none of his raging passion. She kissed him back with equal fervor. The sounds they made created a beautiful, anguished melody. Rasping breaths, groans and moans, grunts and cries. He felt like a predator who'd finally stumbled upon a meal after a too-long drought. Her taste maddened him. Ripened frostberries, more intoxicating than the finest wine.

Her nipples abraded his chest, new flames sparking. When he could take no more, he wrenched from her mouth and returned to his knees.

"Now to prepare the banquet table." He gathered pillows, one after the other, then propped the feathery mounds beneath her lower back, lifting her sex.

Admiring his handiwork, he ran his thumb up her slit. Pink. Wet. Glistening. *Temptation made flesh.* She swelled with need for him, and his mouth watered. He used the pad of his thumb to torment her, massaging her little bundle of nerves.

A whispery moan parted her lips, panting breaths fast on its heels.

"Is there anything you want to tell me before I begin, Taya?" He draped his big body over the mattress, rested his chin on her pubic bone and met her glazed gaze.

"Did you say *before* you begin?" Had she just gulped?

"I did." Roc sank a finger into her wet heat, wrenching a groan from them both as her inner walls squeezed him. His heart tripped as he slipped in to the second knuckle. "So hard on the outside. So soft on the inside." So slick and inviting.

With his next inward plunge, she rocked with him. Divine. He added a second finger, driving both as deep as he could get them without stealing her virginity. Preparing her?

No, no. He wouldn't go too far. Nothing mattered more than the blessings and the weapon. But the sight before him... the gripping heat... *Glorious. Only want more.*

Taliyah's honed and toned body was angled for his pleasure, her arms stretched and spread above her. White hair lay in tangles on the pillows. She remained partly suspended in the air, with her legs remaining spread as far as they could go. Her breasts bounced every time one of them moved.

Made for me.

Again, he used his thumb to torment her bundle of nerves. She quickly soaked his hand. "*Yesss*, Taya." He circled, circled, circled, applying more and more pressure. "You love this."

A choked sound escaped her. "I do. I do love it," she admitted. Then she added, "Almost...almost ready to spill my secrets. Promise! Whatever you do, don't stop this torture."

Viper. "You love the way my heat overtakes you. How I warm you inside and out."

"I do, I do, I do," she repeated. "Mmm. It's good, Roc. It's so good." As he worked his fingers deeper, harder, she cried, "Yes, yes! Don't you dare stop. You promised." She planted her heels and lifted her lower body off the pillows, attempting to *force* him deeper.

She needs more of me. "What would you do to get another finger inside you?" He plunged and circled her clitoris. Plunged. Circled. Stardust glittered, shimmering in the firelight. "Do you need to be filled?"

She gasped. She groaned. "Yes. Filled. Another finger." She watched him, as if she couldn't not watch him, her teeth bared. So fierce. So wanton. *So perfect.* "Give it to me."

"Will anyone's fingers do?" The question left him without thought, and he didn't have to ponder why. He hadn't forgotten her boasts about Hades. Still, he worked those two fingers in and out. In, out. In...he used them like scissors, reminding her of the prize—more. "Or do you need mine, and *only* mine?"

"I need nothing!"

Possessive instincts surged, torching layers of his control. "You need me, and I'll prove it." Chest rumbling, he fed her a third finger, then pressed the pad of his thumb against her clitoris.

Incoherent words left her as she bowed up and threw back her head, those drenched inner walls clenching as the orgasm ripped through. Her breasts bobbed; those pink-as-coral nipples puckered, begging for his mouth. The onyx piercing looked wicked against her pale skin.

Sweat beaded his brow, and strain caught him in a vise grip. He didn't touch her as she came down from the high. He stroked himself slowly, waiting. An act that required every ounce of his remaining control.

Finally, she sagged over the mattress and pillows and offered him a wicked smile. "I almost hate to break it to you, baby, but I'm not talking. You're going to have to try again."

How many males had she slain with such a smile?

"If you need help keeping up," she added, "just imagine me clad in more stardust and deeper satisfaction."

Curse her! Now he could do nothing *but* imagine. "Go ahead. Keep teasing. See what it gets you."

"You mean another orgasm? Taste what you've done to me, warlord." A command disguised by a throaty entreaty.

He shouldn't obey. He should deliver her second climax another way. Following the advice of your prisoner never ended well. But *not* taste her? Impossible. "Think I'll work my way down first."

She trembled as he settled in for another kiss. With his big body resting between her legs, his shaft had a direct line to her sex. The bliss of it. Of her. He rocked his way to heaven, to hell, making her come a second time. But he didn't stop kissing her, their tongues dueling. He continued to rock, thrusting against her, driving her pleasure ever higher—overseeing his own torment.

"Yes!" she cried. "Work your way down, Roc. Give me more."

"You'll hunger for *me* every time you desire a male." He would make sure of it. He must. He wouldn't be the only one to suffer.

A warlord hyperfocused on his goal, he ran her earlobe between his teeth and tongued the tendon running between her neck and shoulder. He laved, kneaded and sucked on her breasts, her nipples and her navel. Anywhere he put his trembling hands, he left a trail of stardust behind. *His claim.*

Her breaths grew more labored. Her frostberry scent strengthened, fusing with the stardust, becoming *their* scent.

"Look at you," he said, awed. He stared down at her flushed, writhing form. "In the throes for your male."

Your male. The words reverberated in his head, reminding him of her earlier taunt. She was his *gravita*, but he wasn't her consort.

The scales couldn't be balanced until she viewed him as her man.

And then? What purpose would balanced scales truly serve, if he killed her as planned?

Maybe…maybe there was another way?

18

Taliyah peered up at the warrior who'd played her body to a fever pitch—twice! Thrice? She'd lost count. He looked on edge. Angry and frustrated and seething with lust. Teasing him had thrilled her, but this intensity thrilled her more.

Roc was done playing.

With a snarl, he dragged a stiff tongue along the center of her sex. He massaged her clit with the tip. She... This...

What is he doing to me?

She undulated beneath his heady assault, wild for him. Despite the other climaxes, she ached beyond reason as he drove her need higher. One sensation blended into another, her body a live wire, her cells aflame.

It wasn't fair! Roc had pinned her wings, caging her harpy-strength, making her feel as weak as a mortal. Horrifyingly vulnerable again. He'd ratcheted up her sexual hunger and toyed with her emotions. Twice, he'd called her Taya. An endearment. A *personal* endearment. One she adored.

How was she supposed to feel about that? How was she supposed to react? Part of her wanted to push him away. Part of her wanted only to tug him closer. All of her just…wanted.

If other Generals could say no…

I can. "Unfasten the chains, Roc. Let me touch you." To feel his strength beneath her palms, to torment his body as he'd tormented hers, she would…she… Ah! His merciless tongue-lashing persisted, razing more and more of her hard-won control.

Oh. Oh! *Too good.* He flicked, rubbed and lapped, firm and unyielding. Perfect. Too much! But she only wanted more. If she could just make him come, the game would end and calm would return, and, and, and… Thoughts muddled, another climax barreling through her hard and fast. World-rocking. But Roc still didn't stop.

He was a man of his word and kept going. And going and going. She soared and she crashed, soared and crashed, again and again and again, but she never begged, and she never told him what he'd wanted to know…whatever he'd wanted to know. Somewhere between the fingering and the feasting, she'd forgotten his demands.

"Roc… Roc," she chanted, unable to say anything else. She existed in a daze of pleasure, fire and desperate need, swinging from one extreme to the other.

No man had ever focused so fully on her body.

Licking and fingering her in conjunction, he drove her to another climax so powerful, she nearly screamed the palace down.

"Tell me how much you want me," he demanded when she quieted.

"Only want…more orgasms," she slurred. She wouldn't beg. She wouldn't…

"Tell me *something.*" He wrenched upright, glaring and panting, the brutality of his nature undeniable. Harsh lines etched each of his features. Veins bulged, and muscles flexed. His broad chest appeared packed with bricks, and his tattoos were…not moving, she realized.

That seemed like an important development, something she should consider. Later. He required some kind of information? "Hot off the press. I'm going to touch you, too, Roc." It was a matter of necessity. "Free me so I can." She tugged at the chains. "Free me now."

"Yes. Can't deny you. Will free you. You'll give me what I want." He snarled the words, and she wasn't sure if he'd threatened her or warned her. *He* might not know. He was a man on the verge of losing control. A warrior gripped by excruciating pain and primal aggression.

No matter how many times she'd reached her peak, he'd denied himself an orgasm. "I'll give you what you *need*." What they both needed.

In a frenzy, he yanked the metal binding from her wrists. She wrapped her arms around him, holding on as tightly as her shaky limbs allowed. With another yank, he freed her ankles.

Taliyah slung a leg over his lap and rose above him, straddling his thighs. A mere heartbeat separated her core from his huge erection, and they both froze, not daring to breathe.

"Do it," he said, his voice hoarse from exertion. "Make me come."

"Yes." She raked her nails over his chest and kneaded muscles as hard as stone, learning how he liked being handled. The answer delighted her. Roughly. She rolled her hips, the action unstoppable.

The tendons in his neck distended. "Yes, Taya! Just like that."

The sight of him… Frothing passion barely banked. Like her, he had no modesty. He unabashedly enjoyed her and their actions.

With the next arch, he trapped her nape in a tight grip, locks of her hair threaded through his fingers. "Stop."

She obeyed. Their eyes met, hers caught in a gossamer web somehow stronger than the weapon she wielded.

"You need more," she rasped. Instinct demanded she move once more, but he wouldn't let her. "I'm going to give it to you so good."

Sweat dotted his face. "You think because you've told me nothing and you're free of chains that you're winning against me, don't you, little harpy?" A husky chuckle summoned fresh goose bumps to her limbs. "Think again. Even when we part this night, I'll be with you. You'll carry me in your thoughts, and you'll ache for me, singed by my stardust. When I said I'd never stop touching you, I meant it."

"Perhaps," she admitted, a bit unsteady. "But you'll feel me, too." His mark was external; as his *gravita*, she'd branded him internally.

He kissed her then, thrusting his tongue against hers and stopping any other words. Moaning into his mouth, she ground on him harder, faster. Her wings fluttered, empowering her, ensuring every point of contact elicited maximum pressure. Her nipples rubbed him, the friction turning the already-swollen, sensitive buds into buttons. For climax, press here.

In seconds, Taliyah erupted into another earth-shattering climax, coming apart, burning, soaring, only to crash again, completely enveloped by the scent of his stardust and the light glowing from his pores, suddenly so hungry she thought she might die without a sip of his soul.

He made indelible noises in his throat as he clasped her backside in a punishing grip, forcing her to remain stationary. The hand in her hair pulled, tipping her head, exposing her throat to him. Her pulse leaped, cheering him on. How her heart raced!

Head trapped, she slanted her gaze to him, their eyes meeting once again.

"Flesh and blood," he said, his tone guttural, almost unrecognizable.

Shivers rushed through her as his eyes hooded, his lashes nearly fused together as she gave an experimental rock of her hips. When he arched his own to meet her, she gasped. He groaned—and unleashed.

Possessed by need, he jackhammered her, and Taliyah—just—exploded. Unstoppable ecstasy invaded every nook and cranny.

He thrust with more force. "So close..."

As she cried his name, she dragged her claws along his scalp. He loosened his hold and locked his fiery gaze on her, the strain he projected unfathomable.

"Give me my prize, warlord. Come for me."

He obeyed. With a roar that seemed to spring from the depths of his soul, he came on her belly, jet after scorching jet lashing her.

An eternity passed in silence as Roc fought for calm. What had just happened—

He couldn't think about that yet.

The moment his riotous heart calmed, he adjusted Taliyah on the mattress and stood. He kept his gaze from her, not sure he wanted to see her expression. Smug, as he'd pretended to be? Vulnerable, as he struggled so hard *not* to be?

"We need to clean up," he said, the words flat. He strode into the bathroom. Though he yearned to glance at her, he resisted. Half of him expected the harpy to follow; all of him hoped she didn't.

At the sink, he washed his face with icy water. The droplets trickled down. He caught a brief glimpse of his reflection and glanced away. He appeared...crazed.

No footsteps sounded to indicate Taliyah fled, yet he sensed her loss, the fever in his veins cooling. Possessive instincts demanded he fetch her *now*. Self-preservation suggested he stay put. They needed to talk, yes. Their marriage required new rules, obviously. But he should probably calm before they spoke.

Roc showered, the water doing little to ease his mind. Alone, he let his thoughts return to what had happened in that bed. How Taliyah had done nothing he'd demanded. How he'd wanted her anyway. How he'd *drenched* her in stardust, as she'd drenched his shaft with arousal.

As he'd marked her, sometimes purposely, sometimes unaware, he'd made a shocking discovery. He'd marked himself, too, stardust burning through his resistance.

A dangerous game to continue to play.

But play he would. For twenty-eight days.

He fisted his hands. No matter how much he wanted, needed, wished he could spare her, he couldn't. Forget the blessing and how it applied to him. A good Commander didn't curse his men.

Does a good Commander kill his wife?

Roc barely stopped himself from punching and shattering the mirror.

He stomped into his closet to dress in—what? Would he walk with the soldiers this night, hunting phantoms that would provide more misinformation about Taliyah? At least he didn't have to worry she'd visit the other realm. He'd taken her— No, he hadn't. He'd *meant* to take her key.

A curse burst from him, and he jerked on a pair of leathers. Shirtless, feet bare, he flashed throughout the rooms until he found her. She exited a bathroom, and it was clear she'd showered, too. Wet hair framed her delicate face. And she was naked. The key dangled between her breasts, taunting him. Lucky key.

"Where did you go before?" he demanded.

She shrugged. "The Realm of the Forgotten. I stashed Neeka there, but she's gone now."

He— What? She'd offered the information freely? His shoulders rolled in. Would he ever understand this woman?

She headed for the closet, stopped before entering, then pivoted and marched to Roc. "My selfish husband didn't think to prepare a wardrobe for me. Out of my way. I've got to grab someone else's gear from yet another room."

Her attitude rankled. Selfish? He'd pleasured her well. Many times!

You also left her to deal with her own emotions afterward.

Guilt choked him. What if she *had* experienced the same sense of vulnerability as him?

"Why tell me the truth now?" he asked.

"Because I don't have time for another mantrum. Your murder isn't going to plan itself."

Roc acted without thinking, picking her up and carting her to the bed, where he tossed her. Before she finished bouncing, he flashed to her side, coiled one arm around her and drew her against him.

"What are you doing?" She sputtered. "I'm not going another round with you. We're enemies again!"

He didn't know what he was doing. "We can be enemies tomorrow."

"Fine." Rather than reject him, she snuggled into him, seeking his warmth. "I'll go another round with you."

She *had* experienced vulnerability, and he had no idea what to make of it. All he could do was marvel. The unflappable Taliyah Skyhawk had been flapped. "We're cuddling, not pleasuring." He had some things to figure out first.

"I'm not so sure about that. Mmm. You smell good enough to eat," she said, her voice thicker. She stiffened. "Uh, I should go." Something tinged her words. Panic? "I need to go *immediately*."

Leave him? No. Now that he held her against him again, her cool skin warming, he refused to let her go. "Tell me why you wish to flee, and I'll consider letting you go." *Before I decline your request.*

"Flee?" She balled her hands and beat on his chest. "You take that back! I do not flee. Ever."

"Then settle in and get comfortable. We're having a real conversation. We can discuss what occurred between us."

"What? No! Dude. No. Don't ruin this." Bit by bit, she relaxed against him. Whatever had hurt—or spooked?—her no longer seemed to be a problem. "Nothing happened but a momentary truce. Tomorrow, we return to business as usual. Meaning, yes, you'll stomp around like a drama queen, making decrees that I'll ignore, and I'll learn how to kill you."

Roc heaved with relief—not a whole lot of irritation. "I'm glad you understand how things must be between us."

Must? He was a god. Powerful. A creator of worlds. So he and his men had tried to find other ways to escape the blessing and curse. So they'd found none. Why must the sacrifice roll on? This marriage was different. Shouldn't the ending be different, too?

Thinking like Solar?

"Understand?" Taliyah snorted. "Warlord, I'm demanding it."

In all the worlds Roc visited, he'd encountered no one quite like Taliyah. Even now, in the warmth of his arms after four—five?—orgasms, she wouldn't bend. "How are you not General yet?"

Her little claws curled into his chest as she petted him, and he knew the question pleased her. "Apparently my own sacrifices suck. Even the arm and leg I once amputated on purpose. Did I receive my star? Nooo."

"Why did you offer an arm and a leg?"

"Haven't you heard the old adage about giving an arm and a leg? Well, I had a dagger, so…"

Bad form to discuss your past brides with the current, yet he told her, "Chaos hinted that I've made mistakes with my sacrifices, as well."

"What happens when you make the right sacrifice?"

"I ascend for the second time." He needed to ascend to have a family. Could he have a family without his *gravita*? Here, now, with Taliyah pliant and curious, he thought he…wasn't sure. "I will kill Erebus for good."

She braced, as if expecting a blow. Why?

"Hey, the *alevala* are moving again," she mumbled, resting her cheek on the hollow of his shoulder.

"They stopped?"

"While we were busy negotiating our…one-night truce."

She didn't know what to call what they'd done, did she? Good, because he didn't, either. It hadn't been sex. He'd had every type of sex imaginable, but this had been…better.

"That happens when I'm lost in *anhilla*." To his knowledge, the *alevala* had never stopped due to arousal before.

"That was *anhilla*? Don't take this the wrong way, but I didn't expect your most fearsome state to mimic horniness."

"You'll know *anhilla* when you see it. I destroy every foe in my vicinity without thought, mercy or regret."

"Okay, stop with the sexy dirty talk if we're not going to fool around again." She tapped the spot above his heart. "Stains are growing here. What's that about?"

Tension overtook him in an instant. To distract her from the question, he reached out to clasp behind her thigh and heft her partly atop him. With her sex resting against his and her face cradled against his throat, he said, "Tell me more about you."

She went rigid before struggling against him. "I really should go, Roc."

Why did she keep doing this? "Tell me what's wrong."

"You just…you smell so good." With a moan, she softened. She ran her nose up his neck, just as he'd done to her, gyrating against him.

As he cupped her backside, she wrenched from his arms and sat up—not before he caught a glimpse of her face.

Black lines branched from her eyes.

19

"I'm leaving, and that's that." Taliyah raced around the room, gathering weapons. "Don't try to stop me."

She'd known she'd played with fire. Hunger clawed at her. She'd gone two days without a meal or even a snack. In the past few hours, she'd met and threatened her father, experienced incredible pleasure at the hands of the husband planning to murder her, received an official dismissal from said husband immediately afterward, showered and cursed his name, then enjoyed a royal welcome back into the strong embrace she'd craved more than she would *ever* admit.

She scowled, angry with herself, with Roc. With Erebus. Her emotions had been through the wringer, squeezed within an inch of their lives.

What she and Roc had done... The satisfaction she'd tasted in his arms warred with the uncertainty. She felt as though she'd finally stored the mysterious parts of her life in the same box. A puzzle she had only to complete in order to make herself whole.

What was she to do about this man? What was she to do about her starvation? Ignoring her hunger pains ceased being an option.

Five days was the longest she'd ever gone without a proper meal. At the time, she'd been trapped in a desolate realm devoid of life. By day four, she'd felt as if she were dying. By day five, she'd *wanted* to die.

No reason to panic. This was only day two, and she already had a banquet lined up. *All will be well.*

With daggers in hand, she rushed to the door. Roc appeared directly in front of her, blocking the exit. Too late to slow. She slammed into him. Only the hard clasp of his hand on her nape prevented her from ricocheting. He used his free hand to disarm her and lock her body against his.

The fingers on her nape inclined her face to the light.

She kept her lids low. Looking at him, even for a moment, made her mouth water and her stomach cramp. The hungrier she became, the more his skin glowed. The louder she heard his soul call. Soon, she'd see and hear nothing else. Remembering she couldn't consume him, that he possessed some kind of mystical block—impossible. She would attack.

Even now, she yearned to attack. Standing in place required great effort. "If you're wanting another go at me, you'll have to wait." She began to pant as though she jogged uphill. "The candy store is currently closed."

"What I want is the key to the Realm of the Forgotten." He wrapped his fingers around the little dagger necklace and yanked the cord from her neck. As he traced his thumb over the metal, he frowned. "This leads to Harpina."

He could tell by touch alone? "Why didn't you touch the key while we were making out?" Because he'd wanted to get her into bed, and he'd seized any excuse.

"Give me the other key, Taliyah."

"I can't." If he fought her on this, she'd...what? In this state, what could she do?

He examined her before forcibly turning her around and sweeping her hair over her shoulder, baring her back to him. "The hourglass tattoo."

How did he even know that? "Remove it, and I'll—"

"What?" He traced a fingertip along the image, unerringly gentle. Shivers rained through her. "What can you do to me?"

She didn't know! "Are we done here?" she demanded with enough vim and vigor to terrify anyone else.

With an unnecessary abundance of force, he turned her to face him. He actually recoiled.

"Stop manhandling me, and get out of my way," she said, meeting his gaze. She gasped. Had she ever spied so much malice? Because of a tattoo key?

Cool air bit her bare skin, rousing apprehension. Before this, she'd never experienced a chill in his presence. Why did he no longer give off heat?

"Black lines branch from your eyes, Taliyah. Why?"

The question lashed like a whip, and her cramping stomach dropped. He suspected she was a phantom.

Drawing on centuries of battle calm, she delivered a flat statement. "I'm part snakeshifter, Roc. Why else?" If he knew little about the snakes, he might believe her very truthful claim.

"Snakeshifters do not develop black lines around their eyes. Try again."

Okay, so he knew about snakes, but he might not know about Erebus. "You're right. But how many snakeshifter–harpy hybrids do you know?" Such a combination was a rarity, snakes a difficult species to infiltrate. Their suspicion of others provided a tough hurdle for any female to jump.

He ran his tongue over his teeth, the barest tendril of heat escaping him, fueling her confidence. "You are the first," he grudgingly admitted.

Confidence restored. *I've got this!* "Since we've got *that* cleared up, be my darling and get out of my way. If you hadn't noticed, I'm naked. I seek clean clothes."

His nostrils flared. "You won't traipse the palace in this state."

Oh, yeah. She totally had this. His possessiveness had just reared its big, beautiful head. Going for flirty, she batted her lashes. "Why don't you do your duty as my spouse and provide for me? In case you're wondering, I'm size perfect." Like every woman who'd ever lived.

"Trust me, I noticed." He maintained his hold, studying her face with renewed intent. "We captured a phantom today."

Confidence plummeted yet again. Clearly, she hadn't convinced him of anything. "Thanks for the warning. I'll be on the lookout. No big, bad phantom will overtake me."

"You told me you've never fought a phantom. How do you know you can defeat one?"

Reveal nothing. "I can defeat anyone. Why else? One day I'll even defeat you. So what, exactly, are you implying here, Roc?" Better to confront his suspicions head-on.

The light in his pores brightened, threatening to unravel her composure. *Do not break his stare and lick your lips.*

"Erebus sent me a message," he said. He went quiet again.

Taliyah didn't let herself panic. She knew better. Panic led to mistakes. As casually as she could manage, she arched a brow and braced a fist on a cocked hip. "And?"

"And he says *you* are a phantom."

Shock and fury punched the air from her lungs. Her own father ratted on her? That…that… There was no insult great enough. The urge to kill vibrated in her bones. At least she didn't have to wonder why. Erebus would rather make Roc miserable than protect his own flesh and blood.

"You believe your greatest foe?" She tsked. "Hey, would you like to buy an invisible best friend? I'm offering two for the price of one."

His eyelids slitted. "*You* are my foe. The one who challenges me for the position of Commander."

"Because you selected me, not the other way around!"

"You *demanded* I select you." Lacking mercy, he returned to the interrogation. "Why did you refuse to eat dinner?"

She rolled her eyes. What else could she do? "Some snakes prefer to devour their mates whole."

His eyelids slitted further. "The day you tracked me in the throne room—"

"You mean yesterday?" She tried for flippant. She might have sounded strained. Yesterday felt a million years away.

"—did you use illusion to hide yourself...or did you disembody?"

Careful. "Tell trade secrets to the male planning my murder? Try again."

He remained undeterred. "Are you a phantom, Taliyah? Say yes or no and nothing else."

Hardly. "If I say no, you won't believe me. If I say yes, you'll attack. Why don't we climb in bed and cuddle this out?" He'd fall asleep with her in his arms. She'd push her spirit out of her body and feed. He'd never know she'd left him, and he'd believe her story. Simple, easy. *Won't whimper.*

"Yes. Or. No."

Okay, so, the first stream of panic invaded. What was her best move here? *Think!* Should she flat-out deny it?

No. Misleading an enemy was fun. Outright lying to save her skin was nothing but cowardice. Should she just admit the truth? What would he do to her? His options were limited. Lock her up or kill her.

If anyone had the means to cage a phantom, it was this uncompromising Astra.

"Silence isn't an option," he said, pushing the statement through clenched teeth. "Yes or no. Say one or the other. *Now.*"

"Screw you. I'm fetching clothes. I've been ogled enough

for one day." She braced for battle. "To stop me, you'll have to fight me."

"Very well." He removed his hand from her nape. He didn't strike—he vanished.

Did she relax her guard? Not even a little. Wherever he'd gone, whatever he was doing, he planned to return fast. She knew it.

Taliyah lunged, sweeping up the dagger he'd discarded.

Roc reappeared with a shirt he tossed in her direction.

"Dress." If he noticed the weapon, he made no comment.

Reflexes in better shape than the rest of her, she caught the garment without fumbling. "I don't understand." Had the danger passed?

As she worked the material over her head, Roc stated, "You are without excuses now. Answer my question."

No, the danger hadn't passed. This man was determined, intelligent and ruthless, and he'd already put some pretty solid pieces together.

"What I am," she said, "is your *gravita*."

"You are a thirty-day irritation."

Ouch. Whatever. His opinion hardly mattered. Except, this one kind of…hurt. Only minutes before, he'd held her as if he couldn't get enough of her. And she'd held him right back, because part of her respected him. Maybe even liked him. He was amazingly strong, his battle skill unsurpassed. His intensity stunned. When he indulged his sense of humor, he charmed.

She couldn't help what she was, and she wouldn't apologize for it. Actually, she was tired of hiding her origins from everyone. Why should she?

Her mother had commanded her to do so because of the horrors Erebus had wrought in the past, and what he might do in the future. Because she'd worried harpies would be unable to separate father from daughter. Taliyah's peers weren't so simpleminded. Surely! Only the Astra would fault her.

"Are you a phantom?" Roc demanded.

"What does it matter?" she snapped.

He bowed up. "Phantoms are worthy only of death."

A layer of calm cracked, an astonishing amount of pain spilling out. "Apparently the same is true of your bride."

His lips thinned, and he dropped his chin. Though he remained in place, she sensed movement everywhere around her. Were his warriors appearing? Spinning to the side, she avoided capture... No! His men hadn't surrounded her. Roc flashed in four poles. Two in front, two behind. Made of trinite and six feet high, those poles beamed pure energy, creating a cage without bars.

Hostility vibrated in her wings. Taliyah didn't do trapped. She raced forward, planning to burst through the force field and deal with the damage. She bounced back, her knees buckling.

Unwilling to accept defeat, she fought her way up with sheer grit, shook it off and tried again. And again. Again and again and again. She. Would. Not. Stop.

Roc scrubbed a hand down his face, as if he couldn't believe what he had witnessed. "You are. You are a phantom pretending to be a snake, sent by Erebus to ruin me."

"You ruin *yourself*." *Wham. Wham.* Still fighting...

"How are you able to act so independent?" The more he spoke, the harsher the inflection in his voice. "You cannot be my *gravita*. You tricked me somehow." He scanned her entire form, and his eyes widened. "The ring."

Full-blown panic took over then, and she shrank back. Not the ring. Anything but the ring.

This might be a good time to detonate her bomb. Would he simmer down if he learned of her kinship with Chaos? Or would he rage about Erebus's potential influence over her?

Split-second decision, no thought. She kept her mouth shut. Too much time remained in the game. For now, she stayed the course. "If you want the ring, you'll have to pry it from my cold, dead hand."

He vanished, reappearing directly in front of her, the force field having no effect on him. Already he clasped her wrist. Her stomach bottomed out.

Their eyes met. "Roc," she said, a humiliating tremor in her voice, "don't you dare—"

With a single jerk, he ripped the metal from her finger, screws and all. Frost spread over his skin.

Taliyah's body bowed, a scream of agony leaving the mouth he'd kissed half an hour before. Roc stumbled from her. Blood poured from her finger, spilling down the pale, pale skin he'd caressed. She dropped the dagger and pressed her hands to her ears.

The sight seared his brain, and he nearly glanced anywhere else. He forced himself to stare at her. Forced his heart to harden. This was nothing more than a trick, courtesy of Erebus.

But her screams tolled on. "Make them stop, make them stop!"

"Enough," he shouted, hating her. Hating himself more. "I'll not fall for more of your deceits." This *must* be a trick. Just like everything else. She'd hidden her origins so well.

His bride was a phantom. A soulsucker. Undoubtedly Erebus's greatest creation. What other phantom could lead Roc to consider changing course?

Part of him clung to disbelief, fighting the mounting evidence. How was she so lovely to him, even now? Why were her eyes not milky white? How did she converse so easily, warming with his touch?

Why had Erebus alerted him to her heritage? Without a warning, Roc might have continued in ignorance, allowing Taliyah to spy. Or worse.

Realization: When she'd left the palace, she hadn't visited her friend. She'd returned to her maker.

Rage stampeded him, trampling every other emotion.

"Make them stop," she cried. Her knees gave out, and she tumbled to the floor.

Only doing her master's bidding.

His heart hardened further. What was Roc to do with his treacherous bride?

20

The screams…so many screams. As if all phantoms from all realms stood in this very room. A phenomenon Taliyah had never understood. From everything she'd read, phantoms remained quiet when they gathered, unless and until Erebus issued a direct order otherwise. They didn't even scream when starved.

She needed to… She should… *Can't think. Need to think!* But oh, the noise! How could she ponder *anything*?

The screams grew in volume as the minutes passed, pain after searing pain lancing her. Was she holding the dagger? She couldn't remember. Desperate, she made stabbing motions with both hands, just in case. *Please…*

The screams escalated. "Stop, stop, stop."

Strong fingers wrapped around her wrists. Something cold and wet slapped one of her palms, and she jerked, vaguely aware Roc was cleaning the blood from her wound.

He helps me? No, surely not. He knew what she was. His hatred knew no bounds. The disgust he lobbed at her…

With her defenses down, she couldn't deny the sting of his rejection. An icy tear slid down her cheek.

Roc maneuvered her arms in different directions, her legs here and there. Through the screams, she thought she heard him say, "You will wear this because I'm not sure what you're faking and what you're not. I won't risk someone taking advantage of you in this condition...or you taking advantage of me."

She thought he'd just refastened the chastity belt in place, then dragged a pair of shorts up her legs. She fought, because she couldn't not fight.

So. Many. Screams. A cold, wet trickle leaked from her ears and nose, and a whimper escaped. What if the screams *never* stopped?

Was she floating? A hint of warmth penetrated her awareness. Roc carried her? He'd subdued her so easily?

She moaned. "Make it stop." Screaming, screaming. *SCREAMING.*

The air turned frigid and damp all of a sudden, familiar scents clinging to her nostrils. He'd taken her to the dungeon?

A crazed laugh escaped. Did Roc think to let her rot until the sacrifice?

Well, good luck. If the screams continued, she might off herself before then.

Falling slowly... Lying flat. Roc shoved something onto her finger. The ring! Blessed quiet descended, until she heard only a mild ring.

Taliyah sagged against the floor. Panting, she wiped at her eyes with a shaky hand. Chains rattled as she moved, confusing her. She blinked. What was that heavy weight on her wrists? On her chest?

What was... Why... When the synapses fired off in her brain, comprehension dawned. Roc had shackled her wrists and pinned her wings.

She gasped, dread and fury unfurling. Jolting upright, she ex-

amined her surroundings. She occupied a cell next to the harpies, who watched her through the bars that separated them,
exuding confusion and concern.

Roc stood inside the cell with Taliyah, his expression fright-
eningly blank. Other Astra towered in the space beyond, peering at her with...horror? Even the one who usually paced and
mumbled nonsense focused on her with laser intensity.

Taliyah remained on the floor and jutted her chin. "I distinctly remember checking *no* on my RSVP to the dungeon
hoedown."

"You don't have to worry," Roc told his warriors. Rage simmered in every word. "The stardust means nothing. It isn't real.
A trick like everything else."

The newest rejection wounded in ways she didn't expect. Unwanted by two fathers. Now discarded by the man predisposed
to desire her. Would *any* man find value in her?

Every warrior but the black-eyed hottie with light brown
skin nodded in agreement. Because desiring a phantom was so
far beyond their realm of comprehension?

She forced a smile. "Are you sure the stardust isn't real? Are
you really sure an itty-bitty phantom coerced the beastly Astra
to do something—someone—he despised? Why, only yesterday
you claimed such a feat is impossible."

Okay, she needed to zip it until she figured out an endgame.
Antagonizing a monster might feel good in the moment, but
she'd be better off ensuring every barb served a purpose. The
goal was freedom, not the assuaging of pride.

His fiery gaze scanned her features. "In these chains, you'll
be unable to disembody or use the key to the Realm of the
Forgotten."

Truth? She tried to flash...to mist... She failed. *Don't panic.*
Her options had dwindled, yes, but a few endured. Maybe.
Hopefully. Could she convince him some phantoms were good?

Torchlight cast flickering shadows over his brutal features, blending with the soul-light. Hunger reignited as she imagined suckling at his throat.

Roc shuddered, his expression brutal.

No, she couldn't convince him some phantoms were good. She doubted *anyone* had the ability to do it.

"Erebus sent her to spy on me, just as he boasted. We didn't ice over in her presence because of a mystical ring." Again, he directed his statements to his men. "We'll sweep the palace and the city within the walls. I don't know what she's done to strike at us. I suspect she's helping the phantoms breach our borders without our knowledge."

If glares were daggers, Taliyah would be bleeding from multiple gashes right now.

Which Astra can I tap into?

Murmurs erupted from the harpies. "A soulsucker?"

"As in…a phantom?"

Well, she'd hated hiding her origins. Now the secret was out.

"Boys, I can verify Roc's words this once. I'm afraid I did strike at you." Taliyah exaggerated a wince, all *my bad*. If she kept talking, she might be able to prove herself independent of Erebus. It couldn't hurt. "I know, I know. How dare I strike at the ones who conquered my realm and plan my murder? Lesson learned."

Did Roc flinch ever so slightly? "You are a soulsucker, Taliyah. How are you able to converse somewhat intelligently?"

Somewhat? Jerk. "Maybe I'm gifted," she said with a shrug. "Or special. A new species of phantom, perhaps? Maybe I'm Erebus's daughter. Maybe he's perfected the art of making us. Take your pick." Mixing truth with a misdirection didn't seem as dangerous as avoiding the truth altogether.

Pensive, Roc replied, "You aren't gifted, special or a new breed of phantom. A husk without a soul is always a husk without a soul. You aren't his daughter, either. Erebus is the essence of death. He has no life-giving seed."

Gross. Taliyah vomited in her mouth a little. Roc had no idea he spoke about her father's— No, she couldn't even think it. But no wonder the Big E had possessed his brother to impregnate Tabitha and Tamera. He couldn't get the job done on his own.

Roc continued. "Phantoms are made the way phantoms are made. The method of creation cannot be altered."

"Are you sure? Mortals have babies the old-fashioned way," she said, "or with the help of science."

"Even with science, the same ingredients are used." He stroked his beard, then flipped his gaze to Mumbles. "Visit the Hall of Secrets. I want a report of any whispers involving phantoms like Taliyah."

Hall of Secrets. Never heard of it.

"I will do this." Mumbles struck her as lucid, until he added, "Why don't I remember? The battle raged. She and the girl were in front of me. Then the battle was over. What don't I remember?"

Hold up. Could *she and the girl* refer to Blythe and Isla? Blythe's victims experienced blackouts all the time…when she possessed them.

Blythe might have possessed the Astra to round up Isla and escape unnoticed. But how had she possessed the Astra in the first place?

And, if Blythe got in…when had she gotten out?

Why am I happy to see you? A question Mumbles had asked on Taliyah's first trip to the dungeon. Had he felt *Blythe's* emotions? Was her sister inside him still?

Hope flowered, and Taliyah leveled her gaze on the male. Argh! Roc positioned himself between them.

"What did Erebus order you to do?" he demanded.

Mind on the problem at hand, T. She couldn't help Blythe until she'd gotten out of this mess.

Her neighbors upped their whispers and speculations. Taliyah tuned them out, concentrating on the warrior who was rubbing the bare patch of skin above his heart. Around it, the *alevala* churned, more agitated than usual.

"Taliyah," he snapped.

"Oh? Were you expecting an answer from me?" His scent infiltrated her awareness, and she dropped her gaze to his mouth. Her shackles clinked as she slinked forward. "Come closer, husband, and I'll tell you." Her raspy voice embarrassed her. Onward and upward. "Just a little closer, Roc."

He did move closer, shooting out his arm, wrapping his fingers around her throat to slant her face up to his. "You would drink me down if I let you. You would drain me dry."

"I would," she confirmed. Why deny it? "That was plan A, and it was an abject failure."

His fingers flexed on her. "You tried to suck my soul?"

"Oh, yeah. Big-time. Last night, actually."

He stiffened further, even as he oh-so-gently traced his thumb up the column of her throat. The tenderness was a shocking contrast to his ferocity. "I felt your attempt. For a moment, my dreams changed." He offered the words softly, for her ears alone. "Were those your orders? To drain me and keep me weak? Your master should have known better."

"Or I acted—act—on my own? I'm so different from the others..."

A flash of uncertainty, there and gone. Enough to catch her attention.

She pressed her advantage. "I don't work for Erebus, Roc. I'm a free agent. How can I prove this to you?"

"You can't." His grip tightened. "You will stay here until I decide what to do with you."

Hardly. "If I can mount an escape, I promise you, I will mount an escape."

He scowled. "You are defeated, phantom. Accept it."

"I'm not defeated until I'm dead, warrior. And even then I'll keep fighting."

A storm cloud of fury, he vanished. His men lingered, projecting varying degrees of concern, before following him.

Taliyah deflated against the wall. Had she detected a thrum of heat before Roc's disappearing act? What did it mean?

Ugh. She was too hungry to process her own emotions, much less his.

The harpies erupted into rapid-fire questions, going silent when the handsome warrior reappeared. Dark from head to toe. Looking at no one, he claimed a post between the two cells.

My guard for the night. She sat up, saying, "You're the repairman, yeah? I caught sight of you a few times when I made my rounds."

To her surprise, he replied, "I am." She'd expected to be ignored. "I bear the ninth rank."

"So, last place?" She offered her favorite exaggerated wince while drawing her knees behind her. "That's gotta sting."

"It's deserved. Once, I led the army. I was the first." He delivered the information with a tinge of shame rather than pride. "My brother acted as my third."

"You're Roc's brother?" Well. Sure enough. They shared similar facial features. Did this man love his brother as much as Roc loved him, or did he harbor secret jealousy? "Pro tip. Your bragging needs work."

"I wasn't bragging. I was confessing."

No, he wasn't jealous. The siblings clearly shared the same sense of honor and respect. A sense she admired, despite their treatment of her. When it came to her sisters, from Blythe, the oldest, to Gwen, the youngest, Taliyah would willingly, happily suffer for their good.

"Astra— Hey, what's your name?" Had Roc told her? She couldn't remember.

"I am Celestian. Ian."

"Ian. Why does Erebus hate Roc and vice versa? What started their war?" Would he tell her?

"Erebus hates all Astra," he said, "but whoever is undergoing their blessing task bears the brunt of his focus. The fact that Roc is Commander ensures he is doubly hated." Ian shrugged. "Erebus first hated us because his father loved us."

All this effort for jealousy? Maybe in the beginning. Guaranteed his motives changed when the Astra killed his brother. Now he sought revenge. Loss for loss. And oh, wow, what a beautiful glow Ian possessed! Her mouth watered and—

No! Taliyah turned, ending the conversation. No big deal. She had this under control.

"Female," Ian said, his tone curious, "I have a question."

"I'm sure you do, but I'm busy thinking." *Of someone tasty…* Someone not too many feet from her, perhaps, in the other cage… Mara might make a delicious dessert.

A groan clogged Taliyah's throat. She'd never eaten one of her own—she wouldn't. Probably.

Ian asked his question anyway. "How did you draw the stardust from Roc?"

A query she couldn't resist. "How do you think?"

"I honestly don't know what to think anymore," he admitted. "If you knew how precious stardust is…how few of us make it…how much some of us yearn to make it…"

There was an excellent chance Ian considered himself part of the *some*. "I don't think you're ready for the answer, warrior."

"Tell me." He stepped forward, gripping the bars, his curiosity seeming to veer into desperation.

If she weren't on the verge of starvation, she might have retorted, *Keep ordering me around. It works so well for your brother.* Instead, she sighed, shrugged and told him the truth. "I breathed."

21

Roc blocked every voice from his head and focused on the realm frequency he'd picked up from Taliyah's hourglass tattoo.

He needed no key to enter a realm, only a link. Had she lied about the location and the friend she'd supposedly met, as he suspected?

He appeared in the so-called Realm of the Forgotten, halfway expecting an ambush. Instead, he stood at the edge of the world—at the end of a winding road that stretched over a churning body of water, leading to a steep cliff with a massive fortress carved into its side. Above it, the inky sky offered no hint of light, save for the freezing fog curling into dizzying swirls.

It was a sky Roc recognized. Part of an original realm rather than the duplicates he created for war. Original realms took ages to make and always carried the DNA of their maker. The secrets hidden in their heart of hearts.

This one had been created by Erebus.

Roc's hands curled into fists. Whatever world the god birthed, he ruined with unsustainable weather patterns and that swirling fog.

Icy rage gobbled up what remained of his hope, Taliyah's connection to the dark god confirmed. An hour ago, he'd believed he'd planned for every eventuality. Never had he suspected a phantom possessed the ability to hide in plain sight, driving him insane with lust and possibilities, tricking him, minute by minute.

How had Erebus made someone like Taliyah?

What if she wasn't made? Could she be his sibling, perhaps? Chaos knew of her. Had even mentioned her by name. But...no. If she belonged to the god's familial line, Chaos would've stopped the wedding. The honorable mentor Roc served wouldn't send a daughter to her death. Chaos wasn't like Roc's parents.

There must be another explanation for Taliyah's condition.

Someone somewhere possessed answers. Someone *always* had answers, no truth ever fully erased. If anyone had spoken of Taliyah in dark places, Roc would find out. The Hall of Secrets collected whispers and confessions. A person needed only to sift through the countless voices to learn the most horrifying mysteries. Roux, even in his compromised state, sorted through the deluge better than most.

Focus. Who would Roc find inside the fortress? His nemesis, ready to gloat? He hoped so. He *craved* a battle.

Materializing in the entry, he paused and took stock. In the distance, a clock ticked and a fire crackled. No footsteps sounded. No voices drifted to indicate Erebus remained.

Roc flashed from room to room, scanning and memorizing, collecting data. There was no sign of Erebus or his phantoms. Not right now, at least. The god had definitely been here, his scent fresh. So was Taliyah's.

The urge to commit violence consumed him. The master and his puppet had met here, along with two others. Harpies, most likely. Did they discuss Roc's unprecedented reaction to Taliyah? The stardust he'd left on her skin? Did they laugh at his preoccupation with the woman?

How he cursed the day he'd spotted Taliyah in the market!

Ferreting out her bedroom wasn't difficult. Frostberries saturated every inch. A stench of betrayal.

Betrayal? When she has only fought to survive?

Yes!

As a matter of duty, he examined this room more intently than the others. What better way to learn more about his enemy? The tidiness of the space fit her personality, but not her origins. Phantoms never worried over making a bed or polishing weapons before hanging them in designated spots. Nor did phantoms care about touches of whimsy. A plaque on the wall read *World's Okayest Sister.* A second wall decoration was a painting of stick figures framed in gold. The artist's name was scribbled.

He stalked into the closet to assess the garments she preferred when she wasn't tormenting foolish husbands. Combat gear and more combat gear. Nothing for seduction or relaxation.

How sad.

How foolish of him to care.

Phantoms had no feelings. Although…Taliyah might. Had she faked her love of family, her loyalty to the harpies? He had doubts.

So different from the others. Faster, stronger and, yes, smarter. Charming without effort.

How did Erebus command someone like her? *Could* he? What if she operated outside of the god's orders, as claimed?

Did she *choose* to serve him?

Bile rose up in Roc's chest. What if he won her from— *No!* He wouldn't entertain such a temptation.

Obviously, she'd pretended to desire him. Was she truly his *gravita*?

He rifled through the dresser drawers, where he discovered

sexy scraps of barely-there material he refused to imagine her wearing. Part of her arsenal against him?

His fingers curled around a pair of ice-blue panties nearly the same shade as her eyes. If Erebus sought to tie Roc into knots, mission accomplished. Roc hadn't felt this conflicted since…

His most hated memory rose, and he pressed the panties against the *alevala* in development. A memory of terrible death, incredible loss and unforgivable betrayals.

He captured and cast out the thought before he was forced to relive every horrifying moment.

Though he wanted to shove the underwear into his pocket, he dropped the garment and flashed to his bedroom in Harpina. He eased onto the foot of his bed.

The trip to the Realm of the Forgotten had done him no good. What was he going to do with Taliyah?

Roc rested his elbows on his knees and held his head in his hands. Despite everything, he desired her still, his need burning as hot as ever.

While chained and splayed on a dungeon floor, she'd gazed at him with defiance. How could he not want her back in his arms?

He never should have flashed closer to her. Never should have clasped her throat as she dared him to act. Even now, he fought the urge to return. To splay her lithe body beneath him and touch and kiss until she fully surrendered to his will.

He thought he might do terrible things for such a thing.

What has she done to me?

Halo's hard voice lifted Roc's head. —*At least forty phantoms breached the palace. Looks like they're headed to the throne room. I don't know how this happened. I never saw them approach the palace or the wall. There's no sign of Erebus.*—

He rose to steady legs and pushed Taliyah from his mind. War came first. War *always* came first, no matter how exhausting. The moment he exalted something above it, his past actions would cease to matter; horrors committed for the greater good would suddenly be mistakes.

Roc didn't have to wonder how Halo spotted the invasion while standing on the wall half a mile away. The male used mystical binoculars acquired with Roc's fourth bride, the lenses peering through every obstacle.

Had Taliyah brought the fiends here? She must have. But how had she done it?

He did his best to mitigate his anger and frustration.

—*Hold your positions. I'll take care of the problem myself.*—

He palmed two three-blades and flashed to the action, finding forty-three phantoms. Females dressed in widow's weeds and starved. They walked in circles in the center of the throne room, muttering, "Get to the throne room, embody, walk around, tell Roc. Get to the throne room, embody, walk around, tell Roc."

Another message from Erebus. One he had no wish to hear. The god coveted more of his misery, nothing more.

Roc flashed to the two closest phantoms and rammed a blade in the underside of their chins. Both creatures dropped, soon to evaporate. In unison, the other phantoms turned toward him before freezing in place, preparing to deliver the missive.

"I know every move you will make."

Roc didn't hesitate; he struck again and again and again, thick mist coating the air. The phantoms spoke until the very end.

"I know every move you will make. I have the Blade of Destiny, after all, and you have—" The last phantom died before the rest escaped her.

The Blade of Destiny. He'd *known* the loss would haunt him.

A thrum of aggression brushed his skin. Roc spun, catching a phantom by the throat. Where had she come from?

Her milky eyes were set in solid-black sockets. Graying lips formed a wide O as she sucked at the air between them. She clawed at his arm, desperate to reach him.

Why didn't Erebus send more like her, his usual MO? While

the Astra were strong enough to block ten, twenty, fifty phantoms from feeding at a time, they couldn't block an entire horde.

Blood poured from his wounds, and her suction cup of a mouth suckled faster. Disgusting. Was this the fate awaiting Taliyah, if she went without nourishment?

There was so much he didn't know about her. Did she operate alone, or did she have help? Roc tensed. Were there others like her?

Did any serve in Roc's army? It was…possible.

—*Did you see this phantom enter the throne room?*— He threw the question at Halo.

—*I did not. I got busy performing a sweep of the palace, on the hunt for others.*—

How had this fiend managed to hide from them both?

Roc stabbed the phantom in the temple, then waited, on alert. Minutes passed. No other phantoms appeared.

—*She seems to be the last,*— Halo informed him, broadcasting the information to everyone at once. —*I'll keep a closer watch.*—

Silver spoke up. —*I believe the group entered through an unframed window in the north tower.*—

The windows were Ian's job.

With gravel in his voice, his brother admitted, —*I was too busy repairing Taliyah's traps to finish framing the windows.*—

Taliyah's purpose all along?

—*Remain in the dungeon. I'll summon Vasili.*— The Midnight Sun had never learned to interact well with others, not even his Astra brothers. Usually, Roc left him in the duplicate realm, where the survivors of the conquered realm always slept. —*He'll ensure every exit is completely covered by morning.*—

Roc turned his awareness to the duplicate realm.

—*Vasili, come here and finish the palace fortifications.*—

The response came immediately, barely a grunt. In Vasili Speak, that was an enthusiastic assent.

To the group, Roc confessed, —*Erebus mentioned the Blade of Destiny*—

The other Astra didn't hurl accusations, as Roc deserved. If he'd better guarded his Amazon bride, Erebus would have been unable to sleep with her, winning the blade. But Roc's men went into war mode, discussing something they'd pondered before. How did you form a defense against someone who knew every move you'd make?

Had the male turned Taliyah *because* she was Roc's *gravita*? *Will rip off his head and tear out each of his organs.*

The blame for Taliyah's condition might rest at Roc's door…

He resisted the urge to return to her. No going back until he'd crafted a viable plan and built up an unshakable resistance against her appeal. His fault or not, her fate was sealed.

Roc fired off commands. —*Halo, call the soldiers together. Silver, read their minds en masse. We might have traitors in our midst.*—

If anyone had aided Taliyah and Erebus, Roc had…questions.

22

Taliyah hated Roc, but she missed him, too. She missed his warmth. His intensity. His hard stare and those roaming hands. Mostly, she missed the excitement he incited. For two days, he'd held her dissatisfaction at bay. Now? The sensation proved as relentless as ever.

Her hunger didn't help. *Must eat.* Soon. She kept eyeing her wrist, wondering how her own spirit might taste. Amazing? She'd taste amazing, wouldn't she?

A demented laugh caught her attention. Her own?

The day wasn't a total wash, thankfully. She'd come up with a rock-solid plan: get free by any means necessary, then figure everything else out. Okay, maybe not so rock solid. At least she'd gained intel into Roc's fighting habits.

During their miniskirmish, she'd witnessed one of his many abilities in action. The way he'd flashed those poles around her in a blink, trapping her within, told her he had an invisible arsenal at his disposal; he had only to flash it in.

No wonder he tossed his weapons so haphazardly. He could acquire more with only a thought. She'd bet the same was true for his men.

When she gained the strength, she would mount an escape. Although, honestly, she believed Roc would return sooner or later. He would remember the blessing mattered more than his bride's species. Guaranteed he would glue himself to her side to stop her from meeting with Erebus.

Forget Roc for a sec. The ring presented a major problem. Your crutches became your enemy's best weapons against you. She'd done herself a huge disservice by relying on a piece of jewelry for the sake of her sanity. At crunch time, she'd had to take a time-out to scream.

Now, when she should be fighting for her life, she needed to use days she didn't have to train against the screams.

No one would use those screams against her again. Next time, she would be prepared.

"Taliyah! Psst!"

The whisper-yell penetrated her ravenous haze, and she swung her attention to the harpies. Since Ian's arrival, the girls had avoided speaking with her. They'd only murmured among themselves, recounting history lessons about Erebus and his phantoms.

Mmm. *Did someone just ring the dinner bell?* As she ran her bottom lip between her teeth, the harpies paled.

"Are you really a phantom?" Mara barked the question.

Taliyah had refused to be straight with Roc, but she wouldn't be so stingy with her own people. "I am."

Had Ian's ears just twitched?

Let him listen and inform his boss.

"So you're the puppet of harpykind's first enemy?" Mara demanded. "The god who once slaughtered our people?"

"Not a puppet." A daughter. She almost said *Screw it* and revealed her royal connection. So badly she wanted to witness everyone's reaction. Somehow, she resisted.

"Only a puppet," Mara reiterated with a nod. "And you think to lead us?" She scoffed. "I'll die before I serve you."

"Trust me. I can arrange your death in a matter of minutes."

"Shout it out later," someone else piped up. A younger harpy with pale hair and only three stars. "We need an A-plus plan, like, yesterday."

Everyone looked to her, then Mara, then Taliyah again. What? They expected genius when she struggled to remain upright with her head propped against the wall?

"Roc will return at some point. He's got to keep me alive for another twenty-eight days." Despite the lack of windows, her internal clock told her they'd passed midnight hours ago.

"Do you truly believe you can kill these guys?" Three Stars asked, earnest.

Did she? Eight hard-earned stars, two absentee fathers, one indomitable mother and four feral sisters. "I do," she replied.

"All right. I...I'll let you have a nibble of me." A slim brown arm extended through the bars. "Let's get you strong and racer ready."

Ian stepped forward, but made no other move toward them.

Taliyah reeled at the staggering sacrifice. Then the girl doubled over and screamed in agony. Her knees gave out.

The others rallied around her, cheering her on as she received her fourth star.

Taliyah's chest swelled with pride. Another harpy's win always thrilled her, inspiring her to reach for greater heights, reminding her of why she fought so hard to lead harpykind. Strength like this must be protected and nurtured. But...

Why couldn't this be enough? Why did dissatisfaction remain a permanent part of her makeup? What did the Commander bring to her table that others didn't? Why did she care that he suffered bad dreams?

Why did she want to soothe him?

When the cheering tapered, the newly starred, beaming harpy reached through the bars once again. "Order up."

"Keep your soul," she said with a small smile. "I have faith that Roc will provide. Wait and see." He wouldn't want to, but still he'd do it. He needed her well.

He could take his disgust and shove it.

New resentment welled. Perhaps she didn't miss her husband after all.

Ticktock, ticktock. Roc sat at the edge of his bed. Hours before, Silver had discovered eleven soldiers with ties to Erebus. Ties the god had created days before the Astra first came to Harpina.

As soon as Roc had locked the males in the dungeon of the duplicate realm to await punishment, he'd come here.

One after the other, warlords had requested a telepathic conversation about the phantom. He had issued denials and watched the clock on the wall. Seething. Waiting.

The moment 6:00 a.m. arrived, he rose and showered, removing the *alevala* from his chest. How Solar must be laughing in his grave right now! Without question, the former Commander had once felt as if he stood before his own personal version of paradise, the beauty of it stealing his thoughts, pleasure beckoning... until the whole world erupted into flames.

How many times had Roc discounted the man's obsession with his siren? How often had he advised his leader to ignore her appeal and pick someone else? Now he wrestled with his own desires, unable to take his own advice.

At least he'd decided what to do with Taliyah. An easy verdict to render, since he'd had no other option.

Roc would keep her at his side, always.

Could he handle twenty-four hours a day with an unpredictable phantom-harpy? No. Could he allow more secret meetings with her master? Also no. Sneaking other phantoms into the palace ended *now*.

She would gloat about his predicament, just like Erebus. She'd probably even guessed his strategy. Had probably constructed a counterstrategy to create problems with his men—with his body. She specialized in his sexual torment, after all.

Erebus chose well.

Did Roc have the strength to resist Taliyah, if she turned up the heat? He didn't know. Even now, filled with hate and repugnance, his body craved hers. The rest of him anticipated their next sparring match.

For the first time, he operated without a fully prepared battle plan, complete with a backup and a backup to the backup. He had to take this minute by minute.

Overflowing with dread, he dressed. He opted to forgo a shirt and selected a pair of leathers. He slid his feet into combat boots. Rather than strap up with multiple daggers, he sheathed a small three-blade at his ankle. Give Taliyah easy access to a weapon able to end her life prematurely? No.

Nothing left to do but collect her...

How had she fared throughout the night? He didn't want to care. He *wouldn't* care. Roc lifted his chin and straightened his shoulders, then flashed to the dungeon, just outside Taliyah's cell.

The sight of her hit like an asteroid. She occupied a corner, her legs bent and drawn up behind her. A queen before her people. Around her eyes, black lines had grown together, shading the spaces between them; uneven edges dripped over her cheeks like tears. Her irises had turned fully black and seemed to spin, snaring him in a dizzying maze.

An irresistible, deadly beauty, even now.

Staring at him, she purred, "Hello, husband." She graced him with a slow, wicked smile, and he hissed a breath between his teeth.

He didn't mean to, but he dropped his gaze to her lips. They, too, were fully black…and he wondered how soft they'd feel against his skin.

He stiffened with annoyance. "Hello, soulsucker."

"Aw, how sweet. Another adorable nickname." A Gothic ice queen, she glided to her feet and strolled to the bars, every movement a wonder of sensuality. Thin straps of metal crisscrossed over her chest, turning her T-shirt into a gown.

She'd reverted to predator mode. Having spotted prey, she'd roused enough energy to launch a final stand.

Frostberries perfumed the air, setting little fires in his lungs. Golden torchlight illuminated the stardust smeared over her skin, fueling his most possessive instincts.

You should try to resist, at least.

The other harpies stepped up to the bars between the cells for a closer look at the byplay. Commentary abounded.

"Uh-oh. He looks *ticked*."

"Only because you're staring at his face. Check out the package in his pants."

"I sense a severe clubbing in T-bomb's future."

"If I'm going to stay here," Taliyah said, empress of her audience, "I insist on redecorating. Maybe a couple of tasteful nudes."

He glared at her. A lowly phantom had no right to tease the Astra Commander. "You won't be staying here."

She pouted with feigned disappointment. "Let me guess. You'll be glued to my side forevermore."

"I will." He punctuated the words with a clipped nod.

"Why do you appear so glum about it? You're getting uninterrupted time with the woman of your dreams. I'm the one who deserves to wail. I have to spend time with *you*."

Disregard her words. Move on. "There will be new rules, of course."

"Of course. I'll give them the same respect as the others." She reached through the bars slowly, giving him a chance to protest before she glided a claw around the unstained skin above his heart. "Will I get three squares a day?"

Though he didn't understand the words themselves, he easily deciphered their meaning. He'd thought to keep her hungry and weak. Should he? She'd deteriorated in a matter of hours. How long did she have until her eyes turned milky, her mouth a suction cup?

Not even trying to mask his revulsion, he flashed into the duplicate realm, appearing in the cell with the imprisoned soldiers.

Roc grabbed the closest—a berserker whose jaw had yet to heal from repeated exposure to Roc's fists. He carted the male into Taliyah's cell.

She remained at the bars, her back to him.

"Your breakfast awaits," he said as the male fought his hold. "Compliments of Erebus."

She turned with sensual grace and eyed her meal. "Normally I'd ask what crimes he's committed, but I remember seeing him in the throne room. He's a soldier of yours. That's crime enough."

Roc pushed, and the berserker stumbled to his hands and knees before coming up in a rush, preparing for battle.

Taliyah moved at an incredible speed, even without use of her wings, restraining him against a wall with her shackled hands and forcing his head to tilt at an uncomfortable angle. She pressed her mouth against his throat, like a vampire tapping a vein. The berserker shouted and flailed—at first. He slowed… sagged, finally hanging motionless in her grip. Color drained from his flesh. Taliyah's pinkened.

Roc could barely stomach watching a soulsucker in action… usually. Somehow, as she swayed in time to her swallows, she made the act a sensual dance. He…didn't like it. His bride should not put her mouth on another male.

Jealousy shocked him. Singed him. Infuriated him! *She's a phantom. This doesn't matter.*

Still he fought the urge to stride over and slay the male. Roc breathed with purpose. Inhale, exhale. Slow. Slower. Better. Except it wasn't better!

As he took a step forward, Taliyah released her meal. Nothing but an empty shell. The body fell to the floor with a hard thud, utterly drained and eternally dead.

The harpies withdrew, and Taliyah most definitely noticed, her posture growing rigid as she straightened.

She craned her head to meet Roc's gaze, sending a jolt through him. As the shadows receded from her eyes and mouth, and the onyx vanished from her irises, she smiled, radiant.

In that moment, she embodied each of her species. The seducer, the warrior and the ice queen.

"Haven't drained someone in so long, and oh, the power! I usually only take enough to stay strong." She wiped her lips with the back of her hand and winked at him. "I don't have to ask if you enjoyed the show. Your measuring log says plenty."

Knew she'd gloat. "Come here." Today he issued orders, and she obeyed him. He would settle for nothing less.

She didn't come here. "Is this the part where we kiss and make up? Because—" Her brow wrinkled, and her smile dulled. She clutched her stomach, accusations flickering in her eyes. "Did you poison me, Commander?"

"Not on purpose." Was this another trick?

In response, Taliyah hunched over and vomited a stream of bright light. The more she lost, the faster the shadows returned to her eye sockets. By the end, onyx swamped her irises once again.

No, no trick. Concern seized him.

If Erebus had predicted Roc's actions, he'd known where Roc would source for his phantom bride's food. Had the god purposely tainted the soldiers? Or was this something else?

He didn't know anything anymore.

At her side once again, he removed the shackles, preparing

to relocate her. Chafed red skin ringed both of her wrists, the sight…disturbing. "Has this ever happened to you before?"

"Never."

Chest tight, he clasped her nape and flashed her to the master bathroom. "I'll find you someone else to eat." Another male who would feel the softness of her mouth.

Hot blood rushed to Roc's muscles, stardust singeing his palms.

"Don't worry, Roc." She pushed at him. "I have no interest in you as food. I like my meals with a little less hypocrisy. Beggars *can* be choosers."

A lie. The woman was starved. If he wanted her to eat from him, she would eat from him. But he didn't, so the point was moot. "Explain how I'm a hypocrite."

Shrug. "You judge me for eating souls, yet every five hundred years, you snuff one out."

He huffed a breath. "Better a hypocrite than a phantom." How did she remain so intelligent? So lucid?

"Are you kidding? There's *nothing* worse than a hypocrite."

Her disdain wouldn't affect him.

It wouldn't.

Appearing to stand by force of her will alone, she cast her gaze around the spacious enclosure. Planning her escape?

He inspected the room for anything she might use against him. The former General had obviously adored over-the-top luxury. Gold dragon scales covered the walls. Every faucet and knob boasted an array of precious gems. A beast-skin rug draped the marble floor in front of a claw-foot tub. The shower stall possessed multiple showerheads, a marble bench, a circular glass partition.

Taliyah could use *everything* as a weapon in a thousand different ways. He'd have to remain on guard.

"You may bathe." He turned the knobs in the shower, hot water raining from different spouts. Steam quickly filled the stall.

He removed the pinner, and she sighed with relief, rolling her shoulders and flapping those delicate wings.

Chest clenching, he explained, "I won't shower with you, but I also won't leave you unattended. When I said you'd stay within my sight, I meant it." The phantom couldn't be trusted.

She shrugged and pulled her shirt overhead. "You want to perv out while I shower. No need to explain." With a flirty smile, she tossed the garment at him.

Roc bit his tongue, catching the item while keeping his gaze on her face. *Do not look down.* A single glance at her nipple piercing or the tuft of pale curls between her legs might be his undoing.

"I'll give you a temporary reprieve from your belt." More eager than he would ever admit, he lifted the key from his head and removed her belt. "Don't even *think* about attempting to seduce me."

"Uh, I love to break it to you, Roc, but that ship has sailed. Why would I bother seducing you, anyway? I already proved I could. You're a sure thing."

He pursed his lips. "That was before I knew what you were."

Something akin to hurt flickered in her eyes, there and gone. Her usual irreverence showed up, and she smirked. "You should probably pass the memo on to your penis. You're Roc-blocking it."

Hurt? A phantom? No. "Bodies can be tamed. They just take a little longer than minds."

"Sure, sure." She held her palms up in a gesture of innocence, then stepped into the stall and glanced at him over her shoulder. "I promise to do my very best not to tempt you beyond reason. Do your best to resist." As she entered the water, droplets cascaded down her incomparable form.

As he watched her through the fogging glass, she leaned against the wall and washed her hair, her body. Her weakness displeased him. He had duties; in this state, she wouldn't be able to keep up.

He knew harpies used blood as medicine. Before he could talk himself out of it, he bit into his finger. Blood welled as he extended his arm into the stall.

"Drink," he commanded.

She looked at the finger, then his face. Finger. Face. She wanted to refuse, as evidenced by her glower. But she snapped, "Why?"

He knew what she asked. "I might not like what you are, but I won't leave you in pain."

Glaring, she marched over. With a firm clasp of his wrist, she brought his finger to her lips and…softly licked. The sight of her tongue inspired a string of internal curses.

Her eyes closed as she savored, a little color returning to her cheeks. When she fit her lips over the healing wound and sucked, satisfaction joined forces with possessiveness, and he nearly roared at the rightness. Providing for his wife. Nourishing her.

When the wound closed, she nicked him with a fang. As she sucked a little more and swallowed, he trembled and scowled. He…*wanted*.

Once she finished, she lifted her head. He almost protested. She'd taken a mere handful of drops.

"I won't thank you." She turned to finish bathing. Weakness gave way to sensuality, every move she made meant to rouse a tide of lust. The way the suds sluiced down her curves, her hands following…

He panted. He couldn't look away.

She bent over to soap her calves, and he swallowed a groan. Those legs. Those curves. The elegant line of her spine. Those spectacular wings, fluttering in invitation.

He shifted his gaze to her nape, where an elaborate brand snagged his interest.

Brand? He'd felt the scars when he'd handled her, but he'd

assumed the raised tissue came from a childhood injury, before her immortality took root.

Curious, he stepped into the stall. He even entered the water to clasp her arms and press her against cool tile. He smoothed her hair out of the way, dragging his knuckles over her damp flesh more slowly than he'd intended, saying, "Why do you have the brand of a deity on your nape?"

She didn't fight him—yet. "A deity? What deity?"

He grazed his thumb over the raised flesh, those possessive instincts threatening to engulf him. *She should wear my brand.* "This symbol is the mark of a god or goddess. Not one I recognize." And he knew every faction of royals, from the Titans to the Egyptians, and everything in between.

"And?"

"And brands give another person access to you in lifesaving and dangerous ways." Roc carried the one for Chaos, as well as his own personal mark, and one for each of his warlords. Those brands secured telepathic communications and allowed a summoning. Ian used his brand to locate and flash them all. "How do you have a brand and not understand its purpose? Who gave it to you?" More important, what did they plan to do with her?

"Nice try, but you won't scare me into talking. No, you know what? I'm happy to share this time. Neeka gave it to me, and even when she's being the most annoying person ever born, with questionable motives, she has my best interests at heart. *She'd* never do anything to endanger me. Unlike my own dear husband, who does *everything* to endanger me."

No one executed better assaults against a man's ego than Taliyah and her viper's tongue. "Be absolutely certain you trust her. The brand *can* be used against you. This Neeka has paired you with some unknown deity who might hope to weaponize you for their own gain." Was *this* how she remained lucid, despite her hunger? Did some god use the mystical link to provide her with power?

"I get it. You've seen my taste in spouses, so you doubt my

intelligence. Here's the thing. The guy who plans to kill me shouldn't question my best friend's intentions. She's bled for me. You've made me bleed. So yes, I'm absolutely certain I trust her. Now do us both a favor and exit my stall. I'm treating myself to a spa day. I've earned it."

Exiting is a favor—to myself. But it was too late. He'd touched her luscious body. He'd inhaled her scent and warmed.

Instinct demanded he heat *her.*

Roc stepped closer, urged by primitive forces. He settled his grip on her waist and gently massaged, thrilling when she groaned. No one made sexier sounds than a needy Taliyah Skyhawk.

Had she rolled her hips, as if imagining his fingers inside her? Wishful thinking? Roc couldn't deny *he* imagined it. He'd had a taste of her. For his sanity, he required more.

As always, she rallied quickly, her defenses firmly entrenched. "Correct me if I'm wrong, but this is a little more than watching, yes?"

"Don't care."

"You've forgotten that I'm a disgusting phantom so quickly? How embarrassing for you."

The reminder hit like a typhoon. He skidded two steps back, ripping his hands from her.

She was right. How easily he'd caved. When you played with your temptation, you deserved your inevitable wounds. But he still didn't leave the stall. He couldn't. She'd turned to face him, and his mind lost control of his body.

Water sprayed between them, mist twirling up. She became a dream…a nightmare. Despite the acerbic tone she'd used before, she evinced raw desire now.

Her nipples drew tight as she roved a slumberous gaze over him. Did she note the tension in his stance? The hardness of his shaft? Did she celebrate her effect on him?

Tiny pink claws glided down her torso to tease the thatch of curls between her legs. "I can't help but notice you aren't leaving, husband."

Was it possible... Did she experience the same frenzied tug-of-war? Did her body experience the same ravening hunger as his?

His heart thudded, as if he were a young lad dealing with his first maid. Roc had decided to take his interactions with her one minute at a time. This minute required a decision and the strength to see it through.

Pleasure a phantom and suffer, or not pleasure a phantom and suffer?

Before Taliyah, he would've opted for the second. Gladly. No thought needed. A phantom, much less a sacrificial lamb, had no business in his bed. But a *gravita...a wife...*

He swallowed, different muscles flexing. *Want her? Take her...*

Why *shouldn't* he take her? He was Commander. Why deny himself what he wanted? He'd earned the right to have whomever he wished, whenever and wherever he wished.

Erebus sought his misery. Why oblige his enemy and welcome his own torment? The god expected Roc to fight his attraction, remaining in an aggravated state. He hated what Taliyah was, yes; she would feel like paradise regardless. He didn't trust her, but he didn't need to trust her to protect himself from her attacks.

You will regret this.

"Well," she demanded, anger eroding her softened repose, "are you just going to stand there?"

He met her gaze, fury to fury. She began to pant. A telling sign he didn't have the strength to resist.

Motions clipped, he kicked off his boots and unfastened his leathers. "This means nothing, bride."

She cupped her breasts, eyelids sinking. "It means less than nothing."

They stepped toward each other, bumping together. As he lowered his head for a kiss, she lifted to her tiptoes. Their tongues thrust and tangled together, a fevered madness setting in.

23

Taliyah didn't want to think, but thoughts zipped through her mind with dizzying speed anyway, culminating in a need to both push the Astra away and lock him in place. To savor this sense of satisfaction and curse it.

He'd imprisoned her. Insulted and threatened her. And fed her. Tended to her when she'd sickened. Freed her from the belt. Watched her with undisguised lust. And now he kissed her with stunning ferocity.

She told herself she didn't have to make a lifelong decision here. Enjoying the moment was a perfectly acceptable plan. Right now, the fact that she'd missed him didn't matter. And why bother trying to guess how she'd feel after the shower? She'd feel how she'd feel. She could handle herself *and* Roc then.

Her claws curled into his chest as she returned his kiss with every drop of lust frothing inside her. Lust she shouldn't feel, given her hunger, but there it was. She couldn't slake it. His warmth seeped past her skin, chasing away the dungeon's chill.

Steam enveloped them, and water rained. Warm droplets dripped into their mouths and splashed over their bodies.

He yanked her closer, smashing her breasts into his chest, and she slung her arms around him. With every inhalation, her nipples grazed his ripped chest. She scored his back, lost. Everywhere he touched, sensations left a mark. Hotter heat. Wild tremors. Delicious prickles and tormenting flutters. The aches. Oh, the aches!

As she writhed against him, thoughts fragmented, the rooms in her brain shutting down, one by one. Her body took the helm. The promise of bliss beckoned.

He pushed her into the wall. Cool tile drew a gasp, but hot man added the moan. Leaving her off-kilter, he slicked his hands over her breasts, circled her nipples with his knuckles, then plumped and kneaded the mounds.

"I want to do things to you," he growled into her mouth.

As she quivered, excited by his claim, he stilled. Rage overcame his expression, confusing her. "Roc?"

He peered up at the ceiling and roared, "Not now!"

What? Had she hurt him? "Roc?" she repeated, plucking her claws free of his flesh. She grimaced when she spotted beads of blood. "My bad."

He lowered his head and rested his forehead against hers. "My apologies. I wasn't speaking to you. A phantom horde has overtaken the kitchen, and they're here to feed." The more he spoke, the stiffer he became. When he lifted his head, fury darkened his expression.

"I'm not to blame," she stated bluntly. And what a nice reminder: never mix war and pleasure.

He got his huff on. "I laid no blame at your door, Taliyah."

Please. "You laid *all* blame at my door, Roc."

He glared at her as he summoned more of those trinite posts. One in each corner, trapping her within the stall.

"How wonderful for me," she said, batting her lashes at him. "Another prison."

"In here, you'll be safe while my soldiers dispatch the phantoms." His gaze moved beyond her, and she realized he'd just received another telepathic communication. Whatever he learned didn't brighten his mood. When he focused on her again, he got snippy and said, "Does it gratify you to know we're dealing with your snares and ambushes?"

Well, well. Now he outright admitted he blamed her. "Yes," she replied truthfully, "it does." Cool air enveloped her wet body, chasing away the warmth. "But I didn't bring any phantoms here."

He opened his mouth to respond.

"No," she snapped. "Don't contradict me. I'm not working with Erebus, and I'm not controlled by him. He told me he wanted me to destroy you for him. I informed him I would destroy you for *me*. I've never once done his bidding. The guy's a prick. When I commit a deed, I own it. I *want* you to know I'm the one responsible for your upset. My snares and ambushes are a fine example."

He frowned, but he didn't comment.

Forget assuaging the aches. His attitude was inoculation enough. Smoldering? What smoldering? She'd already moved on. Now she needed to figure out why she'd vomited the berserker's soul.

The problem wasn't the man's origins. Once, she'd gone on a berserker bender.

Mmm. She remembered it well. Their power had been intoxicating. The sweetest wine.

Inner shake. She'd never sickened with a berserker. So what happened today?

"I *want* to believe you," Roc said, and he kind of sounded... defeated. "That's the crux of the problem."

"Dude. Are you seriously feeling sorry for yourself?" Taliyah gifted him with a rude hand gesture. "You know what? Screw you."

He stared at her as if she were some great mystery. News flash. She was pretty much an open doomsday book. Harm her people, and she ensured you paid. The end.

His eyes glazed as another message came in. Whatever was said, his aggression deflated. "The horde has been dealt with."

"Proof I didn't send this ambush. No one died." *Um, maybe don't antagonize the guy with the wing-pinner?* Strength had never been so important, and they both knew it.

He thrust his hand through his wet hair. "I can't trust you."

"Like that's a shocker." She sighed, choosing to release the worst of her irritation. "Look. What's happened can't be undone. We called a truce yesterday. Let's call another one today. Twenty-four hours. That'll give us time to ask each other questions. Tit for tat."

His remaining aggression slowly dissolved. "I don't know how this is possible. How you are a phantom, yet also…you."

She considered telling him about her connection to Chaos, then caught the gleam of the posts around the shower stall and clamped her lips shut. Roc didn't trust her, and she didn't trust him. For very good reasons! For one to survive, the other had to die. Maybe. Probably. What if there was another way?

Stupid thought? Impossible? Whatever. She'd ponder it later. Today, she'd get to know her enemy…who looked adorably, frustratingly lost all of a sudden.

What are you doing? Stop. Adorably lost? An enemy in any form was still just an enemy.

"Whatever happened to your Hall of Secrets idea?" she asked.

He scoured a hand over his face. "I've yet to receive a report from Roux."

Her nose scrunched up. "What kind of information do you think you're going to get?"

"Something!" He slammed his fist into his palm. "That's all I need."

How easily and quickly he swayed from one extreme emotion to the other. But was it good or bad for her?

Taliyah exhaled as her thoughts whirled. Things had changed between them, so she must change, too. From now on, she and Roc were going to be constant companions. Antagonizing him, as she'd done before, wasn't the wisest course.

Want better results? Pick better battles. "Let me reiterate that I *am* a phantom, but I'm not controlled by Erebus. If you'll give me a chance, I think I can prove it."

He opened and closed his mouth before waving her on. "I'm listening."

"Can we agree that there's something Erebus will never, under any circumstances, order a phantom to do?" Actually, she thought her father might rage. "He doesn't want *anyone* to make you happy, even for a moment."

Clipped nod. "We can agree."

"Well, think back. I'm sure you'll remember a specific moment in our history when roses were in bloom and you came like a geyser all over my belly."

Again, he opened and closed his mouth. "This is different. *You* are different. He knows what you mean to me."

She went still. "What do I mean to you?" No. Unnecessary question. Moving on. "Why do you think he told you I'm a phantom?"

Broody silence heralded minutes of reflection for them both.

Impatient, she led him into the realization she sought, a teacher with her student. "He did it so that you'd...what? Stop messing around with me."

Another bout of silence passed before he nodded. "That's true."

Success loomed! "I mean, really." She simpered at him, just

to drive the point home. "What kind of warlord follows his enemy's plan for his life?"

Maybe she'd driven a wee bit quickly. He narrowed his gaze on her. "I know you're manipulating me."

"So? Truth is truth."

He narrowed his eyes further... Holding her gaze captive, he reached for the waist of his leathers. After working the pants from his legs, freeing that impressive erection, he eased onto the shower bench, getting comfortable, Roc-style. In other words, he sat as rigid as stone and glared.

Her wings buzzed, the rest of her fluttering. Well, not all of her. Hunger pangs twisted her stomach.

"If you think I'm ever kissing you again," she said, turning toward the water, pretending to luxuriate in the stream, "you're dumber than a box of Rocs. I'm here for conversation."

He started making those huffing noises again. Didn't like being denied? Too bad. She'd learned her lesson when it came to the Commander.

"How old were you when Erebus turned you into a phantom?" he asked.

Cautious, she replied, "I was very young when I realized I was a phantom." To him, very young might mean two or three centuries, minimum.

"What do you mean, *you realized*? You didn't know the moment he'd turned you?"

She understood his astonishment. Though she'd never witnessed a turning firsthand, she'd read varying accounts from those who had. Erebus ingested some or half or most of the other person's soul, then used his fangs to inject a special death toxin into their vein; what remained of their soul supposedly rotted out of their body, leaving a husk capable of mighty feats, controlled by he who carried what remained of the soul.

Rather than supply an answer to Roc, Taliyah asked another

question. "What makes you hate Erebus so much? What has he done to you guys?"

"Many things," he said, sounding distracted.

She glanced at him over her shoulder, intending to chide him. When she caught him rubbing the bare spot over his heart, she stayed quiet. She'd clocked this action before. A tell of some kind. One linked to a specific memory, judging by the tightening of his features.

"Such as?" she finally prompted, reaching for the soap dispenser. Yes, she'd already soaped up. As long as she washed, she had an excuse to prolong the conversation and learn more about her ruthless companion before he changed his mind. "Pro tip and subtle hint—girls like examples."

He sighed before admitting, "He turned several Astra into phantoms, forcing us to murder our own."

Ouch. "That's tough. I'm sorry," she said, and she meant it. Losing fellow soldiers sucked, but it sucked more when you had to oversee the deed.

He bowed up, as if to accuse her of more trickery, then settled down and nodded. "Yes. It was tough."

"You know I had nothing to do with any of that, right?" she asked, just in case he needed a reminder.

"I know. In that, you are innocent. I…" His voice trailed off, and he gulped, watching as suds sluiced between her breasts. His pupils contracted, glittering like dying stars.

Layer by layer, his calm veneer stripped away, revealing a harsher, rawer, expression. He exuded such intense heat, she trembled.

He sat up straighter, his heels remaining planted on the floor, his hands white-knuckling his knees. Had he grown even harder?

She gulped. Ribbons of thicker steam curled around him, turning him, this moment, into a midnight reverie. Had he ever looked sexier? Water darkened his hair, droplets clinging to his lashes and beard.

When he rubbed his palms together, she suspected he'd produced more stardust—and she wanted it. As his *gravita*, she deserved every speck. *Not real? Try again, Astra.*

"I want to do *bad* things to you." The gruffness of his voice
made everything better and worse.

She'd thought to curtail this part of their...relationship. His
mid- and post-coital glow sucked. But, as she breathed him in,
she couldn't stop herself from rasping, "Yes."

He required no other permission. He lunged for her, clamp-
ing her waist, then settling in his seat, pulling Taliyah between
his legs. The firmness of his grip suggested the Big Bad Wolf
had his Red Riding Hood at long last, and he wouldn't be letting her go anytime soon. But...he did nothing else. He simply
held her in place as tension thrummed from him anew.

Trying to talk himself out of this? Too bad. What he started,
he finished. Commanders weren't quitters.

Taliyah suspected she knew a way past his defenses. A risky
gamble. Dangerous, even. If it backfired...

Whatever. She was going to attempt it anyway. Though Roc
was Commander now, he'd once been a soldier, expected to
obey the dictates of another. Hadn't his own brother mentioned
being his boss in the beginning? What if she *told* Roc what to
do to her? Things he already wanted to do?

Had any other female dared? Probably not. Why would they?
They'd held no sway over his emotions. But she did. *Despite*
her origins.

Taliyah placed one knee outside his lap, then the other, straddling him. Slooowly she sank down, gliding her wet sex over
his. He uttered no protests. No, he tightened his grip, his gaze
rapt on her lucky, lucky nipple piercing.

Emboldened, she pinched his chin and forced his attention up.
Again, he allowed her command of his body without protest. "I
want your hands on my breasts. Touch me there."

He searched her gaze, anger clearly rising. But still he peeled his fingers from her waist and dragged his hands to her breasts. As commanded, he cupped and kneaded her. With his thumbs, he teased the piercing.

Satisfaction beckoned, within her reach once more. This big, strong brute of a man had just acquiesced to a phantom's command. How he must be castigating himself right now! And yet he never stopped kneading and teasing with a reverent touch.

Did he secretly *want* her to take control?

Such a heady thought. Something she planned to explore further.

"That feels so good," she said, offering praise. "You're making me ache." She gyrated against him and cried out. The pleasure! "Don't stop."

"Won't." He kneaded her breasts with greater force. "Can't."

"I'll make you feel good, too." She grazed the tip of her nose over the tip of his, about to claim his lips in a hungry kiss. His lips were parted for her, ready. At the last second, she rerouted and pressed her cheek against his. What if she couldn't curb her hunger? Even though Roc possessed a block, preventing her from feeding, she might try. He would absolutely know, and he would absolutely rage.

His hatred for phantoms spanned centuries. He'd known Taliyah for a matter of days. Maybe in time…

Inner shake. She drew his earlobe between her teeth. "Put your biceps to good use, baby, and turn me around." Lifting her face, she grazed the tip of his nose again. "Your *gravita* has a craving."

"Does she, then?" he asked, then growled. He popped his jaw, a telling sign. He'd realized she'd been issuing orders.

In a flash of insight, Taliyah realized he'd never hand over the reins of control without a fight. He might enjoy her leadings, but he didn't believe he must obey—yet. If she wanted control… and she did…she would have to *wrest* it from him.

The thought of winning such a powerful man…did things to her.

"Turn me around," she repeated, rubbing against him, "so you can get your fingers in nice and deep."

He nipped at her bottom lip, roguish but fierce.

"Turn me, and I'll let you touch me anywhere you wish." She let her voice drop. "However you wish..."

With a snarl, he lifted and spun her. His chest seared her spine, his heartbeat suddenly thumping between her shoulder blades. Fast. Faster. He lightly gripped her throat, his arm draped over her chest. With her legs slung over his, her thighs remained parted.

Wings flattened and of no use to her at the moment, she gripped the edges of his thighs. Cool, damp air teased her aching core as he drew his knees farther apart, forcing her legs to spread wider.

"I'll touch you anywhere I wish," he rumbled into her ear, applying pressure to draw her head to the hollow of his shoulder.

Goose bumps only he could rouse spread over her in seconds. "Touch me, then."

With his free hand, he palmed her breast, kneading it with more pressure than before.

A moan escaped. No stopping it. Taliyah rocked her hips, grinding her backside against the white-hot, steel-hard length cradled there. His inhalations sharpened with every brush of contact.

A snakeshifter wielding her charms, she asked, "Do you like touching me, Roc?"

He didn't try to deny it. "Yes." A snarl. "You know I do."

She didn't stop. Rocking, rocking. "You want more of me. You want me to make you come."

"Yesss," he hissed, sliding the hand at her throat to her breast. He trapped the nipples between his knuckles and tugged and gently twisted.

She swallowed a cry born from razor-sharp pleasure. "Put your fingers inside me," she commanded, unable to filter out her neediness, "or I stop moving." *Could* she stop? Roll. Roll... She must. Stop.

Taliyah could do anything she needed to do. She always got the job done.

He hissed once again before running her earlobe between his teeth, sending shafts of greater arousal careering through her. His cheek pressed against hers. "Still trying to manipulate me, harpy? You want control, and you seek to drive me mad to get it. But I can wait you out. Move your body against mine, like before, or I won't give you my fingers." He traced his fingertips down her belly. "Do it, and I'll sink them deeper than before."

"Put your fingers inside me," she repeated, nearly choking on her need. *Not enough. More, more.* "I'll make you come so hard."

"Move against me, and I'll ensure you come first." He combed through her tuft of curls and tapped her clit, making her gasp.

More! No, no. *Must. Resist. Never accept a picture of defeat.* "Put your fingers inside me," she croaked, reaching up and behind to grip his hair. The new position thrust her breasts forward.

"I want your fingers. I need them. Mmm. You'll stretch me so good. I'll moan so loud. All my aches will go away." She scraped her nails over his scalp. "Make my aches go away, baby...or I'll do it myself. Do you want to watch me? Hmm?"

"Your pleasure is mine!" He thrust two fingers into her, robbing her of breath, of thought. "Can't get enough of you," he confessed against her flesh. His husky voice vibrated through her bones, raising new goose bumps on her limbs. As he thrust his fingers in and out, he stroked her little bundle of nerves with his thumb.

Her inner walls clenched to hold him inside. She moved with him, chasing her orgasm. "Already so close."

When he stopped and withdrew his fingers from her, Taliyah nearly threw fists of fury. He'd given her a taste, then taken her drug away. Payback was going to suck for him. Except, his power play never came.

He ran his tongue up both fingers, his eyes closing. "The sweetness of you." The noise he released then…unfathomable need. He dropped his chin to her shoulder, telling her, "I want more—straight from the tap. Give it to me."

His voice had changed. He sounded like a man possessed.

"Yes," she rasped.

The next thing she knew, they were standing. Once again, she faced him. He towered over her, panting. Strain etched each of his features. He looked harsh and battle-ready, his muscles like rocks.

"If you want more," she told him, noting her voice had changed, as well, "get on your knees and take it."

Their gazes clashed.

"You wish me to kneel before you." He gritted out the words.

"No," she said, and he flinched with disappointment because he *wanted* to kneel. He could have flashed her flat on her back in bed. He hadn't. He'd flashed her to her feet. "I *expect* you to kneel before me."

Would he do it?

She lifted her chin, adding, "You'll get what you want no other way."

A single minute stretched into eternity. His breaths grew more laborious. Then…

Inch by agonizing inch, he lowered to his knees, settling between her parted thighs. She gaped down at him, astonished, amazed, baffled, confident, vulnerable, unsure, dazed and so aroused she wondered if she might be forever altered.

He licked his lips. Awaiting permission?

"Do it," she commanded.

24

Roc dragged his tongue through his wife's honey, rapturous. The taste of this woman! Nothing compared to her. She was a wonder without equal, and he feared he might crave this— her—for years, decades...centuries to come.

A fear he would dissect and destroy later. For now, he wished only to enjoy. He was Commander of the Astra Planeta, and if he wanted to bed his phantom, he would bed his phantom.

He had *earned* the right.

As he feasted, greedy for every drop of arousal she ceded, he ran his hands up her legs...higher, squeezing and kneading firm muscle. Every soft mewl and ragged moan made him burn hotter.

She writhed against his mouth, so sexy he feared he would come far too soon. *Must savor.*

He wouldn't be satisfied until she'd fallen apart in his arms. Licking... Laving... Addicted.

Hadn't she once promised to maneuver him to this point? To

make him mad with desires he couldn't control? Where everyone else had failed, she had succeeded. In record time. But soon
she would realize her victory came with a cost.

For the rest of the month, Roc intended to glut himself on
her. Whatever happened with Erebus, whatever happened with
the sacrifice, Roc would have her. To the best of his ability, he
would endeavor to forget her origins. For the rest of the month,
he would allow pleasure to matter more than duty. He wouldn't
steal her virginity, but he would take her in every other way.

His control frayed when she pricked the tips of her claws into
his scalp. A silent command to pleasure her faster. How could
he not oblige her? She was his greatest temptation. His temporary queen of passion and ice. A symbol of unbreakable strength
and power. And his. Even now, his palms sizzled with stardust.

He struggled to convince himself of the truth…of the lie. He
was beginning to suspect the stardust was…real. What if his
gravita was a phantom?

"Yes! Right there," she praised. "Just like that."

Releasing a sound of animalistic aggression, he tongued on
her swollen clit. As she rocked against his face, he gripped the
backs of her knees and forced her legs wider. He plunged two
fingers into the tight clasp of her feminine sheath.

A broken cry left her, her body bowing. Roc luxuriated in
her sweetness. In every new sound and sight. Her breasts were
thrust forward, her nipples tight little buds. His heat painted her
damp flesh with a rosy undertone.

She was the picture of carnality, her image forever burned into
his memory and the measure with which he judged every other.

For a reward such as this, he would willingly go to his knees
every day for the rest of etern— The next twenty-seven days.
Only twenty-seven days before the ceremony and life returned
to normal. The blessing. Their predetermined outcome. He
wouldn't…pine for his phantom *gravita*. Not for a phantom,
period.

Taliyah pressed her claws deeper and applied pressure, forcing his face to angle upward. Those ocean-water blues glittered down at him.

I might pine for a phantom gravita.

"Am I interrupting reflection hour?" she asked with a dry tone. "Should I leave you alone with your thoughts?"

Leave him with this throbbing erection? No! Gaze tangled up with hers, he dragged his tongue up her sex once again and plunged two fingers into her opening.

As a cry of surrender left her, thoughts fled. Pleasure awaited.

Roc set in, a man dominated by need, swiftly losing himself in the act.

"It's good, baby. It's so good," she gasped out. "I'm so close. Don't stop, don't stop, don't stop."

Never. He scissored his fingers, stretching her, and Taliyah screamed, a climax ripping through her. Those slick inner walls clenched and unclenched, tension dissipating from her body. Satisfaction pulsed from her.

He wanted more...*more.* Refusing to relinquish his prize, he continued tonguing her even as he wrapped a hand around his length and stroked up. Passion boiled in his blood, her pleasure his fuel. His cells buzzed with life. Pressure built. Pressure so sharp it shredded any remaining threads of his control. His testicles drew up, his seed at the ready.

Taliyah shocked him. She gripped his hair and drew him to his feet. He let her, offering no resistance. What did she plan to do?

When she gripped the base of his shaft, he couldn't stop the escape of his next word. "Please."

Heartbeat...heartbeat... A moment suspended by anticipation... Would she do it?

Their gazes met in a haze of sultry awareness and...she stroked him. A hoarse shout burst from him. He coiled his arms around her, gathering her hair, fisting the strands. "Nice and tight, Taya."

She stroked again and again, her grip unyielding, and nothing else mattered. This pleasure. This woman. The feminine power she exerted so easily as she pumped his length… She *enjoyed* driving him to the brink.

Had he ever experienced such pleasure from another's touch? Curses bubbled up. Thoughts burned away. Muscles bunched. This…this… He was going to—

She stopped, and Roc grunted.

He planted his palms against the stall walls behind her, caging her in. Voice rougher than sandpaper, he snarled, "Woman?"

The hottest, coldest seductress looked at him through a thick shield of lashes. Her pupils were the size of dimes, her irises glazed. Enveloped by steam, appearing both satisfied and hungry, she was his wildest fantasy come to stunning life.

"I just want you to know…" She grazed her thumb over his slit, collecting a bead of moisture. Moisture she sucked into her mouth, her eyelids hooding. "I like your taste, too."

His chest heaved, things inside him cracking. "Finish me," he commanded. A prophetic statement? Did this woman mark his end?

When she pumped him harder, faster, he couldn't bring himself to care. He fed a finger into her mouth, undone as she sucked. His mind wiped clean. Anything he'd hoped to say got lost as he panted. The rightness of this. Of having Taliyah attend to him, *after* being attended to *by* him. He was…he was… Yes, yes!

"Just like that, Taya. That's the way."

Pumping up and down. Sucking. Pumping and sucking. Biting. Roc existed in a world of pure sensation, his blood like fire, his every nerve ending humming a siren's song. He hovered between utter bliss and torturous hell. The two remained at war, locked in a final battle to the death.

He rocked his hips in time to her strokes, pressure continuing to build. Too much… He pulled his fingers from her mouth and slapped his palm against the wall. Rocked. A wonderful madness took hold. If Erebus himself had dared to ghost into the stall, Roc wasn't sure he'd galvanize the will to fight. Nothing mattered but release.

Leaning into Taliyah, pressing her back against the wall, he plunged two fingers into her core and bit the tendon running between her neck and shoulder. She hurled into another climax and…

Bliss won.

Every muscle tensed as Roc roared, coming and coming and coming against her belly.

"Mmm." Her panting breaths fanned his throat. "Have I ever told you how good you smell?"

He rested his forehead against the cool wall…until Taliyah reached up and cupped his cheeks. The temptress glided her cherry-red lips up his neck before lifting her head and…giggling? She offered him a drugged—drugging—smile, the shadows fading from her eyes.

"Don't be mad, okay, but I must have… Didn't mean to… So sorry… I…I think I'm drunk. Roc? I didn't suck your soul, did I? I didn't think I did, despite my hunger, but I must have. Do you 'member?"

Sated from his explosive climax, Roc struggled to make sense of what was happening. He hadn't felt as if she fed from him. His block remained in place, unaffected. But…

Another giggle escaped her. A giggle. From Taliyah Skyhawk. "Oh! Oh! The room is spinning. Spinning is fun. So is sucking on you, even if you only fed me your finger." She focused on his length, and he could almost see the gleam of a fork and knife in her eyes. "I want to feed on another part of you. Let me! We should test to find out if I did or didn't feed on you.

That makes total sense, right?" She reached for his shaft, but he caught her wrists.

"Taliyah?" Shock held him immobile. And enthralled. Who was this adorable creature? She *must* have fed from him, his power too much for her, but...he wasn't sure.

She pouted, and all he wanted to do was laugh. "You're playing hard to get. *Really* hard. Yes... Getting harder by the second."

"Give me a moment to process this." The sight of her was maddening him all over again, yes. She swayed and slid to the floor with a laugh, letting him tower over her.

He maintained his clasp on her wrist, keeping her arm lifted. Warm water sluiced over her upper body, raining over her legs.

Languid and sated and rosy, she stretched. "I feel absolutely... wonderful."

He swallowed. "Do you react this way every time you feed?"

"Nope." She nibbled on her bottom lip, enchantingly confused, and then brightened. "Roc. Roc. Roc! Guess what?" Not waiting for his response, she climbed to her knees and rushed out, "I think you're hot. Like, seriously hot. Sizzling. You make me hate the cold."

How was he supposed to respond to that? He was becoming more charmed by the moment, and he needed it to stop.

Was this a trick?

No. Everything he'd learned about this woman told him she wasn't attempting to part with her virginity. She wasn't a woman who admitted information easily or dropped her defenses ever—and never with him. Though she must do so with her friend Neeka, because she trusted the girl enough to brand her.

He curled his hands into fists. No, Taliyah definitely didn't trust Roc, nor should she. And that...he didn't like.

Twisting me in knots again. "Stand up for me, Taya."

To obey, she used his body as a climbing post. "Guess what else?" she said, claws in his chest. "I'm not hungry anymore. Look at me. Look!"

"I'm looking." He might never look away.

"I'm so full. The fullest I've ever been!"

Full? How could she partake enough to overflow, while he remained unchanged? Had his block failed for a second, the slightest sip satisfying her?

"Do you feel sick in any way?" That *is your first question, Commander?*

"Nope. Roc!" she repeated, clinging to him, and he couldn't not respond as he turned knobs to shut off the water.

"Yes, Taya?" What would she confess next? He must know.

"Your body is sublime. My most favorite one. Your muscles are so…muscly."

"I'm glad you think so." The corners of his mouth twitched as he toweled her off. Amusement now? "You don't know how *not* to arouse me, do you?" he muttered. "Fair warning, Taya. We will be repeating this experience tomorrow. We need to learn how you feed." He ignored the newest round of throbbing in his shaft.

Will never get enough of her.

"You're smiling so big right now, and I'm living for it." She giggled again, and he swept her off her feet.

Roc dismissed the posts, carried her out of the stall and set her on her feet, the obstacles between them coming into focus once again. "We should dress." Despite this…whatever this was, he had a job to do. An altar to craft. To perfect. Precision mattered.

Ignore the rise of tension. Nothing's changed.

Beads of sweat popped up on his brow. Nothing had changed? He couldn't lie to himself. *Everything* had changed.

Soft, so soft, she told him, "There's a little boy buried inside of you, I just know it." Features glazed with sadness, she petted his beard. "He has bad dreams. But guess what? My mother trained me for war since before I could walk. I never got to play games like the other little harpies. Before this, I never thought I wanted to. Now I think I do, so get ready!"

At top speed, wings vibrating, she raced out of the bathroom and into the bedroom, where she jumped on the bed while clutching a pillow.

He remained behind her, but didn't climb beside her. "What are you planning to do with the——"

Smack. She smacked the pillow into his face and laughed.

He stood immobile, his mind playing catch-up. She'd never played as a child. He didn't like the thought of young Taliyah training without cease. He, at least, had played with his siblings before his parents destroyed his entire world.

"Harpy smash!" she called, hitting him with the pillow a second time.

He didn't think about his next actions, just picked her up and tossed her to her back. The giggling resumed as she bounced on the mattress.

She wanted to play? They would play.

Roc dived on her and tickled, delighting as she laughed and wiggled.

As wily as she was, she worked free of his weight and darted through the bedroom, calling, "Find me if you can, Astra!"

Though she moved like a wild wind, he tracked her without trouble as she hid behind the curtains. Her feet stuck out from the bottom. He was grinning as he stalked over and swished the drapery aside, intending to press her against the wall and kiss the air from her lungs. But she no longer stood there.

A rush of cold swamped him just before she giggled behind him. Realization: she'd ghosted—phantomed—straight through him.

Reminded of her highly dangerous abilities, *hated* abilities, he sobered and pivoted. Time to put a stop to this.

In front of him, only a heartbeat away, her icy blues were soft and luminous. "You lose, and I win," she sang, then yawned. "Better get used to it, Rocky, baby. I *always* win."

His chest clenched tighter than ever before. What was she doing to him? "You think you can defeat me so easily, Taya?"

"Mmm-hmm." She jumped on him, winding her arms and legs around him. Clinging again. "I can do anything. I can have you as many times as I want. You'll see. I could even ride you hard."

Foreboding crept down his spine. His shaft throbbed anew. "What of your bid for General?" If ever she gave herself to Roc, he would thrust so hard and sure—

Enough! "Never mind. Let's tuck you into bed. You should rest."

"I'm not sleepy." A second yawn punctuated her words.

As he peered into her beautiful face, the tightness in his chest worsened until…crack. Inside him, something warm oozed out. Something akin to tenderness. For a phantom. A bride.

Harden your heart. Enjoy her while you can.

Or find another way…

He gulped. "Rest anyway."

"Never," she called, pumping her fist at the ceiling.

"Why don't we chat, then?" If she wished to reveal secrets, why not accommodate her?

He carried her toward the bed, moaning as her body molded to his. The rightness of their position both eased and tormented him.

—*Commander?*— Halo's voice cut into his awareness, and he ground his molars.

—*Yes?*—

—*A patrol found three other phantoms. Females, like the others. They come with another message for you.*—

Done with Erebus's game, he snapped, —*Kill them. Erebus only wishes to inflict more misery.*—

If Halo disagreed with the command, he said nothing. Proof of his brilliance. —*I'll see to it personally, sir.*—

"Where'd you go?" Taliyah asked, stroking his beard once more.

He leaned into her touch without thought. He realized he'd

stopped next to the bed, with the harpy clutched against his chest. "Doesn't matter." Roc readjusted her before settling atop the mattress, ensuring her body draped his.

Curling into him, she sighed, mournful. "I really miss your fingers."

He nearly choked on his tongue. "Do you, now?"

Stop! Do not travel this road. He had a prime opportunity here. He could pleasure her or question her while her euphoria lasted. He couldn't do both.

Though he might later hate himself, he said, "Never mind about that. Tell me about your father the snakeshifter."

"No. Don't want to," she told him, tracing a circle around his nipple.

Why not? "Just one detail? What's his name?" So Roc could find and question the male directly.

"Nope."

Even drunk, she refused him. In the shower, she had *commanded* him...and he had obeyed.

"Your turn to answer a question." She crossed her arms over his chest and propped her chin at the center, gazing up at him. "Did you miss me last night? Be honest."

Well, if he were being honest... "I couldn't think of anything else."

—*Roc?*—

He scowled. —*Yes, Vasili?*—

—*Done.*—

The warlord had completed the door and window frames, then. —*You may return to the duplicate realm.*—

A soft caress along his sternum returned his attention to Taliyah. "War business?"

"Yes." And he should resume it. If Erebus stuck to his usual methods, the god prepared bigger and bigger hordes for invasion. Simply to annoy Roc and keep the Astra busy, so that the god could get to the bride. Although, this wasn't a normal situation. Erebus already had an in with the bride.

Roc's mood darkened considerably.

If Taliyah sensed the change, she didn't reveal it. "Do you have time to give your wife another orgasm? I mean, it *is* your husbandly duty."

Hesitation, temptation's fondest companion, crept through his mind. "We shouldn't," he said, hedging. If she wasn't going to answer his questions, he might as well pleasure her.

"You're right," she agreed, and he stifled a groan. Why hadn't he agreed outright? "Before we tackle today's duties, I should probably speak a few inspiring words into your microphone."

She inched down his body, positioned herself between his legs and tapped the head of his shaft. With her lips hovering directly over the tip, she said, "Testing, one, two, three."

The most undignified laugh barked from him, and he couldn't regret it.

—*Commander?*—

Silver's voice popped the balloon of hilarity. No doubt the warrior had finished the new cuffs Roc intended for Taliyah to wear. She might object, this truce between them over.

Might? The woman would erupt.

Guilt welled, tinged with shame. —*We will talk later.*—

Roc prided himself on being available to his men. Today, he sought a mere hour of peace.

Taliyah crawled up his body, refitting herself against him as her eyes glittered with mischief. The cracking restarted in his chest.

"You said you might want me to feed on you for real," she said, "so we can learn how I did it. Want me to feed right now?"

Now? Maybe she should. They absolutely needed to know what had happened.

"Yes. Do it." Reluctant, he tilted back his head. Would he hate this, like he'd hated every other feeding before it?

Would a part of him enjoy it?

"Nah," she said, tucking her head into the hollow of his shoulder. The mischief had dispersed, her tone hollow. "Changed my mind. I'm not hungry."

He wasn't disappointed.

He wasn't.

25

Taliyah sat atop the meteorite she'd dubbed *the murder stone*. She swung her legs as if she hadn't a care, watching as Roc got his chisel on. Meanwhile, she had a freaking care. He'd been working furiously for over four hours, completing the first step and working on the next. Soon, he'd chisel out a platform and the altar itself. For her death.

How easily he'd returned to planning her end. Why had she missed him before?

The more he worked, the more crazed he appeared. He was silent and shirtless, his biceps bulging with his every move, sweat trickling down his tattooed flesh.

At least she had a decent view.

"Are you hungry?" he asked. He'd asked every hour on the dot. Or so it seemed.

"Nope," she said, taking great enjoyment in the refusal. Would she like to feed? Yes. Taliyah had no idea how she'd gotten so drunk on him. Had she truly stolen some of his soul without realizing it? She *had* been ravenous. But she'd never before reacted to a soul in such an undignified manner. She'd love to compare what happened in the shower with a true, non–lust tinged feeding. Well, as non–lust tinged as she could be with a man like Roc.

But, after glimpsing his dread as he'd canted his head for her… No. She wouldn't be feeding on him anytime soon. Or ever.

Actually, her refusal to do so now stemmed from a whole lot more than the guy's dread. Before flashing her to the garden, the awful man had picked up the wing-pinner.

"I'm not wearing that," she'd spit at him.

Expression grave, he'd told her, "Harpy, I promise you—you are. I'll take no chances with you."

Not only had he won their grappling match, putting the pinner on her as promised, he'd secured thin metal bracelets around her wrists, too. The shackles looked like jewelry—nice. They also prevented her from misting. *Not* nice.

Taliyah wore every piece of metal like a mantle of betrayal. So he'd treated her body like spun glass while she'd pummeled him, fighting to avoid the application of her bonds? So what. So he'd pleasured her in the shower and played with her after? So what. So she still wanted him. So. What.

"I'm bored," she told him, just to be contrary. She was irritable and horny and mad about both. Somehow, she needed to earn herself a little alone time. That way, she could practice removing her ring and resume her search for Blythe and Isla, just in case. "I'm unused to doing nothing."

"Tell me about your father. That's doing something." His ears twitched with…eagerness? "Recount tales of your childhood."

"Tell my captor about the childhood I spent in the land he conquered?" At this height, she spotted the moat that surrounded the palace grounds; a massive stone hand with moss-covered claws reached from the pink waters. How many times had she swum there? Flowers of every color bloomed from dew-kissed foliage, emitting the sweetest perfume she'd once breathed every day. Birds soared and sang familiar songs. Frogs croaked and crickets chirped. "I'd rather listen to tales of *your* childhood."

His biceps flexed. "Before or after I was sold to Chaos?"

Her grandpappy C *purchased* him? Had she known that? At the moment, she struggled to remember how much she longed to punch his face…and the way his powerful body moved against hers. "Revealer's choice."

He shrugged. "After my purchase, I traveled from world to world with the other Astra, learning weaknesses, gaining strengths. Through pain and tragedy, Chaos taught us to value control and harness rage. To create and destroy. To overcome any situation."

Oh, really? "How are you in control, yet shackled to a curse? If you can overcome any situation, why can't you save your *gravita* and your men? Asking for all my friends."

Roc chiseled a side of his finger and cursed. Blood poured from the wound.

He said nothing else, prickling her temper. When a bead of sweat trickled from her temple, she banged her fist in frustration. Though she thrived in cold—or she *had*, pre-Roc—she wore the suffocating garments he'd foisted upon her: a long-sleeved shirt and leather pants, both lined with some kind of fur. She wore these *despite* the warm temperature.

"To help you stay warm," he'd told her with determination, as if he should get an A-plus for his thoughtfulness. "The ground is cold—"

"I know," she'd snapped. "My homeland, remember? You're the intruder here."

Lack of sleep was getting to her, too. Since coming to Harpina, she'd slept a total of zero minutes.

"I told you not to bother me while I work, harpy." *Clink,*

clink. Clink, clink. "Yet there you are, bothering me. If you're not going to tell me about your childhood, do nothing."

"I *didn't* do anything! I didn't even say anything."

"You breathed," he bellowed. "Isn't that what you told Ian?"

He'd heard her? Or had his brother ratted her out? Whatever. Truth was truth. Now she wondered… What if Roc, the mighty Commander of the Astra Planeta, was falling for his phantom wife?

What if he fell for her so soundly, he picked her over his men?

Would he? Probably not. But he might be inclined to help save her *and* the Astra.

She admitted it; she liked the idea. A lot. Why accept a picture of defeat for the first time in her life, when the stakes had never been higher?

"Hey, Roc?" she asked with a sweet tone.

He groaned.

"Did I forget to mention it's Topless Tuesday?" She wiggled out of the shirt and tossed it in his direction.

He caught the garment with ease. As he stared at her, hard, she lay on the flat surface of the meteorite, stretching out.

"Ah. Much better."

"Taliyah…"

"What? I'm developing my wing-pinner tan line. A constant reminder to turn you down when I turn you on."

Did a muscle jump under his eye? "Put the shirt on before you burn." He tossed the garment back to her.

Taliyah caught it, smiled and threw the stupid thing over the other side of the meteorite. "The shirt stays off. It's a million degrees out here and someone conveniently forgot to give his precious captive a bra. So, I think we both know this is a sorry-not-sorry situation for you. Complain one more time, and the pants go, too."

He unleashed a series of caveman-style grunts, but he said nothing else.

"Tell me more about the blessing, and I'll behave," she said. "But only as long as you're talking. Just so we're clear."

She expected another refusal. Instead, he told her, "After the Astra ascended the first time, one after the other, we had a choice. Remain as we were, never gaining new power, or enter a door to great suffering and greater heights."

"A literal door?"

"Yes. It appeared before us. We don't know who made it, how or why, but it wasn't Chaos. When we stepped through, we entered a world of darkness. We fought our way free, each killing a monster along the way. That kill decided our original rank, determining our helmets as well as our blessing task. Our rank has changed many times, depending on our performance during our battles and our tasks. Every five hundred years, we must repeat our specific task, in order of our rank, whatever it is. If we succeed, one after the other, we receive the blessing. We win every battle we fight. If even one of us fails, we're all cursed to *lose* every battle."

That was a crap ton of pressure for each warlord to carry. "How does Erebus fit in?"

"We'd been at war with him for centuries already. He ascended before us, and yes, he entered the door first. We couldn't allow him to gain new power while remaining stagnant ourselves. As soon as we received our ranks, we found ourselves bound to him through the blessing and curse. He fights to complete his task—stopping us."

Ohhh. No wonder Roc remained confident in his ability to resist the ultimate temptation. No wonder he'd kept that tidbit hush-hush.

Why tell her now?

The answer marched itself into her head, and she gasped. "You're reinforcing your first warning to me, aren't you? Even though you're sexual with me, something you've never been with another bride, you'll kill me because I'm a phantom. That's almost sweet of you. Know what would be sweeter? Saving everyone."

He flinched. "You think we didn't try in the beginning?"

What would she do if the situation were reversed and she fought to protect her sisters and all of harpykind?

An easy question to answer, since she actually did fight to save all of harpykind. She would do whatever proved necessary.

"You've never wanted to make *yourself* the sacrifice, sparing your bride?" she asked.

"I can't. Our first Commander attempted that." His voice tightened. "The blade crumbled before ever making contact with him."

"So I can end you with a blade. Good to know."

He did the Astra equivalent of an eye roll—he got back to work. Chiseling once more, never glancing up.

"What else have you attempted?" she asked.

"Bargaining. Magic. Vows. There is nothing we haven't tried." He exhaled with force. "I wish there was a way."

Well, that was a huge first step. Definite progress. Would it help her in the end?

"What is the Commander of the Astra going to do after he ascends again?"

He blinked, pausing. "Enjoy peace. Start a…real family."

Her claws sharpened with…jealousy? Gross! *She* flinched. "You want peace, *and* you're attracted to bloodthirsty females? Explain that."

"A man can't have complicated, dueling desires?"

He could, yes, but she thought Roc's motivations delved deeper. "Maybe you admire strength rather than bloodthirstiness. A strong woman won't die easily. You won't ever have to worry about losing her."

He tensed but said nothing else. Because he didn't relish a future without his *gravita*, even if that *gravita* was a phantom?

A sudden crack of thunder boomed, shaking the garden.

Frowning, she pressed the side of her hand to her forehead, shading her eyes, and scanned the area. A storm approached from the north, dark clouds sweeping across the sunny sky. Would Roc work through the rain?

Cold blustered, wind whistling, cooling her off fast. Tossing her shirt had been a really bad idea or a really good one.

"Have you ever lost a blessing and won a curse?" she asked, not yet ready to give up on the conversation.

"Twice, with the two leaders before me. We were forced to hibernate, like the harpies are doing now."

"How does this forced hibernation work, anyway?" Another crack of thunder boomed, an icier blast of wind speeding past.

"Astra are able to design and craft entire worlds. An original world takes centuries. A duplicate requires mere months. We can control what chemicals and gases are released into the air, where and for how long."

Another good thing to know. Her thoughts returned to his varying reactions to her, and she decided to switch gears. "If you aren't letting me out of your sight, why do I need the chastity belt?" Yeah, he'd locked the stupid contraption in place, along with everything else. Another whistling wind stirred up fallen leaves as she asked, "Does someone require help resisting his magnificent phantom?"

His chisel missed the stone and fell to the ground. He bent to pick it up, the storm clouds dancing closer, an electric charge crackling in the air.

If he controlled chemicals and whatnot, he might control weather, too. Was *Roc* causing the storm?

Someone does *need help.* "Say goodbye to my pants." She stood and shimmied out of the fur-lined leather as he pretended to resume his work. Wearing only the wing-pinner and the chastity belt, she launched the leather at him.

He caught and dropped the garment without glancing up, lightning flashing. "Must you?" he inquired with a sigh.

"Yes, Roc, I must. I'm preparing for the wet-skin contest." Resettling on the murder stone, she said, "Ah. That's even better than better."

"You lie. You're already freezing. Your nipples are as hard as diamonds."

"Thanks for noticing."

The first raindrop splashed on her belly, and she gasped. He groaned. This might not be a terrible day after all.

Taliyah spent the entire night tucked against Roc, warm, relaxed and utterly miserable. Her eyelids weighed as much as boulders, but she refused to sleep. Which wasn't easy. When he'd manhandled her into bed last night, she'd anticipated another orgasm. He'd drifted off instead. With a hard-on! She'd expected his bad dreams to return and keep her awake while granting her deeper insight into his personality. But the big lug slept soundly, one arm under her nape and the other draped over her belly. Basically, the giant spoon swallowed the tiny spoon.

What was she going to do about him?

When the sun dawned and chased away the remnants of yesterday's storm, she crossed another day off her mental marriage calendar.

She needed to figure out a plan of action, fast, but a film of grogginess shrouded her mind. In this condition, she couldn't possibly decide what to do about Roc.

Shucking off his arms, she lumbered to an upright position, then twisted to glare down at him. His chest! The spot over his heart had filled in.

She leaned down to inspect...

He slapped a hand across the writhing image and jolted from the bed. After swiping a dagger from the boot sheath he'd dropped on the floor, Roc stomped into the bathroom.

"Drama queen," she called.

"Stay in bed."

Hardly. She followed him. "You said we had to stick together at all hours of the day and night." Why had the *alevala* appeared in his skin overnight? What did he plan to do with the knife? "What kind of captive disobeys a direct order?"

"The kind I've been dealing with from the beginning," he retorted, sealing himself inside the stall and erecting two trinite posts to keep her out. It wasn't long before the steam coated the glass, blurring his form. "Go away, Taliyah."

"What's your problem?" she grumbled. "*You* got a good night's sleep."

"I never slept. I communicated with my men. Since I've refused to listen to Erebus's last two messages, he sent phantom hordes to visit my warlords every hour, telling them my stardust is genuine, you are my *gravita*, and they should lock me away until the day of the sacrifice."

"In all fairness, it is, I am, and they should."

"I can't disagree. I...don't want you dead, Taliyah."

Stunned, she faltered. He was falling for her. He must be. Mind. Blown.

A squelching sound came from the stall. A sound she recognized. Was he *removing* that section of *alevala*?

Her eyes widened when the metallic scent of blood wafted to her nostrils. He *was*. But why? What didn't he want others to see?

She opted not to ask him—yet. In his current mood, he'd only refuse to respond. *Pick your battles.*

As she padded out of the bathroom, he called, "How are the phantoms getting past the wall, Taliyah?"

She stopped, his flat tone sending a chill down her spine. Yesterday, she'd thought she'd made headway with him. That he'd accepted her claims of independence. At least partially. Apparently, she'd been wrong.

"I don't know. Want me to ask Erebus about it the next time he ambushes me?"

A vile curse served as his answer. "How often do you need to feed?"

The change of subject threw her, but she hurried to recover. "Usually daily. Why?"

"Do you need to feed now?" He didn't even try to mask the thrum of hope.

Again, she took great satisfaction in telling him, "Nope. I promise you, I'm quite good." Truth. Whatever she'd taken from him had done the job and then some.

As he huffed with either relief or disappointment, Taliyah kicked into gear, leaving him to his shower. She had better things to do. Like practice removing her ring. Just for a second.

A naked, soaking-wet Roc with a newly healed patch of skin above his heart materialized in front of her. He grabbed her and flashed her to the shower, where he removed all of her hardware before leaving her alone.

Such an underhanded warlord. But oh, she loved being free!

He remained in the bathroom, dressing as she soaped up and pondered what might drive him to remove an entire hunk of flesh. Guilt? He wasn't the type. Fear? But fear of what? Embarrassment? But why?

"What's on today's agenda?" she asked as she shut off the water and toweled off.

"The same thing as yesterday."

Ugh. More altar-chiseling.

"Out," he commanded.

"I can't exit the stall until you remove the trinite."

"Why don't I come to you?" Once again, he appeared before her. He was shirtless, wearing leathers and combat boots. The same as usual, mixed with a different expression: chilling determination.

In his hands, he held all the metal, and an ice-blue tank with matching short shorts.

"Hard pass," she said, barely able to stop herself from retreating. "Metal is so last season. I'll take the outfit, though, if you promise not to drool all over me."

His eyes blazed. "This is happening, Taliyah. I can't trust you, and I can't watch you. I'll be busy doing other things. Accept it."

Never! "Want to know something? Before this, I played with the possibility of us being a team. A real one. Me and you, out to conquer the world and save everyone's day. That is now officially off the table. Do this, and I become your enemy, our truce over for good."

He flinched as if she'd slugged him. He also stood his ground. "So you plan to fight me again?"

"What do you think?"

Though he appeared resigned, he fought her until the bitter end. Once again, he treated her like spun glass, careful not to harm her as she used him as a punching bag.

When her hand "slipped," cupping his shaft, he growled. She couldn't stop this, but she *could* ensure he regretted it.

After that, *his* hands slipped on a regular basis, lingering on her breasts, stroking between her legs. When his eyes narrowed, his breath shallowing, Taliyah knew she'd have no trouble tempting him to keep her in bed, metal-free. And she wanted to. Oh, she wanted to! But she resisted. Why reward him for a temporary freedom?

"Took you twice as long this time, huh, baby?" Let him stew in his desires. Since she must wear his metal all day, he must deal with a steel-hard erection. She lay on the floor, panting, every shackle in place. "Either your reflexes are slowing or you can't keep your hands off your phantom."

He stood over her, his chest rising and falling in quick succession. "Yesterday's time in the sun put freckles on your nose."

Oookay. He'd issued the accusation as if it were a treasonous offense, leaving her sputtering for an insult. Wait. Why was she feeling defensive about this? Obviously, he *liked* the freckles.

"What's the matter, baby?" She glided to her feet and traced a claw along each of his shoulders. "Are freckles your other fetish?"

"I have no fetishes," he said, letting her touch him without complaint.

"Mmm-hmm. Freckles and submission. Yours, in case that wasn't clear." She melted into him. "In bed, you crave a woman unafraid to demand what she wants. You want to be dominated."

His entire body jerked, but he didn't deny it. "We won't be discussing fetishes." He latched on to her waist and flashed her to the meteorite, where he released her and gathered his tools. "Unless you'd like to dissect yours?"

"I don't have a fetish," she told him, confident.

"So you don't get wet every time you win a challenge?"

"I…" Did she? "What can I say? I like power."

No response. A familiar *clink, clink, clink* rang out, his body evincing nothing but calm.

That calm…stung. "Go ahead. Pretend to ignore me." Taliyah worked her way to the top of the murder stone and stretched out. In an hour, she would sport countless freckles. He'd pay *so bad* then.

Who are you? Her weapon of choice had never been *beauty marks*.

As she relaxed, though, she realized she'd made a mistake, stretching out as she'd done yesterday. The rhythmic sounds of his chisel nearly lured her to sleep.

Will not succumb. No way a man who hated her origins, refused to trust her and wouldn't commit to searching for a way to save her life was her consort.

As much as she enjoyed teasing and fighting Roc, she acknowledged that he wasn't her friend. He'd pinned her wings, stealing her strength, and stifled her ability to mist, leaving her vulnerable to attack. And attacks were coming. If old phantoms breached the palace, new phantoms would breach the palace. What would she do if one attacked?

"Be honest, Roc. You bored your other brides to death. You did, didn't you?"

"You've seen how the others died."

Yes, she certainly had. But did he really have to remain so calm while they discussed matters of life and death?

After a few minutes of silence, she groused, "I'm giving you such an amazing view, I should charge by the hour."

"By that logic, I should charge by the inch," he muttered, never glancing up.

Oh, no he didn't. A small little laugh escaped her. She did like his sense of humor.

His gaze flipped up, landing on her. As he searched her face, his calm veneer stripped away, the truth suddenly clear. He wasn't calm. Not by a long shot. A seething animal lurked beneath the surface of his skin, scheming violent ways to escape.

He looked fierce and furious, guilty and regretful. He looked...hungry.

Her smile fell, her heart skipping a beat. Another truth revealed itself. *I'm not seducing him. He's seducing me.*

26

Day five of Roc's new marriage dawned just like the fourth: with the indomitable Taliyah curled against him after neither one of them had slept. All night, fatigue and frustration had pursued him like hellhounds who'd finally sniffed prey. Furious, frothing desire had become his constant companion.

Holding the sensual beauty without pleasuring her proved an unmitigated torture and a true test of his strength. A test he'd passed—just barely. Would he pass again today?

He must. How could he take pleasure from her, then lock her in the metal she despised immediately afterward? How could he take pleasure from her, then toil over her death altar? He was despicable, but he wouldn't cross that line…not again. Not until she required sustenance from him. When she needed, he would give.

Never mind that she breathed, and he grew aroused. Never mind that she challenged and amused him at every turn.

He rubbed his tired eyes. Twice she'd mentioned saving herself and his men, compounding a sense of guilt he couldn't shake. He hadn't lied to her. The Astra had studied and researched and *lived* the situation countless times. There was no way out.

He wished he could offer her hope.

As soon as the sun filtered through the curtains, he pretended to sleep, just as before. How would Taliyah react to waking in his arms a second time?

The harpy gently wiggled around, doing her best not to jostle him. Clearly, she intended to study the regrown *alevala* at her leisure.

He would *never* let her see it.

He maneuvered her over his chest, pinning her against him. "Do you need to feed?" How eager he sounded. The desire was so new. So unexpected. Shameful? He didn't know anymore. To cede a piece of his soul, strengthening an enemy while weakening himself... Only a fool would do such a thing.

But he still wanted to do it. Roc *yearned* to nourish her. He alone would keep her sated. In every way.

"Why?" she asked. "Do you *want* to feed me?" She undulated against him, getting more comfortable and driving him mad. "The boner between your legs says yes."

"I don't want you eyeing my people with a mental fork and knife today." Truth, in part.

She held her breath. "I get to see your people?"

"You do. There's something I must do on the wall." Last night, Roux returned from the Hall of Secrets. He'd been an incoherent mess, and Roc made the call to keep Ian in the dungeon, putting Roux outside with Halo.

"Well, what are we waiting for?" Taliyah bounded up and tugged on his arm, dragging him to his feet. Pale hair tangled around an exquisite face lit with excitement. "Come on! We have a defense to mount? Soldiers to rally? Whatever! This is the most eventful day we've had."

This shouldn't surprise him. She enjoyed the intricacies of war, another fascinating facet of her personality he lo—liked.

He swiped up a dagger and marched into the shower stall to properly start his day.

When he finished, Taliyah took his place and he removed the metal. Just as before, she fought him when he appeared with her metal.

"I'm not going to run from you," she snapped.

"I know. Because I won't let you." He dropped everything but the cuffs. They'd start with those. "Come here."

"No." She prepared for battle.

He almost couldn't bring himself to mount an attack. The more he performed this act, prohibiting her freedoms, the faster the glow in her eyes dimmed. The more her shoulders slumped in disappointment when they interacted.

How could he hurt one like her? The woman who refused to surrender, no matter the odds stacked against her. Taliyah did nothing halfway and played games with him when drunk. As a phantom, she was the essence of death...yet she lived her life in ways he never dreamed possible. His snarpy had a thousand different moods he could never predict. She was a temptress. A warrior. A brat. An ice queen. A student. An assassin. The General. A goddess who twisted him into more and more knots. He liked each facet of her personality in different ways. *Enjoyed* each. She excited and tormented him. She taunted, defied, amused and confused him.

She reminded him that life beckoned outside of war.

The newest clash raged, all business, unlike yesterday's skirmish with wandering hands. As he snapped the last piece of metal in place, he left smears of stardust on her skin.

He liked seeing it there. He wanted to spread more.

He hated himself. Because he knew. In that moment, he knew. The stardust was genuine. He produced it for Taliyah because she *was* his *gravita*. The very reason Erebus had targeted her.

Roc's guilt surged with new life. *My fault.* Maybe she'd told the truth, and she didn't work with or for the male. Unlike Erebus, a known liar, Taliyah delivered hard truths with a sharp edge. But what did her innocence change?

"I must speak with one of my men inside the tower," he explained. "You'll be surrounded by trinite."

She glared at him. "I've been surrounded by trinite before, and I did just fine. Remember happy-shower time?"

He missed her good mood as much as a limb. "You were surrounded by poles, not walls."

"And I'll still be just fine." She stood in front of him, winded but defiant. "Let's go to work."

The pink tank with matching shorts he'd selected today turned his warrior harpy into a young twentysomething ready for a day of fun in the sun. Golden light had left its mark, leaving her with a rosy glow and more of those adorable freckles.

The crack in his chest widened, a painful and unwelcome sensation as he drew Taliyah against him. He flashed her to the guard tower on the north side of the wall.

"Okay. Yeah," she said, swaying. "I get it now. There's a weird crackle of energy in the air. But guess what? I'm fine, as predicted."

Despite the reappearance of the sun, yesterday's storm had ushered in a cold front. Without thought, Roc spun his snarpy around, so that she faced his men, and wrapped his arms around her, shielding her from the wind that poured in through the open windows. Her backside cradled the erection currently being strangled behind his zipper. Desire remained a fire in his blood.

"Commander?"

He slid his gaze to Roux and Halo, who stood at the window, once deep in conversation, now silent, watching him with astonishment.

He lifted his chin, saying nothing.

"Nice digs." Taliyah shifted this way and that, examining the trinite more intently. "I would've gone with something a little more intimidating, but to each his own, right?"

Roc told himself not to do what he was about to do, but the words left him anyway. "Taliyah, this is Halo and Roux."

Introductions were an honor he'd never bestowed upon another bride. His men graduated from astonishment, appearing shell-shocked.

"Aren't they supposed to bow or something?" she asked. "I'm their *queen*."

The corners of his mouth quirked before he had the presence of mind to blank his expression. "Explain what you learned in the Hall of Secrets," he ordered Roux.

"Time-out." Taliyah created a T with her hands. "What's the Hall of Secrets? You never explained."

He nuzzled his cheek against hers. "Our home realm, Nova, draws and collects whispers from other worlds. They are stored in a hallway of our palace. We have only to sift through them." He nodded to Roux. "Go on."

The male had recovered significantly from his trials. Though red-rimmed irises and strain added lines to his face, he had a steady gaze. "I heard whispers from a woman. She never mentioned her name, but she has a higher voice than your bride. Animated, even. As far from monotone as possible. She told someone she's more than a harpy-snake, and she cannot accept him as consort until he knows the truth about her origins, that she's also a phantom."

"So there's a second harpy-snake and phantom able to communicate with intelligence." Did she operate independent of Erebus, as well?

Tension stole through Taliyah. Did she suspect the identity of the other female? Did they share a connection? They must.

"And?" he prompted Roux, impatient for more information. "Did the woman say anything else?"

"Nothing that mattered." Roux's gaze dipped to Taliyah. "The woman who vanished during our invasion is this second phantom,

I'm certain of it. I believe she possessed me, though I'm unsure how. I don't even know how she exited without my knowledge. But she must have. Her emotions no longer muddle my own."

No movement from Taliyah during his speech. No emotion, either. Oh, yes. She knew the identity of the second phantom.

"Did she feed on you?" he asked.

Roux shook his head. "She did not."

His snarpy had once mentioned the atrocities committed against her people, courtesy of Erebus and his brother. Roc had thought nothing of it because the twins had slaughtered *countless* species. What if they'd somehow altered the DNA of some of the survivors? But...

Taliyah hadn't been part of the original slaughter. She'd claimed to read about the event in history books. Had the altered DNA caused phantom...births? Was such a thing even possible?

There was so much he didn't know.

Had the other woman exited Roux and spoken with Taliyah at any point? "Be on the lookout for the second phantom. She might return." When Taliyah braced, he added, "Don't kill her. Contain her for questioning." When her posture softened, he put his lips above her ear. "Is there something you'd like to say to me, snarpy?"

"Plenty," she snipped, as if he hadn't granted her a great boon, providing safety to a phantom. "I don't think you'll like any of my chosen words."

"You know about this second phantom."

"Yep." She didn't endeavor to deny it.

"And you'll tell me nothing?"

"Bingo."

Halo blinked at him, as if he'd never heard Roc make a request rather than a demand for information from a person of lesser rank. He'd definitely never heard Roc accept a denial.

What would it take to win Taliyah's loyalty? To induce her to offer it, of her own free will?

Not planning her murder, for starters.

He worked his jaw. "I'll learn all your secrets, one way or another."

"I could make her talk without killing her," Roux stated. He peered at the snarpy, as if he was already imagining her guts spread out on his table of torture. "She has answers about the other one, and I want to know what they are."

Protective instincts pitched and swelled. He barely wielded the wherewithal to remain silent. Torture Taliyah, dimming the light in her eyes and the fight in her heart for good? Never.

Never? "I will handle my wife," he intoned, making it clear the subject wasn't to be broached again.

Both males jerked, as if they'd been gut-punched.

"Wife?" Halo spread his arms. "You mean the *bride*. Or the *phantom*."

Wife. A term he'd never allowed himself to use with the others. He'd preferred the term *bride* because his marriages never developed past the wedding.

"Look," she said, "let me save you all some trouble. You can remove every limb and organ and I won't talk. Kudos to anyone who can make me cheer their efforts, though."

How proud she was. A perfect queen, unwilling to be cowed by anyone. "No one will be removing your limbs or organs."

"Too bad. I was really looking forward to making fun of your *torture*." She used air quotes, then extracted herself from Roc's embrace to skip to a window, where she leaned out to examine the realm beyond. "I've never seen Harpina from this angle or filled with this many males. Not outside of Harpy Gras."

The sight of her bent over the ledge, wearing only those tiny scraps of pink... He scrubbed a hand down his face. *Not strong enough to resist.*

He closed the distance, coming up behind her and bracing his hands beside hers. At this angle, his body molded to hers, all but engulfing her smaller form.

"How'd you recruit so many different species?" she asked.

He looked out. Men crowded the area below, standing in formation. Shifters of every kind. Berserkers. Banshees. This particular contingent of soldiers awaited a command to attack, should one need to be issued.

"My soldiers come from worlds we've conquered," he explained, "as well as those who thought to try and conquer us."

She whipped around, remaining in the space between his arms and glaring up at him. "If you're planning to enlist harpies—"

He snorted. "As if I would dare. I can't even control the one under my direct command."

"Okay. All right. I guess I won't decapitate you right here and now, before your men can stop me." Pure, sensual grace and languid carnality, she traced a finger down his sternum. "By the way, your *alevala* stopped moving again."

He glanced down, and sure enough, the images resembled any other tattoo. All because he caged the snarpy in his arms, and she seemed content to stay put?

When would she need to feed? When could he pleasure her again?

Perhaps he'd made a mistake, not bringing her to climax these past two nights. Soon, her beautiful life would be cut short. Didn't she deserve to indulge every desire beforehand?

Remembering the two warlords standing behind him, listening to every word, Roc called, "Meeting adjourned."

He flashed Taliyah to the garden, next to the altar.

She groaned. "Not this again."

"No, not this again." He couldn't bring himself to work. Instead, he sat on his bench and pulled her into his lap. "Let's talk."

Taliyah had fought low-level panic ever since Roux's shocking announcement. Roc now knew about Blythe. He might go searching for her.

She scrambled to her feet, not an easy feat when you were

straddling a man. As soon as she achieved success, he resettled her against him.

She didn't want him searching for Blythe. Or anyone! For all Taliyah knew, there was a third harpy-snake-phantom. Another secret daughter from Erebus's line. A sister she'd never met, and someone she wanted to save.

At least Roc hadn't ordered the other phantom's death.

"Let me go," she insisted. "You have stuff to do, and so do I."

His brows furrowed. "What *stuff* must you do?"

"Lots of things. Train without my ring. Catalog the identities of the sleeping harpies. Study. And that's just the start of my list!" There was so much she didn't know about phantoms, Astra and Erebus. Maybe she'd find a book in the library titled *How to Bypass Stupid Trinite Posts*. Maybe?

Never accept a picture of defeat.

"We can do those things later." The cold air should have chilled her, but his heat engulfed her. He traced his fingers up the ridges of her spine. "Right now, we stay here and talk."

Stubborn warlord. She did want to talk with him, to tell him what worried her and analyze the problems and solutions together. He could help; she knew he could. He knew more about phantoms and Erebus than she did. She'd read stories, but Roc had lived them.

If Blythe *had* possessed Roux and *had* exited him outside of Harpina, where was she? Why hadn't she returned for Isla? Unless she'd already found and stashed the girl away? But why not alert Taliyah to her presence?

Either the phantom wasn't Blythe, or something had prevented her dear sister from reaching out.

Why am I happy to see you?

Roux's words replayed in her head. Okay, so the phantom was definitely Blythe, and Blythe had definitely possessed the Astra. But how had she escaped him? What if she *hadn't*?

Taliyah's eyes widened. Could her sister be trapped in there, buried so deep Roux no longer sensed her?

The questions almost tripped from her tongue. *Say nothing!* Roc was the source of her panic in the first place. Frustrated, she griped, "We only ever do things you want to do. When is it my turn?"

He nuzzled her with his beard, just as he'd done in the tower. "That depends on what you want to do. I offered conversation."

"And I turned it down. Twice." Despite herself, arousal swelled. With him, arousal *always* swelled. He knew just how to touch her...

The pleasure they'd shared before... She longed for more. But, for two days, he'd barely touched her. Resisting the urge to initiate contact had proved challenging.

Be the one who caved? No. So, the satisfaction she'd grown to adore had remained at bay.

Now he stared at her lips, as if he imagined kissing her. "I can scent how much you want me, snarpy. I...want to be on your team, but I can't give you false hope. I—" He quieted. His head canted to the side, his gaze going far away.

A telepathic conversation ensued, and it definitely wasn't a good one. More and more aggression pulsed from him.

Did he say he wants to be on my team? "What is it?" she asked, focusing on war rather than emotions. She scanned the garden, expecting to discover an invading army.

From unguarded, sensual, and sexy beyond imagining, to the stone-faced Commander, Roc transformed before her eyes. He stood abruptly, setting her on her feet. "A phantom army has appeared at the wall. The soldiers are embodied, in formation, unmoving and silent. Which means they have orders to do nothing until an appointed time or event."

She really hated her father right now. "So what's the plan? Fight them?" Yeah. He itched for a fight, didn't he? "Remove the metal, and I'll help."

He blinked in surprise. "I— No." A shake of his head for emphasis. "I'll lock you in the bedroom. Posts will ensure no phantoms are able to enter."

Anger sprouted fast and sure. "Hey! You can't just change your rules whenever it suits you. We stay together, remember?"

He turned stubborn. "I can, and I have. This is for your safety."

Her safety? Taliyah scowled at him. "You'll leave me weakened while an enemy attacks?"

He flinched. But did he relent? No. "I'm sorry, Taya, but this is the way it must be."

"Liar." How dare he *Taya* her at a time like this. "This isn't the way it must be. This is the way you *want* it to be. No one can force you to do anything you don't want to do, remember? Well, I've had enough. Before this, I dealt with you fairly because I understood your motives. Were the situation reversed, I would do the same thing, only better. But this… You've gone too far!"

Torment stamped his face, but she didn't care. "The risk is too great," he said, as stubborn as ever.

"That's right," she replied with a bitter undertone. "You've got to protect your investment. Never mind that the enemy might breach your posts and attack while I'm unable to properly defend myself."

"Taya—"

"No! Don't tell me they can't breach the walls. They've already entered the palace without your knowledge on multiple occasions. So, no," she repeated. "Any man who kisses me then puts me in unnecessary danger isn't worth my time."

"I—"

The temperature dropped from chilly to arctic in a blink. Despite Roc's furnace-like temperature, Taliyah's next exhalation crystallized in front of her face.

Apprehension prickled her spine. "The weather in Harpina is weird, but it's never gotten so cold so fast."

"Phantoms approach," he said, palming a blade.

A curse exploded from Roc as great gray clouds filled the sky, blocking the dueling suns. She glanced up. No, not clouds. Her heart thundered. An army of embodied phantoms whirled through the air and descended over the garden.

27

Phantoms. Thousands of them. Aggression charged the atmosphere, inspiring the first flame of *anhilla*. Frost grew over Roc's skin, but that flame melted it away.

A thought streaked across his mind, a mental asteroid, leaving destruction and ruin in its wake. Threaten his wife? *Die.*

He could deal with anything but her loss.

He prepared to flash Taliyah to their bedroom, as promised. She might hate him for a time, but she would live. Nothing else mattered right now. But, though he strained, the ability to flash failed him. No time to figure out why. Collision was imminent.

Not knowing what else to do, he wrapped his arms around her, shielding her as the hordes of phantoms descended en masse.

Whoop, whoop, whoop. The noises registered first, and he braced for impact.

Wham, wham, wham! Repeated blows shoved him left and right, but he held steady. Bones fractured and broke. A myriad of claws raked him. Lips attached to him and sucked. Cold invaded his veins, threatening to weaken him. The *anhilla* flooded him with new strength, keeping him on his feet.

As every inch of his body was battered, he shouted information at his men. How had an army this large gotten past the trinite without notice? Why couldn't he flash?

—*The army at the wall attacks. Silver's men approach on foot; they can't flash. Neither can I.*— Halo threw the words like daggers. —*Ian, if you can, put my men behind the army and yours in the garden.*—

If only Ian could flash *phantoms* in large groups. But they didn't bear the mark of the Astra.

—*I'm unable to flash myself or anyone at the moment, so I'm on foot myself. I'm headed for the garden.*—Ian had slipped into battle mode.

His brother would show no mercy.

"Roc?" Taliyah shouted over the commotion, more and more phantoms crashing into them.

He knew what she requested. With great effort, he worked a hand under the wing-pinner to unhook the two pieces of metal. Metal malleable only to the touch of an Astra. Though he tried, he couldn't do the same with her wrist shackles, the phantoms repeatedly knocking her arms from his grip.

Stomach turning over, he told her, "I need you to fight, Taya. Fight as you've never fought before. Don't stop until the last phantom is dead, and don't you dare die." A battle loomed. There was no avoiding it.

He should have freed her from every bit of metal when she'd asked. He hadn't. He'd held on to his fears instead, for reasons he hadn't wanted to admit or accept. Fear of her motives. Fear of what his men might think. Fear of what *he* would think. Now he and Taliyah would both pay a steep price.

As he well knew, a warrior's unused strengths became their biggest weaknesses. His woman wasn't used to fighting without her ability to disembody.

He told himself it didn't matter. She had many other skills.

She would survive this. More than being a deathless phantom, she was a centuries-old harpy-snake who had outlasted a multitude of wars, betrayals, tortures and ambushes. This was nothing.

This had better be nothing. She had better survive.

"Do you understand me?" At some point in the coming fray, Roc and Taliyah would be separated. She would be without his protection. She would be weakened without full use of her abilities.

"Not my…first rodeo…baby." The newest round of hits jostled her as she spoke. "No worries. I got this."

The ice that had spread over his skin had somehow spread to hers. The brand on her nape flecked with frozen crystals as his mind whirled with plans. "I'm going to count to three and release you. When I do—" A frigid wind slammed into him, tossing him across the garden, wrenching Taliyah from the shelter of his arms prematurely. A phantom clasped her wrist and yanked her in the other direction, ensuring they parted.

Air abandoned his lungs when he crash-landed a dozen feet away. With a roar, he sprang to his feet. Dizzy. Inhale, exhale. He took stock. Shattered ribs. A bone fragment had punctured his lung. Limbs had sliced his side. All insignificant. Where was Taliyah?

He scanned… Phantoms, phantoms, everywhere. No sign of his snarpy.

Racing forward, Roc slashed and clawed anyone in his path. He attempted to flash once more, desperate to reach Taliyah's side. *Nothing* kept him from his wife. But again, he failed.

Where was she? Where, where? "Taya?" Raw panic engulfed him, *anhilla* snatching it up to use as fuel.

His next roar made a mockery of the first.

Going low, he crouched and spun on the balls of his feet, withdrawing two three-blades stashed in his boots. As he straightened, he slashed in a crisscross motion, killing two phantoms with ease.

Destroy them all. The words filled every corridor of his mind, every cell in his body, becoming an eternal battle cry. The beginning of the end.

Roc utterly unleashed, tearing through his enemy. He stabbed with new vigor. Slashed with crueler purpose. Clawed, punched and kicked. Black blood spurted over him. Each kill strengthened him and powered another. A stream of thought refused to die, even in the heat of battle. *Protect my Taliyah. Must protect my Taliyah.*

Heads toppled and limbs thudded to the ground. The plop of organs followed. More blood sprayed in continuous arcs. He killed with abandon, with joy. Bodies and their parts piled around him, soon to vaporize. Carnage littered the battlefield.

The Astra Planeta, creator of worlds, were often touted as the essence of life. Now Roc existed in a haze of death, the scent of it pungent. His limbs shook with exertion, but he didn't slow until—

Had he just heard a woman's pained grunt? Where was Taliyah? He needed to see her. He needed to see her *right now.*

"Taya?" He prepared himself for what was soon to occur. Finding her. Seeing injuries. Blood. He reminded himself she would heal, no matter the injuries she received. She must. That's what phantoms did. They fed, and they healed.

How often had he lamented a phantom's regenerative powers when struck with anything but trinite? Now he relied on the ability.

Get to her! He swung his arms faster, every strike true. Blood splattered his face and dripped into his eyes, blurring his vision. He suspected he looked like an animal. He felt like one, emotion beyond him.

In his world, you killed or you were killed. So he killed. Again and again and again. Phantoms screamed and phantoms died, but their numbers never dwindled. More arrived, each new group ignoring him completely. The entire horde swarmed in one direction—Taliyah's.

To feed on one of their own or to kill? Either way, she would hurt.

Aggressive noises left him as he fought with new purpose. Slash, slash. Kick, slash. Different fiends and their various severed parts evaporated after death, a cloying fog coating the air.

New arrivals. Thicker layers of ice spread over his skin. His joints hardened, but he refused to slow.

Just get to Taliyah. The words were a mantra. More fuel for his *anhilla*.

If she died and failed to revive… "No!" More maddened by the second, Roc swung his arms in opposite directions: one descended at his left and one at his right, each stabbing a phantom in the top of the skull. Kick. Elbow. Hip-bump, slash. Claw. Rip. He utilized his entire body, felling opponent after opponent, steadily moving forward. A man obsessed, he remained in a constant state of motion.

Movement behind him. He spun, a soulsucker slamming against him, ignoring him as much as the others, reaching beyond him to make grabby hands at Taliyah.

A flick of his wrist, and the phantom died.

He fought on. Finally a path opened up, granting him a first glimpse of Taliyah since their separation.

He wasn't prepared, the sight nearly sending him to his knees. Though she fought with expert skill, the sheer number of phantoms overwhelmed her, the fiends landing multiple blows. They battered her with their fists. Others tore at her with their claws. Blood poured from countless gashes, soaking her precious skin.

With Roc on twenty-four-hour watch, Erebus had no more use for her. Had the god settled on overseeing her murder?

When a set of claws raked through Taliyah's throat, tearing out her trachea, a helpless Roc could only watch in horror.

"Taya!" At the sight of her blood, her fall, his *anhilla* redlined.

He roared at the sky as a bright, blazing light burst through his pores. His eyesight dimmed, the world around him slowing. His own blood rushed and boiled. Muscles bulged with new power.

A living wrecking ball, he heaved his big, shining body into the thickest midst of the phantoms, cutting through, sometimes three or four at a time. Soon he lost track. He killed, and he killed.

His enemies must pay. Everyone must die. Destruction would reign. *Will drown this world in blood and pain!*

In the back of his mind, he thought he heard his brother's voice calling to him, telling him to cease. But he didn't want to stop. He wanted only to slay more phantoms. He wanted to dismantle everything standing between him and his *gravita*.

Hurt her? Hurt my woman? You won't just die. You'll suffer your worst nightmare first.

A weight smacked into his chest. Cold. Slight. A familiar voice called, "Shut up, Ian. I've got this."

Taliyah's voice. Roc slowed his swinging arms. She had revived?

"See? Told you I've got this. Right, Roc? Babycakes? Because your sweet, perfect *gravita* is A-okay, honest. She's all better, so the temper tantrum can end, all right?"

Soft fingers petted his cheeks, his beard, and he slowed a bit more. "The phantoms are dead?"

"Oh, yeah. You did so good. Everyone's real proud. There's talk of an award. MVE. Most volcanic exterminator."

Jumbled thoughts attempted to straighten out. "Everyone?"

"Mmm-hmm. Just your brother and a few hundred soldiers. They arrived a while ago. I'm told the army at the wall retreated as soon as you finished off the last phantom here." She chuckled. "When you decide to make a grand gesture, you *really* make a grand gesture, huh?"

Roc blinked into focus and surveyed the battlefield. He stood at the altar, still punching one end. Cracks had formed. Taliyah clung to his chest. Around him, piles of phantoms lay in various stages of evaporation. Ian stood mere feet away, as shell-shocked as the few hundred soldiers stretched out behind him.

"What's up?" Taliyah called to someone over his shoulder. "I'm with him. He's, like, claimed me or whatever."

Gripping her waist, he demanded, "You are unharmed?" He needed to hear the words from her mouth.

"Mostly."

Not good enough! When he darted his gaze for a new target, she chuckled again.

"No, don't go trying to kill anyone else. I'll be patched up in a matter of minutes, I swear. If you want to continue murdering the altar, though, go for it."

Was she nearly patched up? Roc cupped her cheeks with hands coated in blood. The sight bothered him. Release her, however? No. "You stayed and fought with me."

"Of course I did." Those icy blues watched him, open and honest…and gleaming with irritation. "I told you I would, didn't I?"

He scanned her face, searching beyond her expression, trust budding. He called for his brother. "Ian?"

Knowing he expected a report, Ian wasted no time with incidentals, getting straight to the point. "We lost a handful of soldiers."

He pressed his tongue to the roof of his mouth. A single loss was too many.

"The altar—" Ian began.

"I can fix it," he muttered without conviction.

Needing reassurance Taliyah was all right, he pressed her against the side he'd punched, right against the cracks. After bracing her weight, he looked her over thoroughly.

She let him. Ocean-water eyes remained warm without a hint of ice, her gaze inviting him in. A soft smile stole his breath.

A handful of gashes had yet to heal, and she was smiling?

He glared. "How are you in a good mood? Before the battle, you hated my guts."

"Let's be clear. I hated more than your guts. Then you had to go and prove your undying love for your most precious treasure, your darling Taya. You're so whipped."

Too keyed up with aggression, he had no idea how to respond to her...teasing? Bragging? "I had to protect my investment," he said, spouting words she'd once tossed at him.

"Now, we all know better than that." Her chiding tone bore a hint of her smile. "After such a magnificent display of manly prowess, you're only embarrassing yourself with your denials. Well, you're also embarrassing me, since I'm the object of your desire and all. Enough chatter. We've got cleanup to do." She pressed a swift kiss into his lips, hopped down and pushed past him.

He silenced a command—or a plea—for her return and faced his brother. "Assemble and prepare the armies for the next attack." Knowing Erebus, he'd burned through a small piece of his army to make a point, proving he had other ways to reach the blessing bride.

"There's *more* of these things?" Taliyah wrinkled her nose. "After all that, we didn't just save the day?"

Roc almost closed the distance. Almost dragged her into his arms. The need to hold and touch her refused to fade.

Ian frowned at her, then Roc, then Taliyah again. His brother didn't know what to make of what had just happened—what was still happening. Neither did Roc.

Ultimately, Ian settled on Roc. Incredulous, he thrust a small purple stone in his hand.

"What am I looking at?" he asked, rubbing the stone. Dense. Rough. Powerful. *Familiar.* His brows drew together as cold spread over him. "No. I cannot be holding what I think I'm holding. We destroyed the last piece thousands of years ago."

Ian's expression acquired a grave edge. "Apparently, Erebus found more. He hung the stones from a leather cord."

"Someone tell the rest of the class," Taliyah said, tossing up her arms.

"This is firstone. What trinite does to a phantom, firstone does to an Astra. It's the reason we couldn't flash during combat."

Ian gaped at him. "Why don't you make a list of the few ways to kill us and help your bride study it, brother?"

"Because he isn't a tool?" Taliyah asked calmly. "Not all the time, anyway."

Roc replied to neither of them, his mind whirling. Erebus had sent these hordes as a warning shot. He wanted Roc worried. Which meant Roc shouldn't worry. He should enjoy his wife.

His brother said something else, but Roc lost track, too busy observing Taliyah, who unabashedly amassed a sizable firstone collection in a matter of minutes, stuffing the pebbles in the pockets of her shorts. She wasn't even trying to hide her actions. When she came upon the wing-pinner, she grew rigid before bending down to gather the pieces.

She whipped around to face him, their eyes meeting. Pure defiance, she hurled the metal as far as harpily possible, daring him to complain.

Hobble her again? No. Something had happened to Roc during the battle. Something significant. He didn't yet understand the intricacies or complications of it, whatever it was, but he knew his relationship with Taliyah was forever altered. If he had lost her today...

He stalked to her, removed the wrist cuffs and hefted her into his arms, carrying her straight to their bedroom.

28

As the Astra drew a bath, Taliyah remained in the doorway of the bathroom, caught up in an unexpected quandary. She and Roc had reached new territory today. Like, serious couple territory. She knew it. The metal was no longer an issue. They were past it. Roc was choosing to trust her to keep her end of the original bargain and stay put to fight him.

He had killed and bled for her.

He desired her more intensely than anyone else ever had.

He longed to save her. She knew that, too.

The brutal way he'd dispensed of the phantoms to rescue her... Had any male ever looked so sinfully seductive while exuding such evil intent? The warlord had attacked their foes so viciously, so savagely, he'd morphed into the monster her mother had warned her about. More frightening than the hordes—and okay, yeah, the creepiness of the phantoms had taken her by surprise. Mouths with hundreds of tiny suction cups remained wide open, at the ready.

The fiends had iced her brand, just as Erebus had. They'd attempted to feed on her. Her. One of their own. Well, almost one of their own. She was nothing like those ravenous shells.

No, not true. She was absolutely, positively ravenous. Already she could taste Roc's power...

As soon as the number of invaders had dwindled, she'd had the distinct privilege of watching him. He'd awed her. The mastery he'd demonstrated over his body had been so complete, the fight appeared choreographed. He'd known when to go high and when to shift low, displaying the perfect ebb and flow of offense and defense.

The way he'd used his claws and three-blade to tear his victims into too many pieces to identify had been a real eye-opener for Taliyah. As skilled as she was, she realized she stood no chance against him—yet. He was faster, moving at warp speed. He was stronger by leaps and bounds. Anyone who'd come into contact with his otherworldly glow had caught fire. Not with literal flames, but mystical. So, anyone who'd come into contact with his otherworldly glow had died in unbelievable agony.

And this is the male I've challenged? She would have preened, if tears hadn't welled.

He didn't know Erebus was her father. While she refused to lie, she wasn't ready to tell him. Not yet. This—whatever this was—was too new, her trust not yet fully established.

How would Roc react to the news?

So badly she yearned to hurl herself at him and demand everything he had to give, parting with her virginity, forgetting the complications, shedding the past and grabbing hold of the future. But she wouldn't.

Now more than ever, harpies required a strong leader. The strongest. Enemies they'd never before faced lurked about—enemies only the granddaughter of a god could take down.

If other Generals can resist temptation, so can I.

Would Roc understand? After today, she knew there was

no way he would sacrifice her. Disgust for her origins? He had none, not any longer. The man had killed hundreds of phantoms to reach her, shouting her name in panic, erupting into those mystical flames when she got injured.

Which was great—for her. But she kinda sorta didn't want him and his men cursed, either.

Before, she'd toyed with the idea of being with him for a few months or so. To be honest, the option hadn't really struck her as a true possibility until Roc had willingly released her from the metal. Now he had.

What should she do? Take what she could, while she could?

If Roc upended his entire world for her, he would demand everything. She had no doubts about that. He would never be satisfied with a temporary arrangement, and he certainly wouldn't agree to a sexless pairing.

If the Astra were anything like the demon-possessed Lords of the Underworld her sisters scored, they were possessive and obsessive to the extreme. So. Yeah. Roc would insist on forever and lots and lots of sex. Taliyah would be forced to choose between her consort and her people. If he was her consort. *Was* he? Here, now, with his body covered in the blood of their foes, she wondered…

If only she could chat with her sisters. They would offer advice and pep talks, helping her see what she needed to see and ignore what must be ignored. They would also make fun of her for the rest of her life. When every joke was deserved, however, you just had to laugh with them.

"What is this?"

She shook her head, clearing her thoughts and finding Roc in front of her, concern carved into his face.

With a small smile, she told him, "Nothing I need to decide now."

The bathtub was partially full, the surface covered in sweet-smelling bubbles. Aw. Did the big, bad Astra sometimes enjoy a little pampering?

"If you're debating the merits of feeding from me," he said, "let me put your mind at ease. You will do it, no matter what. I want those gashes gone."

See! This man could never end her. "Healing from my injuries requires blood, remember, not soul. Or, uh, seed." They had yet to confirm if she'd sneaked past his defenses and taken his soul. Or if that little bit of seed had done the trick, when she'd licked her thumb in the shower. "My phantom side remains nourished." Mostly.

"Doesn't matter. You can do it now or later, but you will do it. The blood you'll take before we settle into the bath. Come. Let's shower off the phantoms before we enter the tub." He said nothing else as he drew her tank over her head.

She stripped herself the rest of the way, watching as he undid his leathers. That mouthwatering erection popped free, making her belly clench. When she dropped her shorts, the firstones she'd stuffed in the pockets thudded. She planned to study them. And yeah, okay, she also kind of wanted Roc to work with them to develop an immunity to their effects. If anyone ganked him, it would be Taliyah, not phantoms or Erebus.

To her surprise, his lips curved with amusement as he lifted the shorts and walked them out of the bathroom, disappearing from view. No words of rebuke from him?

"Hey," she called. "Those are mine."

"I put them in a safe you can easily open. This is for our protection. I must be able to flash, especially while I'm…otherwise occupied."

Okay. All right.

In front of her again, he lifted the key around his neck and removed her belt. "You did well out there."

"Are you kidding? I got my butt handed to me. I'd never fought phantoms before. They disembodied and embodied at random in ways I never perfected because I was too busy pretending I was only casting illusions. Which changes now. Never again will I attempt to hide what I am."

"Why did you hide your origins in the first place?" He stepped into the shower stall and extended his hand. "Did you expect ridicule from the harpies?"

If she was going to consider being with this man for any length of time, she'd have to share a little about herself. "My mother wanted me to avoid drawing Erebus's notice."

When his hand remained outstretched, despite the mention of his foe, she placed her fingers against his.

"Wise of her," he said, drawing Taliyah closer.

Well. He'd accepted the confession better than she'd expected.

He fiddled with knobs until warm water burst from the overhead spouts. Once the blood and viscera rinsed from their bodies, he pulled her against his chest and bared his neck. "Drink."

Her gaze dropped to his racing pulse, visible beneath his skin, and she trembled. "Are you sure? If your block is down, I might accidentally steal some of your soul. Before you force me to feed, I mean."

He gripped her by the nape, his eyelids hooding, his pupils pulsing. "Take whatever you need, Taya. I'll recover."

"Okay, but only because you're insisting." With a moan, she leaned forward...and sank her fangs into his vein.

He tightened his hold. And yes, his block was down. As hot blood trickled down her throat, she fought not to imbibe any of his soul. *Must resist.* He'd offered what she needed, but she declined the option of taking what she *didn't.*

Heat cascaded through her as she drank, and her veins fizzed. The most powerful medicine she'd ever consumed. Incredible strength flooded her limbs. Gashes wove together at last. Any fractured bones mended.

"That's the way," he told her, cupping her backside to grind her against his length. "That's my Taya. Take more."

More. All. Everything. What could be better than this?

Drinking him while he thrusts inside you...

Spooked, she gently plucked her fangs from his flesh. "That's... that's enough." Her tremors worsened as she wiped her mouth, scooping up any remaining beads of blood and licking her fingers. "I'm healed."

"But you drank so little." He pouted with keen disappointment. "I have more than enough. I can provide *all* you require, Taliyah."

"I'm sure you can." Shivers and pangs blended together, revealing unknown vulnerabilities. This new dynamic between them might require some getting used to. "I'm good, I promise."

The disappointment dulled, flames of arousal flickering in those golden irises.

They exited the shower. He led her to the tub, eased down at the far edge and pulled her between his legs. Splayed out before him, she presented a veritable buffet of pleasures, giving him full access to places she ached. Fragrant steam enveloped them, painting the air with a dreamy haze.

"I think I know how you are a phantom and...you." He settled his hands on her shoulders and massaged, her eyelids sliding shut. "I suspect Erebus and his brother did something to your people during their raids."

He was so close to the truth, yet so far away. "Yes and no. No," she added when he prepared to comment further. "I'll say no more on the subject right now."

"Very well." Leaning over, he collected a vial of soap and lathered her up. He took great care with her breasts, kneading to make sure they got *extra* clean. Especially her lucky nipple piercing.

Her arousal accumulated in select locations, sharpening the delicious aches between her legs. As she rocked her hips, seeking a touch, a kiss, *something*, the water rippled.

"Is there something you *wish* to discuss?" he rasped near her ear.

Goose bumps spread over her limbs. "So many things," she admitted. "Let's start with your safety. What are you going to do about the stones?"

"Fight, despite them. Begin training with them. But let's not talk about that, either." He ran a hand down her left arm and traced his thumb over the stars on her wrist. "How did you earn these?"

Every touch electrified. His curiosity produced a similar effect. "Well, for this one—" she pointed "—I won my first Harpy Games. That's our version of the Olympics, mixed with MMA, mixed with *The Amazing Race*." Not that he knew what any of those things were, probably. "I won my second Harpy Games just to prove I could and took first, second and third place because no one was willing to stand on the podium with me. Apparently, I didn't play nice during either event."

"That, I believe." He tapped another star. "And this one?"

Before she responded, he used his free hand to pluck her nipple piercing. Pleasure arced through her. "Wait. What?" She'd already forgotten his question.

His husky chuckle caressed her heating skin. "How did you earn this star?" His naughty hand moved to her navel, his fingers gliding around and around, teasing and tormenting.

Stardust glittered there, distracting her. Somehow, she rallied. "I led a successful military campaign against a prick of a king who had enslaved some of our people. I put his insides on his outsides. And yes, I said *outsides*, plural. At the time, the king was in pieces." She lost her train of thought when Roc reached the apex of her thighs.

Tremors rocked her as she waited for him to initiate a more intimate caress. Seconds passed. Minutes. The teasing and tormenting persisted...

Breathless, she gave herself an inner shake. "Comments? Questions?"

"I have created and destroyed worlds, conquered kingdoms

and claimed other men's armies as my own. But I've never faced an opponent quite like you."

She arched, thrusting up her breasts, reaching overhead to fist his hair. "That might be the sexiest thing anyone has ever said to me." And if he kept his hand where it was much longer, she would go insane! "Tell me about you. What are your likes? Your dislikes?"

"I like—" he kissed her cheek and finally glided a finger through her silvery curls, rubbing her clit at long last "—slippery snarpies."

Her eyes nearly rolled back in her head. "And?"

"I like—" he stroked the throbbing bud "—moaning, gasping snarpies."

"Oh, yeah?" She couldn't catch her breath. "Anything else?"

"I like...my *gravita*." He applied more pressure, right where she needed it most.

A cry tapered into a moan. "Roc." She didn't pretend not to want this. Didn't tell herself this was merely another test of wills. She knew the truth. This was two people who shouldn't like each other exploring what could be.

New tests would come tomorrow; an inevitable outcome, considering their situation. Today, though, they celebrated a victory.

"Don't stop. Whatever you do, baby, don't stop."

"Never, Taya." He rubbed, glided, then plunged his fingers inside her, just the way they both liked. Stretching her. Then he did it all over again. Rubbing. Gliding. Plunging. Keeping her suspended at the threshold of an earth-shattering climax.

"The things you do to my body." Taliyah writhed against him, water lapping at the sides of the tub.

"Look at you." Awe thickened his voice. "Has there ever been a more exquisite sight?"

"No," she told him, and he rewarded her with another of those husky chuckles.

Her lids grew heavy as sensations replaced thoughts. Arching further, thrusting her breasts higher, she steadied her head on his shoulder, letting herself feel and enjoy...everything.

She thought he might be gentling her, a feat no other had managed. But then, she gentled him, too. The more he touched her, the more he trembled.

Suddenly desperate for him, she angled her face, seeking his kiss. He gave it to her eagerly, his tongue twining with hers. Their breaths mingled, heat and passion consuming her, setting off an avalanche of shivers.

His groans sent a second wave of heat crashing through her and...

"Yes!" The kiss broke as she climaxed, her inner walls clenching around his fingers.

"Do you know what you do to me, woman?" He heaved every breath. Working her. Grinding his erection against her. Relentless. Ruthless. Wonderful.

"The same thing you do to me?" Quaking, far from finished, Taliyah leaned forward, freeing her wings. With an expert spin, she faced him. Water splashed. The kiss resumed, hotter and more frenzied by the second.

He ground his length against her sensitive core. His flesh sizzled, branding her, and she cried out again, her need reaching new levels. Grinding. Grinding harder.

Desperation returned. The bliss! Her thoughts fractured. *More. More.*

Pressure built. "Just a little more." She chased her next orgasm. Never had she wanted like this. Never had she felt so empty.

I'll say no. I will. She just wanted...more.

He spun them both, pushing her against the back of the tub. Gripping one of her legs, just above her knee, he settled his full weight against her. All ferocity and wonder, he rotated his hips.

"Yes!" Taliyah clawed at his flesh, urging him on. "Like this." So good, so good, so good.

He whispered every wicked thing he planned to do to her body, driving her wild with lust. Each time he drew back to thrust against her again, he bent his head to lick or lightly bite her nipples. When he vibrated his fingers against her clit, she became incoherent, losing herself in the throes, the hot, sexual haze.

Strain contorted his features, any veneer of calm stripped away, his expression savage and primal with barely harnessed aggression.

He flashed her to the bed. Sweat beaded his brow as he stared down at her, heaving his breaths. "I want inside you."

His voice was…unrecognizable. A culmination of inconceivable arousal and unmitigated power, making mincemeat of her common sense. Because she wanted him inside her, too. Somehow, she resisted. "We—we can't."

He didn't try to change her mind, as part of her…hoped. With a growl, he claimed her mouth in another fierce kiss, thrusting his tongue against hers. Gentleness? He had none.

Caught up in the frenzy, Taliyah *needed* his aggression. The next time he ground against her, she lifted her hips to meet him. Greater pressure, greater pleasure. Greater torment.

The tempo of the kiss quickened. They devoured each other. He rolled his hips faster, his shaft gliding over her slick clitoris again and again. She rolled her hips in turn, meeting the sensual assault with one of her own. Their bodies mimicked the motions of sex, straining together. Desperate, so desperate, pleasure and pressure still building…

Any moment…

Yes! Taliyah exploded. Without thought, she bit the cord of his neck. The second her fangs pierced his flesh, he roared, jetting hot seed all over her belly. She clung to him through every white-hot lash, pure satisfaction pouring through her.

Let him go? No. Not now, not…ever?

29

Roc reclined in bed with Taliyah longer than he'd intended, loath to leave her. They'd calmed and cleaned up hours ago, and he had things to do. But his mind remained in torment.

Holding her like this, he thought he might prefer to die in her place. If only he had the option!

How could he ever dare to harm this woman?

He loved the feel of her, especially after he'd pleasured her well. Though not as well as he'd wanted. Multiple times, he'd had to remind himself of the blessing, of her dream to become General—of anything but sinking his shaft deep into her sex.

She yawned, and he kissed her temple.

"Go to sleep, Taya," he said, playing with her hair. She was draped over his chest, boneless and sated. "I'll keep you safe." He needed to brief and question his men about the latest battles. They must discuss the stones and what was soon to happen. Even still, Roc stayed put, content.

"Nah. I'm good." A second yawn nearly cracked her jaw, but still she held her eyes open.

He scoured a hand over his face, but said nothing else on the subject. Harpies only slept around their consorts. He knew that. What he wouldn't give to be that blessed male.

Could she ever accept him as such?

What have you done to earn such a position?

What *could* he do? He was a man tugged in two different directions. Duty versus duty. Love for his men versus…whatever he felt for his wife. Adoration? Definitely obsession. He couldn't get enough of the woman. But the duality of his desires left him fumbling, as evidenced by his torment. No longer could he rely on a once-prized possession: his resolve.

The events of the day had scrambled his thoughts. Nothing made sense anymore. Not his past. Not his present. Not his future. He owed protection and provision to his soldiers, but he also owed protection and provision to Taliyah. He had no desire to give her up in twenty-five days. Or ever. Could he even manage such a feat?

Guilt and shame collided as he recalled the terrible things he'd done and said to her only yesterday. The terrible things he'd done and said to Solar, all those centuries ago.

Solar had hungered for his siren bride with the same intensity Roc now hungered for his snarpy, yet Roc had—

"Shhh, shhh." Taliyah stroked his chest. "Everything will be all right."

He jolted, shaking the entire bed. Soothed by her words, her tone and her touch, he relaxed.

If they weren't going to sleep, they might as well chat to keep him out of his head. "Do you know the other phantom-harpy?" he asked softly, not wanting to rouse her defenses.

Strain emanated from her. A long while passed before she nodded, shocking him. "I do. She's my cousin. And my sister. Long story. But she *isn't* controlled by Erebus, either, so don't even think about reneging the orders to your men and harming her."

Such loyalty. His admiration for it, for her, only expanded. Could she ever feel so fervently for Roc? He longed for such a time.

The fact that she'd shared so much with him, well, Taliyah must be as confused as Roc. The realization helped settle him further. At least he wasn't in this alone. "Trust me, Taya. I've learned my lesson. I have come to believe there are two kinds of phantoms. I won't harm those like you, unless attacked. You have my word."

Her sigh fanned over the ridges of his stomach. "There you go again, saying sweet, sexy things."

"You've searched for her with the crystal?"

"Yes, but I haven't found her."

"If she exited Roux, as he suspects, she didn't do it here. We would have found her already."

"I know, but I must complete my search. She has a daughter, and she wouldn't leave the girl behind. And for all we know, there are other harpy-phantoms I know nothing about. Although…"

"What? You can ask me anything."

"What if Blythe hasn't…moved out?"

He stroked his beard, pensive. "It isn't probable. If she's as indomitable as you, however, it's possible. Before we go poking around in Roux's head, let's scour the entire palace and market. If she's sleeping in the duplicate, we'll find her."

A pause. An inhalation. "Okay, yes. You can help me with my search."

Roc felt his chest swell with pride. She was choosing to trust him with more. *I must be her consort.*

If ever she accepted him as such, he would…what? Promise not to slay her when the time came?

Agitated, he scoured his free hand down his face.

She petted his chest the way he loved. "You need to speak with your men about what happened in the garden, yeah?"

"I do." Among other things. Less than an hour ago, Roc had almost claimed Taliyah's virginity. A welcome and horrifying admission, but there it was. The truth was unalterable and undeniable. Had she given permission, he would've breached the barrier and come inside her with no thought to the blessing or his men.

A mistake he couldn't make a second time. Because he would slip again. He knew this. Why deny it? One day, Taliyah might say yes.

No virginity, no General. *If* she lived past the month.

A barbed lump grew in his throat.

"Uh-oh. I sense some drama coming on," Taliyah said, before kissing the pulse at the base of his throat. "What's this about?"

"My men aren't going to be happy with me." But he wouldn't stop this. He must prepare for *every* eventuality, even sex with his *gravita*.

"Well, go get the conversation over with. I'm staying here to practice removing my ring. Any protests about leaving me on my own?" she asked, lifting her head to meet his gaze.

"No protests." Never again. "But I hate the thought of you in pain."

A relieved, teasing smile lit her face as she sat up. "Are you sure you don't like me in pain? Because I specifically remember a time when you held my wrist and—"

"We don't talk about that moment in history," he interjected, guilt and shame colliding again.

"Uh, that doesn't sound true at all." Those ocean-water blues glittered down at him. "I defeated you that day. I'm going to brag *forever*."

Minx.

"Are you sure you want to forgo the ring before the month's

end? If we're attacked again and you're incapacitated..." If she were gravely injured, unable to protect herself...

"I'm sure." Seemingly timid, she asked, "Are you afraid you won't desire me anymore if I remove the ring and you ice over?"

Roc came up fast, pressing a swift kiss into her soft lips. "I enjoy everything you do to me." Even that. He got to melt them both. "Will you feed before I head out?"

"No. I probably won't feed later, either."

He sighed and forced himself to rise to dress before he gave in to the urge to flip her over and feast, tempting her to do what he wanted.

After donning a clean pair of pants and boots, he weaponed up, then returned to the bed. He smoothed a lock of silvery hair from Taliyah's brow. With the touch, slight though it was, a rosy shade spread over her skin.

Perhaps crawling back into bed— No! "I'll be thinking of you while I'm gone," he admitted. "Will you be thinking of me?"

She wrinkled her nose the way he liked. But then, he was beginning to suspect he liked everything about her. "Roc, darling. I'm going to be screaming. Of course I'll think of you."

He almost grinned. There was none braver or more resilient than his woman.

Pride straightened his spine and puffed his chest as he flashed to the throne room and eased onto the cathedra. He broadcast a message to his men, even those in the duplicate realm. Only two would be left out.

—*Vasili, watch the wall in the duplicate realm. Ian, watch the wall here. The rest of you assemble in the throne room now.*—

Silver and Halo appeared first. Then Sparrow, the Peace-maker. Bleu, the Spymaster. Azar, the Memory-keeper. Roux materialized last, his red-rimmed gaze clear.

Could the other phantom be in there, as Taliyah suspected? Everything Roc knew of Astra and phantoms told him *no*. But he understood so little about Taliyah and her kind.

He looked over the rest of his men. None appeared confused by the summons. A few evinced concern. Most revealed dread. Only Halo conveyed anger. Roc's second feared a repeat of the past, with good reason.

Despite their array of emotions, no one spoke. The honor of beginning the conversation fell to the Commander, and they awaited his first words. He suspected they cared more about the problem of Taliyah than Erebus's stone.

Very well. "Long ago, Solar refused to sacrifice his bride. Each of you witnessed my response to his failure." Roc pounded a fist against the patch of bare skin above his heart. With his next words, he gave voice to the worst memory inside a head filled with countless wars, cold-blooded murders, vicious deeds and vile decisions. "I killed his bride. I'm also responsible for the death of Commander Solar himself. But even still, I was too late to stop the curse. We were condemned to five hundred years of defeat."

No one moved an inch.

"I want to be with Taliyah," he announced. "If she'll have me, I will be with her. In every way." Let there be no mistaking his meaning.

When many of the men opened their mouths, he raised a fist. A bid for silence. Lips sealed shut, warriors awaiting his words.

He nodded in acknowledgment of their restraint. "I know if I do this, we'll lose the weapon and Erebus will gain it, as he gained the Blade of Destiny. That's why I seek a unanimous agreement from you first. In return, I'll willingly accept…the last rank." His decision solidified. "I won't challenge Commander Halo for five hundred years." He would do this. He would exchange less for more—for Taliyah.

Halo's anger dissipated, replaced by bafflement. "You want her that badly?"

If the way inside Taliyah Skyhawk was five hundred years as this man's errand boy, so be it. A small price to pay. "I do."

His second-in-command assumed a battle stance. "In twenty-five days, you'll do your duty? You won't hesitate to slay the phantom?"

He...couldn't answer that question honestly. Because he didn't know. What he *could* promise? "I will always do what I believe is right."

"A phantom is worth this?" Silver asked.

"This one is." Taliyah was so much more *everything* than Roc had ever expected for his *gravita*. Matching wits with her wily mind was a drug. Her unshakable will astounded and humbled him. He was never not aware of her scent and taste. Every time he warmed her, he thrilled. The mere thought of her ignited a fire that burned through his control in record time.

She had done the impossible. She had brought the most powerful Commander in existence to his knees. And he was willing to stay there.

"So I ask you," Roc said. "Who agrees?"

Taliyah gave herself a grand total of two minutes to remember the ferocity Roc had displayed when he'd wanted inside her... to lament and relish her cracking resistance to him.

Would she have the strength to refuse his advances a second time? Part of her still tingled from his touch, reckless for more.

Only part? She laughed without humor.

She'd have to be more careful going forward. Right? She shouldn't give her virginity to him, ruining her dreams. But... why couldn't a General have a man? Why, why, why?

When the two minutes ended, she booted the Astra from her head. War was afoot, and she must be at her best. So, she would train as she had always trained. Lots of pain, lots of gain.

Abandoning the warmth of the bed and the haze of Roc's scent at long last, she bounded to her room to dress in battle gear, boots and weapons. From now on, she would practice without the ring a minimum of three times a day. She'd start with a minute. Quick and easy. A confidence booster.

Decided, she grabbed the stopwatch she'd found in a nightstand. It belonged to General Nissa's sister, who'd stayed in the room before Taliyah.

Once she discovered a way to save everyone, she might turn the room into a gym.

With the thought, supposition became plans etched in stone. Yeah, she was going to do it. Not the gym, but the saving. She would save *everyone*. Find a way to be with Roc, salvaging their relationship for however long. Circumvent the curse over him and his men. Free her harpies. Avoid hibernation.

The tasks mounted, the stakes critical. But when had she ever shrunk from a challenge? There would be no more weddings. No more sacrifices. No more blessings or curses. There was a way; there was always a way. You just had to find it.

As Taliyah moved to a spot clear of furniture, her stomach churned. Inhale. Exhale. A familiar pep talk rang inside her head. The one she'd chanted every day at harpy camp, as she'd learned to kill her foes more efficiently.

She glanced down at the ring and gulped. *Do it. Do it now. What are you waiting for, Terror? Do it! Dooo it.*

Taliyah did it. She activated the stopwatch...and removed the ring. Immediately the screams tore through her ears at full volume. Pain engulfed her, so much pain. Excruciating. All-consuming. Warmth poured from her eyes. Her vision blurred.

A minute might've been too ambitious. She squeezed her eyes shut and clamped her hands over her ears, the ring slipping from her grip. "No!" Taliyah dropped to her knees and blindly patted the floor. "Make it stop, make it stop!"

Where was the ring? Where? No, no, no. A scream barreled up, but she swallowed it. If she screamed, Roc could come. If Roc came, training would end. Something cold grazed her fingers. There! She snatched it up and, with a trembling grip, shoved the band into place.

Silence arrived, and she sagged against the floor, blindly patting for the stopwatch. Thirty-three seconds.

Tears of frustration gathered. Thirty-three might as well be thirty, and thirty might as well be zero. Not good enough!

She banged her fist into the floor. Why did she hear those screams? Why didn't Blythe? Where did the screams even come from? Every phantom in every world, as she'd always imagined?

With a screech, she sat upright. *Never accept a picture of defeat.*

Taliyah reset the timer. She hadn't lied to Roc. The phantoms had worked her over today. She'd stood no chance against them. An intolerable outcome, since she would be fighting many other phantoms soon. Probably even Erebus himself. So, she would remove the ring once more—and go *two* minutes.

She climbed to unsteady legs and jutted her chin. The wife of the Astra Commander was the future harpy General. Two titles without equal. She would do this.

Nothing would stop her.

30

The search for Blythe and Isla proved disappointing and un-eventful. For hour upon hour, Taliyah glimpsed faces through the crystal. She saw women she knew and those she didn't, but not her sister or niece. They *must* have gotten away, but oh, what she wouldn't give for proof. At least the other harpies had healed from their injuries. They slept peacefully, even comfortably, on cots the Astra provided.

As she and Roc wound through the empty streets to return to the palace, she glimpsed a patrol unit marching by.

"Don't worry. I'll arrange a meeting with Roux," Roc said. He had remained at her side the entire day, not to keep tabs on her but to shield and protect. To comfort and encourage. The difference in him, in his treatment of her, left her reeling. The monster she'd sworn to kill had become a…friend?

"Thank you," she said.

"I'll also send spies to search Nova, with orders not to harm her."

"That's a sweet offer, but Blythe will view your men as enemies. There *will* be a fight, and someone *will* die."

"Even if they bear a message from you?"

"Maybe even then." Roc looked good today. Well, he always looked good, but he looked *really* good right now. He exuded no animosity or malice. Only contentment. Despite the cooler weather, he'd opted to go without a shirt—of course—donning only leathers. A fashion choice she gave five orgasmic stars.

At the moment, she kinda matched him. She wore a barely-there halter, her wings wonderfully free, and a pair of leathers, with thin, lightweight pieces of armor strapped to each of her limbs.

He clasped her hand, drawing her to a stop when they reached the heart of the courtyard, where the most famous landmark in all of Harpina grew. The Tree of Skulls.

"Let's not hasten to the palace just yet," he said, surprising her. "If Blythe *is* inside Roux, she's safe. I'd like to hear about Harpina—your Harpina. Tell me what it's like as if I've never before visited. Take me to your favorite places. Let me view the world through your eyes."

"Like we're on a date or something?" Taliyah had never actually gone on a date. To grant the first one to this smoldering mountain of a man... *Yes, please!* "All right. Fine," she said, and he grinned. "You talked me into it."

For just a little while, they could pretend. He was a normal man, and she was a normal woman, every mystery between them revealed. There was no curse or sacrifice, only admiration and desire.

"You picked a good place to start." She motioned to the Tree of Skulls. The enormous structure was wider and taller than many skyscrapers in the mortal world, blooming with red flowers shaped like, well, skulls.

Usually countless harpies gathered here to carve the names of slain enemies into the trunk. A beloved tradition. Afterward, carvers enjoyed a day of shopping and pampering with friends. Nearby retailers offered everything from coffee to vibrators.

He brought her hand to his mouth and kissed her knuckles, making her knees go weak. "Tell me all about it."

Though she hated to sever contact, she released him to climb the tree, perch in one of the branches and dangle her legs from the side. Well, well. At this height, she had a full view of him and all his tattooed goodness.

Gorgeous warlord. His hair had grown some, giving him the same boyish air she'd noticed the night she'd sneaked into his room. He seemed lighter, as if his mantle of discipline no longer proved such a heavy burden to bear.

This morning, he'd removed the *alevala* over his heart, just as he'd done every other morning, but this time he'd let her inside the stall while he did it. She'd asked a million questions, but he'd answered none of them. Out of respect for him, she hadn't glanced at the image when it landed on the floor fully intact. He'd tell her when he was ready. Just like she'd tell him about Erebus when she was ready.

Foreboding prickled the back of her neck. Would either secret tear them apart?

"Soon," she said, forging ahead, "these flowers will become bloodfruit." A tasty citrus with a soft pink skin and a pulpy crimson center, which acted as medicine to harpies no longer able to consume blood because they'd lost their consort or—

The thought skidded to a halt. Harpies who'd found their consorts lost the ability to drink blood from anyone else. When they tried, they vomited. Taliyah had vomited soul after feeding on the berserker. Because she'd already met her consort? Could she consume blood and soul only from her consort now?

She wheezed her next breath, the next question stinging. Had she already met her consort?

"Taya?" he asked.

With great effort, she shook off her concerns. No worries.

Not today. This was her first date, and she wouldn't ruin it with suppositions about lifelong mates.

She plucked a bloom and tossed it his way. "Erebus and Asclepius slaughtered thousands of harpies here. The tree grew from the blood-soaked ground."

"A rebirth of sorts," he said, smelling the petals.

Yes. Very much so. She liked that he understood the importance the tree represented to her people, and to her.

A mix of hot and cold wind blew through the area, and he frowned. "I must admit, I've never gotten used to the seasons of Harpina."

"No one has." There were eighteen seasons in total. Winter, Fool's Autumn, Fifth Winter, First Spring, Spring of Indifference, Hurricane, Tornado, Third Spring, Pre-Summer, Summer, Mid-Summer, True Autumn, Post-Summer, Second Winter, Third Winter of Fall, Fourth Winter of Spring, Final Summer and All Seasons Day, which lasted six weeks, except in August and never on Sundays. "As a girl," she said, patting the limb, "I called this my thinking spot."

Interest perked him up. "And what did Little Taliyah ponder?"

Pulling her legs up, crouching, she admitted, "She pondered running away." A secret she'd never shared with another.

Roc did a double take. "She did? Why?"

Shrug. "I was fifteen, and I'd just come home from a successful vampire raid—they'd taken some of our girls to feed on, and we slaughtered them all. I had a history paper due the next morning, so I came here to figure out a topic when suddenly I got hit with a tsunami of panic. Was this going to be my life? Killing, losing friends in battle, then coming home and acting as if nothing had happened? The expected temperament for a General. At the time, my future seemed…too much. I contemplated running somewhere no one knew me. To just…be."

He listened, hanging on every word. "What changed your mind and kept you here?"

"Family." She leaped onto a higher branch. "I have baby sisters. The twins were five at the time. At ten, they were to be sent to Harpy Camp to learn to fight, just like I was. The wrong leader takes people down the wrong path. If something happened to my loved ones because I refused to do my duty—to fulfill my destiny...I would never forgive myself."

"A selfless leader, even then." Paling slightly, he asked, "Being General is your destiny? You're sure of this?"

"I am." *And your dissatisfaction? What of that?* "I was born to rule."

Can't have the crown and the man. You know this.

"I must have been...right?" she asked.

Appearing distressed, he said, "You are the only one with the answer."

Well, he wasn't wrong about that. "What was fifteen-year-old Roc like?"

He held up his arms, and she willingly jumped from the branch. Catching her by the waist, he eased her to her feet. As her body grazed his, a moan lodged in her throat.

Hands sliding over her, eyes twin flames of gold, he said, "Fifteen-year-old Roc was training in a sightless, soundless void, dreaming of a time he would meet his *gravita.*"

And now you have her.

He had a family. A wife he had yet to claim. He *needed* to claim her.

His talk with his men had gone better than expected. For a higher rank, each male had agreed to relinquish the weapon prize. All but Ian...at first. His reason had astonished Roc.

You will make a terrible ninth, Roc. I don't want that for you. But I don't want you without your gravita, *either. So I'll do this. I'll agree. Let's hope you never come to regret it.*

Though Roc yearned to kiss Taliyah in the glow of sunlight,

he merely took her hand and led her toward the empty shops. "I'd like to speak with you about something important, Taliyah."

He'd hoped to wait for the most opportune moment to bring this up. As she'd shared tales from her childhood, however, fear took root inside him. Why not do this now? She deserved to make the choice; he had no right to make it for her by keeping quiet. Because she couldn't make a choice without options.

"Uh-oh. You used my name." As they strolled, she rested her head on his shoulder. A perfect fit. "All right. What's up?"

"I have a confession." *Here goes.* "I don't need to sacrifice a virgin, only a bride. By sacrificing a virgin, I receive a special weapon on top of the blessing. If the bride isn't a virgin, Erebus receives the weapon instead."

She yanked her hand from his and glared up at him. "You've got to be kidding me. You've been running a side hustle all this time?"

"Not on purpose." *Messing this up.*

They'd reached the Well of Wanting, and he took a moment to center his thoughts. Harpies used to come here to make a wish and toss a coin into the water. Some of those harpies received their wish. Most received a warped version of it. None had ever known what they would get until it was too late.

He almost tossed in a coin and requested a do-over with Taliyah. How could things start off worse?

"Have you ever tossed in a coin?" he asked.

"Once," she admitted. "I requested a new sword, and I got it. Right through the gut. But we're not talking about that. I'm not over your confession. You let your other brides try to seduce you, hoping to save themselves from death?"

He bristled at that. "I did, and I won't carry guilt for it. Before the wedding, I told them I couldn't be seduced. Is it my fault they chose not to believe me?"

"You could have told them sex wasn't a lifesaver."

"Should a Commander *ever* explain his thoughts to a foe?"

"Are they really a foe or a means to an end?"

"They get my army if they succeed. They are foes."

She sputtered for a moment, pointing a finger in his face, then retreating, only to get in his face again. "I hate when you make sense."

The fire in his blood died. "I'll never understand you, will I?"

"Probably not." With a sigh, she deflated. "Why are you telling *me* this? I'm your foe."

"You know you're more. You know I desire you," he told her, suddenly hoarse. "I want to be with you. I crave you more than I've ever craved anything. I need to save you, if there's a way. I yearn to save you, even if there isn't. I'm willing to give up the weapon for you. I just want you."

The rest of her anger dissipated, leaving a conflicted female with troubled ocean-water eyes. "My virginity and future in exchange for a weapon?"

"That isn't… I'm messing this up worse than I imagined."

"Wrong. The *truth* is messing everything up. I suppose I should be flattered. You desire, want, crave, need and yearn for a disgusting phantom."

"You are *not* disgusting," he burst out. "The problem was never you. The problem always lay with me."

Bit by bit, she softened. "I admit I want you, too. Okay? Does that make you happy? But," she added, "I won't rewrite my dreams. I will be General."

"Of that I have no doubt."

Pleased with his confidence, she wound her arm around his, snuggling into his side and nuzzling against him for warmth. They resumed their trek.

"How can I be with you *and* be General? All other Generals had possessed the strength to say no to the men they'd wanted."

"That isn't true. Your General Nissa wasn't a virgin."

"How do you even know that unless… Is there something else you need to confess, Roc?" She gritted out the question.

Sheepish, he told her, "She slept with Ian, often. He approached her before our invasion. She wasn't a virgin the first time."

"Nissa and Ian... My world is suddenly topsy-turvy. But this just reinforces a General's need to stay away from horny men."

"A friend is just as likely to betray a General as a lover. Why not have both?"

"Argh! I mean it, Roc. Stop being logical."

"How can anyone be General when there's no General to fight?" he said, pressing. No topic had ever meant more. "An acting General must take the reins before a new General can be named a new way. Why must the new leader be a virgin?"

"Because...because...tradition!" she shouted, as if the word carried significant weight.

"What if some traditions are unfounded? How many other Generals allowed the present and the future to eclipse the past?"

"And if you forgo the tradition of the ceremony?" she quipped.

He heaved a breath. "What's the purpose of this particular tradition?"

"The General gives her body to her people," she grumbled as she calmed.

That, at least, he knew how to counter. "I give myself to my men without denying my body's needs. Why can't you? Why can't there be a new breed of General? A new regime with modern laws?"

Her claws embedded in his bicep. "I should risk everything for the man who will kill me in twenty-four days? And you do plan to kill me, if you can't find a way to save your men. Do you deny it?"

Desperation shredded his mask of calm, until he felt as if he chewed on glass. He couldn't offer her reassurance because he didn't know what he'd do at the appointed time. "I'll do everything in my power to save everyone involved. I won't stop until I've found a way."

"I...need to think about this," she said, and it was a better response than he'd expected. "You know what really sucks, though? I'm sacrificing a dream. You're sacrificing a dumb weapon."

He wouldn't tell her about his deal with the others. Wouldn't add that kind of pressure to her.

They entered a part of town known as the Green Light District. According to flashing neon signs, *Anything goes!* Karaoke bars abounded. So did happy-ending massage parlors, where patrons punched their attendant. The harpy version of a happy ending.

As they rounded a corner, ice glazed his arms, and he cursed. Phantoms.

Roc withdrew two three-blades. Taliyah reacted to his sudden aggression and palmed daggers. Together, they halted.

There, at the far end of the street, congregated at least fifty fiends. All were females dressed in widow's weeds, of course, sporting a firstone necklace to prevent the Astra from flashing.

His ears twitched, and he homed in, listening more intently. The phantoms chanted, "Go to town, walk around, tell the girl. Go to town, walk around, tell the girl."

So. Erebus had a message for Taliyah. What would it be? What could the god say to incite more misery?

"Stay here," he commanded, summoning posts to lock the phantoms in place. He stepped forward.

"Oh, no, no, no." Taliyah jumped into his path. "That isn't how this is going to work. This is the perfect practice herd to bone up my skills. *I'm* doing the killing."

This idea he liked. The more prepared she was for the next attacks, the safer she'd be. He slapped the hilt of a three-blade into her palm, saying, "Don't stab yourself."

She flipped him off as they strode forward side by side. "Trust me, I know the effects of trinite. A shot to the heart is supposed to kill me for good. Having fought the other herd, however, I'm skeptical. I shouldn't die like other phantoms. I'm…me. And I've recovered from a thousand other things."

"Is this how you focus on a fight? Get your mind on your job—staying alive."

"Sir, yes, sir." She offered a jaunty salute, only appearing halfway mocking. So, he'd clearly made progress. "Let's skip 101, and go straight to the advanced class. Any tips for the teacher's pet?"

Hundreds. But few involved the battle. "If a phantom disembodies to avoid your strike, don't change your position. It—she is coming closer. Keep stabbing."

"Or I could disembody with her and take her down in spirit form? It's a skill I've always hidden. Maybe it's time I show off. It's worth a shot, anyway." Taliyah bounded over before he had a chance to respond.

She delivered a flawless first strike, hitting her mark: a straight shot to the heart. As the phantom dropped, Taliyah spun, coming up behind the next one, three-blade already in motion. Contact. The second phantom dropped, beginning the process of evaporation.

The others sensed her and halted. Quieted. In unison, they pivoted toward her to relay their message. "Will you truly ruin your dreams for the man planning to kill you, Taliyah Skyhawk?"

Hate Erebus. Hate the Blade of Destiny.

Ready to feed, the phantoms attacked her in unison. Taliyah stutter-stepped before going low, avoiding their grasping hands. There was a thoughtful glaze in her eyes, the wheels in her mind obviously turning. She pulled her next strike, and the next, working her way behind a phantom.

He frowned. Why did she do this?

Roc rolled his weight onto his heels, preparing to launch forward and offer aid.

"I think they're harpies," she called. "I might be seeing wings under those dresses." Blink. She vanished, not flashing but misting to escape a tangle of arms and legs. Blink. She reappeared behind the farthest fiend, away from the others, and ripped the back of her gown.

Taliyah froze and gasped, allowing two phantoms to ghost closer. Embodying, they crashed into her. She let them. Because of their origins, she'd stopped playing offense.

"They are! Let's capture and confine them," she called. Because of course she did.

"Never tell me I do nothing for you, wife," he grumbled and made his way over.

31

Days passed. Ten of them, actually. To Taliyah's surprise and appreciation, Roc kept his word and allowed her to meet with Roux. Though she'd questioned him, slapped him around and shouted to Blythe, her sister had made no attempt to communicate. Maybe she *wasn't* in there.

Afterward, she'd retreated to the bedroom and fell into Roc's arms, forgetting her disappointment for a little while.

To her added surprise and appreciation, he never pressured her for sex. As he waited for her to render a decision, day by day, hour after hour, he never mentioned the possibility again.

Did his mood darken while he waited? *Oh, baby.* Dark only scratched the surface.

At first, all went well. Each morning, they woke and bathed together. He removed his *alevala*, asked if she wanted to feed, and when she declined, he pouted but said nothing else as they dressed and headed off to accomplish their respective tasks. In the evenings, when they came together again, they acted like long-lost loves who'd finally found each other. Orgasms abounded. She *might* have giggled again, without his soul or his seed.

Each of those ten days, he labored over the altar for several hours. He labored on it even now. Did she understand the need to do so? Definitely. At the appointed moment, *some* kind of sacrifice had to take place. But oh, wow, she resented his job, too. And as *her* mood darkened, his got worse.

He'd kept his word and sent his best spies to study sacrifices, loopholes, blessings and curses. He'd left Harpina to meet with other gods. He'd called in favors and chased every possible lead. He'd even requested a meeting with Chaos.

The god had yet to respond. Taliyah had gone ahead and requested a meeting, too. Because why not? She'd been ignored just as soundly.

She spent her days ravaging the palace library, determined to do her own research. She focused on the same topics as the spies, but she also added Chaos, Erebus and his twin brother, phantoms, Astra, and harpy traditions into the mix. Not that it had done any good. So far, she'd made no progress.

Still, she treated each new piece of information like a big, juicy soul and *devoured*. And yeah, okay, so she might be a wee bit hungry again. Nothing critical. Not yet. Just a few minor pangs. In the shower this morning, she'd almost asked Roc for a top off, but she'd quickly changed her mind.

He'd woken up with a hard-on and a major attitude. The worst so far. "I really need to kill someone today," he'd grumbled as he dressed.

"I can give you a list of candidates," she'd offered helpfully. She kept multiple lists drafted and at the ready. People to kill. People to torture before she killed them. People to consider torturing or killing. Just the basics, really.

"If Hades doesn't have the number-one spot," he'd snarled, "I don't need to see it."

A sweet thing to say, right? Until he'd added, "Why is having a *gravita* so difficult?"

Did he think he'd be better off without her?

Last night, Roc had lain on his side of the bed, and she'd lain on hers, each facing a different wall, a great divide between them. For the first time since their date, neither had reached for the other.

Did he fear they were going to fail at crunch time? She had to admit, holding on to her optimism required a Herculean effort. The struggle was compounded by her refusal to sleep. Oh, she'd caught herself drifting off a couple of times, lured by the sweet scent of Roc's stardust and the heat emitted by his furnace of a body, but Taliyah had continued to resist the urge.

If Roc was her consort—and she dared to admit it—she might do as Blythe and abandon her dreams. Already temptation whispered, *Enjoy the moment.*

Choose a temporary pleasure over a future dream? Foolishness! But what if Roc was right? What if they could have everything they wanted? Roc, free of the curse. Taliyah, leading a new, modern regime as harpy General.

What if they couldn't? *No closer to a solution.*

Bottom line: Taliyah and Roc had no business being together. If he spared her life, they were doomed. If he didn't spare her life, they were doomed. If she saved herself, they were doomed. If she didn't save herself, they were doomed. And yet...

Still she hungered for him. Desperately. Her dissatisfaction had returned with a vengeance. Even the nights Roc filled her with his fingers and loved her with his mouth, she felt empty.

With increasing desperation, she yearned to say yes to his possession. But how could she? Her people needed her more than ever.

Nissa had lied to everyone. Warriors and hard workers who deserved only candor. How many other Generals had done the same? Taliyah vowed to never lie or mislead her harpies *ever.*

Sacrifice their happiness for her own? No. She would fight for what was right, and she would *never* accept a picture of defeat for them.

What other contender for General could say the same?

But.

Was denying Roc what he craved, what *she* craved, an admission of defeat?

With a grunt of disgust, she closed the book she was not really reading and stood. She headed to the dungeon to check on both her harpies and her phantoms.

Though it had left them exhausted, Taliyah and Roc had corralled the phantoms she'd fought. Well, the harphantoms. They now wore cuffs, as Taliyah once had, to prevent them from disembodying.

With three harphantoms per cell and new members added every day, the dungeon bustled with activity.

As Taliyah passed, old and new harphantoms did their best to fit their bound hands through the bars. Any messages had been delivered, the women able and eager to feed.

Roux stood guard near the harpies, staring her down as she approached. In front of him, she held his gaze, new hope stirring, but…no. Again, she found no sign of Blythe. Where had her sister gone?

He said nothing. Neither did she.

Taliyah pivoted, relocating the bulk of her attention to a new captive. Someone she recognized from drawings in history books. An infamous warrior named Dove who'd once fought alongside Tabitha Skyhawk, counted among the number to die by Erebus's hand.

Another of Taliyah's research projects: find a way to fix the harphantoms. If father had broken them, surely daughter could patch them.

"Hello," she said with a gentle tone. As always, the harphantom paid her no heed. "I'd like to help you. Soon, Roc will cave, and you'll dine on immortals." Truth. So far he'd refused, unwilling to give anyone under Erebus's control added strength. Which was understandable. She kept pushing anyway.

Nothing. No flicker of intelligence inside Dove's milky eyes.

"T-bomb," the harpy named Athena called. Miss Four-stars herself. Taliyah had finally learned everyone's names. "We demand to speak with your manager. Our new neighbors *suck*."

"I'm working on it," she vowed. And she was. Harpies could assist Roc with his war, if only he'd let them. She'd revisited the topic twice, but he had yet to soften.

"You think you can fix these phantoms," Roux said, speaking up for the first time. "You are wrong."

She knew his words conveyed a double meaning. *You cannot fix yourself, either.*

"Roux," she said, turning away. She glanced at him over her shoulder. "I wouldn't bet against me. I tamed the Commander of the Astra. I can do anything." Maintaining a sedate pace, she left him stewing.

Do you truly believe that? She must. The alternative was intolerable.

Taliyah stalked to the master suite, where she crouched on the balcony railing to watch Roc. A chilly wind blew her hair around her face, and she shivered. Another storm brewed in the distance, approaching steadily. The sky had already turned a deep gray.

Energy charged the air as the Commander chiseled at a furious pace. Any vestiges of civility had been removed from his features. He was a man overcome by frustration, strain and anger, his control in tatters.

The steps were complete, the platform set. Only the altar remained. Already he had repaired the cracks he'd caused in the midst of *anhilla*. Huh. Maybe the deepest, most primal part of him considered the meteorite an enemy?

An acute pang left her panting.

Lightning flashed, and for a moment, Roc looked like a possessed man battling all his inner demons at once. Her heart raced, desire for him surging, never far from the surface. She longed for him, all of him. She *always* longed for him. Taliyah coveted every experience life offered, nothing held back. But...

But what? *Never accept a picture of defeat.*

The mantra beat through her head, unleashing a new flood of righteous indignation. Why *couldn't* she have everything she wanted? Just because she didn't have solutions for her problems didn't mean those solutions didn't exist. The problems were not insurmountable. Nothing was.

If she fought hard enough, she *could* forge a new army of harpies. And she should!

Want something different, do something different.

This was an opportunity for harpies to choose their own futures. To stick with the old ways, what they knew, or reset with different—better—rules. They knew what aided, and what hurt. Those who decided to follow her could. Those who opted out shouldn't. She could rule her own army *and* have her man. Her...consort.

The truth infiltrated every cell, and she could deny it no longer. Roc Phaethon was her consort, her man, and she thought she might be falling in love with him. The unshakable warlord who shook from bad dreams and his woman's touch. The Commander who'd always craved a family of his own.

Satisfaction took root inside her, no longer a fleeting thing but a permanent part of her makeup. It grew and grew, internal cracks quickly filling, broken things mending.

This was her path. She knew it was. Never had she been so certain.

She and Roc were only doomed if they gave up.

Thunder cracked, pulling her from her thoughts, and more lightning flashed. Taliyah straightened, perfectly balanced on the rail as wind danced her hair around her face.

Roc had ceased chiseling. He leaned his head into his hands. A position of agony. Of despair. As much as she needed him, he needed her. She *required* this man, and she would have him.

Decision made.

There was no need to worry about a possible pregnancy: harpies were only fertile at certain times. The only question now? Tell him about Erebus before or after?

The man she'd grown to admire wouldn't fault her for her parentage. He just...wouldn't. But either way, he deserved to know before they took this final step together.

Why wait? She wore a halter and pleated skirt; she was ready for war. No matter her foe.

Though she battled apprehension, Taliyah stepped from the railing, falling, falling, landing in a crouch. The time had come.

Roc sensed Taliyah's presence. He always sensed her presence. He always wanted her and he always needed her, and he'd grown to hate himself for it. Asking her to abandon her dreams had been wrong. Especially when he'd found no way to circumvent the curse. No way to escape this living nightmare.

The more time he spent with the woman, the more he liked her. The more he liked her, the more hopeless their situation seemed. And he had no one to blame but himself.

He remembered how confident he'd been with Chaos. *I will kill her.*

How could he *ever* bring himself to kill her?

Keeping his back to her, he called, "This isn't a good time, Taliyah." The past few days, Erebus's message to her had played on constant repeat in Roc's head. *Give up her dream.* And for what?

"I don't care. I will have you. All of you. I'm done waiting."

What? Roc whipped around, the tool falling from his hand. The next flash of lightning revealed a harpy warrior with oceanwater eyes set aflame. "All?" *No. Pick up your tool. Turn around.*

Do your work. Don't make her choose between her future and yours.
Let her grow to hate him? No. Then he'd hate *himself* more.

"All," Taliyah confirmed. "But you gotta take all of me, too."
She shifted, as if uncomfortable. "I...I'm ready to tell you my
connection to Erebus."

In his chest, old cracks spread, creating new ones. Since
their date, they'd spoken only of innocent things. Moments in
their pasts, teases and taunts. "You can tell me," he assured her.
Whatever she said, he wouldn't care. Nothing mattered but the
woman herself. A woman who demanded her right to him...

Am I truly to have her? "Tell me."

"He...he's my father. He possessed his brother, and they were
with my mother. Together. They're both my fathers. It's complicated. The reality is confusing but true."

"Possession," he said, with a nod. He should have guessed.
The brothers had always been close. But this meant... Roc went
rigid. Chaos had willingly sacrificed his own granddaughter.

The father who had refused to abandon his son, no matter
the vileness of his crimes... The mentor who had refused to
pick between his son and his guards... The god Roc had faith-
fully served for eons had thrown his own family to the wolves.

If he could do such a thing to the indomitable Taliyah, what
would he do to the Astra?

"I promise I'm not working with him," she said in a rush.
"I've only spoken to him once, and you already know what we
discussed."

"I trust you, Taliyah." He fought hard to temper his rage,
lest she mistake the source. "We aren't our parents. I despise
my own."

"So..." She glanced at him through the thick shield of her
lashes, almost shy. "You still wish to be with me?"

"I want to be with you more than anything." He took a step
toward her, then stopped. "But your dream..." How could he

steal it from her? How? "I never should have asked you for this. I've taken so much already. I can't take this, too."

"You're not taking anything. I'm giving. And I'm going to be harpy General. I've decided I can bed whomever I please."

His chest threatened to burst. *Magnificent female. No lovelier sight.*

Nothing could stop Roc from closing the distance. The moment he reached her, he clamped her by the nape and waist and yanked her against him. As she gasped, he fused his mouth to hers.

What the—

Roc had let his beast out of its mental cage, and Taliyah loved it. For a moment, she stood stunned as he kissed her; she was defenseless against the frenzied, sensual onslaught. He was a starving man who'd finally stumbled upon a meal.

As lightning flashed and thunder boomed, she gave herself fully to the kiss. To Roc. They devoured each other, exchanging breaths. When the first raindrops fell, splashing against their hot skin, she lost all control.

With one hand, she sank the tips of her claws into his scalp. With the other, she tore at his belt until his rock-hard shaft filled her hand. He hissed. She moaned.

"I've been without you too long." He picked her up and flashed her to their bedroom, easing her upon the bed.

He kissed her hard, harder, kneading and plumping her breasts. Beneath the fabric, her nipples puckered. Her next inhalation sent an arc of pleasure from piercing to her core.

"Roc!"

He ripped her top, shredding the garment as easily as paper. Her skirt fared no better. When she lay naked beneath him, he wrenched from the kiss to lift to his knees and admire what he'd bared. His fierce gaze worshipped every inch of her, and she fought a moan.

Being nude while he still wore his pants acted as a titillating aphrodisiac. She shivered, her airways thickening.

He cupped and tugged his testicles before stroking his length with languid ferocity.

There was no stopping her next moan.

"Is this what you crave?" he rasped.

"Every inch."

His pupils pulsed. "Never has there been a lovelier wife. And you're mine. Only, ever mine."

He leaned over, flicking a stiffened tongue against the bit of metal. As she gasped and writhed, he glided his hand up her inner thigh.

As he penetrated her with two fingers, never relinquishing his languid pace, his intensity remained barely banked, different muscles quivering. Taliyah nearly came, the sensations maddening.

"My Taya is soaked already." He pressed the pad of his thumb against her clit and thrust his fingers with more force.

Another gasp, this one ragged. Another moan, the herald for a hundred others. The pleasure he elicited... Her mind shut down gradually, one light going out at a time, until a single thought remained: *more*.

"More, more, more." Never had she been so greedy for it.

He sucked the piercing harder, her every pulse point pounding, pounding. The constant rubbing and thrusting and sucking pushed her to the edge faster and faster until—

Taliyah's body bowed, a scream barreling from her as a swift, violent climax tore through her. But, just as swiftly as it hit, it dissipated. She crashed from the high, need resurging and redoubling. Control? She had none.

She cupped Roc's face and drew his mouth to hers. Their tongues met in a wild tangle. Outside, the storm continued to rage, raindrops beating against the balcony. Lightning struck near the window, flashing through the air.

Amid the dance of light and shadow, her consort lifted his head. Lust boiled in his eyes as he panted. His pupils pulsed *continually.* "I wanted you. I won you." He stood. Moving more slowly than before, he removed his weapons. "Now I will have you."

Glorious male. A proud warlord, fierce beyond compare. A true god among men. *And he's mine.*

He crawled up the bed to fill the space between her legs. More lightning flashed, momentarily setting him ablaze. She gasped at the seething intensity in his expression, at the *alevala* frozen on his skin.

He smiled at her with panty-dropping carnality. "Now we begin."

Begin? Hot tremors shook Taliyah.

"Today, I'll show you the benefits of choosing a warlord whose stamina is unparalleled." With the warning ringing in her ears, he set out to make her lose her mind. And he succeeded!

Roc was merciless. He kissed and licked every inch of her, his mouth searing. Anytime she neared a second climax, he stopped what he was doing and selected another part of her body to torment. Rapture beckoned alongside crazed desperation. She panted and she thrashed, soon muttering incoherent nonsense.

"I love the way your body warms for me," he praised.

Her head whirled with fragmented thoughts—a condition only he inspired. Her body pulsated with sensations. Nipples throbbing. Belly fluttering. Her heart beat out of sync. Between her legs, the ache grew and grew and grew. "Give me what I want. Give me... Now, Roc!"

"There's my little commander." Sweat trickled from his temples as he rose above her. He draped a forearm over the top of her head, an authoritative hold she couldn't break with her wings pinned underneath her. Strain etched his every feature. He looked like a wild man, an animal barely caged. "You want this, Taya? You want me? We're in this together?"

Panting, she peered up at him, meeting his gaze. "Together."

A thousand emotions stared at her as he positioned the head of his shaft at her opening. Anticipation and dread coiled. He was so big. So...aggressive.

She sank her claws in his shoulders, preparing for a siege. "Do it."

With a slight push, he breached her an inch, maybe two. There was a twinge of pain and a promise of pleasure, but he went no further, leaving her suspended and gasping.

"More," she demanded, marveling at the incredible rush of heat.

"I'll *always* give you more."

When he rocked his hips with verve, sinking deeper, stretching her inner walls, she experienced a sharper twinge. But still pleasure beckoned.

"So tight. So wet." He rocked, gaining another inch.

Oh! That one had more bite than the others. *Not enough.* He had more, and she wanted it. Needed it. "Give me."

His lips peeled back over his teeth. "Just...give me a minute," he gritted out. "Don't want to hurt you."

"I'm hurting *without* you." She undulated, stealing more of his length. The stinging intensified, but Taliyah hardly cared. She needed her consort seated firmly inside her. He wasn't the only one staking a claim here. "Give me more. Give me everything. I can take it, baby."

He lifted his head to meet her gaze. *Eyes like starlight.* "Caused you so much pain already. Only want to make you feel good."

He decided to indulge his guilt *now*? "Roc! Snap out of it, okay?"

With his next slight surge forward, her sex squeezed him, the fit tight enough to empty her lungs. But the ache...oh, the ache! This partially in, partially out business only made it worse.

Wait. What was she doing? She was a harpy General in the making, and she took what she wanted.

Determined, Taliyah hooked her leg around his waist, sank her claws deeper and yanked him down while lifting her lower body. He plunged the rest of the way, impaling her with his shaft.

Roc hissed against her lips before steadying himself, remaining motionless as she adjusted to his invasion. Sweat dampened his skin. "You're mine now."

"And you're mine." Taliyah panted, a twinge of pain there and gone. Her heart raced, rapturous heat flooding her from the inside out. "Give me more, Roc, or I take it," she vowed. Rolling her hips, she tested the new sensations. "Oh. *Oh*." With the next roll—

He gripped her waist, pinning her to the mattress. He kept his other arm draped over her head, ensuring his body covered every part of hers. Then...he thrust.

Ecstasy! She mewled. Another thrust. She cried out. Another. Harder. Again. Harder! Restrained by the male she craved. Covered by his strength. Filled with his girth. Straining together, becoming lost in the throes. Consumed by indescribable bliss, pressure mounting.

"So close. So close," she said with a keening moan.

With his next thrust, he pinched her pierced nipple, propelling her to a new pinnacle. Just like that, all torment morphed into rapture, cascading through her.

As her inner walls clenched around his length, he continued hammering into her, hard, harder. Faster. "You're not done yet, wife."

Just as her spasms tapered off, the evil male nipped her lower lip, reached between them and strummed his thumb over her sensitive clitoris.

Satisfaction fled. "More," she commanded. The pleasure robbed her of all sense, all thought.

"Never letting you go. Never. Never. Now drink from me, wife." He fed the words into her mouth. "Drink all you need."

Taliyah hesitated only a moment before thrusting her tongue

into his mouth…and sucking, drawing in a tendril of his soul. The heat she'd experienced before? Nothing. The power? Less than nothing. The drunkenness? Not even a blip. His energy hit her full force, and she erupted into the most frenzied orgasm of her life, whipping beneath him. Bright lights exploded behind her lids.

"You…you're…" Roc bellowed loud enough to shake the palace, following her over the edge, filling her with lash after lash of his heat and, and, and—

"Yes!" The heat, power and drunkenness overwhelmed her. The lights behind her eyes brightened, blinding her to anything else. Contentment like she'd never known infiltrated every cell.

As he collapsed on her and rolled to the side, sliding out of her, the light remained, attempting to carry her away…

No! She fought to stay awake, unwilling to miss a single moment of this literal afterglow. Never had she felt like this, and she wasn't ready for it to end.

Groaning, Roc pulled her to his chest and kissed the top of her head. He was panting. Wheezing, really.

I did that. I exhausted the Astra Commander. She wanted to see him. The light…

"Sleep, Taya."

How could she refuse him anything? Even this? "Just gonna take a little nap, okay?" she muttered, finally letting the light carry her away.

32

Different emotions swelled inside Roc. At the forefront? Astonishment. This had truly happened? He had truly claimed Taliyah, willingly handing Erebus a weapon to use against him and his men? The harpy had truly fallen asleep atop him, trusting him to keep her safe, accepting him as her beloved consort? She truly glowed as bright as a sun, blazing as he often did, because he had fed her a soul whirring with pleasure and power?

A smile broke free, pride puffing his chest. Roc had many names, but he thought this one—*Consort*—might be his favorite.

To his surprise, he had *loved* nourishing his phantom. Warming her from the inside. Sharing his strength. Knowing a part of him flowed through her now... *Want this every day for the rest of forever.*

He had expected weakness and cold to accompany her suckling—the first true feeding they'd shared. Instead, he'd experienced only delight, feeling as if she caressed every inch of him at once. Nothing at all like a typical phantom meal. Because of her parentage? Or had Erebus and his brother engineered other phantoms to consume souls sloppily, just to cause Astra more aggravation?

Hate him. The male had to die, and stay dead. Soon! The curse needed to be circumvented. Roc must save this woman. This contentment wasn't something he could give up. No wonder Solar had fought so hard to rescue his own *gravita*.

Roc hugged Taliyah close. *Worth dying for.*

He rubbed the spot over his heart and peered up at the ceiling, a strange desire surfacing. He thought he might want to show Taliyah what he'd done to Solar. She had trusted him with her secrets, and he'd only wanted her more. Shouldn't he have the courage to trust her with *his* secrets?

That was what family did. They exchanged secrets and offered support.

Family. The word echoed in his mind, and he fisted his hands. Chaos owed him answers. Owed Taliyah. Why had the man not protected his precious granddaughter?

Though his heartbeat had yet to slow, Roc kissed Taliyah's smooth brow and rose from the bed. Did a grin hover at the edge of her mouth?

He grinned in turn as he strode into the bathroom to clean up. When he finished, he gathered the things he required for his wife, then cleaned her up, as well. Though he had much to do, he couldn't resist crawling under the covers and curling around her once more. She nuzzled closer, sinking her claws into his chest to keep him in place.

His snarpy wanted what she wanted when she wanted it. *No woman more perfect.*

Some men thought they had the best wife. Those men were wrong. No one had a better wife than Roc. He had the unstoppable Taliyah, who never gave up. Even her surrender to him came with demands.

As he sifted his fingers through the silk of her hair, he halfway expected his men to interrupt, telling him of a new phantom sighting. A new message. Had Erebus foreseen this bedding? Did the god know he was soon to receive a new weapon?

Let him have it.

Taliyah had gifted Roc with her body, her future—her heart?—and there was no greater prize. He'd given up his place as Commander of the Astra for her, and he had no regrets. He would give up a thousand ranks for a moment like this.

The brand on his nape heated, and Roc stiffened. A royal summons *now*, just when he cradled a sated, naked *gravita* against him? After ten days of making inquiries and receiving silence? A curse exploded through his head.

For the first time in his life, he resisted the pull. The burn agonized, but he didn't care. He stood and shoved his legs into a pair of leathers, then informed Halo of his upcoming absence.

—*Guard her.*— The command allowed no argument.

Sounding mildly offended, Halo replied, —*I will die before I allow her harm before the ceremony, Commander.*—

The warlord still watched the palace from the wall, and no matter what he thought of Taliyah, he *would* protect her until the day of the ceremony. Anything for the blessing.

Mired in resentment, tasks completed, Roc ceased fighting, letting Chaos's power tug him through the realms. When he came to a stop, he found himself ensconced inside a throne room. One he'd never before visited. Gold...everywhere, from the ceiling to the floors and every wall in between. Chaos perched atop a golden seat, draped in a black robe.

Roc forced himself to bow his head.

Chaos didn't speak. Testing his loyalty? Roc waited him out, the minutes ticking away.

Finally, a greeting came. "You come with many troubles. Mostly, you are disappointed in me."

Yes! "Taliyah Skyhawk is your granddaughter."

A dark brow lifted. "This isn't news to me."

Accusations detonated inside him, fury gaining new ground. "You let me wed her. You knew she belonged to your family line, that she fell under your authority and protection, and you did nothing to save her. Why?"

Roc comprehended he wasn't to question someone of higher rank. He let the question stand, regardless. If he received punishment for his actions, so be it.

Silent, never looking away, the god waved two fingers. Within seconds, Aurora and Twila flashed onto the dais while already in motion, appearing from thin air. They took up posts beside the throne, both sisters wearing worried expressions and flowing gowns.

If Chaos hurt them...

"We spoke of this." The god reclined into a more comfortable position, casual and at ease. Except for his gaze. His gaze leveled Roc. "When questioned about choosing your *gravita—your* family—over your men, you chose your men. You did that, not I."

Guilt sliced him to ribbons. "I did, yes. But I'm not that man anymore." Taliyah had changed him. "You were and are and will always be her grandfather."

"Yes." A nod. Chaos said nothing else.

"Is there a way to stop this?" Desperation plucked the words out of his mouth. "Is there a way to save Taliyah as well as my men?"

"What's done is done and can't be undone. You know this. If she dies, she will never return. If she lives, your men die."

No. There *must* be a way around this. "Let me take her place."

"Solar once issued the same request. I'll tell you what I told him. You may die in her place, if you wish, but your men will be cursed."

Frustration boiled over. "Release me from this! The blessing has become *my* curse."

"You think I'm the one binding you to it. Did I walk through the door. Did I allow years to grind on without change. Did I fail to ascend before this moment."

Every question was disguised as a statement, and every statement stabbed him with an invisible knife. "I can't let her go. I can't hurt my men."

"Yet you must do one or the other."

Unless he ascended. Which he couldn't do until he presented an acceptable sacrifice. But how was he supposed to kill someone he...cherished? The very key to his happiness?

"Ah. Now you see the crux of your dilemma. You've never truly offered a sacrifice before. You created the appearance of giving without actually giving. While you killed the others, you never hurt afterward. To ascend, you must hurt like never before—and overcome it. With pain comes weakness or power. The choice is yours."

"And you?" he demanded. "Will you hurt if she dies? If your Astra do?"

Chaos canted his head, his expression unchanging. "Never doubt that I love you." He used the same unyielding intonation to gift this tender truth as he'd used to wound with the heart-wrenching ones.

"Help me save her." His chest cracked wide open. No more fissures—no more shields. Hurt like never before? *Already there.* "Love without action means nothing."

A heavy pause, tension thick. "We must *all* make sacrifices, Roc."

The words reverberated in the space between them, a new truth crystallizing, upending everything Roc had come to believe and admire about this man. He stumbled back. "You seek your own ascension."

Disappointment glittered in the god's dark eyes. "If you are not gaining power, you are losing it. I taught you this. Yes, I seek another ascension. Something you should have realized long before now."

Betrayal gutted him, the blow nearly knocking him off his feet. "I'm to be your sacrifice."

"In part. I will lose you or I will lose the harpy."

"Will *you* hurt?" he snarled. Roc didn't think about his next actions. He strode forward. No, he ran. He sprinted across the throne room. Blood would flow.

"Don't," Twila called.

Roc hadn't heard her voice in so long, he skidded to a halt, his gaze shooting to her slight form. The petite beauty who looked so much like Ian projected abject sadness—the same sadness he remembered seeing in her eyes the night their parents had sold her.

A tear slicked down her cheek, razing what remained of his calm. "You are embroiled in one war right now, brother. Don't start another."

Aurora stepped forward. "The bride I met doesn't need you to save her. She needs you to love her. So go. Love her while you can."

While he could? Roc refocused on Chaos and took another step forward, only to lose sight of the throne room as he fell into another realm, then another and another, returning to Taliyah... to defeat?

Bad dreams sneaked up on Taliyah. At first, she floated in the light. But all too soon, darkness came. Though she couldn't see her hand in front of her face, she knew she stood in the midst of an army, one of thousands, pressed in from every side. Screams, so many screams. The same screams she heard when she removed her ring, and they sprang from the women crowding around her...women who made not a sound. The incongruity of it all confused her.

What am I seeing? What is this?

Whoever they were, they needed her help. Their desperation felt like acid on her skin.

"I'm here, Taya. I'm here. I won't leave you again. Rest easy. You're safe."

Safe...yes. Roc's voice chased away the darkness. The light returned, and Taliyah sighed, slipping away...

Minutes or hours or days later, she roused. Consciousness came slowly as she stretched, waking from the most amazing slumber of her life. She was all set to bask in it, and the incredible power flowing through her veins, when she detected a thrum of aggression. A vibration along her bones.

Remembering her nightmare, she came up swinging, heart pounding, gaze darting, seeing little. She noticed enough to realize she occupied the master bedroom. Where was that light coming from?

Frowning, she scanned herself. Okay. Oh, wow! The light came from her. Her skin emitted a soft glow. But...was a threat nearby?

Another scan. "Roc?"

"I'm here." He sat in a chair by the dying hearth, and the sight of him nearly broke her brain.

He wore a shirt and a pair of leathers but no boots, and he looked *devastated*, as if everyone he'd ever loved had died at once. What had happened while she'd slept?

Taliyah leaped across the room, throwing herself against him. "What's wrong? Tell me!"

He kept his head bowed as he coiled his arms around her. Her big, powerful Astra was trembling.

Panic surged. "Roc? Start talking before I start throwing fists."

"I can't lose you." His narrowed gaze jerked up, landing on her. "I *won't* lose you."

Fear of losing her had reduced him to this? The realization eased some of her apprehension. "You won't lose me, baby. There's a way out of our predicament, I know it." She'd just found him, had just altered the course of her life for him, and she wasn't willing to lose him, either. "Maybe you can kill me without ashing me, fulfilling the sacrifice, and I'll revive. Maybe Chaos knows a way? Let's not dread anything until you've had your meeting with him."

"No," he croaked with a shake of his head. "Chaos won't help us."

Ohhh. He'd had the meeting, and it hadn't ended well. Well, Pawpaw Chaos could choke on hairy balls.

Roc reached out to clasp the edge of a blanket draping the top of the chair. He drew the material around her and settled in with his arms wrapped around her. As she melted into him, resting her head upon his shoulder, different parts of her body ached, reminding her of everything they'd done.

After thousands of years, Taliyah Skyhawk had given up her V-card. To her husband and consort, no less. She had no regrets. Her satisfaction remained.

"Tell me what happened with Chaos," she requested. Morning sunlight poured through a crack in the curtains, and she barely stifled a groan. A new day meant a new check on their thirty-day calendar.

Only thirteen days remained.

"He...betrayed me," Roc croaked. "He betrayed us both. We are to be *his* sacrifice, so *he* may ascend."

She cringed. "Roc, I'm sorry for this. I am." Did her grandfather's betrayal suck for her? Yeah. Of course. But she'd never met the man. He'd exhibited no real interest in her, and that was his loss. But this *really* sucked for Roc. He'd loved and admired Chaos.

"I thought he cared for us. All the while, he did to us what I did to my brides. I am reaping everything I sowed." Bitterness laced his tone. "How do I fix this, Taliyah? I've racked my mind to no avail."

Well. No need to stone and ash her. His anguish was killing

her quite nicely. "We're going to overcome, Roc. We're going to make him pay. And we're going to have a good life together. I'll allow nothing less."

He tightened his hold on her. "How can you want a life with the man who once planned to kill you?"

"For starters, I have yet to meet a man who *doesn't* want to kill me."

A strangled laugh. A sharp inhalation of breath, as if he couldn't believe he'd found humor in the situation, even for a moment. "I want to show you the *alevala*. The one I remove." The torment he projected...the grief. "You haven't seen the lengths I've gone to ensure we receive the blessing, and you should. Today, you will learn about the man you're fighting for. If you decide he's not worth the effort, I...will understand. Just give me a chance to change your mind. Please."

Taliyah jolted. Please? He'd actually asked nicely for something outside of sexual gratification? She gulped and cupped his bearded cheeks. "Baby, I know you've had a rough day and all, but this poor-me attitude gets two thumbs down. You buck up, and you buck up now. I chose you as my consort for a reason. There's nothing in your past that will change my mind. You're worth *every* effort, I promise you. Okay?"

He gazed at her with haunted eyes. "Look, then. See."

She wanted to...and she kind of dreaded to, but she clasped the hem of his shirt and lifted, baring his chest to her view...

Out of habit, he covered the area with his palm. He realized what he'd done, however, and fisted his hand. Slowly, he lowered his arm and gripped the arm of the chair.

Taliyah strove for an encouraging expression as she studied the area. No longer a blank canvas or dotted with the beginnings of an image. The *alevala* writhed in all its horrifying beauty.

An expected spike of dizziness, a shroud falling over her mind. A memory weaving into her thoughts, taking shape...
Here we go...

Roc stands before a lovely woman with hair as black as night, skin a magnificent shade of umber and eyes a rich brown. A sheer white dress billows from her slight form. An exact replica of what the Amazon wore in the first vision. A vision Taliyah had seen from Roc's point of view. This time, she was removed from him and purely a spectator. Did he *feel* that way, when he thought of this moment?

"Please don't do this," the woman cries, clutching her belly. The altar blocks her escape, the usual crowd in attendance. The man in the black robe, a smiling Erebus and an army of motionless phantoms wearing widow's weeds. "I've done nothing but love him."

Taliyah almost felt the frigid bite of wind past, almost scented the array of roses blooming from surrounding shrubs. They occupied a garden similar to the one in Harpina, with four full moons twining eerie pink light with gray shadows.

"We won't lose our Commander because of you," Roc bellows.

Beyond them, pained grunts and groans mixed with broken cries—war's melody.

Taliyah scanned the scene. There. Eighteen other Astra battled a single male. She recognized the four she'd seen with Roc, plus three she'd spotted in the crystal. The others were new. They fought a madman willing to strike anyone in his path. Rage and desperation accompanied his every blow.

This was combat at its most brutal. Brother against brother. Swords and other weapons swung. Flesh ripped. Limbs got hacked, while organs were sliced and diced. Blood arced through the air, creating ribbons of crimson.

Some of the warlords glowed, reminding her of stars. Others possessed iridescent rings around their bodies. Weapons? A type of armor? Two warlords blazed with literal flames, while a few spewed blue-tinged ice from their fingers. The rest cloaked themselves in some kind of thick cloud.

"Solar," someone calls to the one fighting so fervently. "Stop this!"

He—Solar—screams, "Don't touch her, Roc! She's mine. Do you hear me? Don't touch her!"

A warrior pivots into Solar, blocking his view of the bride. He sinks his teeth into the male's throat, shakes his head and wrenches back, taking the jugular with him. As his opponent drops, he spits out his bounty.

Taliyah pressed a hand to her churning stomach. She'd witnessed countless horrors on the battlefield before, had participated numerous times, but this...

From the sidelines, Erebus taunts, "Time ticks away, Roc. Do you wish to acquire the blessing or the curse? You decide..."

Her stomach churned faster as she zoomed her gaze to her husband.

Roc lifts the bride off her feet—by the throat. She flails and kicks, fighting for freedom, for life.

"You have pitted us against one another, making our Commander—our brother—despise us," Roc snarls at the woman. "You aren't his family! We are."

Her eyes bug, her face molting. "Love...him."

"How can you love the man who once planned to kill you?"

Similar to the words he'd spoken to Taliyah only minutes ago.

From somewhere in the battle zone, Ian shouts, "Ten seconds remain, Roc. Strike!"

"Roc! No! Please! Do not do this," Solar screams.

"Do it," Erebus urges. "You know what happens if you fail. You activate the curse—you activate me."

"Five seconds," Ian yells, panicked.

"Roc! Please. I beg of you. I love her." Solar's hoarse voice cracks. Realizing he cannot fight his way to his woman in time, he drops to his knees, uncaring what becomes of him. "I love her. Please."

Still Erebus taunts him. "Three. Two..."

Roc grips the woman's neck so tightly, blood vessels burst in her eyes. The molting worsens as her mouth flounders open and closed. Gray spreads over her skin. Before she finishes turning into stone, he roars, grips her hair with his free hand and yanks. Her head detaches, taking her spine with it.

"Nooo!" Solar shouts, reaching for her.

By the time her pieces hit the ground, she's fully stone and already ashing.

Erebus laughs and laughs and laughs. "Her death came too late. She died, and you're cursed anyway."

The other Astra focus on the jubilant god, raising their weapons. But as they rush for him, the phantoms come alive, swarming the entire group of warlords. Their weapons fail, swords break and daggers shatter before contact. The men trip over their own feet, barely able to remain upright. Solar is swarmed.

A blood-coated Roc rushes toward his Commander. As soon as Solar notices his approach, he jumps up, swinging a sword.

Roc dodges and unsheathes a sword of his own. Metal clangs against metal as he meets Solar's next strike. There's a wild, grief-stricken glaze in the male's eyes.

"You killed her," Solar snarls. "You killed my Allanah."

"I thought to spare you from... I hoped to spare us all. I..."

Solar launches a second attack. Roc blocks and returns a blow. They are predators, and they make no mistakes between them. Unlike the others, they encounter no problems with faulty weapons, every strike true. They fight with sublime skill, exuding a rare mastery of their bodies, each able to predict his opponent's every move and adjust his stance accordingly.

Two bears locked in a cage, neither willing to retreat.

"I don't wish to kill you, Solar."

"If you hope to survive this day, you'll have to."

"I did what I thought was right!"

"Because you saw no other way. But I did! Why didn't you trust me?"

They scream the accusations at each other, Solar's combat growing more vicious. They move so quickly, wounds seem to appear out of nowhere. A gash here. Swelling or a bruise there. Neither male heals. Because of the curse?

Roc releases his weapons long enough to slash with his claws, then crouches to catch the daggers before they ever hit the ground. He stabs his friend, his Commander, in both of his thighs.

Solar stumbles, and Roc presses his advantage, moving behind him and placing a dagger at the hollow of his throat.

Erebus claps, as if he's witnessing a sporting event, his team winning. His phantoms rip through the Astra with ease.

The man in the black robe displays no emotion. The women at his sides sob.

Between harsh pants, Roc pleads, "Don't make me do this, Commander. You won't recover."

"I'm no longer your Commander, and I'm no longer your brother." Solar laughs, crazed, blood staining his teeth. He continues to hold the sword, the tip resting in the ground. "The curse is indeed upon us. Can you feel it? I've lost my love, and with my death, so will you. You, the challenge winner, will take my place as leader. You'll become the one to wed and slay the virgin bride. One day, you'll find your gravita. *If you don't kill her, Erebus or your men will do it for you, and my pain will become yours. Enjoy it with my compliments, Roc."*

With that, Solar swings his sword, the tip arching up. His head flies off his neck, his body turning to stone as it topples.

As Roc falters with shock, blood pours and spurts from severed arteries. Half his hand is missing.

Taliyah was panting as the real world replaced the memory. A flush seared her cheeks and hot tears slicked down her cheeks.

Roc peered at her, the torment in his eyes tangled with a toxic mix of grief, guilt, sorrow and regret. Because he'd killed his Commander's wife. Because he'd killed his leader. Because Solar's prediction had come true.

No wonder he'd refused to sympathize with any of his brides. Deep down, he'd feared this very thing. Of living Solar's nightmare.

"Now you know my shame," he said, his tone flat.

"Yes." He'd gone to great lengths to avoid the curse, and he'd still failed. He would *always* go to great lengths. That he'd pleaded with Chaos to be with Taliyah, well, it meant tons. But in the end, he would take her life if necessary. "Now I know."

33

Just love her.

His sister's parting words played on repeat within Roc's head, causing an excruciating tightness in his broken chest. Far worse than ever before. He felt as if someone had wrapped barbed wire around his heart and now squeezed the life from him one drop of blood at a time.

He did love Taliyah. He knew that now, the truth as bright as she was, chasing darkness from the deepest corners of his mind. She'd become a part of him. The most important part. To have her in his arms every night…to awaken with her every morning…to witness her battles and protect her when she required it…to spar with her, talk with her, tease her…to anticipate what she would say or do and always end up surprised…

He would do anything.

From the beginning, she'd given him her best. He'd only shown her his worst. That needed to change.

Perched on his lap, she said, "Tell me everything about the blessing, and I mean everything. Leave out no detail, even those you consider dangerous for a bride—"

"Wife," he corrected.

"—to know."

Very well. He would do anything she asked. He explained how everything worked. How Halo would begin his task upon the completion of Roc's, then Silver after him. The order depended on the rank.

"So nine tasks in total. Nine chances for Erebus to initiate the curse."

He toyed with the ends of her hair. "He strikes at us in varying ways. Sometimes to cause failure. Sometimes simply to torment. If one of us fails, all other tasks are moot, and his fun is over, which is why he mostly toys with us and strikes at Ian the hardest."

"Why do people stand around watching the sacrifice?"

"They serve as witnesses. On the thirtieth day of our marriage, the trinite wall comes down early in the morning. Soon after, Chaos arrives." *Must save my sisters from the god.*

"Chaos," Taliyah muttered. "Of course."

"Erebus attends, as well. He brings his army, but no one is allowed to act against us once the ceremony starts. Anyone who attacks the participants dies before a blow ever lands. When the ceremony is complete, a battle always breaks out."

"But I saw you and your men fighting during the ceremony, when the bride still lived."

"We are participants. We can fight whenever we want."

Pensive, she tapped her bottom lip. "What kind of sword killed Solar?"

"Firstone."

"Like the stones the phantoms brought here?"

He nodded. "Firstone swords kill other gods as well as mere immortals. Most beings are vulnerable to firstone. After Solar's death, we labored to eliminate any trace of it. We thought we'd succeeded."

"So I can kill you with firstone, and you can kill me with trinite *and* firstone."

A denial rushed to his lips—a lie. He barely stopped its break-out. "I cannot halt the ceremony unless I ascend. I cannot ascend until I make a proper sacrifice. I refuse to kill you. I refuse to curse my men. I don't know what to do," he repeated.

"You and me both." With a sigh, she hopped to her feet to prepare for the day ahead. "You've given me a lot to think about. I'm cleaning up, then going to the library to study."

His chest squeezed tighter. Did she want to escape him? "I'd like to spend the day with you." The altar could wait. If he ever returned to it. Resentment flared. "If you welcome me?" *Please, welcome me.*

"Sure," she said, and he exhaled. "But you're going to have to be on your best behavior. You *must* resist my irresistible appeal."

She teases me? An agonized smile broke out. "Taya, I'm afraid that's the one thing I cannot do."

They showered, and for the first time in thousands of years, Roc left the *alevala* over his heart intact. Once they'd dressed, he escorted her to the library, where they sat at opposite sides of a table. As he read the passages she slid his way, he rejected them as the answer to their problems.

Yesterday, she'd gifted him with her virginity, willing to fight time-honored traditions on his behalf. She'd given him so much. But what had he given her? Grief. A possible promise of death.

After hours of scouring, he sent a quick message to Vasili, then tugged Taliyah to her feet. Her beauty never failed to mesmerize him. In a tight black T-shirt that ended well before her navel, and shorts made of a tough blue material known as *denim*, she nearly stopped his heart. Pale skin flushed for him.

"Be my precious and pause your studies? I have a gift for you," he said.

Never, not in the whole of his life, could he have predicted her reaction. Squealing, she pushed him back into his chair and straddled his lap, making his chair skid back. "A gift for me? Gimme! Immediately. I'll be your precious!"

The tightness in his chest dissipated completely. *I will give this woman a gift every day for the rest of her life.*

All thirteen days of it.

The thought torched what happiness he'd rallied.

"Roc! My gift. I believe I mentioned I wanted it *immediately.*" She bounced against him. "Is it a sword? I bet it's a sword. I love it already."

"Give your husband a kiss first." Would she do it, or would she challenge him?

She smiled down at him. "If you want a kiss, baby, you're going to have to take it."

With pleasure. He clasped her nape and brought her mouth to his. The sweetness of her taste drove him wild. *She is...home.*

As he thrust his tongue against hers, he stood with her in his arms and flashed her into the duplicate realm. The master suite, to be exact, where he'd stored the nine- and eight-star contenders for General. There were twenty-four in total. There were over a hundred others with one to seven stars. Those females he'd placed in the surrounding rooms.

He ended the kiss reluctantly, brushed the tip of his nose against hers and set her on her feet. "Behold. Your gift."

For a moment, she remained captivated by him, leering at his lips and licking her own. The sight of her aroused him painfully, even as he grinned, so pleased with her he could burst.

Her attention veered, and she caught sight of the harpies. Mouth agape, she spun. "The duplicate realm." She clapped while jumping up and down. "Oh, Roc! I do love it." She rushed from cot to cot, touching faces and patting hands. "Wake them up. Come on, come on. Wake them up, and I'll do dirty things with you later."

"Do you attempt to bribe the Commander of the Astra, wife?" How he managed to deadpan the question he might never know.

"Yes! But full disclosure, I plan to do dirty things to you regardless. I *have* to. Your kiss was begging for it."

Every inch of him begged for it.

"Hey! Everyone here is vying for the title of General. I didn't notice that detail with the crystal. Why are they together like this?"

Oh. That. He pulled at the collar of his shirt. "Each of my men selected a potential bride for me. They chose from the surrounding rooms."

"You have eight men. There were ten harpies in the throne room."

Her tone had sharpened. Did Taliyah think he'd chosen the other two? Was she...jealous? "I'm supposed to pick the woman I'm most attracted to, which is usually the most bloodthirsty." He'd always enjoyed a good challenge, and he must admit, he'd always experienced disappointment when the bride gave up and accepted her lot. "Ian and Halo discovered my preoccupation with a certain blonde, blue-eyed harpy-snake, so they selected two in her image."

"Tell me when and how you first noticed me." She climbed into a cot and stretched out beside a harpy with sable hair and skin a shade lighter. "Go on."

"I saw you at the market. I wanted you."

She wrinkled her brows. "That's it? How shallow of you, Astra. I, at least, observed how scary you were before I admired the battering ram in your pants."

He barked out a laugh. How he loved this playful side of her personality. Few had the privilege of experiencing it. "You want the harpies woken up, Taya. So be it." He made a few mental adjustments to the air that flowed into the room. Right on cue, the females began to stir.

Some stretched, others moaned. Most threw fists around as they lumbered to their feet.

"Hey, hey, hey!" Taliyah called. "It's okay. Everything's okay. There's a lot you don't know."

Roc was spotted, and every harpy leaped up, assuming a battle position. Hisses and the most vicious threats were tossed in his direction.

"No one touches him," Taliyah screeched. Everyone went silent, every gaze swinging her way. "You want to fight with him later, fine, go for it. Until we've killed Erebus Phantom, the commander of the Astra Planeta is your best friend."

Shouts rang out. "Nissa is dead."

"He tore her to pieces."

"I lost my beautiful hands!"

"Yes," Taliyah said with a dry tone, "I'm familiar with his fighting style." She stalked to his side in a show of support. "We have no General. We need one, and I'm it. No, don't say a word. Just listen. You've all read reports about Erebus from the women who came before you. You know our people couldn't stop him as he ravaged our villages. Well, good and bad news. He's back, and I'm his daughter. I'm also the wife of his greatest enemy, and the reason you're awake right now. If anyone or everyone wants to challenge me for the title of General once Erebus is dead, I encourage it. In fact, I'll insist on it."

As she spoke, his chest puffed up with an infusion of arrogance. There was no *gravita* more amazing.

After receiving nods and grudging acceptance, she smiled up at Roc with expectation. "We're ready to return to Harpina now."

The harpies with stars took over the palace in the original realm, and Taliyah loved it. Roc had also freed the ones in the dungeon, and she'd taken charge right away. So far, everyone had followed her orders, as promised. Even Mara. Roc and his guys were a little traumatized, though.

To everyone's surprise, the two groups—Astra army versus harpies—got along well...mostly. There'd only been a few dozen losses on Roc's side. So hardly any at all! She wanted her girls to know what they were up against, so she sent them to train and patrol during the day and battle as needed.

Yeah, Erebus kept sending new hordes of phantoms. A glance out of any window revealed a fight of some kind. To be honest, her father had proved more of an irritant than a threat. Because he didn't want Taliyah to die—before the ceremony. No, he wanted Roc to be the one to kill her, forced to live with his guilt and regret for the rest of eternity. All along, she *had* been her father's weapon of destruction.

Only eight days remained until the ceremony, and her nerves were...frayed. They were no closer to a solution. Doom loomed ever darker on the horizon.

Taliyah kicked a boot someone had dropped in the middle of the hall, punting it out of the way, and marched on, heading for the dungeon. She'd been practicing with her ring and studying like crazy.

She'd finally picked a major. Sacrifices. Forget everything else. The crux of every problem revolved around the sacrifice. The linchpin.

Roc's sacrifice spurred his ascension to god, just as hers spurred an ascension to General. Motives mattered, the impact of the loss important.

His loss—his dream of family. The death of his *gravita*.

Hers—life. Willingly dying for her consort.

Yeah. She'd entertained the possibility a time or twelve, but had always backtracked, a dead General doing no one any good.

Never accept a picture of defeat.

If only she could sleep! When she tried, she dreamed of phantoms trapped in a tunnel or cave, pinned in by countless bodies and starving. The real-life harphantoms were well-fed, at least. Yesterday, Taliyah had convinced Roc to serve up his naughty soldiers.

Sweet Roc, who had refused to work on the altar.

His men had completed it for him. The murder stone currently resembled every altar she'd seen in his memories. Anytime she spotted the stupid thing, she imagined sacrificing Erebus and Chaos there. They *deserved* to die.

In the dungeon, she breathed deep. The place had been scrubbed clean. Harphantoms rushed to the bars of the cages as she passed. Like every time before, they reached through the barriers as much as possible, their mouths open and sucking.

Roux stood at the end of the corridor—nope, he sprawled today, his shoulder propped against a wall. Drag marks suggested he'd crawled there. Blood trickled from his nose.

Taliyah sprinted over, her wings flapping. She crouched beside the blond giant and lifted his head into the torchlight. His pupils were huge.

"Roux? Tell me what happened so I can help make it better."

He blinked rapidly, doing his best to focus on her. Suddenly his pupils consumed his irises. "Aunt Tal? Aunt Tal!" Relief lit his features. "Help me! Please. I don't know how much longer I can keep control. Mom's trapped in him, and I'm trapped in her. We're real hungry. Aunt Tal? He's fighting me, and I don't…" He shook his head and blinked again.

Taliyah fell, hitting the bars of the nearest cage. The harphantom inside it grabbed her hair, but she misted, solidifying a few feet from Roux. Roux, who carried her sister and niece. Shock flash-froze her veins, answers clicking. Isla had possessed Blythe, and Blythe had possessed Roux. Like Russian nesting dolls. If his block was as powerful as Roc's, Blythe had been unable to break free. The longer they'd stayed, the deeper they'd gone, and the less Roux had sensed them. Because they'd become more a part of him.

How had Blythe entered him in the first place? He must have dropped his shield. But why would he do so? And how had seven-year-old Isla penetrated her mother's shields *and* the Astra's? No way he'd dropped it a second time.

Roux glowered up at her before coming up with a roar, getting in her face. "Why did I black out? What did you do to me?"

Rather than return-shout at the warlord, as part of her demanded, she held up her hands, palms out. "Let's de-escalate a notch, soldier. I did nothing, but I now know what's wrong with you. I even know how to fix you...kind of." She had theories. She'd never had to do this before.

That got his attention. He rocked on his heels, easing off. "My...apologies." He dipped his head in a show of respect. "You have answers, General?"

Okay. How to break this to him? "The woman you saw during the battle did, in fact, possess you. I can confirm that." He tensed as she continued. "Here's the thing. Her daughter possessed her first. Meaning, yes, you're carrying both mom and child. Knowing Blythe, she hoped you'd whisk them to safety, where they could exit without your knowledge."

"The little girl. Yes. I saw her. Then she disappeared, and *she* appeared. The woman. But I stopped. I was swinging, but I stopped. I would never hurt a child. By then, they were already gone. Then the darkness came." Creases appeared in his brow. "If they remain inside me, why do I feel as if they're gone?"

"They're buried deeper. At least, that's what my niece told me when she took over your body. No big deal. Nope!" When he opened his mouth to complain, she extended a finger. "Let your shields down, and I'll draw them out."

He crossed his arms over his chest. "Lower my shields for a phantom?"

"Yes. Do it willingly, or I'll make you do it by force." She infused her tone with steel. "One way or another, I'm getting my girls out. No, you know what? You don't get to think about this, and you don't get to fight it. Kneel."

He laughed without humor. "I will not."

"I wear your Commander's stardust. I'm his wife and *gravita*. I'm Acting Harpy General, and I'm the granddaughter of Chaos. You will show me the honor owed to me. Kneel."

He peered at her for a long while, fuming—but he also knelt.

"Good boy. This might sting a bit." Charged with confidence and Roc's electric energy, Taliyah pushed her spirit from her body. Cold washed over her, and she whisked to Roux, where she hovered directly in front of him.

His soul glowed as brightly as Roc's, but cracks fractured the shell. Interesting. She stepped into his body without an obstacle in the way. He'd truly dropped his shields, as ordered.

I was born to rule. She bumped up against his soul and hissed. Ouch! Not cracks after all, but lightning zaps. Gritting her teeth, she sank deeper into his conscious.

"Blythe," she called. "Isla. I'm here. Follow my light and reach for me. I'll do everything else. Isla, help your mother. Blythe, you'll both be safe, I swear it. I'm not sure what you've witnessed, but you have my word the Astra won't hurt any of us."

Finally! A cold brush against her fingertips. Taliyah clasped onto her sister and gently separated her from the Astra.

34

Three of Erebus's kinsmen lived under Roc's roof and protection. Harpy-phantoms filled his dungeon, the number growing daily. The non-phantoms worked with his army. He had his wife in his bed every night. He knew utter joy and the most gut-wrenching panic in equal measure. Joyous one minute, despairing the next.

Perhaps he *was* a drama queen.

Taliyah studied all the time, obsessed with sacrifices, the motives behind them, and the meanings. She wasn't sleeping. Even now, she tossed and turned in his arms, his coos of comfort doing little to soothe her. He'd hoped the rescue of her sister and niece would calm her nightly terrors. Alas.

Mother and daughter had moved into Taliyah's old room, where they'd stayed for the past two days, sleeping and recovering. The mother's condition continued to decline. She'd attempted to eat fruit from the Tree of Skulls thrice, but even that she vomited. She needed nourishment from her consort, but he'd died during the invasion, killed by Roux.

Roc didn't know how to help the woman. He didn't know how to help *Taliyah*.

Must save her. His objective had not changed. Living with her was a drug he couldn't quit. Roc loved seeing his wife's things strewn everywhere. Since he'd returned the key to the Realm of the Forgotten, she'd brought her treasures over. A vast array of weapons. Clothes she hung next to his in the closet. Something called a *lava lamp* without actual lava. An autographed photograph of Taliyah and a human male named Jason Momoa, taken at something she called a *con*.

He'd wanted to toss the thing, but she looked too cute as she pretended to be a human who pretended to be an immortal version of herself. The signature? Taliyah's. She'd said, "I'll mail it to him as soon as the restraining order is lifted."

The tasteful nudes she'd once suggested now hung on the walls of their bedroom, portraits that featured Taliyah herself. To *stimulate his creativity*, as she'd put it. When he glanced at them, he smiled. And hardened.

She'd placed a bottle of Sex Panther cologne on their mantel, as if it were a treasure. Upon his first and only sniff, he'd wondered if two panthers had actually peed in it.

He'd asked her, "Why do you have this?"

"First of all, *we* have this, and it's for our street cred, obviously. Speaking of, how do you feel about getting my name tattooed on your only available blank canvas? I'm talking about your penis, in case it's not clear. And my full name. I promise I'll only ask you to whip it out and show the relatives on holidays, my birthday and every get-together from now until the end of eternity, and *only* then."

Her words acted as a kick in the gut. She still planned their future.

A future they might not have.

Agony ripped through him. She was the guiding star he'd needed for so long. *Icy with others, even as she melts for me.*

How could he destroy her? How could he curse his men? The questions plagued him. They plagued his wife, as well; he knew they did.

His spies had learned nothing of value. Roc had called in every favor from every god who owed him, the number vast, but none had provided an answer to his dilemma.

Taliyah jolted upright with a loud gasp, startling him. "I know where they are." Tremors shook her as she scrambled from the bed and tugged his discarded shirt over her head, covering her nakedness.

"Who?" he asked, throwing his legs over the side of the mattress and standing. He reached for his pants.

"The rest of the harphantoms." With that, she vanished.

"Taliyah!" He loved having an independent wife; he didn't hate it sometimes. Trying not to worry, he finished dressing and flashed from room to room, on the hunt. All the while, he shouted commands to his men.

—Sound the alarm and prepare the armies. Something has happened. What, I don't know. Prepare for anything. Alert me the moment you spot Taliyah.—

Despite their feelings toward her, they issued speedy agreements. He knew many fretted about his obvious love for the woman and debated whether or not he would perform the sacrifice…and what they would do if he didn't. If they would take matters into their own hands, as Roc once had.

Wonderful. Another internal battle. His panic and joy, always at war. He was raw inside, his aggression always high.

Taliyah was nowhere in the palace. He braced to flash into the Realm of the Forgotten when Halo's voice stopped him.

—Found her. She's in the marketplace, near the Tree of Skulls.—

Roc switched gears, landing where he'd last stood with her. His eyes darted. She knelt on the ground, her body heaving as she pounded her fist into dirt. Great, agonizing sounds rose from her.

"Taya!" He flashed to her side and slung an arm around her. "What is this? What happened? Tell me!"

Her sobs continued. With her next punch at the dirt, he captured her fist.

"Taya!"

Crying out, she threw herself at him, clinging and shaking and breaking the heart she had just welded together. "He buried them, the harpies of old. The ones he and Asclepius killed. The brothers turned my people into phantoms and forced them to go underground." The more she spoke, the less she heaved and the more fury she broadcast, until malice sizzled in her every word. Heat boiled from her. "They forced the slain harpies to disembody and sink. Ordered them to slowly re-form and wait, silent, becoming one with the earth, tree roots growing through them."

Had Roc re-created the horror of this in the duplicate realm?

"He hid them from you," she continued, "so he could raise them up whenever he wished to toy with you."

"Taya. I'm sorry."

"He planned this!" she screeched. "They've been screaming silently for centuries. They've been screaming, but I refused to listen. Well, I'm listening now, and I. Will. Repay." A bright, blinding beam of light exploded from her.

No, not just a light: incredible power. Her own, mixed with his. The heat of it melted her ring and singed Roc. He didn't ice over as the mighty force threw him down the street. The light shot through him, too, across, above and below the land; he felt it penetrate the duplicate realm. Not once did his hold on Taliyah loosen.

Taliyah collapsed against him with a gasp. He cradled her to his chest and flashed to their bedroom.

—*Commander, all phantom attacks have ceased. They've collapsed.*—

—*The light. What was that?*—

Roc had known Taliyah was the daughter of a god and the granddaughter of a higher god, but he hadn't expected…this.

—*The light came from Taliyah. I'll explain later.*— As soon as he healed her and figured out what had happened. —*Put the phantoms in cuffs and cells. Do them no harm.*— Standard operating procedure, nowadays.

He gently laid his wife upon their bed. Dark lines branched through every inch of visible skin. Black shaded her eye sockets.

Remembering the care and feeding of harpies, he sliced into his wrist and held the wound above her mouth, while forcing her lips to part with his free hand. A crimson stream trickled down her throat. But, as the minutes passed, she didn't rouse.

Desperate, he leaned down while lifting her head, pressing her lips into his throat. "Feed, Taya. Please."

Again, nothing happened.

Fighting a stronger deluge of panic, he raced to the other bedroom, shouldering past the door. The daughter sat at the edge of the bed with her legs folded. The mother rose, as well, vibrant color restored to her once-pallid skin. When she spotted him, hatred filled her eyes—eyes so like Taliyah's.

She sprang to her feet, shielding her daughter and gearing up for attack. Whatever Taliyah's light had done to the phantoms outside had also helped this phantom greatly, her strength restored with the same intensity as her color.

"There's no time for that. Taliyah won't wake. Come. Wake her." Unwilling to wait, he flashed to Taliyah. No change in her condition.

The sister and the niece rushed after him. Both dived on the bed.

"What did you do to her?" the sister demanded.

He explained as he paced, ending with "Wake her," he repeated. "Whatever is needed, wake her. I think she burned through her life energy." His woman, starve to death? Denial roared from him. "She needs my soul, which I'll gladly give her. Just wake her! Make her feed."

"You can't make a phantom feed, you fool." Blythe frantically tapped Taliyah's cheeks. "Come on, T-bone. Wake up. Do you hear me? Wake! That's an order from your more powerful sister."

A horrifying thought occurred to him as Taliyah's words echoed in his mind. *He planned this. She was right.* Erebus had absolutely planned this. But he'd done far worse than Taliyah realized. Erebus hadn't just stored the phantoms below the earth to use as toys. He'd planned Taliyah's burnout to save them.

Erebus had known she would find the harpies underground, guided by the Blade of Destiny. He'd wanted Roc to taste the loss he was soon to experience.

What should he do?

What should he do?

"She has a friend," Blythe blurted out. "An oracle."

Roc made and tossed the sister a key to Harpina within the same second. "Fetch her."

"Yes." The sister caught the three-inch stone and reached for her daughter, who currently sat on Taliyah's chest, cupping her face.

"Aunt Tal is in there. She's fighting, and she promises she won't stop. She won't accept a picture of defeat. She says you gotta hurry, though. The little light is fading fast."

Another denial boiled in the core of his being. "Get the oracle. Now."

"Hi, guys." The bright, cheery voice came from behind him, and he spun. A beautiful black harpy stood in the doorway. "I prefer the name Great and Mighty Oracle Neeka." She skipped into the room and handed Roc a piece of paper. "This is a list of her sisters and where they're located right now. Also her mother. Sorry. If you want T-rex fixed, you'd better gather the girls quick. Chop-chop."

Roc glanced down at the list before her words pierced his

thoughts. Comprehension dawned, and he flashed to the first location with no goodbyes. First up, a woman named Gwen.

Neeka had given him more than names and addresses. Notes with arrows pointing here and there littered the margins, offering warnings. Everything from *A bark worse than her bite* to *Already plotting your murder.*

He materialized in a spacious bedroom, standing behind a strawberry blonde throwing a crystal vase at a big, dark-haired man, while shouting, "Yes, I *can* start a war with gods just because I want to."

For a split second, he locked gazes with her male, who rocketed from amused frustration to unending rage. No time to explain his actions. He simply grabbed the woman and flashed. Not the best introduction to his new brother, but what else could he do?

Roc dropped Gwen in Harpina and flashed off just as she tore into his throat. Up next, the sister named Kaia. A redhead. This one was busy stuffing a grenade into a purse, telling a dark-blond brute, "When I have this Alaroc person's balls dangling from my fingers, I'll return yours to you."

Again, Roc snatched and flashed. This male caught sight of him, too, and reacted just as fiercely.

Problem: when he dropped Kaia off in Harpina, she deposited the grenade in his hand—with the pin pulled. He barely managed to toss the weapon into an empty realm before detonation.

Two more names left. Up next? Bianka, another sister. Roc took the lovely brunette from a warrior with gold wings. This male lunged at him, grazing his cheek with a sword of fire as he vanished.

One female to go. The mother, Tabitha. She fought him through the flash itself. By the time he landed in the master bedroom, she had three daggers embedded in his shoulder. He plucked the weapons free and pointed to Taliyah. "Fix her."

All of the sisters congregated on the bed, cheering encouragements at Taliyah. Neeka commanded, "I said louder!"

"Come on, T-bag!"

"You can do this!"

"Don't be a slacker. Fight harder!"

"Lie next to her, Astra," the oracle instructed. "Warm her. Stardust her. Give her the works. Remind her what she's fighting for."

Hisses sounded and claws were bared as he shouldered past her family and gathered Taliyah into his arms. He didn't care, and he didn't withdraw. He willed his body to produce more heat for her.

"I didn't say to stop cheering, did I?" Neeka boomed, a true dictator. "You know General Taliyah performs best when she's being praised for her efforts. Or am I the only one who has foreseen this?"

New cheers erupted, filling the air as Roc's heat warmed Taliyah's chilled skin. As stardust singed his palms, he stroked her face, her throat and collarbone. Her arms. Under her T-shirt. If he could reach it, he touched it.

"Come on, Taya." He kissed the shell of her ear. "Every harpy in this room wants to kill me. Only you should have this privilege, yes? You did promise me at our first meeting."

A light moan parted her lips, and the crowd instantly quieted down. She tried to open her eyes, her lids parting slightly, but the effort proved unsuccessful.

Relief and panic colliding, he drew her face toward his neck. He didn't need her lucid right now; he just needed her feeding. "Drink me, Taya. Drink all you need." Words he hoped to say to her every day for centuries to come.

She stirred a little more, wiggling against him. Breath snagged as he waited...a stroke of her tongue.

"Yes, love. Yes."

Fitting her lips against his skin, she fed at last.

35

Roc peered down at the goddess stretched out beside him. And she *was* a goddess. The granddaughter of Chaos. The daughter of Erebus. The only female in existence who possessed the strength and cunning to challenge the Commander of the Astra and win, claiming him as her very own.

She had fed, her skin glowing with power once more. Stretching her arms overhead, with eyelids flittering open, she graced him with a soft, intimate smile—until she noticed the other harpies occupying the bed.

"How long have you been boning the enemy, General Hussy?" the one named Kaia asked.

Her eyes flared, and she muttered, "You've got to be kidding me. Well, why not go with it? Neeka! You owe me answers."

"Deal with your friend in a minute." Blythe returned her hate-filled gaze to Roc. "I'm going to ruin your man, Roux. He killed my consort, and I'll not stop until he pays."

Was stubbornness woven into the Skyhawk DNA? "I'm sorry for your loss, but I will not let my warlord be punished for defending himself during battle."

—*Commander?*— Halo didn't wait for permission to continue. —*The phantoms have awoken, and they're speaking. Intelligently! They demand a meeting with Taliyah.*—

Roc marveled. Her light had healed the phantoms Erebus made? —*The phantoms will have to wait. She's recovering.*—

—*They don't strike me as the patient types.*—

—*Handle them anyway.*—

Taliyah sat up and threw a pillow at her sisters. "You guys suck. Get out so I can speak with my consort. When I'm done, I want to have that chat with Neeka. *Then* I'll deal with the rest of you and explain everything that's happened."

Boos erupted.

"Guys," Gwen said, dead serious. "You'd better do what General Horny orders or else she'll give you a stern talking-to."

Or *not* dead serious.

Snickers abounded, the harpies remaining in the bed.

—*Commander?*— This request came from Silver, and he didn't bother waiting for permission to continue, either. —*A group of males known as the Lords of the Underworld and some Hell kings are at the wall, insisting on an audience with you. At least, that is my assumption since they're attempting to tear down our wall piece by piece.*—

—*Is Hades among them? No, don't answer that.*— Roc would deal with him soon enough. —*Tell the Lords and the kings I'm sending their wives back to them.*— As soon as possible.

"Get out, and go visit my phantoms," Taliyah insisted. "They could use some friendly faces. I can feel them now. They're going to be all right. I healed them, and I think I might have even...branded them." She rubbed the scar on her nape. "I'm not really sure how. I didn't use an iron."

"You did brand them. Mystically," Neeka explained with a

wide grin. "The symbol I burned into your nape is your own. And I'm so proud of…myself for making it possible."

Taliyah possessed her own brand?

Of course she did. *My goddess.*

"Wait. Are the big guy's tattoos moving?" The entire group of harpies crowded around Roc, studying him as if he were a bug under a microscope.

Taliyah draped herself over him before anyone could relive his memories, shouting, "Get. Out!"

"Okay, okay."

"Fine! I can take a hint. Even a subtle one."

"I call dibs on the room of my choice!"

They filed out of the master bedroom, finally leaving him alone with his wife.

When he opened his mouth to inquire about her state, Taliyah pressed a finger into his lips. "Don't speak until you undress me."

The command held more power than her sister's grenade, summoning a tide of passion.

With slow precision, he lifted her top over her head, leaving her bare. Silvery-blond locks tumbled down her arms. He swallowed. As gently as possible, given the strength of his arousal, he urged her to lie on her front.

She obeyed, a willing queen.

"I want to worship you. These wings…" He smoothed her hair over one shoulder and kissed along her spine, nestling against each appendage. Her backside received a few nibbles. When she rocked her hips and gave a rough moan, he slipped a hand between her legs. Wet. Soaking. He thrust a finger deep, filling her with his heat. Gloriously tight. His shaft throbbed as her silken walls squeezed him.

He kissed his way up, up. While licking her brand, he reached beneath her to knead her breasts. "I want to possess you."

Tremors shook her, her heart racing against his hand. "I want to worship you, too, Roc," she said, already breathless.

"Anything, Taya." Everything. "But first I need to touch you more." He couldn't stop. How close he'd come to losing her.

"Why don't we get a little more comfortable, then?" She dematerialized slowly, ghosting through him, chilling and thrilling him. Then she solidified on top of his back. He flashed to face her, there and gone before she could fall. With her mouth just above his, she rasped, "I'll let you play with me. Make me scream. Your every demand will be my every desire. But then... I get a turn. You'll do whatever I tell you."

He groaned. "You want to tease your man?"

"I do and I will. Just know when the time comes, I'll be playing only as hard as you do."

"That sounds like a declaration of war, love."

"Oh, good." She ran his earlobe between her teeth. "You understood."

Wicked temptress. No one had ever meant more to him than Taliyah.

He turned his head to kiss the corner of her sexy mouth. "Your own sexual torment is assured, wife."

"Then my job is halfway done."

With a husky chuckle, Roc flashed around, facing her. He slanted his mouth over hers, pushed her down and followed, rising above her. As she snaked her arms around him, he tore at his fly. When heated sex met heated sex, the kiss paused, the ecstasy too much. Not enough.

"More," she said.

He was panting as he slanted his mouth over hers a second time. This kiss had a slower but far more powerful start, their tongues tangling together, savoring. *No woman sweeter.*

Their scents combined, creating an intoxicating perfume. He grew light-headed. Heat pulsed in time to his heartbeat, as if he lived for this alone.

A rosy flush spread over her, starting up top. He trailed it, licking and nipping along the elegant column of her throat, over her breasts and past her navel. Lower...

As she undulated, crying out, he teased the edges of her sex, then lightly bit the tendon in her inner thigh. She gasped, her wet heat glistening.

How she craves me!

"Kiss me there," she demanded.

"My Taya aches, hmm?" He settled in, getting comfortable between her legs. As she undulated with increasing veracity, the breadth of his shoulders kept her legs apart for him, her body bare and vulnerable before him. "Does she ache enough?"

"Do it," she pleaded when his warm exhalation fanned her most intimate places.

His mouth watered for her sweet honey, that plaintive tone fraying his control beyond repair. He licked her little slit and groaned. *My paradise.*

He set in, sucking, flicking and circling. Taliyah scraped her claws through his hair, sinking the tips into his scalp to guide him where she wanted him. Tremors traveled through her limbs.

Her reactions ignited his. His throbbing intensified. His breathing quickened. *Nothing better than this.*

"Roc," she cried when he flicked his stiffened tongue over her swollen clit. Her breathy moans filled the sultry air, and his pleasure surged.

He licked and laved with abandon, driving two fingers deep into her channel. Thrusting in, pulling out. In, out. Licking, laving. Indecipherable words left her. As her voice grew higher, a climax nearing, he stopped and climbed to his knees.

Taliyah cursed his name—that, he understood. The next thing he knew, she'd flattened her foot against his chest and put him on his back. High with excitement and triumph, he gloried as she rose over him, her pale hair tumbling around him, a curtain separating him from the rest of the world. She raked a heavy-lidded, smoldering gaze over his body. There was no hint of ice. "I've made a decision. We're not going to do this in order. My tit then your tat. We're mixing things up."

Her lips were red and puffy from his kiss. Firelight danced over delicate features softer than ever before. *A fantasy made flesh.*

"Is that so?" he rasped, swiping the pad of his thumb over her distended nipple.

She arched into his touch. "Yes, it is. Also, I'm tagging in."

Taliyah studied her prey. How sensuous he was, with his hair in disarray and her essence sheening his mouth. His skin shimmered with layers of his stardust, just as hers did. Muscles flexed with tension.

Tracing a fingertip down his sternum, she told him, "Put your hands over your head." She nipped his bottom lip. "And don't come until I give you permission."

His pupils pulsed, a sure sign of his pleasure. He offered no resistance, reaching overhead to grip the headboard.

She petted his chest and bent to lick his nipple. His entire body jerked. As promised, Taliyah played with him, letting her tongue dabble here and there while caressing the very soft skin along his very hard shaft. She cupped his testicles and tugged the way he liked. Anywhere she touched, she kissed. When hinges whined, she feared for the safety of the bed.

"Grip the sheets," she commanded, and he immediately obeyed.

His claws ripped through the fabric. Sweat dotted him in places, and he pumped his hips every time she moved, his motions growing more and more forceful. Aggressive snarls brewed somewhere in his chest; she felt the vibration as she let her lips hover over his erection.

Roc went still. "Enough teasing, Taya."

"Are you sure?" She held his gaze and licked a bead of precum from his slit.

His head fell back with a mighty groan. "Teasing is fine. Continue to tease."

As Taliyah sucked on the top, his gaze snapped back to her. His eyelids slitted. He heaved his breaths. On the edge?

"Take another taste, love. Just one more. Then another."

She dragged her tongue across his entire length, and he shook the bed.

"Whatever you do, Taya, do not stop."

No, she wouldn't be stopping. He *needed* her to do this.

And she needed to do it.

Aching for him, she sucked his length down her throat. A hoarse cry left him, emboldening her. He was so big he stretched her jaw and so long she nearly gagged a time or two, but oh, she loved every second of it. She'd felt so empty without him; she'd craved some part of him inside some part of her.

"Never felt...anything so...good, love. It's so good." He released the sheets to comb his fingers through her hair, then fist the strands in his very Roc-way.

Mmm. She tasted pre-cum and wanted more. It was just as drugging as before. *Need more.* So she took it. She sucked him, sliding her mouth up and down, pumping her hand in sync. Every time he thrust his hips, as if the pleasure had become too much for him, he cursed and stilled.

He showed concern for her, even when frenzied with lust.

When her teeth lightly scraped the head, he shouted her name and bowed his back. Hot seed flooded her throat, as drugging as before. After swallowing the last drop, she smiled up at him, dazed.

Power suffused her. Life.

"More," she told him, dizzily hurrying to her knees. He'd already hardened again. "I want you inside me."

"Ride me, Taya."

Trembling, she lifted up just high enough to place the tip of his erection at her opening. Then she slid down...

He thrust up with a roar, meeting and filling her.

"Yes!" The stretch! The heat. The *rapture*. Taliyah nearly climaxed. *So close.*

Though her body shouted for hard and fast, she rocked her hips with precision, easing into a slow rhythm. Rocking again. Just as he got used to the pace, she snapped her hips. They both gasped.

With a growl, he clamped onto her waist, lifted her body from his—and thrust her down. Her back bowed, his length sliding deeper. There was no going slow after that.

She was in heaven as he jolted up and kissed her. The kiss only grew more fevered as he stood, remaining deep inside her. His biceps flexed as he carried her to the desk, every step bouncing them together, wringing another gasp from her.

In classic Astra fashion, he went the extra mile to remove anything in the way of what he wanted. He gripped the side of the desk recently installed to aid her studies, yanked it to its side, dumping everything off the surface, then setting it in place. He did this without ever releasing her or sliding out of her.

After splaying her upon the surface, he hooked his arms under her legs, spread her knees wide and hammered into her. It was brutal—thrilling. He took her hard and fast, plunging deep.

Unbearable bliss. Skin too tight, heart too fast. Muscles tightening, desperate for a release. And he wasn't finished with his torment. He stroked her clit with his thumb.

Guess he'd tagged in. She thrashed atop the desk, an eager vessel for his merciless thrusts. Her breasts jostled, her nipples throbbing. "Yes, yes. More, baby. Harder. Faster."

Harder. Faster. He made the most delicious, guttural noises as he rammed into her. Losing her mind for him, she raised an arm up and behind to grip the edge of the desk, sending him deeper. Almost...

"Look at you," he said, awed. His tempo eased, until he slowly ground against her. Never had he appeared more ruthless. "You are pleasure itself, Taya. And you are mine. I'll *never* part with you."

He released her legs and leaned over, cupping her nape and yanking her up. Suddenly they were chest to chest, their mouths fused together, tongues dueling. Her fangs nicked him, and a bead of blood welled. As the sweetest whiskey teased her taste buds, pleasure itself, Taliyah screamed, her inner walls clenching all over his shaft as she climaxed.

He hissed as her spasms continued on, his next plunge as frenzied as before. A vein bulged in his forehead. Breath sawed in and out of his mouth. He gripped the desk outside her thigh, his claws embedding in the wood.

"Come with me, baby," she pleaded and set her mouth over his pulse to suck the barest hint of his soul. "Let me feel your heat."

He bellowed, an orgasm ripping through him. His hips continued thrusting until she'd wrung the last drop of his searing seed.

The agony that had etched his features only moments before softened into ecstasy, and he sagged against her, resting his forehead against her shoulder.

They clung to each other, breathing each other, calming slowly. When he lifted his head, he shifted to the side and took her face in his hands.

All gooey inside and still a bit dazed, she met his stare. Those magnificent golden irises glowed with tenderness.

"We'll find a way to be together," he vowed. "We must."

Taliyah might—big *might!*—have misted up. Despite what he'd done in the past, Roc was choosing her over the sacrifice. He was all in. They *would* succeed.

Time was running out. Options, too. Only two days remained before the countdown clock zeroed out, but Taliyah and Roc were no closer to a solution. Her sisters, mother and consorts-in-law were working on a "quick fix." So far, no luck.

Neeka had bailed before Taliyah had gotten a chance to speak with her. Though her trust in the oracle endured, her irritation had reached new heights.

There'd been some good news, though. The Astra and the Lords of the Underworld hadn't killed each other. Best of all? The Astra had maybe kinda sorta fallen in love with Taliyah, as their leader had. Well, not as fervently as Roc. And not even to a degree anyone else would recognize. But she'd gotten to know the warriors, and their stoic acceptance screamed *we adore you, o great one.*

Once, Silver had marched up to her and groused, "Control your harpies."

She'd winced for him. "Aw. Is the Astra not strong enough to handle the job?"

He'd stormed off and had glared at her ever since, which was Astra Speak for *I think you're amazing.* Just ask Roc.

She'd had a similar experience with Halo. He'd stalked over to demand, "What have you done to my Commander?"

"Nothing," she'd sworn. "I didn't shoot him in the face again, I swear!"

He'd pinched the bridge of his nose, as if praying for patience. "I meant he's smiling. Make it stop. It's scaring the soldiers."

As if she could.

When the warlord named Vasili had visited, she'd heard him mutter, "The Commander should spank you," as he'd walked away from her.

She hadn't hesitated to respond. "Why? Does he want to lose a hand? Silly man. Doesn't he know I'll remove it for free?"

In Taliyah's spare time, she'd managed to forge a dagger with pieces of stone the phantoms had worn during their attack in the garden. She carried it always, hoping her father would dare to make an appearance.

Her desire to kill him flourished daily. The way he'd tortured her people… He *must* pay.

The harphantoms had recovered significantly, at least. They communicated without problem, and so far, they had refrained from feeding, filled up by the power Taliyah had released. But they were…feral. For everyone's protection, Ian had moved them to the duplicate realm and brought the rest of the harpies here.

The two armies worked well together, when they weren't bickering. Would both groups be forced to watch as either Taliyah or Roc lost everything during the ceremony?

Stomach churning, she hunted for her husband. She found him standing before the altar, simply peering at the stupid thing, his expression dark and brooding.

The churning worsened as she slipped her hand into his. His posture immediately softened. So did his expression.

He brought her knuckles to his lips and kissed. "I missed you, love."

Love. She chewed on her bottom lip. "What are we going to do, Roc?" Worry poured from her. So often lately, she'd felt as if she swung from a pendulum, one side panic, the other hope. Mostly, she'd felt as if the weight of the world balanced on her shoulders.

No, that wasn't true anymore. She no longer carried the weight alone. Roc bore the other half.

"We're no closer to a solution," she said. "There's no way around the curse. For a sacrifice to gain acceptance, someone's gotta give up something for a better cause. The more the object means to you, the more power your gesture generates." Before Taliyah, he hadn't known his brides, and he hadn't cared for them. He hadn't longed for their return. "For the first time, the loss of a wife will matter to you. You care, and you'll long for me after I'm gone. This will be a true sacrifice. That's why you'll ascend."

Today, she'd thought more about *her* sacrifice. Willingly dying the last death to aid the Astra. Not just Roc, but all Astra. She was their queen now. As much as she owed the harpies, she owed the warlords. Men who would look after her harpies long after she was gone.

"I don't think you understand, Taya." Night had fallen, a new storm brewing in the distance. Lightning flashed, highlighting sinister features. Thunder rumbled, shaking the whole realm and every dimension in between, she was sure. Leaves gusted about, spiraling this way and that, as if the world reacted to his mood. "If you die, I will follow."

"No!" The thought of death repelled her. Die? She *loathed* the very idea. But she loathed the idea of Roc's death even more. He'd come to mean so much to her in so little time.

How could he not? The man cherished and challenged her. He made her feel as though she lived for the first time. If she had a need, he met it. If she had a want, he provided it. If she were injured in any way, he raged, then kissed her to make it all better.

She feared for anyone who harmed her, anyone who attempted to harm her and anyone who even briefly considered harming her. "You're not going to die. I'm not going to die." They weren't there yet. "What are we missing?"

A brighter flash of lightning couched his face in an eerie haze of shadow and illumination. When minutes dragged by and he said nothing, she released his hand to pace before him.

"We must be missing something," she chattered. "But what?"

Roc flashed in front of her. She crashed into his chest, unable to stop her momentum, and he banded his strong arms around her. He held her, just held her, and the frantic energy seeped from her, leaving her exhausted.

She couldn't fight his embrace and didn't want to; Taliyah sagged against him, resting her head on his capable shoulder.

Roc didn't falter. He held her steady.

Finally he spoke, his voice rougher than sandpaper. "Nothing will separate us. Not now, not ever."

36

One day until the final ceremony. A mere twenty-four hours. *No closer to a solution.* Standing on his balcony, peering out at the garden—the altar—Roc pulled at his hair, his frustration razor-sharp. He'd failed his wife.

He had no one to blame but himself. He alone had put Taliyah in this situation. Now he cursed his arrogance. Too strong to resist temptation? Him? Hardly. He'd lost the war the moment he'd first spied her; he just hadn't known it.

He wished Solar were here. He would beg for his Commander's forgiveness. *I'm so sorry, brother. I didn't know. Forgive me.*

Roc hated Erebus. He disdained Chaos. But Roc despised himself the most.

All around, wind blustered and lightning flashed. The newest storm had yet to break. He could relate: he struggled to contain the worst of his emotions, even now.

Erebus had ceased his attacks. But then, he'd had no more

phantoms buried in Harpina. They'd all been unearthed and transferred to Taliyah's control.

"Like there's really something I can't do." Taliyah crouched atop the desk, wearing her battle gear. Mesh leather halter, pleated skirt and metal shin guards. She was on a *video call* with her sisters and some of her friends, whom she'd barred from her bedroom, demanding to spend this last day with her husband.

Last day. He gripped the railing so tightly, the metal bent.

Taliyah could've run from this at any time, saving her life and dooming his. She had the power and means to do so. Yet here she was, fighting for him. Fighting for *them*. Her courage and loyalty astounded him.

"Guys, enough. Everything's going to be all right," she said with a forced smile, and Roc's chest clenched. "I never accept a picture of defeat, remember? I always save the day. That won't change because I'm getting boned on a regular basis."

Roc moved to the balcony doors, leaned against the frame and crossed his arms, watching his wife. Strain emanated from her. Though her nightmares had ceased, she wasn't sleeping. Of course, neither was he.

"Neeka," she said, as if barely clinging to hope. The oracle had, apparently, hacked her way into the conversation from an "undisclosed" location. "Let's say the worst happens and I kick it. Erebus resurrected after the Astra killed him with their super-weapons or whatever. Why can't I?"

"Because you can't?" Neeka responded.

"You aren't going to die again," he shouted. Taliyah made his life worth living. When he fueled and stoked her desires, he experienced more satisfaction than he'd ever earned winning a war. Anytime he held her in his arms, he experienced con-tentment like never before. The too-fleeting moments he fed her his soul, blood or seed, sating her hunger and keeping her strong, his pride knew no bounds.

He'd chosen a warrior queen. A goddess. A fierce protector

to those she loved. A stubborn enchantress Roc would destroy worlds to possess. He wouldn't give her up.

She glanced up from the phone as her sisters called out, "Don't hang up!"

"I have so much more to say!"

Taliyah said, "Guys, know that I love you more than life itself. Know that I regret nothing." She hung up.

"Come to me," he said. And she did.

Taliyah lay in bed with Roc, naked and tucked into his side, hysteria teasing the edges of her mind. How had she failed her mission so grandly?

She croaked, "If Neeka is right, if I die for good—"

"Taya—"

"Y-you and your guys will look after my people, right, if necessary?" A lump grew in her throat. "And don't say you won't kill me. I've been thinking about this, and I know you're as torn as I am. One part of me wonders what kind of Goddess General can condemn the Astra to five hundred years of loss. They're my people, too. But the other part of me screams to keep fighting, no matter what."

"Taya," he repeated, misery crackling in his voice.

"I...I don't know if I'll lie down, a willing sacrifice, or if I'll fight till the end." Tears welled, clouding her vision. One droplet escaped, sliding down her cheek to drip onto his chest.

He hissed upon contact, then braced a hand over his face, rubbing his eyes.

"If we do end up fighting," she whispered, "I won't hesitate to take my shot against you. Okay? But you don't hesitate to take yours, either. Okay? If you can kill me, do it. Our fight will be fair."

"Taya," he repeated yet again, heartbreak in his tone.

"No, no more talking," she pleaded. "I just... Help me forget, Roc. Love me all night, and help me forget."

"I will love you forever." With a hoarse cry, he slanted his mouth over hers. The kiss was as heartbreaking as everything else, their tongues making love slowly.

He kissed every inch of her body, branding her with more and more and more stardust. From the beginning, his strength and intensity had drawn her. His willingness to do anything to complete a job…his ferocity…his ambitions…his loyalty to his men…his Roc-ness. He'd been made for her, and she'd been made for him.

Could she bring herself to fight him? Taliyah had no idea what she'd do tomorrow or how she would react. But here and now, in this last stolen moment together, it didn't matter. Roc mattered. Her guiding star. Her *final* star.

When he positioned himself above her, he slid inside her as slowly and carefully as if they were making love for the first time. Her thoughts fractured, shattering on the jagged edge of rapture. Taliyah felt him in every cell of her aching body.

With his next inward surge, he curled one muscular arm over the top of her head, caging her in the way she loved, holding her too tightly—perfectly. The way she needed.

They peered into each other's eyes and rocked together. His irises were luminous, an endless night sky. She lost sight of the bedroom.

Roc reached between them and pressed his thumb against the heart of her need, ensuring pleasure lashed her with every move. As she erupted with a devastating climax, he twined his free hand with hers and lifted their arms over her head.

At this angle, she had better access to his throat.

Inhale… Her nipples grazed up his bare flesh. Exhale… The sensitive buds swept down. The friction was *indescribable*.

She knew he wanted her to feed, but she refused. She wouldn't weaken him the day before the ceremony. Taliyah kissed him instead. For minutes…hours…an eternity, a blip, they continued rocking together, the sense of connection unparalleled.

Another climax hit, the force of it staggering. She scored Roc's flesh. He must have liked the sting, because he followed her over, collapsing and rolling to the side.

Out of nowhere, Taliyah burst into tears, ugly-crying, overcome by the emotion of it all. Always before, she'd felt vulnerable after lovemaking. But this? This was full exposure, something she'd never really experienced. She had no defenses against this, no secrets, no hidden agenda.

No hope?

He lifted her to his chest and cradled her tight, giving her the same words he'd given her before. A soothing balm. "Nothing separates us."

The next morning dawned as any other. Unstoppable and unavoidable. The rainless storm seethed with untold fury, an accurate portrayal of the cyclone raging inside of Roc. Mere hours remained on the clock.

When the bedroom shook, Taliyah jolted upright, instantly awake.

"It's all right, love. It's all right." He traced a hand down the ridges of her spine. "The wall came down, that's all."

The beginning of the end, then.

A curse brewed in his throat as she settled against him.

"Erebus is free to come and go now?" she asked.

"Yes. But he and his phantoms aren't allowed to fight us."

"I want to kill him," she snarled, her little claws sharpening at the tips.

He fell in love with her all over again.

As Roc sent orders to his warlords to prepare for the ceremony, he drew Taliyah closer. "We have hours to go. Shall we study? We might find a last-minute save."

"No, the time for studying is over." No emotion laced her tone. "The time for action has come."

Always in the past, Roc had left the bride locked in her room alone on this day, to mentally prepare for her end. Her favorite foods. Wine of her choice. Whatever she asked for, within the scope of his abilities, he provided. This time, he refused to let Taliyah out of his sight.

"H-how is the rest of this day going to go?" She conformed her body to his, her icy blues stark. "I should've asked before, but I don't think I was ready to hear the answer until now."

Linking their hands—one or both of them trembled—he told her, "Two hours before the ceremony, my sisters Aurora and Twila will arrive to help you bathe and dress. When they finish, they'll leave and join Chaos, who will be waiting in the garden. At the altar." His voice cracked. "At eleven fifty, my men will escort you to the garden, where I, too, will wait."

"No. I'll walk on my own," she said with firm assurance. "Astra guards will give the appearance of force. I'll not have *anyone* thinking the harpy General and wife of the Astra Commander is unwilling. I do what I want, when I want."

Killing me. "You'll come to the garden on your own, then."

Inhale, exhale. "What happens next?" she asked softly.

"You walk to me. To the altar."

She averted her gaze for a moment. "Each of your brides was the fiercest of her species. Some ran. Some cried. Some fought. As your *gravita*, I will prove myself the fiercest of them all. I won't run. I won't cry."

A terrible choking sound left him. "With my entire being, I wish you would run."

"Sorry, baby, but that's not my style."

He cupped her cheek and kissed her brow. "I know that well, love."

"Tell me the rest," she said, though she'd watched it occur to twenty others.

Roc could deny her nothing, not even this. "Usually I deliver the blow at midnight. The death is to occur in that window of time between the first and last bell."

She nodded. "If I die—" A familiar denial sprang from him. She continued anyway. "If I die, know that I meant what I said to my sisters. I have no regrets. I wouldn't trade our time together for anything."

His eyes burned, his line of sight wavering. He pressed his fingers over his lids.

She kissed his cheek. "There's one more thing. If I die, you are not to follow me. You *are* to forever compare every woman you meet with me. And make sure they understand why they're inferior to me in every way. I mean that. It's not optional."

His heart broke. Right there, in that moment, his heart shattered into too many pieces to ever weld together. She had never accepted a picture of defeat—until Roc.

From this, he would not recover. Erebus had wanted his misery. The god had gotten it.

37

The rest of the day passed in a blur for Taliyah, her emotions chaotic. As Roc predicted, his sisters arrived with a gown and toiletries. They didn't speak to him, and he didn't speak to them, but tension arced among the trio.

Taliyah thought his eyes glinted as he left the room, and she almost broke into another round of humiliating sobs.

The two females pasted on smiles before introducing themselves and drawing a bath.

"You won his heart," Aurora said once Taliyah had stripped and settled in the warm, perfumed water. "That's good, and that's bad."

"Roc is going to hurt when you're gone," Twila added with a sigh.

A barbed lump grew in her throat. She couldn't discuss Roc's feelings right now. Not while her own were such a jumbled mess. "Come on, now. I'm the harpy General. I have skills. Who says I've got to lose?"

The girls made *tsk*ing sounds.

Whatever. "What's it like, working for Chaos?"

"He's…complicated. Complex." After lathering her hands, Aurora washed Taliyah's hair. "He seeks power, whatever the cost."

"Is that why he keeps you separated from Roc?"

Twila shrugged. "As acolytes, we owe our loyalty to Chaos." The words gave off a *rehearsed* vibe, as if drilled into her head.

Been there. "Does Chaos deserve your loyalty?"

"I'm sorry, but we aren't allowed to discuss our time with him."

Silence descended as they completed their task, everyone lost in their own thoughts. Once Taliyah emerged from the bath and dried off, the sisters helped her don the ceremonial gown. An ivory beauty with a deep V, ensuring megacleavage, and a split skirt.

She strapped on every piece of her armor. The breastplate, the limb guards. The weapons belt.

Because everyone should look their sexiest on their proposed death day. She laughed, nearing hysteria again as she tugged on a pair of combat boots and sheathed a dagger at her waist.

The dagger was one of her own creations. The weapon she'd made using the firstone. She'd promised Roc a fight, to give her best. How could she give her best without a proper weapon? Something able to kill a god.

The moisture in her mouth dried. Would she truly fight him? How could she not? She'd finally found her purpose. To rule as harpy General beside the Astra Commander. The consort she loved.

Tremors racked her. "Will you guys—" Well. She was alone. When did the sisters leave?

She glanced at the cell phone her sisters had given her. It was 11:48 p.m. Almost showtime.

Ignore the tremors. Her family waited outside, forced to stand side by side with the other spectators. Chaos should be in place. Erebus, too. Grandfather and father. The rest of the Astra. Even the harpies had agreed to serve as witnesses without interfering, whatever happened. Of course, they expected her to fight and to win. The only ones missing were her harphantoms. She missed them.

Her brand heated, and she frowned. The harphantoms misted into the bedroom, rubbing *their* brands.

Uh, what just happened?

"You summoned?" Dove said with a cock of her brow.

I did? Dove was best known for committing harpykind's cruelest acts on a battlefield, so she was a true role model. Taliyah had been eyeing the woman as second-in-command. Once Dove could go an hour or so without trying to murder everyone around her, she'd be perfect.

Taliyah spun in a slow circle, looking over her new army. They'd ditched the widow's weeds and now sported proper war gear. Malice iced their expressions.

You know what? Yes. I summoned them on accidental purpose. "Here's what is about to happen, girls."

She explained the ceremony and Erebus's part. Just the mention of his name earned curses, promises of violence and soul-searing aggression.

"You should get to face your tormentor, and you will. In the next ten minutes, in fact. However," she added, "you can't attack him until after the ceremony, no matter what happens. Do you understand?"

Hisses of assent sounded. Another glance at the clock revealed 11:51 p.m. Oops. Past showtime.

Feet suddenly as heavy as boulders, she trudged to the door and turned the knob. Hinges squeaked as she exited. The army let her pass, ghosting through the midst, then followed behind her, embodying as they marched.

Only yesterday, the palace had overflowed with immortals.

Today? The rooms remained empty. Through the throne room she went. The doors to the altar, to Roc, waited ahead. Her tremors intensified. Head high. Shoulders straight.

She strode outside, a cold wind blustering, though the newest storm had passed. The trio of blue moons decorated a clear night sky, each one full and luminous. The stars around them appeared brighter than usual, as if every celestial body stared into the garden, waiting to discover what would happen next.

She paused when she reached the walkway to the altar. Her army paused with her. Roc stood in place, and her breath caught at his magnificence. He was a dark god alight with stardust. A warlord without equal. And he was looking at her as if he'd never beheld a more glorious vision.

Four of his men stood to the right, and four to the left. All Astra were shirtless, their *alevala* on display, wearing leathers and combat boots.

Harpies fanned out everywhere. They perched on statues and trees and crouched before bushes. Her mother, sisters, consorts-in-law and even Hades observed from the sidelines. Everyone watched her with pride. They still expected a win.

Behind the altar stood Chaos, draped in his black robe. A sullen Erebus towered next to him, shirtless like the Astra, his muscular chest dominated by a tattoo of his brother's face. Aurora and Twila watched from behind Chaos.

Wings fluttering, Taliyah lifted her nose into the air and met each man's stare. Erebus. Chaos. *You mean nothing to me. Less than nothing.*

Without saying a word, she raised a hand and motioned for the harphantoms to join the others, which they did, spreading out. They glared at Erebus all the while. No matter where or how they moved, they never veered their gazes from him.

Had he just shifted from one foot to the other, as if uncomfortable with their scrutiny?

Good! Hatred for him threatened to boil over. Stronger tremors invaded. She returned her gaze to Roc and strode forward, closing the distance, approaching the male she loved. The man she would die to protect.

When she halted before him, drawing in his beloved scent, she forgot everything else. They were the only two here, the only beings who mattered. His heat prickled her skin, warming her. Always he warmed her.

Golden eyes tormented but determined, he raised his chin, telling her, "You have no reason to worry, love. I won't fight you, and I won't kill you."

Okay, so pretending they were alone stopped working when a collective gasp rose from the crowd. Only the Astra remained unfazed. Rather, they, too, tilted up their chins. Because they agreed with him?

A light bloomed inside her heart, her mind. Suddenly Taliyah knew the answer to the question in the center of her struggles: Would she become his willing sacrifice, giving all of herself to ensure his—their—well-being?

She offered her husband a sad smile. "It's okay, baby."

"No." He gave a clipped shake of his head. "Don't insist I kill you."

"I won't. You have my word." Most of her life, she'd fought to become harpy General, to lead and protect her people to the best of her ability. Finally, she'd done it, and she'd gained an amazing consort in the progress. He'd given her everything, and she would do the same for him. "I love you."

"I love you, too, Taliyah." He sounded relieved. Resolute.

Erebus's laughter rang out, raising her hackles. The fool thought he was winning. Just wait until he had to battle her harphantoms. Then he might not ever laugh again.

Ding. The first toll of the bell rang out. The curse approached.

Roc offered Taliyah his hand. "When the ceremony ends, we'll flash away and hibernate. We'll figure out a solution when we wake."

Ding.

No. She had already figured out the solution. "When the ceremony ends..." she told him, accepting his hand.

Ding. As he drew her closer, she peered up at his beautiful face.

"...kill Erebus. Make him scream." That said, she unsheathed one of Roc's three-blades, ripped off her breastplate and thrust the weapon straight into her heart.

Horror contorted his face as pain exploded through her. Then she knew nothing more.

Ding.

"No!" Roc caught Taliyah as she collapsed.

As gasps, curses and denials rose from the crowd, the Astra closed in around him, forming a wall. Just before the ceremony had begun, they'd come to him as one, supporting his cause. He'd been humbled. He'd been overjoyed. More time with Taliyah, even slumbering—it was an end worth any price. But she...she was...

Ding.

"Wake, Taliyah! Revive! I command it," he shouted down at her.

"No, no, no." Erebus tore at his hair. "That wasn't supposed to happen. She wasn't supposed to die like that."

Ding. Shock punched him. As the warmth faded from her skin, cold spreading, grief finished the job, slashing him to ribbons.

She had sacrificed herself.

Ended her life.

Ding.

She was dead, parts of her already evaporating. Soon, her body would be no more.

Different faces displayed different levels of shock.

Chaos...grinned.

Rage hit Roc with the force of a nuclear bomb. Rage like he'd never known. Something beyond *anhilla*. He focused on it, letting it blanket everything else. He'd told Taliyah he would follow her, and he'd meant it. With her, he lived. Without her, he merely existed. He could no longer do the latter. He wouldn't. But first...

"Flash our sisters to safety," he commanded Ian, barely able to recognize his own voice. He unsheathed Taliyah's handcrafted blade and leaped to his feet, facing Erebus.

The frantic god paced, running through his playbook. "Create the army of phantom-harpies, spawn a Skyhawk daughter, defeat Roc."

Roc would deliver Taliyah's vengeance before turning his focus to Chaos and delivering his own.

All around, the phantoms whom Erebus had tortured for so long screamed so loudly that Roc's eardrums burst. Then they charged at Erebus. The god vanished before contact. Many of the phantoms gave chase, quickly returning him. Gashes littered every area of visible skin. Blood soaked his torn robe.

Not escaping me. "Release him," Roc thundered, the entire realm shaking. "His death is mine."

The phantoms...obeyed, releasing the god and floating back.

With a war cry that sprang from the depths of his soul, Roc launched forward. His feet hammered at the ground. In his bid to reach his enemy, he knocked over anyone in his way.

Two cannonballs of hatred, he and Erebus slammed together, flung to the ground and pinwheeled.

Roc slashed, bit and clawed with a savagery that surprised even him. He showed no mercy. Erebus was unprepared—at first; he sustained injuries that would've killed any lesser being.

"Drink them," Erebus bellowed at his army when Roc circled him. "Drink them all!"

War erupted around them. Astra, harpies and harphantoms swarmed by the enemy.

For a moment, a split second, Roc caught sight of Chaos's smiling face. His grin had only grown wider.

Bellowing his wrath, Roc advanced on Erebus once again. Flames sizzled over his skin, the fiends who threw themselves into his path evaporating upon contact. Nothing possessed the strength to stop him.

Roc slashed and ducked, locked in hand-to-hand combat until...he stabbed Erebus in the gut. Bits of firstone crumbled into the wound, weakening the god further, preventing him from healing.

Brilliant Taliyah, designing a weapon meant to cause maximum and lasting damage.

"It wasn't supposed to end this way," Erebus spit. "The blade showed me the arrival of the curse. You were to refuse to kill her. The two of you were to fight, and she was to kill you. The curse...the others should be cursed. It wasn't supposed to end this way," he repeated, swinging his dagger.

"Your daughter is not only smarter than you, she's better. She bested you." Roc grinned. "Ruined your plans."

A new dance ensued, the force of Roc's blows unleashing one avalanche of pain after another upon Erebus.

"I can see you tiring. Do you sense your own death, Phantom? Know that I plan to make it hurt."

The male grew paler than usual as Roc herded him into the arms of the other Astra. They shackled his wrists and snaked their arms around his throat. A team worked together. With no hesitation, Roc drove his dagger home—

The blade cut through Chaos rather than Erebus. He struggled to make sense of the mistake. The god had materialized?

Will kill him, too. Roc gave the blade a cruel twist, but Chaos remained in place, seemingly unharmed.

Roc released the hilt and drew back his elbow. Putting all of his strength, all of his might, into his fist, he rammed Chaos's face. His former mentor bobbled a moment. As he straightened, he wiped a trickle of blood from his mouth.

"Son," he said, speaking to Erebus while staring at Roc, "the Blade of Destiny reveals exactly what will happen...but it doesn't account for free will and a goddess's ability to change her mind, and her destiny, with a single decision. Which Taliyah did today. Quite spectacularly. Leave now, before I give Roc another crack at you."

"You don't deserve to be proud of her," Roc spit at Chaos as Erebus flashed away. *Will hunt him, find him, end him.* "You will move out of my way. You cannot deny me my right to avenge my woman."

"What crime did my son commit?" Chaos asked.

"Roc?"

Taliyah's sweet voice pierced his mind, a whisper from the beyond. His guts twisted as if he'd driven the blade there.

"Roc?" she asked more forcefully.

Taliyah? His heart leaped and he spun, gaze darting. Enemy phantoms evaporated on the ground. The winning team was spread throughout the garden, daring anyone else to appear. The Skyhawk sisters surrounded Taliyah's body and—

She lived!

He flashed over, shoving everyone out of the way to crouch at her side. She was alive, her eyes open, her chest rising and falling. With a cry, he yanked her into his arms.

38

Seconds after stabbing herself and awakening fully healed, Taliyah found herself in bed with Roc. He'd flashed her out of the garden, away from the action and her concerned family. Not to mention the prying eyes of both Astra and harpy alike.

He eased her onto the foot of the bed and knelt before her, his body between her legs. Gripping her thighs, pouring warmth into her flesh, he issued a one-word demand. "How?"

"I don't know!" Darkness had come; then consciousness had returned. As if her pilot light had been blown out, then relit... with a hotter flame. Power flowed through her veins, a newly awakened river of lightning.

"How else?" The harsh voice came from across the room, where Chaos appeared. "A true sacrifice is power, and power is life. Had you, Ian or Solar ever earned such devotion from a bride before, you would have returned to your brides, the cycle ended."

Roc bowed his head with shame. "You told me she would not recover."

"No. I told you Taliyah would not return, and she hasn't. She is a new creature." The god continued, oddly proud. "She made her sacrifice, earning her ninth star. As the current harpy General, she has now fought herself and won, earning her tenth. She has ascended. Death won't come so easily for her."

She glanced down at her wrist and gasped. He was right. Ten stars!

Chaos shifted his gaze to Roc. "You made your sacrifice, as well, by placing another's well-being above your own. But you will not ascend until and unless your men complete their coming tasks, as well. You entered the cycle of blessing and cursing together, and you'll leave it together. Just know the tasks and the order are…twisting. Prepare your men."

Maybe PopPop wasn't so bad? "What of Erebus?" She wanted her father dead as soon as possible.

"Like you, Erebus won't be so easily defeated next time." Chaos arched a brow. "He has won the newest weapon, after all."

Roc tensed up. "Which is?"

The god shrugged. "You'll find out soon enough."

"What of you? Have you ascended?" Bitterness, joy and fury layered her husband's tone.

Chaos merely smiled and flashed away, husband and wife alone.

Roc wasted no time, throwing his arms around her. "You were willing to die for me."

"Um, I *did* die for you," she teased, returning the hug with all her strength. "You gave up everything for me."

"You *are* my everything."

The door burst open, her family flooding into the room, demanding a full accounting for what had transpired. Even Strider, Sabin and Lysander entered, though her consorts-in-law glared murder at Roc the entire time. The Astra arrived next, barely beating the harphantoms, who ghosted through the walls.

A thousand voices tangled together. Some she heard louder than others. "What happened?"

"Did you *see* T-bomb defeat death itself?"

"*Now* can I punish the Astra for putting my sis in danger?"

Well. He'd once wanted a family of his own. Now he had a brood.

Taliyah laughed at his bemused look. "Christmases are going to be fun."

Roc sat on the Harpy throne, with the General perched on his lap. Only a day had passed since the ceremony, but so much had changed.

Taliyah had already received six challenges for General, all of which she'd won. Actually, she'd received eight others, but those eight eventually rescinded their challenges after watching her fight. She no longer hid her phantom abilities and utterly *destroyed* her opponents, misting and embodying at will. They survived only because she had willed it so.

Roc had cheered her on, calling out, "She's mine. Do you see her? Mine." His men might have been a little impressed, as well.

Usually after a ceremony, the Astra returned to Nova to prepare for the next task. This cycle, they'd chosen to remain in Harpina and celebrate their victory with everyone involved.

The harphantoms stood lined up by the walls, watching with haunted eyes. They had suffered for so long. With time, effort and Taliyah's help, they would recover.

The Lords of the Underworld had decided to mingle a bit longer, as well. No matter where they stood, they continued to glare at Roc. Apparently, his *I will not apologize for aiding my wife* speech hadn't gone over well.

Blythe sat on one of the many chandeliers hanging from the

ceiling, observing Roux's every move. Judging by the stiffness of the warlord's posture, he was not unaware.

Isla danced in the middle of the room with Taliyah's sisters. The little girl smiled, yet she projected sadness. She'd lost her father, and Roc...regretted. If there were something he could do, he would. Already he had an idea. But Roux would need to spend more time in the Hall of Secrets first...

Laughter caught his attention. He glanced about the room, where his army mingled with Taliyah's. Both groups were having fun.

The Astra stood in formation behind the throne, choosing to remain set apart from the crowd. Roc had delivered Chaos's message, so the warlords remained keyed up. They didn't know what weapon Erebus received, or who would be given the next task, or even what that task would be.

What Roc did know? With a woman like Taliyah on their side, they couldn't lose. Failure wasn't even a possibility.

"I wish Aurora and Twila were here," Taliyah said.

"One day, they will be. When I ascend, I'll be taking them from Chaos." The god might have come through in the end, but he'd also made a choice. He'd saved Erebus from Roc's sword, proving where his loyalties lay. So, he would share his son's fate.

"I'll help."

As soon as she'd learned how Chaos shielded Erebus, she'd viewed the god as a major foe. Because of this, Roc knew both males had numbered days. Taliyah the Terror of All Lands didn't accept defeat. Ever.

He traced his thumb over the seam of her cherry-red lips. "You appear starved. Shall we adjourn?"

She snorted. "I fed this morning."

"Who can survive on one meal a day?" He loved feeding her. Loved providing for his wife, his family. He had so much to give. Whatever she took, he regenerated—and then some! Truly, the more he gave, the more he produced. Roc's body *hummed* with power. He'd never felt stronger. "Also, you need more stardust."

Another snort. "Baby, I'm a walking glitter bomb. I sparkle from head to toe, which makes it a little hard to intimidate my foes and my people, by the way. But okay, you talked me into it." Smiling, she smoothed her hand over his cheek. "I love seeing my stardust on your skin."

Powered by his soul and her return as a Goddess General, she'd begun producing a stardust of her own. He loved it, too. More than he could ever say. "I want more."

He geared up to flash them.

"Wait," she said. "I want to try something."

He didn't flash, but the next thing he knew, he was sitting at the edge of his bed, Taliyah reclined in his lap.

A laugh sprang from her. "I did it! I flashed us both. Because I'm amazing!"

"That you are." What other powers had she developed with her ascension? They would find out…later. Roc divested his wife of her stunning scarlet dress and set out to show her just how much he loved her. He was living a life he'd never dreamed possible, loved beyond reason, accepted and supported by a warrior of incomparable resilience.

Whatever came next, they would overcome. Together, they were unstoppable.

★ ★ ★ ★ ★